Lori Adams

Father of Lies

Father of Lies

Susan C. Ryan

RESOURCE *Publications* • Eugene, Oregon

FATHER OF LIES

Resource Publications
An Imprint of Wipf and Stock Publishers
199 W. 8th Ave., Suite 3
Eugene, OR 97401

www.wipfandstock.com

PAPERBACK ISBN: 978-1-6667-0331-3
HARDCOVER ISBN: 978-1-6667-0332-0
EBOOK ISBN: 978-1-6667-0333-7

06/03/21

For Matt

Acknowledgments

This novel wouldn't have happened if I hadn't been dreaming at my day job with my wise and good friend Kristen Connolly. My sister-in-law Paula Bodah, a gifted writer and editor, contributed her considerable talents to this book.

Mark, Linda, John, Katie, Jamie, Ken, Henry, Tim, Paula, and Alan are the best family anyone could wish for.

Special thanks to my sister Carol Ryan, whose belief has sometimes sustained mine and whose support has made all the difference in my life.

Finally, my husband Matthew Bodah, who has been the greatest gift of all. There isn't a kinder, more generous, more loving soul on earth. My gratitude to him, and for him, is endless.

1

At this hour, the city belonged to birds. Other mornings he'd watched them rise from the bushes as if spawned by the dew. A rustle from an impenetrable interior, an indistinct shape forming among the leaves, and finally a small burst, bringing a sparrow or a chickadee, a finch or a wren, to the top of a buddleia or the side of a hedge. Along with blue jays, crows, robins, starlings, grackles, and woodpeckers, they called and cried and chattered and warned, establishing their territory just as the generations had done before them a century ago, two centuries, three centuries, and nearly four now since the city had begun to grow around them. In another hour, the first rumbles of noise would interrupt the symphony as the Boston commuters started their cars. A little later, as the city awakened, the cars and the motorcycles of the Providence commuters, the landscapers with their mowers and blowers and trimmers, and a hundred other man-made noises would all but extinguish the sounds of the city's birds. He lay in bed a few moments longer and, as happened most days, the breathing in his ears became insistent and, incrementally, the birdsong retreated beneath it. He said his prayer to Agrippina, the syllables skimming lightly over the surface of his brain, the words so well-worn they were nearly without meaning, then rose to begin his day.

James Ennis had been pastor of St. Patrick Church for four months. It wasn't the plum of the Aquidneck Island parishes; that was St. Mary, the oldest and largest Catholic parish on the island, the church that had married a young senator who would become the country's first Catholic president. St. Patrick was old, though. Built in the 1870s, the church was an enormous brownstone with a cavernous interior that always felt cold. The brick rectory, with dark paneling in every room and stained glass on many of the interior doors, had been intended for a cohort of three priests and two visiting clergy but nearly one hundred fifty years later, the rectory housed only Jim and Father Leo Sullivan, seventy-four and retired and, he had been reminding Jim lately, unable to tolerate the heat that seeped through the gaps and the cracks that time and weather had inscribed on the building. St. Patrick was expensive to maintain but St. Mary would have been worse; not an ambitious man, Jim was glad he hadn't been given that parish.

The first hour of the morning, he prayed for everyone who would suffer that day. Years ago, he'd listed the causes: wars, famines, fires, floods, illness, injury, everything consequent of malice, greed, envy, lust. As if God needed him to detail the causes. As if God might miss something or someone. In his mind now, Jim drifted over the world, praying for an end to suffering, for an increase in love. After that, he sat in the chair by his bed and opened his breviary for the morning prayer. Feast of St. Thomas the Apostle. One of the less endearing disciples. You've seen a man cure lepers, blind men, deaf men, walk on water, appear with Moses and Elijah, raise three people from the dead, and you still don't believe he himself can be resurrected?

The chair was one of two varieties of furniture installed in the rectory; both were dark and oppressive. The dressers and tables and cabinets had stood in place since the rectory was built; the curtains and upholstered furniture had been purchased in the 1940s and 1950s, judging by the style and, sometimes, by the fabric, although he was no expert. No matter when it had come to the rectory, however, the furniture was heavy, the massive dressers and sideboards and tables and cabinets fashioned out of mahogany, the fabric of the chairs tending to damask reliant on navy, burgundy, browns, and black. He expected that in every season he would find his surroundings oppressive; meant, he supposed, to reflect the solidity, the permanence of the Catholic Church, the murky fabrics and stained glass, the peat-colored carpeting and looming furniture seemed to repel all light or, when a stray beam found its way past the stained glass and the curtains, to swallow it down without a trace. But there it was; he had no mind to redecorate and couldn't afford to, even if he had.

Along with the bed, nightstand, and chair, his bedroom held a tall chest of drawers and a dresser, chunks of mahogany bitten off along the bottom. Atop the chest of drawers were framed photos of his parents' wedding and Lizzie's wedding, as well as the most recent school portraits of his niece and nephew. Candid photos of the children were stuck into the wide mirror atop the dresser. Willy on the family's day sailor, reaching to a gull that was hovering a few feet above him and intent on the bread in his hand. Triona, red hair streaming behind her, galloping into the surf at Second Beach. The two of them, making a snowman with their father, so wrapped up in coats and hats and scarves there was little of them to see but their joyous grins. Their happiness piercing the gloom, a charm against irritation, anger, fear, and despair, he lingered a moment, as he always did, before crossing through one of two common rooms—his alone now, since Leo was at the end of the hall, away from the street. He was also in sole possession of the bathroom on the west side of the building. And, in fact, he never saw Leo until he went downstairs to breakfast.

The kitchen most felt the rotation of pastors through the years: an enormous six-burner stove had been in place since the early days of the twentieth century; the original wood floor had been smothered by gray-and-black-flecked linoleum sometime after that; enamel sinks had been replaced mid-century by aluminum; the avocado countertops were a vestige of the 1970s; and very likely a decade later the original oak cabinets had been torn out to make way for mahogany-stained, engineered wood with jarring white knobs. The refrigerator, a stolid steel thing, looked to be the most recent replacement. The effect was a little dizzying at first, a sort of early morning funhouse. In the midst of the funhouse, bent over a table meant to seat eight, was Leo. Who more precisely was arched over a homemade coffee cake, methodically breaking off chunks as he reviewed the other offerings: glazed doughnuts, banana bread, Italian pastries from Federal Hill in Providence, blueberry muffins, a strawberry rhubarb pie, and several plates of cookies. People still baked or bought for their parish priests.

"I can get you a knife for that." And immediately, he was sorry. It was no way to start the day.

Leo straightened, unabashed. "Shouldn't be eating it." He brushed crumbs from his fingers. "Bad for my diabetes."

In some ways, Leo had the appearance of a priest as Hollywood in the last century would have imagined him. Well over six feet, with thick white hair, the bones of his face sharp. Not genial, though. You wouldn't mistake Leo for someone who'd start Boys Town, crack little jokes and thus win the hearts of young thugs. Leo had a wintry expression, except when his features eloquently conveyed distaste.

As they did now, at the thought of a more healthful meal.

He took a bowl from a cupboard and, opening another, selected from an assortment of cereals. "Why anyone comes to Newport in July is beyond my understanding. It may be a degree or two cooler but really it's just as hot as anywhere else. You feel it acutely when you're trying to sleep at night."

The complaint was a familiar one, and, in fact, Jim responded not to the words, which didn't fully register, but to the music of it, which he knew well. "You didn't use the fan?"

"I'm too old for a fan. All that hot air blowing through the room; it's not cooling, you know, and I prefer not to wake up some morning to find my flesh has been steamed like a bucket of clams. Point is, I don't regulate well. Once upon a time I regulated, but now I don't. Not at all."

Jim checked his watch, which told him that he didn't have time for coffee before Mass. Resigned, he nodded at Leo from the other end of the table. "I'll stop by Seaside Heating today."

Satisfied, Leo opened the paper, but a moment later let the corner drop so he could see Jim.

"It's a peculiar thing. If the parishioners don't like you because the homilies are too long or you don't give them the hymns they like best or don't make endless small talk with them after Mass, or do one hundred other things that suit them, they desert you for another parish. But if you please them in all things, they're more likely than not to give you cookies and candy and everything else that will kill you as quickly as a knock on the head. You really can't win, can you?"

Jim was scanning the headlines of the Providence paper and only half-attending. A crash with multiple fatalities, a dolphin pod stranding on Cape Cod, a list of fireworks displays throughout the state. "They mean well."

"Which reminds me. I had a call from John Ferguson, up at St. Columbkille. Anselm Chace passed."

Jim didn't respond.

"I suppose we'll go up for the Mass," Leo continued on a sigh. "I suppose we must, though it's in western Massachusetts and long rides tend to nauseate me. However, I did serve with Anselm at St. Clare. And do I remember that you were an altar server at Blessed Sacrament?"

They didn't have to go. At least, Jim didn't have to go. But Leo wanted to and Leo's car never left Rhode Island. Leo's friends would be there, and plenty of time to talk.

"I served there briefly," he said. "Just before I went to the Abbey. A few months, maybe."

Leo closed the newspaper, turned a cool hazel gaze on him. "Eighty-nine when he died. Brilliant man. Absolutely brilliant. Convert—did you know that? Always wonder about the converts. Most of them are fine, I suppose, if determined to out-pious the cradle Catholics, working themselves to the bone and on their knees twenty hours out of the twenty-four we've been allotted, but some of them are just looking for an outlet for general looniness. And so it was with Anselm. You knew he lost his last parish before he was sixty." Leo drew out the last word; between his careful enunciation and the lingering final syllables, his homilies tended to run long. "The sisters have been taking care of him forever now; what's the name of that place?"

Jim shook his head.

"Practically in the Berkshires? The Benedictines run it? I'm sure you know it." Leo waited for an answer. After a moment, "Well, it'll come to me eventually."

Blessed Sacrament was less than a mile away but Jim hadn't crossed its threshold in more than twenty years. Thank God Lizzie hadn't been married from it. It was small—cozy, almost—and brighter than St. Patrick, the pews some sort of light wood, and the ceiling painted a sky blue with gold stars. It had felt dark, the last time he was in it, so dark it was hard to breathe, and then he'd never had to go back. He'd caught a late-summer cold, or at least he'd told his parents he had, and by the time he was feeling better the school year was beginning. He'd been accepted to Portsmouth Abbey School and he preferred to attend Sunday Mass at the abbey's church; his parents had thought it a natural thing and had been happy to go with him.

He sometimes felt that he was circling it, going from Salve Regina University to St. Patrick Church in Newport, would have been happy for a parish in Westerly, at the southwestern tip of the state, or Woonsocket, far to the north, because you couldn't get far enough away from it, though there were other considerations. However, as much as Jim disliked him, he never said no to the bishop, and took what he was offered.

After Mass, Lizzie came at him like a blowtorch. He stood just outside the front door, trying to ignore the heat that was rising from the concrete and pouring thickly from a cloudless sky, prickling the skin under his clerical collar and vestments. He was trying to concentrate on the people he'd been charged to serve, trying to get to know them and their needs. The hands he shook, the skin dry and loose over the bones, belonged to the daily Mass crowd. Many were in their seventies and eighties, had grown up in St. Patrick when it was an Irish parish; now, Portuguese, Brazilians, Central Americans, and a few African-American families occupied the pews on Saturday nights and Sunday mornings. The children of the older congregants had moved on, out of the city or just out of the church.

Lizzie was three years older than Jim and medical director of the emergency room at the local hospital. Small, slender, she had the translucent skin of redheads and eyes such a pale blue they were nearly transparent. He was always a little afraid when he saw her coming.

She had been at him for months to let Willy and Triona train to be altar servers. He'd known she'd badger him if he became pastor at St. Patrick; in fact, the knowledge had made him hesitate when the bishop had offered him the parish. Heaven knew he needed altar servers; sometimes a lector would have to do double duty. But it wasn't going to happen; he loved the children as if they were his own.

"Jimmy, it's like the church is driving people away. Who can come to an eight o'clock weekday Mass? Everybody works. Will someone please tell the bishop that? Obviously he has no clue."

He hazarded a covert glance around but he knew before he looked that she had an attentive audience. Gave Lizzie a bit of a smile, which usually was the best you could do with her.

"And no server again; it's not like Triona or Willy have anything else to do. You have to be settled in by now—it's been months—and anyway, Mass is Mass; it's not like you have to learn something new."

He started to explain that altar-server training was only held in the fall but Lizzie was running ahead. "Look, I've gotta go." Impatient, as if he'd been keeping her. "We've been slammed for the past three weeks and Fourth of July weekend is always the worst, so I told Adam Baker I'd come in today, even though I was supposed to have the day off. Adam's a complete idiot. He couldn't diagnose a PE if it hit him over the head. Who hires these people?"

Relief. "Well, it was nice seeing you, Liz."

Lizzie wasn't leaving quite yet. "Summer in Newport. Drunks. Fights. Crashes. Swell." She suddenly focused on Jim, a terrifying white gaze that concentrated light and, penetrating, saw everything. "Anyway, come early tomorrow, so we have time to eat before the fireworks. Unless a meteor hits the island, I'm not working, Adam or no Adam."

The crowd around them hadn't dispersed. They were waiting for their turn to say hello and shake his hand. For some, it might be the day's only contact with another person; for others it might be the opportunity to ask for prayers or help for a spouse or child. He braced himself, knowing what was coming. "What time? I told Kevin I'd take the five-fifteen at St. Rita."

"What does the man do?" You couldn't stop her voice: she was used to shouting the length of the ER, over chaos and impervious to interruption. "You take his Masses, you visit his sick, you bury his dead. What does he do all day? Jimmy, I love you, but you're a pushover. The word is 'no.' Practice it a few times, will you?"

Jim, who half-suspected that he'd been given St. Patrick for precisely that reason, refused to look around. "It's a corporal work of mercy."

Lizzie might not have heard him. "Well, come as soon as you can. Don't bring anything. Just show up, okay?"

And as Lizzie was winding down, Maria Estrada checked her watch and hurried away. She'd brought her children to Salve when he was there and had followed him to St. Patrick. Two children in high school, a husband who never attended Mass; Jim had never asked why and Maria wasn't a chatterer. He wondered what she would have said if she'd had time, was sorry that she hadn't.

But now it was nine o'clock, the last of the congregation dispersed, the vestments put away, and the third wave of the city was making itself known. The Boston commuters gone, the Providence commuters at their jobs or still on the highway, the local commuters took their place on the city's streets. The shopkeepers who would open at ten o'clock, the waiters and waitresses who staffed the lunch shift, the day-trippers from Warwick and Cranston and other West Bay towns, and because so many had made it a long weekend, cars from New York, New Jersey, and Connecticut, looking for coffee or coffee and breakfast. Along with the engines and old mufflers and the occasional shriek of a police car or ambulance, a steady current rode underneath, creeping into the ears as a pulse, then as reverberation, before an angry male rapped at maximum volume over a woozy beat. It didn't matter whether the car's windows were open or closed and it made you wish cars came with soundproofing. Lizzie called them the noise-induced-hearing-loss crowd and now Jim thought of them as the NIHiL-ists.

Newport sat where Narragansett Bay met Rhode Island Sound, and the city had grown from the waterfront. Thames Street, running north/

south, was closest to the water and retained remnants of colonial Newport: at the northern end, houses dating to the eighteenth century lined both sides of the street, and the southern end was distinguished by a parade of docks. Spring Street ran parallel, on higher ground, and while it, too, retained homes and churches from the colonial era, a gas station squatted over the spring that had supplied the colonists with fresh water. Bellevue Avenue, on the highest ground, paralleled Thames and Spring streets. Hotels had sprouted along Bellevue Avenue to accommodate nineteenth-century summer visitors but the sole survivor now housed several businesses; along the southern end of the street, Bellevue Avenue, with its grand wooden homes, became Ocean Drive, famous for the enormous stone constructions of the Gilded Age. Thames Street, Spring Street, and Bellevue Avenue had been remade again and again, but what hadn't changed despite the centuries was the width of the city's roads, which had been designed for horse and carriage. The third wave was the final wave in winter, but in summer, a fourth wave crashed over the streets of Newport and was absolutely confounded by the seventeenth- and eighteenth-century roadways.

This fourth wave was dangerous, a tidal surge that swept into the narrow streets and pushed relentlessly south to the tip of the island and west to the waterfront, oblivious to the man-made barriers that had been created to direct its flow. Between ten o'clock and noon, the tour group buses, the mansion visitors, t-shirt shoppers, restaurant goers, downtown wanderers, honeymooners, destination wedding crowds, bicyclers, kite flyers, waterfront strollers, bay cruisers, and thousands more, determined to have a great day/weekend/week, poured into Bellevue, Spring, Thames, and all the little streets, hardly more than alleyways, that connected them. Informed and propelled by some recondite force, they were oblivious to the one-way street signs, were prone to sudden stops and reversals mid-street, indicated their intention to turn left and then abruptly turned right. They ran stop signs and red lights and double-parked where parking was prohibited.

If someone wanted him, he used the car to bring the Eucharist to the ill or injured or to administer the Anointing of the Sick to the dying. That was the calling: to go where you were needed. But he preferred to walk rather than drive during the fourth wave and if he had to drive, realized afresh, every time, that he preferred a white-out blizzard to a sunny day in July.

Dodging a bicycler at a street crossing, he nearly collided with a pair of runners. Several obstacles stood between reality and Leo's dream of central air. One was the rectory: it was large and old and it might not be possible to install central air without significant disruption, which he thought would be no more welcome to Leo than the summer heat. Another was cost. The parish could pay for it, but strictly speaking, did the rectory really need it? So then he could ask Leo to pay for it, since Leo wanted it, but Jim wouldn't ask. Which meant that, in the end, Jim would end up paying for it, unless it was beyond his means. Which it could very well be; he wasn't a great saver. And if beyond his means, then what? A question for his invisible companion, who never answered and did not do so now. It was a decision deferred: Seaside Heating and Cooling, he discovered, wasn't open; he'd have to call later.

It was no use being angry at Leo, who couldn't be blamed for wanting to attend the funeral Mass of a fellow priest. Leo always went to the funerals. Jim did, too, though he wouldn't have gone to Anselm's; he would have had a reason ready, though he doubted anyone would have asked.

He was thirty-six years old. Old enough to know that people didn't vanish simply because you wished they would. He had known in some part of his brain that Father Chace was living and breathing somewhere—he just hadn't wanted to know where. He also was old enough to know that the past is the present vanished. Once an hour was gone, it never came back. And if you weren't done with it, if you wanted to call it up in memory, it would not be that precise hour; instead, it would be what you took of that hour, what you thought you saw and thought you heard and, in fact, it might not resemble the actual hour, might be completely your invention. That's what made him angry: it wasn't Leo's news, it was the instantaneous flare of fear the news engendered.

His mother on the phone, explaining that she would no longer be washing and ironing Blessed Sacrament's vestments, that Jim would no longer be an altar server. His heart pounding as he listened on the stairs, as if something could shoot through the telephone line and find him.

He was thirty-six years old. And Anselm was dead.

The most unpredictable part of the day was the hospital ministry. It should have been Kevin's but it was a ten-minute walk from the rectory and so not burdensome. The hospital was a small community hospital surrounded by old homes that tried their best, with hedges and trees, to pretend they were located elsewhere in town. As Lizzie said, its ER could be chaos during the summer but the rest of the hospital was quiet, relatively speaking. The ill and injured of Aquidneck Island occupied the rooms and most patients were elderly. No amount of cheerful paint and light wood confused the senses: as the elevator doors opened, the inmates announced themselves with the clamor of televisions and, more powerfully, the earthy odor of old flesh.

Staff at the nurses' station greeted him with a glance or a nod; instructions were being issued, notes tapped into computers, phones answered, and several conversations were jogging alongside the rest of the noise. Nurses were pushing rolling computer stations from room to room, housekeeping staff were pulling linen carts, transport was maneuvering a gurney through an open door, and breakfast trays were being cleared, but the rooms themselves, even with the televisions, were oddly still. The work of healing and the work of dying were inner processes and sometimes so hidden that they weren't recorded by all the machines designed to detect the most subtle workings of the human body.

An odd thing sometimes happened, a transformation particular to no specific age: one minute, it seemed, the patient was ill and furious about it, fighting with everyone; either that or pleading for any help that would prevent them from dying, though they could hardly know whether they were truly in danger of death. Then awareness crept upon them, and when they knew that life was ebbing away, the flailing and the pleading stopped. Some reached out, as if afraid to make the journey alone. Others grew increasingly inward, while others seemed to step away from themselves, seemed to see the doctors, the nurses, the priest, friends, and family with a kind of fondness, seemed to sympathize with the struggle to do and to be, which they themselves were no longer part of. Those who had been angry and rude during one visit could be gracious the next day, agreeable to everything, thankful for everything that was done for them. It was always unexpected and when the transition happened, he still couldn't help it: it made the hair stand straight up on the back of his neck.

That was animal instinct, the primal revulsion of death, part of a primitive mandate to put distance between oneself and the dead and the dying, in case the dying was contagious. That's what he told himself anyway, usually when he was examining his conscience at the end of the day to see where and when and why he had fallen short. It was perfectly natural, he told himself, like shivering on the way to morning Mass in January. It was natural and normal and nothing to be ashamed of. But he was. Every time it happened, he was ashamed. Every time, he promised himself not to flinch if it happened again. He tried to see these dying women and men as they wanted to be seen, tried to love them as children of God, which, after all, was what he was called to do.

He wondered how Anselm had met death. Loony, Leo had said, which wasn't a charitable word but also was curiously nonspecific for Leo, whose precision was so striking it sometimes got under Jim's skin. Loony could have meant anything, from a collection of odd habits to an absolute break with reality. Loony said nothing, although the care of the nuns suggested a bit more than eccentricity. Eccentricity had become tolerable in today's church, as had a bit of forgetfulness. With no replacement waiting in the wings, priests doddered on into their eighties, quavering their way through Mass, sometimes dropping a line or two of the Nicene Creed, sometimes forgetting one of the antiphons altogether. To lose a parish before you were sixty—that said something more than odd habits or the vagaries of an aging brain.

And that was why he'd never heard any mention of Anselm, not in twenty years. Anselm hadn't been forgotten; there simply was nothing to say about him. He was in a nursing home run by nuns, had been there for years. Old news by the time Jim had been through school and the seminary. He'd never heard anything about Anselm and he'd never asked. Perhaps he should have; if he had, he wouldn't have been rattled by Leo's news.

Checking the number beside the door against the list in his hand, he walked into a room brilliant with summer light. The single bed was occupied by a heavyset woman in her mid-forties who was working on a crossword puzzle in the newspaper. Ghastly. Surrounded by a nimbus of wiry hair gray as a pewter platter, her face looked like she'd been buried and dug up a month later: two black eyes, a wide scrape running the length of her nose, her upper lip swollen. One leg in a cast.

"Mrs. Acker, I'm Father Ennis."

"Yes. You used to be at the college. Kit Acker. Not a Mrs. I shed that when I shed 245 pounds of laziness disguised as thwarted ambition." She took a careful breath. Bruised or broken ribs, he thought; beaten by the estranged or ex-husband?

"How are you this morning?"

"Anxious." She set the paper aside. "Actually, let me clarify: I'm always a bit—it's in my DNA—but now I'm extremely anxious." Another painful breath. She put her hands flat on the mattress and tried to push herself up in the bed; her eyes went wide with the sudden surge of pain. Shifted, more pain, and he saw more anger than frustration in her face;

she was used to doing things for herself. In the end, though, she admitted defeat, dropping her hands in her lap. "I wonder if it's the medications they're giving me."

"Possibly. I wouldn't be surprised, but you'd have to ask the doctor about that. Maybe it's being in the hospital?" Trying not to look at the bruises, he opened the door to whatever she might want to say. "Or is something particular on your mind?"

"This is no place one wants to be but I cope well enough with most things. Though I do think of my grass getting longer and my hanging plants withering a little more with every passing hour. Did you know that plants can hear? Studies have documented roots growing toward the recorded sound of a stream. And plants bending away from the sound of predatory insects though no actual insects were present. Amazing what there is in the world that we haven't discovered."

Some patients, he'd learned, asked for a clergy visit just to have someone to talk to. Mostly, though, those patients were much older than the woman in the bed.

"If I had my cell phone I could look up the meds myself, but that ship's sailed. I'm hoping to get out today or tomorrow; I think they've run every cardiac test they could think of. I told them we don't have cardiac problems in the family. Dad had lung cancer. Mom's hale and hearty. No grandparents, siblings, aunts, or uncles with heart trouble. Still they test and still no sleep."

Probably not battered, then. "Sounds like you're more aggravated than anxious."

She met his eyes. "I'm being watched."

Not conspiratorially, not querulously. It was purely a statement of fact.

"I'm a fairly well-grounded individual and I am sure there is something in the corner of the room, all the time, watching me. You can see why I'm anxious. I don't know why I'm being watched or, to be more precise, what its intentions are. I think I'd feel a bit better if I knew, but in fact I have no inkling. The presence is so strong right now that I hesitated to tell you because if I did, it would know that I knew it was there."

She had a pleasant voice, if you were just listening to the shape of the words. Educated, lower-pitched, and soothing. Which made her words even more surreal, though he knew that drugs could make a person say almost anything.

"It must be the medication, don't you think?" A fine line existed between reasonable and dismissive; he hoped he was on the right side of it. "Maybe you're having a bad reaction to something they're giving you."

"I know it sounds ridiculous. There's nothing there; I know that." Her eyes, nearly lost in the bruising, appealed for confirmation, but would settle for something lesser—patience, perhaps. "As you say, it has to be the drugs they've given me, but here's the problem: I can't be sure. At first I told myself I was imagining things because I've been lying flat on my back, nothing to do. I teach at Salve; that's how I knew you. Psychobiology. I also do volunteer work; that's how I broke a leg, bruised a rib, and gave myself two black eyes. I was walking two dogs at the animal shelter and my big feet got in the way. My problem isn't my heart, it's my coordination. I fell over the smaller dog and kept hold of the leash instead of putting my hands out to break my fall. Fortunately, my sunglasses didn't shatter. Although this is bad enough. Point being that I'm used to being busy, so I thought it was idleness—I'm not accustomed to that."

Someone was shouting for help from one of the rooms. A rasping voice, more fury than fright in it, which gasped at the end of a string of words, subsided for a handful of seconds, and then started up again. No one seemed to answer the demand, which probably had gone on ever since the patient arrived on the floor. Disturbing at first, but then you almost became used to it.

"That first day I was so busy castigating myself for my stupidity I wouldn't have noticed if the philharmonic had set up shop at the end of the bed. I became aware of it gradually that first night. The next day I awakened expecting everything would be back to normal but it was worse. The first night I felt something was in the room. On the second day I knew exactly where. I suspect hallucinations aren't that subtle, or are they?" Her voice was calm, the words measured out, perhaps the style she'd adopted for the lecture hall—at odds with the purples and reds rippling away from her eyes.

In the short time he'd been taking the hospital ministry, he'd seen delirium, and had held the hands of Alzheimer's patients who thought he was their brother or father or their long-dead son. Once, when he was administering the sacrament of the sick, a previously docile patient snatched his arm and just in time he'd understood that he was about to be bitten. No one had ever invited him to discuss the hallucination they were experiencing. It barely seemed possible that such a thing could happen; surely one obviated the other. A tremendous force of will must be required to describe with dispassion the thing that terrified you, he thought, and he saw her with new respect.

"It has to be the painkillers," he said firmly. "If the doctor switches you to something else or stops them, I bet it'll go away."

She ignored that. "There's another possibility," she said to herself. "Not a good one. I wonder if I injured my brain when I fell. Do you suppose I could have done that?"

"The doctors would have checked for that, wouldn't they?"

"I remember an article in which electrical brain stimulation was applied to a woman's temporoparietal junction and rather than resolving her epilepsy it caused her to see a shadowy figure behind her. I wonder if I fell in such a way that I injured that area of my brain. It was a hard hit: I fell down concrete stairs. I don't remember blacking out but perhaps that's what's happened, although as I said, I don't actually see anyone. I feel something but I don't see anything, not even a shadowy thing. But now that I'm thinking about it, I remember another article that reported that the subject thought someone was actually lying on top of him." She glanced at him. "A little unnerving to contemplate, isn't it? If I recall correctly, it was part of an experiment evaluating the function of various areas of the brain. The subject claimed that the sensation was very strong, though, obviously, he could see no one was there. If I did some kind of permanent or at least lingering damage to one area of the brain, maybe that's what's happening."

He realized she was trying to talk herself into a little ease. One part of the mind rational, reasoning, while another part had gone completely haywire, hallucinating. It had to be terrible for her, for someone who must live most hours of the day inside her brain. "I'm so sorry," she said suddenly. "I know I'm nattering. And unlike my students, no one's paying for you to listen to me."

"I'm interested."

Years ago he'd made a study of hearing, learned about the pinna and ossicles and cochlea and how each hair cell in the cochlea was designed to respond to a certain pitch or frequency. The transference of sound waves from outer to inner ear seemed to him no less complicated than Voyager 1's transmission of sound from interstellar space, and just about as unlikely. If hearing was implausible, and hearing well was nothing short of miraculous, those various tiny and intricate bones and structures were obvious suspects if the sense malfunctioned. "The temper-what junction? What did you say was the name of it?" And when she told him and he'd committed it to memory, "If an injury could make you see things that aren't there, it probably could make you hear things, too, couldn't it? Sounds, maybe. Or voices."

"Voices? I'm not hearing voices," she said sharply. And then, to herself, "Not yet, anyway."

"No, of course not. I'm sure you're not. I was just wondering."

"That's often something else. Voices, I mean. But sounds?" She started to shrug but thought better of it. "We really don't know much about the brain. I doubt we ever will. And just as well, perhaps."

He wasn't sure he agreed. If some kind of probe could isolate the source of alien respiration, he'd happily submit to it. If scientists could create hallucinations by lighting up the temporoparietal junction, they might be able to tell if that area of the brain was malfunctioning or misfiring somehow, or if that area was continually stimulated and consequently reported breathing where none existed, though how it could be stimulated he didn't know. He'd have to look it up when he was back in his office.

"Perhaps I have hydrocephalus," she mused. "Or an aneurysm." She settled in to think about that.

He roused himself to reassure her about those possibilities. "They would have seen those on a scan. And they certainly would have run a scan if you'd hit your head."

Suddenly he had her full attention. "You know something about this?"

"My sister works in the emergency room. She's a great diagnostician. She would have ordered a scan and if there had been something, she would have found it."

Lizzie would have, but what if Kit Acker had come in during her colleague's shift?

She was studying him. Piecing together bits of information about him. Then she retreated to her own thoughts. "There's always another possibility. It could be that I'm not hallucinating at all. We're programmed to dismiss what we can't see, aren't we?"

"Some things," he said, smiling. "I have confidence in God."

She wasn't willing to be distracted. Too confused or too worried. "Enculturation, it's called. The process in which we adopt the norms and values of the culture we live in. It's a survival mechanism. In twenty-first-century academia, we believe in plenty of things we can't see but we require proof to do so. Hard evidence, unbiased studies, formulae: we accept nothing without proof."

She looked at him. "I know it's not benign, whatever it is. I can feel it," she said.

Her voice nearly breathless; he knew where he was now. A place where he fell short, always. If he'd been made differently, he could have offered something soothing, words that were calming and comforting, but everything he thought of sounded patronizing to his ears. That was his chief trouble: he never had the right words when he needed them. He could listen for years but it took him a full day just to write a six-minute homily and three more days to revise it and, even then, it was never quite what he had in his mind.

His deficit wouldn't have been quite as glaring if he'd been able to compensate for it; sometimes, the words didn't matter as much as the way in which they were delivered. He often wished he had Lizzie's self-confidence: if she told you something, you believed it.

But Kit Acker had asked for a priest to visit, and that told him that he did have something to offer her. She relaxed a little during the blessing, and just before he left the room, he found that he did have something to tell her. "I expect you know the great mystic, Teresa of Avila. Her visions were described as those in which no form is seen but the object is known to be there."

"Visions," she said, and at last her eyes lit with amusement. "Something new to think about. Though no one would mistake me for a saint."

2

You went along and went along and what you saw and heard and said and did left a wake, occasionally the wild eruption of a motorboat, but more often, much more often, the gentle ripples cut into water by a sailboat, and you went along because nothing on earth had the power of stasis and the eruptions and ripples of your wake lost their energy and subsided, settling back into the blue water that had its own inviolate movement, the water flowing in over hours and, peaking, flowing out again. Movement was the lesson of the ocean, where nothing ever stilled, where even the air-light scales of fish were swept into marine snow that fell and fell and were scooped up and digested by translucent creatures that beat against the black waters just above the sea bed.

But you did not forget. All that motion, that unstoppable forward movement, brought you to memory again and again. A sound, or sudden silence. The odor of a particular laundry detergent. The light in an empty church. A name. Anselm Chace.

His mother had an unhealthy relationship to dirt. She didn't vacuum a room, she assaulted it with sponges and cloths and dusters and mops before any vacuum was allowed on the battlefield. Her intent was annihilation so complete that anything that smudged, muddied or darkened, or drifted in the air until it settled didn't dare venture anywhere near the site where its comrades had been obliterated. She never succeeded but she also never stopped trying. She said she found it relaxing, but you'd never know from the fury with which she wielded her weapons. That's why you couldn't find your favorite shirt that you knew was hanging on the end of the bed, except that now it wasn't. You could search beneath the bed to see if it had fallen, but it never had. Instead, it had been washed and folded and put back in the shirt drawer, although you'd only worn the shirt once and it was still good. And that's why you found yourself every Saturday afternoon, even in summer when there were a million better things to do, opening the door of Blessed Sacrament with one hand while cassocks and albs flapped from hangers held in the other. On Saturday mornings, his mother washed and ironed the church's available inventory of altar server garments and on Saturday afternoons Jim delivered them.

Blessed Sacrament was the church in which he'd been baptized, the one in which he'd received First Communion, and the one in which he'd been confirmed. Up the concrete walk to the stairs, eleven steps to the wide oak doors in front, over the dark stone floor in the vestibule to the second set of doors. The rows of stained glass windows casting muted colors on the pews in the nave. Thick, sweet smell of beeswax candles and eighty years of incense perfuming the wood. The small red glow of the sanctuary lamp. The life-size wooden cross overlooking the altar. Everything started out big and then became smaller over time, started out intimidating and grew more comfortable.

Standing in the transept, his back to Jim, was the pastor. He'd been pastor for Jim's First Communion and Confirmation. Father Chace wasn't like the church, though: he hadn't shrunk as Jim got older—he always seemed small. Wrists no bigger than Jim's, hands as delicate as rose petals as he lifted the Host during the consecration. Biggest part of him his nose, spread as if someone had taken a rolling pin to it, flattening it against his face.

"Father Chace? I've brought the vestments."

You wouldn't hear people if you were deep in prayer. It had never happened to him, but his experience, with video games especially, had taught him that it was possible. "I'll put them in the closet."

He suddenly felt the silence outside: no low hum of traffic, no sound of birds in the maples that surrounded the church. Stillness, as if when he walked into the church he'd walked out of the day. Or into the day, stopped. No sound outside, but something in. Breathing. And oddly below that—because wasn't breathing the softest sound?—the murmur of a single voice. Praying, it must be, but odd for that, because you knew what praying sounded like, without thinking about it. It was all in one tone, not the up and down of this.

"Father Chace?"

He didn't want to interrupt but he couldn't stay where he was, and he was reluctant to take another step because that would bring him farther into the church and closer to the sound.

Father Chace didn't stir. And now he thought there were two voices. No one there but Father Chace but he clearly heard two voices, low, reminding him of his parents in conversation after his sister and he had gone to bed. Except both voices continued without a break—Father Chace's and a deeper voice. The voices seemed to crawl to him over the floor, and up his ordinary jeans and the t-shirt that smelled of laundry detergent, though he couldn't make out a word or even a clear syllable. Not coming through his ears, but sliding its arms around him, enveloping him, going right through the skin and settling there, penetrating the flesh under his hair and spreading through his brain. Some part of him began to receive a warning. He thought to look to the floor; one body might block another from sight but two sets of shoes would be visible.

At that moment, the priest turned. The hangers with the albs and cassocks clattered against the floor.

Jim ran.

After leaving the hospital, he'd stopped by the parish office. People called the office at any time of day or night. Could Father bless a rosary? Would he change the hymns for the next day's funeral? Would he put an elderly parishioner on his prayer list? Could the parish pay an electric bill? Provide money for gas so a parishioner could get to work that week?

If Megan Marks, the parish secretary, took the call, she steered financial help requests to the diocesan office, where funds were available for basic needs such as food and shelter. Sometimes, though, people knocked on the rectory's front door. The requests were almost always for money. Perhaps they didn't ask until they were facing empty cupboards. Perhaps they were a few dollars away from homelessness. Jim didn't recognize the faces he met at the rectory door but it hardly mattered if need had become desperation. Once he knew he was hearing a well-practiced speech; he'd have to figure out what to do about people who found it easier to make the rounds of the local parishes than to apply for jobs.

He could hear Lizzie telling him it wasn't sustainable, but she'd never know because he'd never tell her. He liked doing it, though it worried him because Lizzie was right: one day someone would ask and he might not have the money. For now, though, it was a great gift that St. Patrick had given him. He could help people here: young families living paycheck to paycheck, the elderly whose Social Security did not cover the essentials, people of all ages who worked hard but still found themselves with empty pockets now and again—his parish had a good share of each.

At Salve Regina, he'd celebrated Mass, performed benedictions during this or that important event in the life of the university, led a Bible study group, heard confessions. Once or twice a student had come to him for guidance, but most must have preferred to bring their troubles to their friends, a professor, or, perhaps, their parents. Though it was a Catholic university, the church was terra incognita to most students.

His primary concern was the spiritual welfare of his parishioners at St. Patrick, but he could hardly ignore their physical well-being. And sometimes one led to the other: for someone facing hunger or homelessness, he could be an answer to a prayer, a way of bringing them closer to God.

As he finished his lunch and began to eye the cookies and pie on the table, he thought of Leo and realized he'd forgotten to stop again at Seaside Heating. Leo, fortunately, wasn't there to ask him; Leo had been born in Bristol, a pretty town farther up Narragansett Bay, and frequently ate out with his fellow Bristolians.

He'd been thirteen when it happened. It could have been the only thing that happened that year but fortunately wasn't. He'd told no one about that Saturday and he'd hoped it would dissolve from memory, but it hadn't; you might forget the good things, but you remembered every bad thing that happened to you. And in case he was thinking he could just drop it in the ocean, let the waves close over it, a constant reminder kept it alive, as if the event were inhaling and exhaling life-sustaining oxygen, keeping the colors vibrant, the sound sharp, continually replaying the feeling that something was crawling over him. Though he wasn't so sure about the breathing as he once had been. He didn't remember whether it began that day or not. It could have been there for weeks or months before, he too unaware to notice it, or even months after, he too shaken to hear it. Even if it had begun that day, it just as easily could have been coincident with the day rather than connected to it. Totally unrelated, an unfortunate byproduct of his growth spurt that year, or a mishap at the beach, a wave knocking him over or slamming against an ear.

Loony. What did that mean? Had they called Teresa of Avila loony because she felt what wasn't seen?

What he needed was a book. Something better than the one he'd just finished; there was a reason some books ended up on the dollar shelf.

The streets were less congested; at two o'clock, people were where they meant to be. With fewer cars on the road, the air felt cooler. And a taste of the afternoon breeze drifted from the waterfront. Some days, walking down Broadway, the air was oiled with the smell of hamburgers; on most summer days it was a dry and gritty mix of car exhaust and heated tires. Occasionally, though, you inhaled the ocean, sharp and sweet.

Dyer's Books was across from city hall. His first view of the store, when he was a high school freshman, was identical to the view now: a worn sign, a dingy façade, and Michael Dyer leaning against the latter, smoking. Michael was a chain-smoker and his shop was smoke-free, which meant he was almost always outside the store and perhaps for that reason knew everything that was happening in Newport.

Straight black hair that never looked combed, a sallow complexion, a button-down shirt, and chinos that appeared to have been pulled from the bottom of a hamper, the effect was slightly seedy: he was a bad advertisement for his business.

"How are you, Mike?"

"Hanging in." He flicked the cigarette into the street.

Like Jim, Mike was a solitary creature; he'd never married, lived alone in an apartment on the Point. Good view, he said, and close enough to walk to his shop if he wanted, although he said he never wanted. He didn't seem to go anywhere—he didn't like movies, wasn't much, he said, for eating out, and thought most bars were too noisy. Instead, he read. Jim liked to talk politics, the news of the day, though he rarely told Mike something that Mike hadn't already read or heard.

Jim followed him into the shop, which was better organized than one would expect, although the rear of the shop always had four or five boxes that were marked Newly Arrived and were overflowing with unsorted books.

Mike produced a small pile from behind the register. "Science fiction for the kid. There might be a fantasy one in there; I don't know since I don't read them, and anyhow, what's the difference."

Jim looked at the titles. They meant nothing to him, either. Jim was less interested in the distinction between science fiction and fantasy than in the difference between books suitable for adults and those for children. Sometimes you could tell from the cover art or the copy on the back cover. Usually, though, he took them to the rectory and sought the help of the web, which was easier than reading the books. At one time he'd thought he might read them so he'd be able to talk books with his nephew. That idea died within thirty pages of the first book he'd opened.

"Cleaned out a house. Estate sale," Mike said, surfacing from behind the counter with another pile. "Ex-CIA."

Jim had taken a paperback from the top of the pile, but looked up, startled. "CIA? What was he doing in Newport?"

Mike didn't quite smile. "Middletown, not Newport. Near Second Beach. And I didn't ask him; he was dead, right? Paid forty-five dollars for a bookcase, floor to ceiling. Still haven't gone through all the boxes but I've got a few good ones: *Quo Vadis*, *Kristin Lavransdatter*, and *All the Names*. You said no particular order, right?"

His nephew and niece lived less than a mile away. He saw them on their birthdays, at holidays, and whenever Lizzie invited him for a meal. He never took them out to give their parents a break, though the parents certainly could have used one when the children were little; never brought them to the movies or the beach. He made sure he was never alone with them, even for a moment. He remembered Lizzie laughing when Triona was born, insisting that babies wouldn't break if he held them, but in his mind's eye he could see something crawling from him to them, dark and formless, and the thought of it terrified him. The price for their safety was that neither child knew him very well, and quite possibly considered him a little odd.

He was a little odd. More than a little odd. A hearer of things. So he became the bringer of books, his sister apprising him of her children's changing tastes. It wasn't much of a connection but it was the best he could think of and it made him happy to imagine that they looked forward to seeing him, the source of new books. Right now, Willy was running through science fiction and Triona had decided to read at least one novel of every Nobel laureate. For the past few years, Mike had been saving books for him. Jim hoarded them until he saw the children. The paperbacks and hardcovers perched on a table in his study and sometimes just the sight of them would warm him.

"And for you." From behind the register a last paperback appeared. "Slim pickings on the nonfiction front but here's a novel set in our fair city. Woman brought this in last week. Looks like it took a bath in suntan lotion, doesn't it? She wanted ten bucks for it. Dripping in jewelry and she thought she could flip it for ten bucks. 'Are you kidding?' I said. 'Who's going to buy it in that condition?' Told her if she gave me five bucks I'd be happy to throw it out for her. Some people have no sense of humor. 'One dollar,' I said. 'Take it or leave it.' God love her, she took it. Shameless, people are."

The reek of coconut oil, the cover cracked and curling. The pages would be stained, and gritty with sand. "So you're willing to part with it for two? Is that it?"

"Anyone else wouldn't have heard that story and I'd be charging four," Mike said. "It's pirates and it's local. These things fly out of here."

Jim looked at it with distaste. Pirates. He did need something to read, though. "Let's split the difference and make it three."

"Come back when you're done with that one. I'll be getting more in every week now and there might be something you'd like. Probably in the same crappy shape. People read while they're getting their party tans. Four big parties going on tonight. You've got the senator's fundraiser, the save-the-land fundraiser, the save-the-theater fundraiser, and last but not least, some swank event at the WASP beach. Disgusting."

Jim didn't feel the same: sometimes an event would benefit the hospital. Good for everyone, not just the rich.

Mike ignored that comment. "Last alleged fundraiser must have cost about one hundred grand, easy: three hundred people, open bar, sit-down dinner after two hours of ostrich and oyster hors d'oeuvres. Oh, and some singer whose name I should know but don't. Not that it would mean much to you—I mean, you never struck me as an *American Bandstand* kind of guy. But one of those ones who just can't commit to a single note but has to go up and down the scale a few times before she lands on something. Not exactly my cup of chowder, but I'm in the minority."

Jim was grinning. "*American Bandstand*?"

"Big show, back in the day," Mike said defensively. "Look it up."

Wanting to get off the topic of fundraisers, Jim said, "Newport was a lot quieter when I was a kid."

"Quieter?" Mike snorted and, reaching into his pocket for his cigarettes, shook one out. "Not in my lifetime. Well, I suppose it was, for about three years. Before your time. Like *American Bandstand*, apparently. When the fleet left Newport in 1973, instant ghost town. Empty storefronts, people selling their homes for pennies on the dollar. Then the bicentennial happened and all the Tall Ships came to Newport—we had more ships than anywhere else, for some reason—and the multitudes descended and our fair city saw big dollar signs. Those few years between 1973 and 1976 were quiet as a morgue. Bad for business, but I limped along."

"You had the store in 1973?" Jim had thought the bookseller was somewhere around his parents' age.

Mike looked at his unlit cigarette, sighed. "No smoking in the shop." And tucked it back in the pack. "Any idea what the city was like before the early seventies?"

"Not a clue. Rougher, I suppose."

"Putting it mildly." Mike was searching his pockets and finally produced a box of cough drops. "I don't have a cold; something about that pseudo-medicinal taste keeps me coming back for more. Probably loaded with THC or something." A glance at Jim. "I like them two at a time. Want one?"

Jim shook his head. "You were here before 1973?"

"Yeah, and it was a jumping little burg before the Navy left. Half the city cat houses and the other half dives. Not exactly a tourist mecca. Wouldn't be surprised if some of the old dives went all the way back to the Triangle Trade—there were eighteen rum distilleries back then—but I'm guessing the Newport Historical Society's never looked into it. After the slavers dropped off their cargo in the Caribbean they'd sail into Newport Harbor and swab the decks with vinegar to get rid of the stink of sweat and piss and misery before they stuffed the hold with rum bound for Africa. All that rum and all those slavers, I'm guessing the City by the Sea wasn't exactly a snoozefest. Newport's always been kind of a horror show; could be all cities are, when you scratch the surface."

It wasn't the first time Jim noted Mike's rather bleak view of humanity. "It's ironic, when you think that the state was founded on freedom of religion. It was such a generous idea."

Mike snorted. "Noble ideas usually die a quick death. Though it wasn't as free as you think: Catholics weren't welcome. You'd have been run out of town. Or hanged, maybe. But I take your point. You start out with a little group that has a noble idea but then all kinds of foulness finds its way in."

"I like that: 'all kinds of foulness.'" Jim let the sound of it roll around in his brain. "It reminds me of Mather's *Wonders of the Invisible World*."

Mike was shaking out another pair of cough drops. "*Observations As Well Historical as Theological, Upon the Nature, the Number, and the Operations of the Devils*. Not exactly a snappy subtitle. Another crazy doing God's work. Thought his merry little band were conquering the devil's territory."

"Weren't you just telling me it is?"

Mike looked blank.

"Newport. New England. Weren't you just telling me it is the devil's territory?"

A half-smile. "You're the priest; you tell me."

Jim was fishing his wallet out of a pocket. He took out a few bills. "Must have been discouraging for my predecessors at St. Patrick."

Mike rang up the sale. "You don't think they'd have been jazzed about the challenge? Saving all those souls from the dives, the doxies, and the devils?"

"Saving them from themselves, really."

"There you go: that's the devil's territory."

Jim opened the pirate book, but his mind began to wander after the first few pages. The afternoon had been hectic: meetings with the altar ministry, two women who fought politely over every petal that adorned the sanctuary, followed by two couples who wanted to marry, although one couple didn't belong to the parish and kept referring to the church as a "setting." Then more phone calls. Leo was right: they did complain if the organist wasn't playing the hymns they liked.

In between meetings, he'd browsed the internet for articles on the temporoparietal junction, and by the end of the afternoon, he'd read accounts of out-of-body experiences, which he found frightening, as well as the connection between the temporoparietal junction and moral judgment, which he found deeply disturbing. The ability to choose between good and evil, he discovered, could be affected by damage to one small area of the brain. If your brain had been scarred, would you know it? Would you realize you'd need to carry a pocket guide to malevolent acts? Don't kill native inhabitants of the land you covet, don't covet the land in the first place, don't enslave people, don't rape or torture people whether enslaved or free, don't procure women for sexual purposes, don't harm children or animals. The list would have to be very specific and therefore lengthy. At the end of your life, would you be judged on the fact that you'd compiled such a list? Where was the action of God in such lives?

However, his order had come and late in the afternoon Jim set up a feeding station, midway between the rectory and the trees, which location he hoped would discourage the aerial assaults of squirrels. The station was like an eight-foot, multi-pronged shepherd's crook. The day cooling, and the sun further muted through the filters of an old red maple and several cherry trees, Jim filled a sunflower seed dispenser, a mixed seed feeder, a suet hanger, and added a solid block of seed. To prevent ground attacks, he fastened a squirrel baffle, shaped like the top of a parasol, around the middle of the pole. He brought the stepladder into the rectory, stored it in the little closet near the kitchen door, and when he looked out the parlor window, he was rewarded by the sight of two chickadees. They were the most curious of birds, hopping from branch to branch to get a closer look at human activity. And nearly tame: his brother-in-law had once held out a hand filled with sunflower seeds and within twenty minutes a chickadee had undulated in, snatched one, and then retreated. Triona missed it, having returned to the house after the first few minutes but Willy had been rapt. Then, recovering, he'd said, "I think I will try that the next time we have asparagus."

Jim cooked for himself because, although he had no culinary ability, he also had little interest in food. He ate the same thing every night: chicken or fish, a baked potato, whatever vegetables had been on sale that week, and a small salad. Sometimes he saw himself, fork in hand, chewing his way through the years. The animal things that were part of being human had always felt odd to him. You thought you were master of yourself, that your brain was in control, but it was no match for the animal urges to drink, to eat, to eliminate the waste of what you drank and ate. He wondered if most people considered at one point or another the creature things they did. The planet gently revolving in space, early evening gradually slipping into night and as it did, from east to west, lights being lowered or extinguished, people undressing and sliding into the little slots that were their beds, perhaps pulling up covers, turning their bodies to the side or lying on their stomachs or backs, closing their eyes and preparing to be insensate for the next six to eight hours. You wouldn't forfeit awareness of your surroundings unless you were forced to do that, and that was the animal ruling the human. Although children didn't go so meekly. Children fought to remain conscious as long as they could, until they'd progressed from silly and slaphappy to wailing (he remembered Triona at four years old) and, if they hadn't been marched off to bed, to sudden exhausted collapse on the floor, on the couch, anywhere.

At some point, rather than going until you dropped, you prepared yourself and went to your sleep area and closed your eyes submissively. Though sleep had been dangerous in another era, when you could be set upon by your enemies or eaten by something nocturnal, the animal urge overpowered every rational consideration. He wondered when people had stopped dropping and begun to keep regular bedtimes.

That conversation at the hospital had given him a little lift. He'd never heard of the temporoparietal junction. At the very beginning, before the terror had passed, he'd adopted Agrippina but after that he'd decided it must be something to do with his ears. Now he wondered if he'd been too quick to diagnose himself. It was more likely that his brain was at fault. Not that you would want your brain to be damaged or malformed, but it would be an answer. If the mind could produce shadow figures, if it could tell you that someone was lying on top of you, a bit of breathing would be small potatoes.

That woman, talking to distract herself. Just as he was doing now. He knew what he was doing; he wasn't stupid.

He washed his few dishes and decided to attend to the small stack of bills on his desk. As he came up the stairs, he heard the racket of a television blasting above the roar of Leo's fan and, as he did most evenings, he knocked on the door to what had been a bedroom but was now Leo's study.

"Anything good on?"

"The nightly affirmation of my vow to be a celibate," Leo said without turning in his chair.

Jim watched for a moment. "You know it's a sitcom. Families aren't really like that."

"You miss my point." And now Leo did turn, revealing a look of extreme distaste. "The idea that I might have spawned the writer of this terrifies me."

Bookcases lined the walls of Leo's study and every shelf was packed. Leo preferred philosophy, poetry, the classics, and modern European literature. Jim was a little intimidated by Leo's library; his own contained a bit of philosophy, a greater share of religious biographies and literature, and was peppered with novels and a few field guides—seashells, mushrooms, the night sky, and birds, the last being the only guide he'd actually used. Also CDs. A few were classical but he preferred words; it was easy for him to get distracted when there were no words. Sacred music, Christmas and the Triduum, especially. Some traditional, a smattering of rock bought during his teens. No rap. No pop, either; Mike had been right about that.

The mahogany desk in Jim's study was a pretty piece, likely original to the rectory, with bronze pulls, a high gloss, and only a few dings here and there, but the chair was hard, narrow, and ruthlessly vertical. As he considered, as he often did, replacing it with a chair from another room, the breathing pushed to the front of his consciousness.

On his better days, he ignored it as he did the sound of Leo's television and the traffic, which was still building on the street—there'd be a peak around eight, a lull around ten, and from eleven on it would be people going home after dinner, after drinks, after the nine o'clock movie, after whatever else occupied people on a warm summer evening.

Jim closed his eyes and listened for birds. They were there if you paid attention between the throbbing radio of one passing NIHiList and the next, one aggressive driver and the invariably outraged blast of a horn that resulted. Crows and gulls were loudest; you couldn't miss them. But a cardinal's chipping notes, the crooning of a mourning dove, and other gentle calls were there, were accessible if you cared to notice them.

Still, there was the breathing. Like a mouth against his ear, steady inhalations and exhalations insistent with propinquity. A burden every morning he awakened to it because there was always the hope, even after years, that one day it would have been borne away with the night. Some mornings he awakened full of the day's plans and he could muscle it aside, but on other mornings it was like a toothache, and tears would come to his eyes because it would not go away. He didn't know what it was or why it was, but like a toothache or a chronic illness, the world came to him through it, distorted. He would resolve to ignore it and then he would see Leo in the kitchen and something small and mean would arise from it and that would be his first offering of the day.

Long ago, he'd been afraid that it was the first symptom, though every year it seemed more likely to be the only symptom. Cause not known, risk to others suspected but also not known, it could be as isolated as it was isolating, but it could also be like the firestorm of pneumonic plague; for that reason, he didn't take chances. Relentless, it kept pace with him throughout the day and was the last sound he heard at night. When he wasn't exhausted, he could lie in bed for hours with that pumping air. Years ago, on a January night, he'd been frantic, arranging and rearranging the pillows, trying to shut it out, the parade of years inescapable; he saw an endless procession of plots and maneuvers and their utter failure through wretched middle age and desperate old age. But then came the call of a great horned owl. The rich, pure notes melting softly into the darkness. He'd fallen asleep immediately.

Since that time, he'd been grateful for birds; they were, in a way, reassuring.

At the end of his evening prayers he prayed for himself, that tomorrow would find him a better servant of God. He didn't seem to grow in love from day to day but he liked to think that at least he'd ended his prayers and the day on an optimistic note.

Jim was in a deep sleep when the phone rang. He fumbled with the sheet and reached a hand from the bed. In the thick darkness of the room he couldn't see his cell phone, but his hand knew where it was. He brought it to the pillow, set it against his ear.

Silence. Then: "Go to the bridge. She's waiting there."

He held the phone away, saw that it was 2:11 a.m. Took a breath and, the temptation overcome, he said in an even tone, "I'm sorry. This is St. Patrick rectory. You have the wrong number."

As soon as the phone was returned to the table, it rang again. Wide awake now, Jim was more forceful. "I don't know whom you're trying to call but this is the rectory of a Catholic church."

The voice was a baritone—flat, determined. "Go to the bridge. Hurry. She's there now."

Now he was annoyed. Prankster, he thought, or one of the kids wandering away from the bars, too drunk to know he'd misdialed. He'd never get back to sleep. For a breakdown, you called for a tow. For a crash, you called the police. But then a thought: maybe it was a bad crash . . .

"What bridge? Which one?"

His caller was gone.

3

Just over two miles long, rising majestically above Narragansett Bay, the Newport Bridge was illuminated against the night, two sets of lights strung like garlands between twin arches at the summit and sweeping down both sides of the bridge, and highway lamps marching from Newport to Jamestown, giving shape and substance to the concrete deck. Its steady companion in the bay was the Rose Island Lighthouse, squat, sturdy, shining an all-seeing red light. Dark ocean, and small lights north and south of the bridge announcing the presence of the little boats catching bluefish this time of year. Newport was a steady glow in his rearview, but at the other end of the bridge the island of Jamestown slumbered in almost total darkness.

There would be a few cars at this hour, people who'd gone to the parties Mike mentioned and then attended the after-parties, and people who'd hung around the city after the bars had closed. A two-car collision, possibly, or more likely a drunk driver who'd lost control. Though an accident would be announced by the flashing light of an ambulance or firetruck in the thin fog blowing over the bridge. Perhaps he was too late. Or had arrived before them.

He tried not to dwell on what he would find, what metal and concrete could do to muscle and bone and the slight barrier of skin. His car creeping along the bridge deck, he shook himself in an effort to awaken those parts of him that mulishly insisted on their need for sleep. He scanned the road ahead but saw nothing, looked over the newly installed jersey barrier and although he could see up to the summit, the road was clear. He was wondering whether, considering the hour, he would be able to do a U-turn in the toll plaza if the car was on the other side of the barrier. Then, out of the corner of his eye, he saw her.

She was on the narrow walk used by the work crews and prohibited to everyone else. A long pale column, was that a nightgown or a dress, solitary, making slow progress. Straight, shoulder-length hair caught by the endless sea breeze, the separate strands lifting independently, silver under the lights, swirling and dropping and lifting again. At this hour, she could have been the last person on earth. At this hour, the breathing in his ears, that constant companion, uncanny on the deserted bridge, she could have been nothing that belonged to earth. A dress, he decided, pale blue or yellow or perhaps white; it was hard to tell in artificial light. So long it nearly covered her feet, so twisted by the breeze that it reduced her progress to small steps.

He drew beside her and lowered the passenger-side window.

"Do you need a ride?"

She was tall. Straight-backed, remote. As she turned he felt a momentary, atavistic fear. But she was mortal, holding up one side of the dress so she wouldn't trip over it. Sandals with thin, high heels that challenged her balance. Her other hand gripped a bag. A quick look to affirm that he was there, that she was no longer alone, and then she tried to increase her pace. One hand fell against the railing as she struggled to remain upright. Her balance shifted; she dropped the bag and struggled until her other hand found the railing behind her.

"I'm a priest at St. Patrick Church in Newport. Can I give you a ride?"

"Fuck you." Spoken carefully, but thickly nonetheless; she was drunk.

"Did your car break down somewhere? Were you in a crash?"

She continued to edge along the walkway, steel painted an optimistic milky green, the color of the sea embracing a Caribbean beach. The lanes going east were empty; he glanced into the rearview mirror to the westbound lanes behind him. No one coming. He turned off the ignition but left the lights on.

"Do you know where you're going?"

"Get the fuck away from me."

It was an attempt that fell short of a snarl; she wanted to sound menacing but she was frightened. She picked up her pace, determined to put distance between them.

He opened the car door and got out. "At least let me get your bag."

He knew she wouldn't like that but he couldn't be patient. At this time of night, anyone coming over the bridge probably was driving drunk. No, that was wrong: the morning of July 4, it was a certainty that anyone driving over the bridge was drunk. Drunk, drivers often turned the wheel to follow their gaze; he'd read enough news reports of stranded motorists being hit as they stood near their cars, of cars slamming into police cruisers stopped to render aid or to ticket speeders. He needed to get the woman—and himself—off the bridge.

She was young. Late twenties, he thought. The light glinting off her eyes without revealing color, the skin beneath them dark with smudged mascara. The damp air caught her hair in strands that seemed to move by a will of their own, dancing around her face and shoulders, lifting and falling. She was shivering and though still regally erect, her voice rose in fear. "Come near me and I'll jump."

He suddenly felt unearthed, dizzy and breathless. The death presented to him might as well have been his own, given his body's response. He yearned for a police cruiser; cops knew how to help suicidal people. It wouldn't look good: a Catholic priest, a suicidal woman, three in the morning, only one car. It wouldn't just look bad, it would be scandalous. Newport gossiped and no one would believe that someone called a rectory rather than a police station to report a suicidal woman on the bridge. Scandalous or not, he didn't care: at that moment he wanted a cop more than he'd wanted anything in his life.

"Don't. For the love of God." He didn't recognize his voice. No one would listen to something so puny, so lacking in authority. He tried again: "I'm a priest. Whatever it is, I want to help. Please."

"You can't help." She leaned back against the railing.

It wouldn't be easy to jump; tall though she was, she'd have to lift herself a little to go over the railing. In the condition she was in, she probably wouldn't have the coordination to do it. Though probably wasn't certainty.

"I know. But wait a minute. Wait a minute. Listen." His mind scrambled for something to say. He never had the right words, never had the right tone; he could have howled with frustration. He felt the needle prick of a mosquito on his left leg but didn't dare move. "You can jump but you know what? Honestly? You probably wouldn't kill yourself from this height. Probably not."

"How would you know? You get a fucking PhD in bridge-jumping?"

She wanted him to feel the scorn, not recognizing that nothing she said would sound as if it had come from strength. "I'm guessing you're from out of town so you don't know. Even at the summit, you might not kill yourself."

The ocean air moved around him, cold, wet, heavy with the clean smell of water. It was like being wrapped in frost; it penetrated his shirt and light jacket and he was shivering badly. Maybe that was fear rather than cold. "It happens. People break bones or break their neck and they end up paralyzed." He'd snatched at the word when he saw that she was listening. "You'd be paralyzed. You wouldn't want to risk that. That would really eat at you, knowing what you'd given up."

That made her angry. "Gave up what?"

"I don't know, but you don't either. Let me ask you something: When you woke up this morning, did you think you'd end the day here?" She was still listening, but she also was leaning farther over the railing now, hands holding on tightly behind her. Goosebumps rose on his arms and crawled up the back of his neck, but he concentrated on keeping his voice steady, despite it. "I didn't know I'd be on the bridge tonight and I'll guess you didn't either. And if you decide to take a chance on another day, when you wake up tomorrow you won't know what's ahead the rest of that day either. You won't know what may happen and what good might come your way. That's the beauty of it, don't you think?"

Another bite. Same leg. A separate part of his mind saw the rectory, dim glow of the lamps, the quiet of the rooms, the warmth, so distant as to feel unreal.

"Look, I don't know anything about you or your life, but I do know about the bridge. I've lived here all my life. Sometimes people die and sometimes they don't. You wouldn't want to take a chance like that. I wouldn't, anyway. Here, I can show you what the drop is. I've got a flashlight. It's sitting right here in my car. I can shine it down to the water and you'll see the drop. You should know how far down you'd be going. Okay? I promise I won't touch you."

Fingers stiff with cold, he grabbed the flashlight and went around the back of the car. Stepped on the walkway a few feet away from her and switched on the light.

The water danced below, dark but glinting in the glow of the bridge lights. His flashlight wasn't needed—they were standing at the beginning of the bridge's incline, not too far above the water—but he trained the light down, to small whitecaps, the chaotic chop as waves collided. He heard a plop that could have been water striking itself, or something that surfaced and then dove again.

"You can see it's a fair drop but then you have the waves and you don't know how you'll hit." He was inventing now, just to keep talking. He thought she wouldn't jump if he was talking. "You hit them the right way and maybe you're gone instantly but probably not. Could be that your neck is broken when you slam into the water and you're aware that you're drowning but you can't do anything about it because you're paralyzed and can't swim to the surface. Or you hit the water the wrong way and you break a lot of bones and maybe puncture a lung or something. That happens, too."

She let out a deep breath that could have been a snort. "So, yeah, you don't shut up, do you?"

"You're making me nervous." A quick glance at her. "I'm usually more of a listener." He moved a fraction closer, not so much that she would notice but enough to satisfy him that he could grab her before she jumped. Looking down, he was fairly certain that the jump wouldn't kill her. But then she might drown. It hardly mattered how she died; dead was dead.

"I'm a good listener. I don't have a lot of talents but I do have that. I'm a very good listener and I can listen right up to the eight o'clock Mass. We could go back to the rectory and have some coffee or tea to warm up and you can talk and I'll listen. If you want to talk. You don't have to talk, though. Not if you don't want to. We could just sit and—"

"It's true about the bridge?" Her words were a little clearer; he thought she was sobering up, which may have been a good thing, or not.

"I am a really bad liar. I've never been able to think up a lie on the spot. My mind just goes blank. It used to drive my sister crazy when we were kids and got caught doing something we weren't supposed to be doing. She used to call me magma brain because she said it moved so slowly."

The last was unexpected and he felt the hot shame of telling a stranger something so humiliating. The worst part of it was knowing she didn't say it to be mean; for Lizzie it was a statement of fact.

But it had a good effect on the woman, who actually laughed. Not out of the woods but some muscles relaxed a bit, though not all—he was cold and damp right through to his bones.

Behind him a murmur became the distinct thump of wheels passing over the expansion joints on the bridge deck. Not two sets of wheels; he thought he heard four separate sounds, possibly five. An eighteen-wheeler, then, the sound sweeping along the bridge, as if with the sea breeze. The vibration of it ran along the concrete, found his shoes and moved up his body. He felt himself rising and falling, sickeningly, as the bridge adjusted to the massive weight of it.

They were both caught, silenced and stilled as the sound approached. He realized that her features should have been lit, her eyes should have been blinded by the penetrating beams of the truck's headlights. The truck was being driven without lights.

Gulls and cormorants, sleeping on the concrete pier and the solitary roofless shack on Gull Rocks, an outcropping just north of the bridge, shrieked and rose and then scattered into the darkness.

The woman staggered, tripping on her gown. The noise became deafening, slamming against his ears, ricocheting in his head. He knew they would be crushed. Knew that the truck would smash into the car and grind them into the railing. But still he couldn't move. Because he couldn't think which way to move, which way would save them. Couldn't think at all. He thought he felt her grab his arm but then she was ripped away and he knew there was no truck. The woman scrabbled for a moment and then kicked back over the railing and was gone.

4

He'd never had a calling to the priesthood, at least not what he thought a calling must be like. There was no growing awareness, no awakening, no loving but insistent voice. If that was what a calling was; he didn't know. Instead, it was a kind of compulsion, like running into the water when the sun on the beach was so hot the sweat poured down the side of your face. You didn't have a choice.

At Portsmouth Abbey he'd barely lifted his head from his books. Latin and German, Christian doctrine, English, history, calculus, physics. You studied from the time you got home until midnight just so you could keep up. Walking between the classroom and the refectory, black robes flapping around their legs, seated on either side of the altar, the monks were calm, were certainty. Were safety. The rule of the order nearly fifteen hundred years old, calling men to silence, obedience, humility. The routine of their days, the community, even knowing that when they died they would lie with their brothers in the abbey cemetery. Emblazoned on the church, reassurance: "You are no longer strangers and sojourners, but you are fellow citizens with the saints and members of the household of God . . ."

He watched them at Mass, listened to them in the classroom and graduated third in his class, but no call came to him. Nothing urged him to join the monks flanking the altar, lifting his voice in praise to God.

Which was not to say they had no effect. You couldn't miss the distinction they drew and tried to live, the clear difference between love and the less austere emotions, kindness among them (one of Leo's set pieces was on American infantilism embodied in the cult of kindness). Love, he came to understand, was emptying yourself as Jesus had done. Giving every creature the love it craved, and to be profligate, indiscriminate about it.

He wished he could do that, but he could no more do that than he could live in an abbey. Rubbing up against the same people every day, year in and out. You couldn't avoid knowing the other monks and their knowing you. Living so closely there could be no secrets. As a diocesan priest, you could decide how close you came to people, could determine how much love could be safely meted out. As a diocesan priest, living alone or nearly alone in a rectory, no one could hear you when you awakened to another day in the company of the susurrant voice or see that, overcome, you'd been weeping.

He remembered the feel of that woman. Not when he first grabbed her; after the immediate shock of finding himself in the bay, he'd been struggling to keep them both alive. He'd lost his shoes going over the railing, but his pants and jacket pulled at his arms and legs as he'd slashed at the waves, closing the distance between himself and the woman. It was brutal work, straining against the sodden fabric as he stretched his arms in a crawl and kicked frantically; he felt he was fighting himself. And in the dark, gelid water, his nostrils burning with salt and the harsh, wet smells that merged in the air, he felt something brush against his legs, as if urging him along. He put out a hand and grabbed the fabric of her dress. It felt oddly like a mushroom cap, smooth and so tender it would rip if roughly handled. But he hadn't had time to be considerate of it; the dress would be pulling her down. The sound of choking momentarily stopped as he yanked at the material, bringing her to him, and then she was grabbing his shoulders, as if she meant to climb over him. With his free arm he'd encircled her and pulled her against him, kicking to prevent them from sinking.

It was after he saw the fishing boat approaching, when it became apparent that he wouldn't have to haul them both to shore but only needed keep their heads above water until they were pulled into the boat. As the skipper cut the engine and let the boat drift the last few feet, Jim had never been so aware of his body as flesh, not because he was gasping with the cold, or that every inch of skin was wet, or that every muscle was straining to keep them from drowning, but because her body had been flesh; frantic, as wet and freezing as his body, but with young muscle and bone beneath. He'd never held a woman in his arms. Never held anyone.

Her name was Emily. She worked at Metropolitan Auctions in New York City. She had attended one of the parties Mike had mentioned and when she arrived she'd discovered that her lover was there with an even younger woman. From what she told him, Jim surmised that she had left the party and gone to a bar, or possibly bars, and had only stopped drinking when the bars closed. From there she had gone to the bridge.

She told him this at 5:30 a.m., when he was driving her from the police station to her rental. Angelo, the skipper of the boat, had called the station. About fifty years old, with a deeply etched face that appeared to have every ounce of fat sucked from it—years of sun, salt spray, and, possibly, drug addiction. Angelo repeated to the dispatcher what he'd been told. He'd pulled two people from the bay: a young woman who had lost her balance on the bridge, and a Catholic priest who had spotted the woman just before she fell in.

Wracked with cold, seawater like a living thing slithering down her arms and back, her arms wrapped around her middle, her body curled in on itself, teeth chattering, her head down, Emily didn't deny the accidental nature of her plummet from the bridge. In the back seat of the patrol car, she had refused a trip to the ER, insisting that no bones were broken and she'd barely swallowed any water. At the station, she'd sat straight in the chair, as if she were being interviewed for a job, but had been unable to stop shaking, whether from cold or shock, replying in monosyllables to the officer making the report. As Jim recounted the call he'd received, the officer, baby-faced and stout, looked up a few times, his expression skeptical, but he'd told Jim that he knew Jim's sister, the ER doc who, he'd said, grinning, was hell on wheels with the drunks who spent their weekends getting into fights.

And now he was in his car again, this time with Leo. Running on two hours of sleep but at least they were going against the traffic. He was trying to replay the sound of the truck that wasn't a truck and finding that he couldn't do it.

"Hot as blazes last night," Leo offered. "I couldn't catch my breath it was so close."

Jim remembered only his own clammy skin, the hair on his arms vibrating with cold, the damp sea breeze and the brutal water, though when he'd checked the car seats after morning Mass, he'd found them warm and dry. "Probably worse at the newer parishes. The old rectories like ours were built to minimize the extremes."

Leo was unmoved. "The only fortunate aspect of the rectory is its propinquity to the hospital. When I am felled by heat stroke, it will be a short trip to medical care. That's *if* I get heat stroke; I suspect what's really happening is that I'm deliquescing, like a bar of soap in water."

"I talked to someone at Seaside. He said he'd have the owner call us back. If the cost is prohibitive, we may be stuck with portable units."

"I can't tolerate the window ones. With the roar it's like trying to sleep in an airport, one of those intercontinental jets taking off right above your head. It's a poor choice: death by dissolution or insanity by 747."

Jim hadn't been surprised that Leo hadn't mentioned the early morning outing. Leo's bedroom was far from the rectory's driveway, but Jim's cell phone was loud, set to maximum volume so it would wake him if he slept. With his eyes still on the highway, "By the way. Last night. You didn't hear anything did you? Late last night?"

"You mean the phone?"

"You heard the phone?"

Leo was looking out the window. Jim saw that he had a blot of something, dark against dark—jam, maybe—on his shirt. "Someone called the rectory?"

"Called the rectory phone? I don't think so."

"If you're talking about yours, I never hear yours. Why, did you get a call?"

Jim hesitated. "It's a little odd," he said at last. "I checked my call log and the last one came in yesterday afternoon. Nothing after that."

Now he had Leo's interest. "Were you expecting a call?"

"No."

Leo's thin lips came together and he shook his head, exasperated. "Well if no one called, why would I hear anything?"

The collation was in the common room of the nursing home in which Anselm Chace had spent the last decades of his life. It was meant to be bright: cream walls, a turquoise chair rail, a large cork billboard papered with greeting cards, a calendar with a photo of the Rocky Mountains, announcements printed on pastel-colored papers. Cold fluorescent lights overhead and in the kitchen, where everything was stainless steel. Scuffed linoleum. Jim found it depressing.

The nuns had set up a table with sandwiches and small pastries, coffee, tea, and water. Priests hovered in groups near the tables, chatting and eating. Jim had greeted one or two as they'd left the church but he was terrible at small talk; usually, he started with a few polite questions, but if they led nowhere, he felt he'd be perceived as prying if he asked more, and so the conversation would fall flat. He recalled Lizzie when they were young, chattering to one or another of the neighbors, perfectly confident, even then, that what she had to say was worth hearing. Perhaps first-borns had that self-assurance; he'd stand by, mortified because he expected her to be rebuffed, but if she was she never noticed, and she'd rattle on until someone else caught her eye. He would never be that outgoing; he knew, even before Blessed Sacrament, that he just wasn't as easy with people as she was.

Jim was near the entrance, watching Leo make a circuit around the table, when he felt someone come up behind him.

"And here you are, now, Jim Ennis, big as life and twice as natural." Martin Reilly, desiccating in his early eighties. Salt and-pepper hair and a face that appeared mild until you saw the eyes, watchful and cool as a lynx. Reilly had left Ireland more than fifty years before but he retained the brogue. Jim thought some people never acquired the accent of the adopted country because they had no ear for sound; he'd noticed those people couldn't sing, either. He didn't think that was the case with Reilly.

"'Man of the Island' I call you. A rare thing, now, serving your whole life on the little island. First at the college there, and now at St. Patrick. Although I hear you're doing double-duty these days."

Jim didn't pretend not to understand. "Well, Kevin is getting older."

Reilly leaned closer. "Still plays a good game of golf, from what I hear."

Jim changed the subject.

"How did I know Anselm? We were both at Assumption; that was years ago. The pastor at the time was Tim Donovan, from the next county over in Ireland. Did you know him at all? You'd remember: past master of the mutter, he was. You could take your ears off, give them a good scrub, stick them back on and still not understand a word the man was saying. Anselm was a terrible mimic." Catching Jim's expression, Reilly nodded. "You wouldn't know that. Brilliant, it was. Not a mean bone in him but he couldn't help himself. Ah, it was great fun and then Anselm was sent to St. Patrick."

"St. Patrick?" Jim felt the blood rush from his face and feared he was perilously close to fainting. He gulped iced tea from the glass he was holding and the feeling receded a little.

"You didn't know? He wasn't there long. Some trouble, I think, though I don't know what it was. He was sent to St. Joseph in Pascoag and after that he jumped around a bit before he went to Blessed Sacrament."

Jim was trying to catch up with it, realized he was panting a little, Reilly observing him the whole time. Took another sip, which kept his eyes averted. "Maybe he didn't get along with the pastor."

"He never said and I didn't ask." Something in his voice made Jim look up. "It wasn't my business."

Anselm facing the congregation from the same altar, saying Mass, his hands holding the same vessels. Anselm pacing over the same walk from church to rectory, his fingers grasping the same handle of the door. Not in the same bedroom, thank God; Jim's bedroom had always been reserved for the pastor. But bad enough. Perhaps Leo would know what had happened. "I served Mass at Blessed Sacrament until I started at Portsmouth Abbey. After that I lost track. Did he have the breakdown while he was at Blessed Sacrament?"

"Breakdown? Is that what people are saying?" Reilly considered it. "You might call it that, I suppose. He's been with the sisters for about nineteen? Or wait a minute, hang on . . . Twenty years. Yes. Twenty."

Only a few years after Jim had fled the church, terrified. Jim suddenly saw the church again, the rows upon rows of dappled pews, the crucified Jesus, the muted glow of the sanctuary lamp, and the absolute stillness inside and outside, the birds as quiet as if the skies had darkened ahead of a storm.

"Someone said he'd been catatonic."

"Did they?" A narrow look, held for several uncomfortable seconds. "Well, nature abhors a vacuum, I suppose. Anselm and I were good friends, certainly, but I don't know anything about it."

Jim had told himself he didn't want to know but now he felt disappointed. "So you don't know how he ended up here?"

Reilly looked away, silent, thinking. Assessing, Jim thought. When Reilly spoke again, it was so low that Jim leaned in to hear. "The 'why' I don't know; that's private, I'm told. Patient confidentiality they call it. But the 'how' is another matter altogether and I suppose I'll tell you. We were to have Sunday dinner and I drove down to Blessed Sacrament and Anselm wasn't in the rectory. So I went out the side door and met a man coming out of the parish hall. Locking up after Mass, he was, and I asked him had he seen Father Chace. 'No,' says he, 'he's not in the parish hall because I've just closed it up for the day.' So I tell him I'll go to the church.

Well, he isn't in the sacristy and I think maybe he's preparing the readings for the next day, so I walk out to the altar."

The brogue receded. "I've kept this close all these years. Never wanted to talk about it. Never wanted to think about it either, truth be told. He was sitting on the deacon's bench, still as a stone. Nothing moving. You didn't even know was he breathing or not. 'Anselm,' I says, 'are you there at all?' And no response. Not a word. Didn't even turn to look. I had the thought that he was having a stroke and I should call for the ambulance. Then I'm right in front of him and him still not stirring. It was then I saw his eyes. God help me, I still see them."

5

Lizzie was an indifferent cook, couldn't tell a flower from a weed, and her interest in the house had waned after she'd chosen the exterior paint. She rarely read novels, couldn't tell you what movies were playing on the island and avoided the computers and televisions in her home. What she was interested in was people. Her house was overrun with medical journals; when the Clarkes had company, the dining room table had to be cleared before it could be set and room made on the coffee table for hors d'oeuvres. Jim had heard the stories from patients he visited at the hospital, how Lizzie had grilled the patient and then ordered a test or bloodwork to confirm her diagnosis, how the doctors in Providence and Boston had been amazed that she'd put her diagnostic finger right on the problem without the aid of the technology the big-city doctors relied on.

Her patients weren't the only ones she grilled: Jim had watched, many times, as Lizzie fired a barrage of questions at a friend, insistent, unrelenting, but so obviously with simple, almost naïve curiosity that people liked her, sometimes despite themselves. She remembered everything she had been told, decades later. She wasn't gathering facts to make a judgment, wasn't compiling fodder for gossip, and people knew that. If you asked why she wanted every detail, every scrap of information, her face would go blank with surprise. "I'm interested," she'd say, as if that explained everything.

He remembered her at their home on Gibbs Avenue, after their father died, people milling around the living room, the dining room, and the kitchen, the solemnity of the day wearing off as the afternoon stretched. He was bringing plates into the kitchen and as he passed through the dining room, he heard Lizzie saying to Frank Silvia, one of their father's oldest friends, "You shouldn't be drinking. Two glasses of alcohol is the limit for men, but you have liver disease in your family and you shouldn't be drinking at all."

Sometimes she exhausted him. Right now, though, he was looking forward to seeing her.

Before the long weekend, Megan Marks, the pastoral assistant, had gathered the booklets the summer session students would be reading, but while Jim knew he was running out of time to order new booklets, he only returned the calls, spending most of the hours after the funeral on the computer in his office. A robin sounded its eight hurried notes in the enormous maple outside Jim's window, and the afternoon breeze was from the south, bringing moist sea air to the office. Today it was pungent; more than a touch of seaweed but also the sharp smell of mud at low tide. At some point in his online search, he realized that if he followed a link deeper and then the next link and then the next, he arrived at divergent diagnoses and was unequal to evaluating their merits. Lizzie would be a help.

The Clarkes lived five blocks away, in a quiet neighborhood in which tall hedges hid Victorian-era homes with lush lawns and graceful landscaping. Lizzie liked old houses but the home was too large for her taste. "Why do we need five bedrooms?" But Sam had wanted it and they'd turned one of the bedrooms into Sam's study, a space lined with bookcases that were overflowing with books on marine biology, Narragansett Bay, astronomy, geology, botany, and guides to all the places they'd been and places they might someday go.

Lizzie had chosen a cheerful yellow for the clapboard, a creamy green for the scalloping and black for the trim. A porch wrapped around three sides of the house and was a resting place in winter for shovels and ice melt, and a parking lot the rest of the time for the children's bikes, racquets, skateboards, surfboards, boogie boards, two kayaks, and other transient artifacts of fun three seasons of the year. Smiling, as he always did at any reminder of his niece and nephew, Jim went around the porch and found the latter and his mother on the patio in the backyard. It was a comfortable arrangement: wicker chairs; a wicker loveseat and two chaises; a glass-topped, wicker coffee table and two end tables. A large grill sat at one end of the patio, away from the seating. Sam had planted a cherry tree in one corner of the yard; an enormous hickory, chosen by an earlier owner, loomed from another corner.

Lizzie was basting chicken on the grill. Wreathed in smoke, she batted the cloud with her free hand when she saw Jim.

"Good night for fireworks," Lizzie said. "Unless the fog comes in."

That made him think of the tendrils that had wrapped around him on the bridge. He closed the space between himself and his nephew, who was sprawled on one of the chaises, reading. Ten years old, Willy was small-boned, slender, blue-eyed like both his parents, and his skin was nearly as pale as his mother's but lacked the freckles. Willy had a wide mouth like Lizzie, a Roman nose like his father, but otherwise he was a mystery. While Triona was maturing in the expected stages, Willy seemed to have been born in finished form, complete.

Jim had thought of Willy as just a calm, happy baby before his nephew's first Christmas. A store-bought Yule log in hand, Jim had gone to the kitchen, where Lizzie was mashing potatoes, and Willy, in a high chair, was pushing dry cereal around the tray. Lizzie asked Jim to stir butter into the potatoes while she checked the vegetables in the oven. They were chatting, distracted. Then Willy shouted, a sharp, unintelligible sound that nevertheless conveyed alarm. They both turned to Willy, but as Lizzie turned, she saw what she hadn't before: Triona had entered the kitchen and was barreling toward the oven. Triona's hand was inches away from the open door as Lizzie snatched her up. Shaken, Lizzie went to find Sam.

Willy had returned to his cereal as if nothing extraordinary had happened. Nine months old, before he even could talk: Jim was staggered.

Everyone liked him, Lizzie said wonderingly: the big kids, the little kids, their parents, the teachers, the neighbors. Willy seemed perpetually alive to the humor in the world and everything, everyone, seemed to charm him. He was funny, but his jokes were never mean and had always been wry but not pointed. But that's not why Triona's friends looked for Willy when they visited. When you were in his company you were happy. Something about him, as if he had been given an extra dose of grace.

"I hope you haven't read these." Willy dove into the paper bag, pulling books out one by one, glancing at the titles, flipping them to read the back-cover copy.

"Thank you, Uncle Jim," Lizzie said.

"What she said." And seeing that he had his uncle's attention, rolled his eyes.

Jim watched in a moment of perfect happiness. "No friends tonight?"

"Just us," Lizzie said. "Caitriona's going to the fireworks with Sarah's family—they have a power boat—so it's just the four of us. I've got chicken and a couple of steaks, potato salad, coleslaw, and island corn, which is one vegetable Willy will eat. You want a beer, don't you?" And without waiting for an answer, "Willy, tell your father that Uncle Jim is here and wants a beer."

Willy disappeared into the house.

"Where should I put Triona's bag?"

"Just drop it anywhere. Sam can bring it in later. Anyway, Willy said he'd like to be an altar server and Triona will be, whether she wants to do it or not."

"That reminds me," he said, "are the kids signed up for the summer session?"

"Did you look at the workbooks they use? You could be an atheist and have no problem with them. I can't believe they're published by a Catholic press."

He chose one of the chairs and stretched out his legs. The friction of cloth against his skin alerted him to the two mosquito bites on his legs; Jim absently leaned down to scratch. "I've already changed morning Mass to 5 a.m. You want new books, too?"

"Five?" Lizzie whirled around, a morsel of chicken flying off the fork, just missing him. She saw his face. "I knew you were kidding."

Jim had hoped to talk to Lizzie when they were alone. Sometimes she frightened the children; focused on some diagnosis or some person, her descriptions could be graphic and her speculation could be chilling. Twenty-four hours ago, he'd wanted to ask her about the temporoparietal junction, which likely would have been a safe topic for children's ears. But that was before the funeral.

"Did you ever see someone who was catatonic?"

He'd tried to make his voice sound casual, but it stopped Lizzie instantly. The fork held like a scepter, she turned on him. "Who's catatonic? You know someone who's catatonic? Is it someone at the hospital? It's not Leo, is it? Considering he eats all the coffee cake and whatever else he can vacuum up, I wouldn't be surprised."

"I shouldn't have told you that; it was petty." And wondered whether he should ask her to stop badgering Leo about diabetes every time she saw him. He gave it a shot.

"Someone has to; it's obvious his own doctor isn't telling him to stop eating junk."

In the face of his silence, she shrugged. "Oh, all right; I won't embarrass you anymore, okay? I know how sensitive you are about everything."

"No, I'm not."

"Mom always said you took everything to heart." As if he hadn't spoken. "Anyway, you don't know who Leo's doctor is, do you? Someone ought to follow up with Leo about his eating."

"Not a clue."

"So what about the guy who's catatonic?"

"It's Anselm Chace. Leo and I went to his funeral. Someone said he'd been in a kind of suspended animation for years. Is that even possible?"

Lizzie laid steaks on the grill and turned the chicken breasts; a new eruption of smoke bloomed outward and the smell reminded Jim how long it had been since the collation. "I've never seen it but yeah, it can happen."

"I looked it up online and came up with catatonia, narcolepsy, and narcolepsy-catalepsy. At least, I think that's what I came up with; the problem with the web is that there's no translation from professional to layman. Could one of those things freeze someone for twenty years?"

Jim felt a small, sharp pain and bent to hit his left leg. "Mosquito. Right through my pants. They've been eating me alive lately."

"You should use spray; you were a super-attractor when we were kids." Lizzie was thinking. "Father Chace. I remember him. He was the one with the limp. Mom liked him because he used his vacation every year to volunteer for Habitat for Humanity and things like that. Maybe he was a good guy but I thought he was scary."

Jim didn't remember a limp. "You thought he was scary?"

"Definitely creepy." Lizzie looked closely at him. "You didn't get that vibe from him?"

Jim was spared a reply as Willy emerged from the house, Sam behind him. Sam had Jim's beer in one hand and a scotch in the other. As they approached, Sam's glass, twin ice cubes rattling, found its way to the back of Willy's neck. Willy feinted, grinning.

Sam had grown up in Portsmouth. Lizzie and Sam began to date when they were in college; Sam had been at MIT when Lizzie started freshman year at Harvard, and they'd found themselves on the same bus to the island a few times. After college, Sam had taken a job in Newport at the Naval Undersea Warfare Center. Lizzie had gone to medical school in Providence and afterward, she'd been offered the job at the hospital. When they'd bought the house, their mother had asked Lizzie if she meant to populate all the bedrooms—Lizzie's directness was somewhat genetic, Jim thought. But they'd stopped at two children.

Every marriage, Jim thought, is a secret. Why two particular people decide to make a life together. What forces hold one particular marriage together, what precise combination of forces, and balance of forces, cause another to break apart. Lizzie gave off a kind of kinetic energy at all times; Sam was calmer, an undemanding and reassuring presence that made it easy for you to just sit with him while the children played with their toys and Lizzie was on the phone with the hospital. And while Lizzie loved people, Sam was content with his own family. He sat back and watched his wife at family gatherings with something like pride, as if her interrogations were a trick that he'd taught her.

"You and Jim talking about priests? They all terrify me. That's why your father never goes to Mass, Willy."

"Also you are not Catholic." Willy's voice had always been arresting. Deep, but so thin it cracked now and then, and each word, each letter, nearly, was distinct. He was a stranger to contractions, which made his speech oddly formal. It had stopped people in their tracks when he was a four-year-old.

"Well, you got me there," Sam said agreeably. "I do know a few, though."

"Sam, did you bring out the stuff in the fridge?"

Sam, who'd just settled in the chair, rose again, uncomplaining, accustomed to his wife's sudden commands.

Lizzie cut into a chicken breast, saw that it was done. "Narcolepsy-catalepsy syndrome is pretty rare. There's also encephalitis lethargica. Did you see that movie about a group of patients who contracted it around the time of the 1918 flu epidemic? I remember reading the book in med school. They could hear and see but they couldn't respond. Do you know if he was aware of what was going on around him?"

"I didn't ask."

"What about symptoms? Was he complaining of anything right before it happened?"

Jim saw she was winding up. "All I know is what I told you."

"How about his family history? Did anyone in the family have neurological problems?"

Jim had a sudden image of Lizzie going around the common room after the funeral, interrogating the groups of priests. He fought a smile. "Lizzie, I don't know and I didn't ask, okay? Can people just go on that way until they die?"

"Yeah," she said flatly. "That's it. You're zonked out for life. Someone tried a course of L-dopa on the 1918 flu group and they came back but it was only temporary. And the drug had serious side effects: compulsive thoughts, spasms. Unbearable."

Sam stopped on his way to the table, cradling a bowl of potato salad. He took in Willy, who was listening intently. Looked at Lizzie, who was oblivious, and frowned.

"What causes it?" Willy asked, his new books forgotten.

"Unknown." Lizzie methodically flipped the steaks. "Possibly an enterovirus but could be a bacterium. Nobody's figured it out."

Sam set the bowl on the table. "But it's rare," he said, leading her. "You've never seen a case, Liz."

Sam's voice brought Lizzie out of her thoughts but she mistook the point. "I don't have to see it to know about it."

"Probably as likely to see someone savaged by a starfish," Sam said.

"Starfish do not have teeth," Willy pointed out.

Sam turned as if he hadn't known his son was listening. "They don't? Well then, maybe someone gummed to insensibility."

With food on the table, Jim thought the conversation was over. Jim declined Lizzie's offer of coffee and Sam's of port. Sam was bringing dishes to the kitchen when Lizzie came back to the topic. "It's possible he had some sort of psychosis. That could have been the vibe I got from him when we were kids. But I don't think so. More likely he had PTSD. Was he in a war?"

"Again, no clue."

Lizzie nodded once, as she did when she thought she'd worked out a problem. "PTSD. He definitely had PTSD when we were kids. Do you remember how jumpy he was? Exaggerated startle. Not normal." She nodded again. "Like he thought someone was sneaking up on him. Hypervigilance is pretty classic. PTSD can cause psychosis. Saw a full-blown case of it last year; the guy thought he was back in Vietnam. It's also been linked to catatonia."

"So something happened to him in a war and that caused all the rest of it." Jim could feel some parts of his brain relaxing: nothing to do with him, then.

"Yeah. Or some kind of trauma. That would be my guess."

The dishes cleared, Sam had appeared with Lizzie's sweater. "Dolphins trapped in fishing nets have been observed to go into a catatonic state. Saw a paper about it, three or four years ago."

"We do not have dolphins in the bay," Willy said. The children were opposites in that way: Triona thought all adults were idiots and not worth her time but, even as a toddler, Willy had gravitated to adult conversation.

"Not usually," Sam said, "but every so often, something wanders in. Common dolphins, white-sided dolphins, harbor porpoises."

"Did you see the story about the stranding on the Cape?" Jim wished now that he'd read the article because if Sam hadn't, he had no more to tell his brother-in-law.

Sam had, though. "Yeah and another one a week ago, farther up the coast. Ten of them last week; it's sickening. They're beautiful animals. Did you see the belugas that came into the bay a couple of months ago? The kids and I went over to Jamestown to take a look."

"They are white," Willy said repressively. "Like enormous slugs."

"Amazing what finds its way in. Right whales, sperm whales, at least one humpback that I can think of, fin whales. We also get a fair amount of tropical fish, because the fry aren't strong enough to fight the Gulf Stream, so they get swept north and end up in Narragansett Bay every year. Of course, almost all of them die during the winter months because the average temperature of the bay in January and February is just above freezing, and it can get as cold as four degrees."

Over the years, Jim had heard Sam discuss the mechanism of avian migration; the use of tree rings to date volcanic eruptions, hermaphroditic marine life, and climate change in the Early Jurassic Period (Triona had gone through a dinosaur phase). Lizzie told Jim, somewhat proudly, that vacations usually involved the howling of oversaturated children; Sam read the history, geography, and everything else about the countries they visited and by the time their bags were checked at Logan Airport and they were boarding, usually was able to conduct a rudimentary conversation in their destination's vernacular.

Willy had been watching his father with waning interest but then he brightened. "Dad is a spy now."

"Willy will need a jacket," Lizzie said.

Sam grinned at his son. "007 and a half." And to Jim, "The new job came with higher security clearance. Not exactly spy stuff. Though something odd . . ." He shook his head and disappeared into the house.

"It also came with a higher stress level," Lizzie told Jim. "Sam needs to cut down on fat and salt if he wants to keep his blood pressure down: no more potato chips. Also he has to start working out every day instead of three times a week."

"Because who doesn't love getting up before dawn to work out?" Sam said agreeably, dropping the jacket into his son's lap. "I have no idea how Willy knew about the security clearance."

"I am smart."

"Or listening at keyholes. It just means I can see more boring stuff than I could before, kid." Sam glanced around the patio to make sure everything had been taken in. He looked weary. "New sonar system that has a longer range. Yet another thing we're going to hand off to a contractor who'll make a fortune manufacturing it. If I had half a brain I would have gone to business school and gotten an MBA."

It was late when Jim returned to the rectory. Tumbling fireworks imprinted on the backs of his eyelids, the cold earth lingering on his palms; Lizzie wouldn't take no for an answer and he was nearly beyond thought he was so tired. He got himself upstairs, saw that Leo had gone to bed, and went to his own bedroom. Turned on the lamp and dropped into the chair. A musty odor communicated itself from the cushions. Years of bodies in all seasons. He thought about the parade of priests down the decades, imagined when the rectory was full and alive with personalities. When St. Patrick was built, the priesthood had been one way for the poor to get an education and steady income. How many men, sitting in the chair he was in, regretted the decision they'd made?

Possibly none; he thought people in those days just got on with it and, too, priests at one time had been given more deference, more respect than they had now. It was possible the men sitting in this chair and the iterations before it had felt pleased with themselves and their station in life. It was different now. You had to be worried about everything: being too friendly with a child, or seen too often with one man, or being alone with a woman. At three in the morning. He should be happy that he'd saved a life; instead, he was worried that talk would ripple outward from the fishing boat or from the police station. It was a hell of a way to live, he thought. And then smiled.

At this hour, most people were done eating and those who were making a night of it at the bars were still drinking. Every so often a firecracker went off. A car or two roared by and now and again, a motorcycle. The birds were done hours ago. An occasional creak as the building cooled and wood contracted. And there was the breathing. Steady.

Jim held his breath, though he'd done it countless times before. The sound continued, long inhalations and exhalations, as if someone nearby was lost in sleep. Or that someone had quieted their breathing, listening quietly, watching quietly. Sometimes he thought it was his own breath, remembered and replayed when he held his breath. He'd had his hearing checked when he'd had his physicals and once he'd seen an audiologist and been disappointed to learn that his hearing was fine. Except it wasn't. Sometimes he could hear around it but most of the time he was hearing through it and it was like seeing something coming toward him through mist.

He never thought about his daily reminder of an earlier time, but now it came to him, the words long broken into syllables that ran together through his brain, almost without thought. Long ago, he'd adopted Agrippina of Mineo, a third-century martyr invoked against evil spirits. That was just after Blessed Sacrament, when he was afraid to sleep, afraid even to turn the light off. He began taking a flashlight to bed and whenever he thought he felt something in his room, he'd switch on the flashlight and slowly sweep the walls and the floor, taking in the signed photo of Red Sox outfielder Ellis Burks on the old dresser, panning over desk and chair, the posters of Dewey Evans and Mike Greenwell and Mo Vaughn looking back at him from the walls. He prayed fervently to Agrippina, right through the abbey and then through Leuven, though the prayer felt less and less urgent over time. He continued the habits, flashlights now beside his bed and in his car, and the prayers, reasoning that prayer never hurt, so why not, just in case. Which wasn't the best reason. The first few months at the American College of Louvain, where no one would give it a second thought, he'd scoured the library for lives of the saints. Teresa of Avila, John of the Cross, Francis, Therese of Lisieux; he'd read all the mystics, looking for clues. John Vianney, who was dragged around the room by the feet. Anthony of Athanasius, who heard voices, the sounds of battle, was beset by demons in the form of wild animals.

Then he'd seen what he was doing, feared that it was rooted in a perverse pride, that it assumed an exceptionalism at odds with the facts of his life. He may or may not have seen something as a child, but he certainly was not beset by anything more than one badly functioning sense. So he stopped reading biographies and autobiographies. Though he kept the prayer to Agrippina, because why not? No reason not to.

He'd never told anyone, not even a confessor.

But now he was rattled. Held up his hands and was surprised to see they weren't shaking, the back of his hands nearly hairless, yellow in the light; noticing the darkness seeping in between long fingers he realized again how dim the rectory was. He was careful not to turn on too many lights in a room. Another thing he would have to look into, especially as summer turned to fall and fall into winter. He assumed the kitchen was better wired but suspected knob-and-tube everywhere else, and some of the fixtures were clearly meant for gaslight but had been converted—who knew when?—to electricity. Probably not to code, he thought.

Hard to be reconciled to an undiagnosed misfiring in the ear or a small part of the aural machinery that didn't work right. The breathing was annoying, maddening, occasionally overwhelming. Assuming that it was a chronic medical condition, he'd tried to live with it. It was like a bad knee, he told himself, which sometimes ached and sometimes subsided to a twinge; people lived with that kind of thing. Like ringing in the ears. Floaters in the eyes. He was lucky to be as healthy as he was, doubted anyone was perfectly healthy. He'd never been hospitalized, never even broken a bone. His familiarity with the hospital was that of a visitor, never a patient.

The eighteen-wheeler that wasn't there. His ears had been malfunctioning for years, but he'd never doubted his other senses.

He leaned back in the chair and closed his eyes. Replayed what had happened on the bridge. He had a flashlight in his hand, had trained it down to the water, and he could discern a pallid shaft of light that dissipated like smoke the further it went from the source. He'd been able to see no more than what the bridge's lights illuminated, although that hadn't mattered; what he'd wanted then was to turn her attention to something other than herself. She wouldn't have noticed the flashlight had been ineffective, not in the condition she was in. He'd been jittery with cold and nerves and then he'd heard the wheels. Had he turned to look? What he remembered was her face, and the thought that it should have been lit by the headlights. So no, he hadn't looked behind him. Nothing wrong with his eyes, then. Perhaps his hearing was moving into a new phase. But then he remembered: the bridge deck had risen and fallen under the weight of something massive.

Anselm sipping coffee in the funhouse kitchen. Padding down the dark halls. Sleeping, possibly, in Leo's room. Loony, Leo said. What did that mean, anyway? He'd asked Leo on the drive home and the best Leo could offer was that Anselm had spent an inordinate amount of time on his knees, praying. One man's pious, Jim thought, was another man's loony. It was relative, a matter of perception, and perception was as individual as one human to another. Take color, for example: one person would see a color and say it was gray, while another would interpret it as blue. Who decided which person's pronouncement was correct? Because the decider would have his own vision of that color, his mind interpreting in a unique way.

Sanity was like that. One person could be talking incoherently and to one man it would be completely unintelligible and obvious that the speaker was no longer functioning in a sane manner, while another man could interpret it as speaking in tongues—mystical, certainly, but no indication that the speaker had broken with reality. Some people thought the moon landing was trickery. Some people called psychics a thousand miles away to have their future told. He'd read about a millionaire who was funding research to make humans immortal. Josef Stalin believed he could determine a person's character by examining their stool and when Chairman Mao visited Moscow, Stalin had the toilet disconnected from the sewer line in order to procure a specimen. Stalin was an abomination but would anyone have said he was insane?

When he'd adopted Agrippina, worried that something evil had attached to him, he'd been a child, and children were credulous. The fact that he'd continued the prayers was unremarkable. It was habit, only habit; it didn't mean he was loony.

Was it possible that his ears were fine, that it was his brain that was malfunctioning, the junction between his temporal and parietal lobes damaged somehow, making him hear things that the rational part of his brain recognized as hallucinations? If it was a lesion on the brain, a long-ago injury that had damaged the temporoparietal junction, he could live with that, too, as long as it didn't get worse. But the eighteen-wheeler. He was sure he'd felt it as it barreled along the bridge. Could his brain conjure up feeling, imagine movement when there was none?

He decided to add one more prayer to his nights, because why not? Dymphna. Lived in Ireland, father a chieftain, deranged with grief over wife's death but cut off his daughter's head when she refused to replace her mother in the marriage bed. Bad parenting, even in the sixth century. Invoked for mental and neurological disorders. Had Anselm started that way? With an ever-growing list of saints invoked for help?

He was listlessly scanning the summer session workbooks, waiting for a reasonable time to go to sleep, and jumped when his phone rang. Hesitated before answering, thinking of the other call. Calls.

"Is this too late?"

Her voice was different, softer. "Emily?"

"I just called to let you know I sent you a check today." The tone was formal, but he heard the uncertainty behind it. "Dry cleaning, detailing your car. I just called to let you know."

"You didn't have to do that. Really. A corporal work . . ." He swallowed the rest of the sentence. Not a corporal work of mercy and he didn't want credit for it. Fear had driven him into the water; the desire to save her had come sometime after that. Also, the words might sound dismissive to her ears.

She took a long breath, willing her next words. "I also wanted to apologize to you, Father. I think I have a lot to apologize for."

The words had been rehearsed. Not in the way people did when they had a list of minor sins to confess and wanted to make sure they included them all, but in the way people did when they felt compelled to confess but didn't want to air the words. She'd said them over and over until she thought she'd escaped the meaning of them, but saying them aloud, understood that she hadn't.

It might have been the difference in their ages but more likely it was the clerical collar. In the confessional, words could bring you close, but outside the sacrament, the collar was a white wall that kept you separate, apart. Even from the family you'd been born into. And that might have been another reason he'd chosen the life he had. Safer for everyone, he'd thought. "You just had too much to drink," he said. "You were upset and you drank too much, that's all."

". . . and then I jumped off a bridge." Marveling a little, as if she were still trying to convince herself it happened. "People get drunk every day but they don't jump off bridges. If you hadn't been there I would have died. Though small loss, right?"

"No," he said firmly. "Not to me and certainly not to God."

He had been absently rubbing one leg against the other; now he reached down and scratched. When Lizzie and he were kids, their mother had plastered every bite with calamine lotion. Jim didn't remember it doing any good. Ice would be better, numb the area. But he was too tired to move.

"My friends think I went swimming. Yeah, so, not real friends, not really. Coworkers. Everyone at work has heard the story and they think it's hysterical. Not that it matters. I told them I got a ride to the beach, went swimming in my dress and then walked back to the house we'd rented. If they ever knew I jumped . . ."

"You fell," he said flatly. "You had too much to drink, you walked onto the bridge and then I came along and you lost your balance. If I hadn't been there, you probably would have found your way back to Newport. Or maybe you would have crossed to Jamestown. I don't know what you would have done but I'm sure you didn't mean to go over the railing."

"I would have drowned," she said, more to herself than to him. "The water felt like it grabbed me and was pulling me down. I know I was drowning when you found me but I don't know whether I wanted to be saved. You know? Maybe I didn't want to be saved."

The breathing had become louder in his ears but her anxiety cut through it.

"You grabbed my shirt." And was grateful for the thought. Lizzie would have been better at this. Firm, positive, but sympathetic. "Remember that? You got a pretty good grip on my shirt. And the other hand latched onto an ear. You must have been going for my collar but you got my elephant ears instead."

"I'm sorry."

He'd hoped to elicit a laugh but he thought he could hear her crying.

He didn't know this woman. Who thought she might have wanted to die. A great distinction between comforting someone who'd had a frightening experience and counseling someone who wasn't sure she wanted to live. He was an amateur at this, had no carefully considered words, no practiced strategy to guide her away from uncertainty and dark thoughts. Arrogant to think he could help her; he might accidentally say the wrong thing, do more harm than good. "Maybe it would help if you talked to someone about it? Someone with training."

"I'm sorry," she said again. "Sorry. I know it's really late. This was probably a bad time to call. Sorry about that. Anyway, thanks for saving my life."

"It's not that late." Sleep called to him. He ached in odd places; muscles he rarely used had been strained by the plunge, by the effort of keeping their heads above water. He was still cold from sitting on the ground, watching the fireworks with Lizzie's family, and he was itchy where he'd been bitten. Because he was so tired, the breathing grated on his nerves. Despite that, he was struck by how quickly the words had come to her. As if she had been waiting to be dismissed and had the words ready. "I won't be going to sleep until the neighbors exhaust their supply of fireworks. And I don't have to get up early for a long commute to work. One of the benefits of being a parish priest."

"I'm probably taking you away from something."

"Not really. I was looking at some workbooks but it's hard to concentrate with fireworks going off every few minutes."

He asked her what she liked to read and led her away from the subject of the bridge, though he badly wanted to know if she had seen the eighteen-wheeler that was there, then wasn't. He could still hear it, the motor, the wheels thumping as they rolled over the expansion joints. The rhythm not breaking even when the driver must have seen the car. If she'd seen it coming, and she must have, why invite her to relive the experience? But if she hadn't? Did he want her to confirm that he'd imagined it?

She returned to the bridge on her own. She'd talked a little about growing up in New York and about her job. Then she took a breath.

"The person who called you, was it Rob? I know it doesn't matter," she said quickly. "We're over. I get that. I was stupid to get involved with him. I get that, too. I'd just like to know. Just to know."

If he could tell her that her boyfriend—former boyfriend—had sent Jim to the bridge to find her, would it make her feel better? Would she try to rekindle the relationship? But was it really any of his business? The day fully caught up with him then, and the day before came hard on the heels of the other, and every bone in his body felt weighted, and every muscle, jolted by sudden use and from the strain he'd put on it, felt as if it were being hammered. He wished he could go to bed and pull the covers over himself until Christmas. Dear God, he was tired.

He tried to infuse some life into his voice and realized belatedly that he didn't need to, because the calls were as strange as everything else. "To tell the truth, I don't know who called. When I got back to the rectory I checked my phone; I was as curious as you are. There was no record of any call after midnight. I thought the phone's clock might be wrong so I looked up the numbers that came in before that. I didn't find a single one I didn't recognize. I have no idea why the call doesn't show up. Calls: he called twice and thank God he persisted. I hung up the first time."

Her voice was desolate. "We're never going to know, then."

"I'm sorry. I know you'd like to know. I would, too. It's odd: if someone had seen you walking across the bridge, why didn't they stop? Even if you didn't know pedestrians are prohibited on the bridge, you'd realize a woman walking alone at that hour must be in some kind of trouble. Why didn't they offer help? If they weren't able to stop, why didn't they just call 911? The police would have come. I don't suppose you remember cars going by when you were walking, do you?"

"I could barely stand upright." She made a noise in her throat. "Disgusting. I never get drunk. Usually I never even finish a glass of wine. My father drove his car into a ditch when I was a kid. So yeah, he wasn't a big drinker, but I guess he was that night."

"I'm sorry."

"It was a long time ago." Dismissive, but he thought she'd opened a door.

He was wrong, though; she was done.

When he'd finally set aside the breviary and went to bed, he couldn't sleep. He fought the urge to scratch his leg, which felt like a thousand needles were pricking him. Mostly, though, the night before was coming at him in flashes of sounds and fragments of images, as if he were in a wind tunnel and pieces of the night were whirling past him. He thought he had the sound of the voice on the phone but then it slipped past him. He thought he saw her tipping and losing her balance but it was gone before he could focus on a single clear image. The only certain thing was the sense of her body against his, and when the feeling surfaced amid all the fragments, he pushed it down, again and again.

He'd jumped because he hadn't wanted to be alone on the bridge. He wasn't thinking he would die, of course; if he had thought he was jumping to his death he might have chosen to stay. Or not, and that was the worst of it: the terror he'd felt hadn't come to him fresh. It was a replay of something decades older.

Keep me safe, O God; in you I take refuge.

She'd surprised him at the end of that awkward, painful conversation: she'd asked if she could call again and he'd said she could.

"I don't like being alone in the apartment," and her need reached across hundreds of miles. "I'm afraid of myself."

6

You'd want to know who it was, wouldn't you? Any normal person would. You'd want to know if it was a friend or an acquaintance or a stranger who happened by. You'd want to thank them. You'd thank them and you'd mean it because otherwise you would be dead. Exactly no one wants to be dead. Even if you think you do, you really don't. You just don't want to be where you are in that moment and you think the only way out of that moment is death. Something whispers it in your ear and you believe it because you're in pain and you're not thinking straight. No one wants to be dead because no mind knows what death actually is, can encompass death, especially its own. It's like trying to wrap your mind around the thing before time began. You can't imagine it, just like you can't imagine where you were before you were born. Salvador Dali supposedly remembered being in the womb but he had more than a bit of carnival barker in him. Also, you'd recall being slapped into life. Dali didn't say he remembered that and you'd think it would be a lot more vivid than floating around in the warm dark.

Maybe thanking someone for saving your life is the first step on the road to Everyone, away from the sorry hamlet of Everyonebutyou. You find out who saved your life and then you thank them, and then they'd know you're grateful and you'd know you'd mattered to someone, at least for a moment. Probably you don't become friends, because that would always be embarrassing, that person a constant reminder that you once tossed yourself off a bridge.

Though maybe the caller didn't think you were going to end yourself. Maybe the caller was thinking that a woman alone on the bridge at that hour might not be alone very long and someone reasonable should get her off that bridge before someone nasty came along. When I started to think about all the things that could have happened, my whole body went cold, even though it was a hot day and I was walking home from work with the sun baking the sidewalk and the grit in the air was being fricasseed and sticking to the back of my throat. So yeah, other than babies being born, nothing good happens at three in the morning.

I live with two other women in an apartment basically designed for two, but most of the time they're not here. They are out with the boyfriend of the moment, and within a few months of our shared existence I discovered that it doesn't matter whether I learn the boyfriends' names because none of the guys lasts more than a few months. They find the guys online and usually have at least two going at the same time, and there are dinners, and parties, and concerts, and then come the overnights and then the breakups. I don't use an online dating service; Jess and Lindsay say I'm practicing natural birth control. I don't have any problem with online dating, though. Jess and Lindsay are looking for love, after all.

Without love, your soul dies. And I know how it happens. First, you get angry at the people who should love you but don't, like your parents or your spouse. Then you begin to harden and that thing that enables you to love atrophies. At that point, you may think you're indifferent but some part of you begins to hate the people who should love you but don't, and over time, if no love comes your way, that hatred ripples outward, to the people in your apartment building and the checkout person at the supermarket and the people you work with—everyone unlike you, everyone who has someone to love them. When that happens, you've lost your soul, another thing that no mind can encompass but it's there, and I've seen it in a million paintings. Your soul pumps empathy and kindness and love and the hope of love, and you know when it has died because all those things are gone, you feel the emptiness and hopelessness, and that can drive some people to a bridge.

Without love, your body breaks down, you get sick more often and you take longer than you should to recover. Some people die because they've lost the person they loved most in the world. Like married couples who've spent a lifetime together; one of them dies and the other follows within a year. Loneliness kills them, you think, but it's more than a longing for company. Those people die because without love there is no reason to live.

Those first few days back in the city my mind was preoccupied with who made that call, who it was who had been worried about me because you wouldn't call a priest if you weren't worried and you wouldn't worry if you didn't care. I was hoping the priest would give me a name and really, it didn't matter if I recognized the name or not. All I wanted was to know the name of the one person, out of the billions on the planet, who cared enough to call. I would have thanked them, just as I thanked the priest.

When the priest said there wasn't a name because the calls didn't show up on his cell, I thought about the four people who'd been in Newport that night. Two were people I work with and one had brought his girlfriend. They had planned to go to dinner and then to the bars. By the time I was on the bridge they might have been sleeping off the evening's excesses. Because they sell art and artifacts to rich men, people at Metro think they're hybrids, part artist and part money—although many of them do come from money—and both groups are famous for being big drinkers, so their belief in their hybrid status gives them twice the reason to suck down oceans of alcohol whenever they can. It could have been Rob, although I don't know whether he saw me at the party and even if he had, it wasn't likely he'd have followed me for hours after I left. Especially if he was in the company of what was obviously my replacement.

It seemed a little odd that the calls didn't show up on the priest's phone. I searched the web to see if it was possible to make a call without leaving any record of it. Maybe I didn't have the right combination of words but I couldn't find anything. Someone had called twice but neither call had shown up on the priest's call log. There might have been something wrong with his phone; the priest didn't say but maybe he'd had that problem before. He could have been lying, I suppose, though I don't know why he would. He didn't sound like he was lying and I think he told me he wasn't any good at lying. He wasn't much better telling the truth: at the station the cop thought the priest was inventing the whole story and pretty much told him he was giving him a pass because he knew the priest's sister.

I got exactly nowhere thinking about the person who'd called the priest but it did start me down another path: back in my bedroom, which was exactly the same overstuffed, sweltering box it had been before I had my close encounter with the bridge, I began to think about the person who'd actually saved my life by throwing himself into the water and grabbing me when my dress had every intention of making me one with the sea bed. I hadn't been discounting him, exactly. I'd just felt that he'd been obliged to do it, given his job. He has a warm baritone, but when I rang off and thought about it, I realized he was even more uncomfortable than I was at the beginning of the call. I'd been determined to charge right through the call, deliver my gratitude, ask my question, and hang up, so

I hadn't noticed at the time. He really didn't want to hear how thankful I was that he'd saved me. And then he'd been floundering for something to keep me on the phone. He's not exactly glib. Not smooth, not glib, not polished, not practiced. Kind of an innocent, in a way. And human. Not the kind of person I often see, except standing at the top of an aisle marrying one of my friends, but human. Vows or no vows, it took courage to hurtle over the railing to unknown water below. So I started thinking about him, the priest.

7

Newport may have been small, but it breathed like a city. It took in immigrants like air, used them as the body used oxygen. Before it was Newport it was something else, something as dense but green. But then it became a different thing—not better, not worse, just different, beating with a changed heart, exchanging air with an altered set of lungs, the metabolism of it speeding up gradually. The English in the early 1600s, the Sephardic Jews shortly thereafter, found a place on an island in Narragansett Bay, grew it from a settlement and kept it pumping, kept it moving, and then it was as if Newport learned the habit of breathing as immigrants continued to flow in. Jim had seen the Chinese and the Southeast Asians; they rode bicycles to and from work for a few years but then they were absorbed into the city. You saw their names in the lists of property transactions printed in the local paper and presumed that before they bought homes they'd bought cars. Now you saw short, square men on bicycles, with dark brown skin, black hair, sharp noses, and high cheekbones. Lizzie called them Incas and she was probably right that they were indigenous people of South and Central America. They worked for builders and landscapers and some had already started their own companies. They would be absorbed just as all the others were, and the city would inhale again.

Maria Estrada was from Guatemala. Small, slender, with light brown hair. Maria's defining characteristic was a kind of grim determination suggested by the expression she showed the world, and validated by her actions. Nearly twenty years before, she'd made her way north from a house that had a dirt floor. She'd worn hand-me-down clothes in Guatemala, and her schooling had ended in eighth grade. She was a housekeeper for two nursing homes on the island, and in between she ferried her children to sports and lessons. Her husband, Jorge, had worked as a cook when Jim had first known the Estradas, but he was now the owner of an electrical business and employed two people. The Estradas lived in a Victorian home that had once been cut into three apartments, and in what little spare time he had, Jorge was restoring the house to a single-family home while Maria scoured southeast New England for original molding, doors, windows, doorknobs, and other architectural hardware. This was their third house in Newport: they bought old homes that had been neglected or abused, moved in and restored them, then sold them at a profit. Their two children were in high school and Maria intended them to go to college, whether they wanted to (in their daughter's case) or not (in their son's case). To keep them focused on their studies, Maria did not allow dating. What saved Maria was her sense of humor, directed most often at herself.

When Maria approached him after Mass, Jim expected that she'd ask him if he needed her daughter's help for the religious education program held during the last two weeks of July. That wasn't it.

The little crowd had dispersed and it was steaming on the walkway so they'd retreated to the sacristy.

Maria always looked directly at you; as he shed his vestments and saw that her gaze never wavered, Jim felt discomfited, though he was only removing one layer of garments. She explained that she had become friendly with a woman she'd met at one of the nursing homes, and after the woman had been discharged, Maria had begun visiting Mrs. Brennan and her husband in their home. "They live alone. I bring food, clean a little but I tell them no pay me. Sometimes I bring Brownie."

Jim knew that dog. A year before, he'd been invited to the Estrada homestead. Brownie had launched itself at Jim's ankle, but before it had a chance to attach, Jacob had grabbed it by the scruff of the neck and deposited it in a bedroom, from which it loudly protested its exile through dinner and coffee. "So you would like me to visit them? I'd be happy to do that. Or do they need help?"

"No." Maria was emphatic. "Last time I go, man is there. He say leave and no come back. He think I steal from them. He tell me he call police if I come back. I no steal nothing from nobody."

"He actually accused you of stealing?"

Although he didn't doubt her. Maria usually wore scrubs to Mass—today's were lavender with yellow, green, and blue balloons—but even with the scrubs there was no mistaking the way she carried herself, that ferocious determination. He wondered a little that anyone would cross her.

Her husband had advised Maria to avoid trouble but she refused to end the friendship. Instead, she wanted Jim to intercede.

"There must be some misunderstanding. I'll talk to him." Mosquitoes at his leg again but if he scratched he'd only be itchier.

Nine o'clock in the morning and already it felt like the high eighties. A hoarse cry from a lone catbird in one of the cherry trees.

Leo was parked in front of the refrigerator, cool air pouring out as he ate the pie that sat on the top shelf.

"Strawberry rhubarb I suppose is as good as anything for breakfast." And there, he had done it again. He didn't believe the cause was anything as familiar as the breathing or as annoying as the bites he'd been getting for more than a week; he preferred to think it was the time of day. He was never at his best before breakfast. Though he had just celebrated a sacrament. How quickly he'd shrugged off grace.

Leo let the door swing shut. "Another blistering night and the worst is yet to come."

Offered mildly but there was no mistaking the accusation.

"The owner hasn't called me back but it's only been a few days. I'm sure he'll get back to me; this must be their busy season."

"Cooling *and* heating is what they peddle," Leo said. "If there are demands for their services, they must come year round. Although given their casual approach to service, perhaps they aren't quite so busy as they otherwise might be."

Back to Spring Street. Though the street was just wide enough for a stationary car and a moving vehicle, there was barely room on the sidewalk to jump out of the way if joggers attempted to flatten him against the pavement. Occasionally, an eighteenth-century house muscled its way onto the sidewalk, its stoop a hazard to distracted pedestrians, its overgrown greenery a threat to clothing. Though rarely more than two stories high, some buildings seemed to lean over you and crowd you to the edge of the sidewalk. Together, they mobbed you; in the colonial era, the instinct to huddle was stronger and there was little separating the houses—an alley, perhaps, or not even that. He didn't know how the painting crews got between some buildings but apparently they figured a way.

No trees; there wasn't room. He felt itchy and hot but perhaps people in earlier centuries were acclimated to the weather, or it was cooler then, or they were used to the misery of stockings and breeches, layers of petticoats, and high-necked dresses with long sleeves. Sterner stuff, people said.

He thought he should return Emily's check. He didn't need it. Would that be seen as a rebuff? Maybe a note to explain that he'd be happier if she kept the money. Certainly she couldn't afford to give it away. He wondered if she was Catholic; perhaps he could include a prayer card. But that would be presumptuous, wouldn't it? Or would it be just what you expected from a priest?

He had been looking at it from inside his skin, at the image of her, at the feel of her, because he didn't want to examine why he'd jumped in. He didn't need to examine it, though; he knew why he'd done it. It was more the fact of facing it. A natural thing, to want to feel good about yourself, to avoid the things that drenched you in an unflattering light. But he had to face it sometime, to call it up in memory and put words to it. He had the habit of it in nightly examinations of conscience. This felt somehow worse. At the margins of it, even, he shrank from it. But with the sun blazing down, alone with his thoughts, with all that was himself, he pushed himself into it.

He hadn't thought of the risk of injury or death because he hadn't been thinking at all. Something else had taken over, the creature part, the part that was unnerved by the stillness of a patient in a hospital room, that had been frightened, long ago, by the sound of a conversation that was quieter than a breath.

What pushed him off the bridge was the need to get away from whatever was on the bridge with him. It had been instinct. Irrational instinct fueled by terror, the roar of the motor and the relentless thunk, thunk of the wheels on the bridge deck lighting up the primitive parts of his brain. Just like that, his brain had shut down and his body had taken over. Panic had galloped through him and he hadn't tried to resist it. In those moments he had been nothing but fear. Two decades after he'd fled Blessed Sacrament he'd been just as terrified and had allowed that terror to rule him again. Then he'd been a child, but he wasn't a child anymore. And that was why he'd been so discomposed by Emily Bell's gratitude: her rescue had been incidental, really, and because it had been, he felt nothing but shame.

Taylor Fine Art was in a handsome, clapboard building painted a dark juniper; cream-and-juniper-striped awnings stretched out above the two wide windows on the ground floor. It looked well-established and prosperous. In recent months, Jim had often passed the building and observed the procession of large nineteenth-century paintings on display in ornate gilt frames. Lots of roiling seas, majestic ships, and pastoral landscapes. A few portraits of stiff gentlemen and rigid women with staring, unsmiling children. He had never been inside.

A large oriental rug covered most of the floor. Small pictures hung on the cream-colored walls. A few easels with larger paintings. Stairs led to another floor, an open door led to another room of paintings. Near the back wall was a dainty, antique desk and sitting there, writing, a woman with blonde hair tightly pulled back.

She looked up and put a smile on her face. Somewhere in her late forties, a face that was sweet rather than kind. A sleeveless dress with pink and red roses running down one side. White heels. Very tall white heels, which brought her nearly eye-to-eye with him. "Is there something I can help you with?"

"I'm Father James Ennis from St. Patrick Church," although he didn't know why he suddenly became James rather than Jim. "I'm looking for Mr. Taylor. The owner of the gallery?"

"Lily, George's wife," she said brightly, although her expression had dimmed a little when she'd noticed the clerical collar. "Unfortunately, you've just missed him."

She looked cool and pristine; in her reflection he was grubby and awkward, a lower order of being. He could practically see her counting the seconds until she could return to whatever she'd been doing. He would not want to come back; better to do it now.

"There's a misunderstanding with a parishioner, Maria Estrada. She's been visiting an older couple in town and she's concerned . . ." he faltered ". . . ah, from what she told me, your husband is worried that she's taking advantage of them. She asked me to," and again he groped for a word, "to reassure him about the nature of her visits with them."

A subtle shift in her expression. The smile became slightly broader, if not warmer. "You must be talking about Mr. and Mrs. Brennan. They live off Thames Street? George has known them for years, of course."

"I don't know where they live, but yes, the Brennans."

"Well. George did mention to me that the woman who cleans their house has been bringing them cake and chocolates and heaven knows what else, and they're both diabetic." Her voice became indulgent, inviting him in.

Perhaps she didn't know. Perhaps her husband hadn't told her what he'd said. Whether or not her husband confided in her, her tone irritated him. "Actually, he accused her of theft."

Her face smooth as glass, her voice soothing. "I'm sure George didn't think the woman was stealing, but you know—blood sugar, diabetes—they just don't understand."

"'They.'" Which could be anything she wasn't: male, old, or unemployed, for example. But he knew what she meant, and wished he could turn on the kind of withering expression that came easily to Leo.

She became brisk. "We have a woman who does a good job and I'll ask her to add the Brennan home to her list. Every other week should do for them."

"Maria isn't their cleaning woman." Knowing he'd get no farther with the woman, but persisting, anyway. "She's a friend."

"Really?" He wasn't taken in by her expression, meant to convey dismay, or by the little smile that replaced it. "Not much of a friend if she's bringing them sugar every time she visits. I'm sure George is right. We don't want them to be killed by misguided kindness."

The door opened behind him. "Good morning," she said, looking around Jim to a couple in shorts and t-shirts. A last glance at him. "Pleasure meeting you."

If you thought about it at all, you would be amazed by the persistence of birds. Even on Spring Street, where buildings imposed on the sidewalk, where no tree provided respite from the summer sun, sparrows hopped along the concrete and dipped into the gutters looking for crumbs. English sparrows, the males with black bibs, the females lighter, with pale eyebrows. Introduced from Europe in the nineteenth century, the noisy, aggressive birds were not his favorite, although it was hardly their fault that they lacked charm.

An image came back to him. Two forms, beating against the sky, brighter than the diffuse yellow glow of Newport, hovering around the boat but keeping their distance, watching. Gulls. Although were they nocturnal? Maybe they followed the fishing boats at night, as they did during the day. They had been silent, though gulls usually were as raucous as sparrows and squabbled just as much. Or perhaps, for once, he hadn't noticed whether they made noise or kept their own counsel.

He was getting hold of himself, finally, having faced the worst of it. He'd reacted badly, mortifyingly, and he admitted that. He wouldn't make excuses. He would try to do better. Otherwise, though, he was exactly where he'd always been: defective hearing and nothing more. As for the bridge: it had been three in the morning, he'd been abruptly awakened from a deep sleep and could well have mistaken his senses. The sound could have come from miles away: sound carried farther at night. The motion could have been caused by trucks leaving the west span of the bridge after completing night work. They seemed to work on the bridge year round; it was likely they were on the bridge that night. He wouldn't have noticed them because Emily had focused all his attention.

When his phone rang he stood in a building's shade while he talked to the owner of Seaside Heating, who said he'd stop by later in the week. One thing moving forward, anyway. New summer session books had to be ordered today if he wanted them in time. Lizzie had been right about the workbooks. He was meeting with the summer school principal, and that reminded him that he needed to meet with the new organist, as well.

Then, as long as he was in the shade, he decided to defer the direct sun a little longer. A call to Maria. Nothing had been resolved, he realized while he was waiting for her to answer, but Maria should know why the Taylors were concerned. Though if he'd found it hard to confront Lily Taylor with her own prejudice, it wasn't any easier airing their bigotry before the object of it.

"He say that? Is not true. They take pill for blood pressure, acid, cholesterol."

"You're sure about that?"

"I work in two nursing homes. He say I steal." Her voice nearly vibrating with outrage. "So I am finish this morning and not work again until later. I go visit Helen and Peter and you come. If George Taylor there, you tell him I no steal."

8

It's been said that Manhattan is for the very rich or the very young. I certainly wasn't the former and barely was the latter. Twenty-seven is more *younger* than *young*. A comparative thing only.

So yeah, I don't think of myself as a kid anymore. That's new this year. I think twenty-seven is the year people pass from childhood to adulthood, if they're going to pass at all. Twenty-seven is the year in which you look at how many years you've been on the planet, where you've been, and where you are, or obviously are never, going. That survey sobers you right up. Kicks out all the silliness and stupidity.

As I say, not everyone passes to adulthood, and for the majority of those people, twenty-seven is not too different from the years before or after it; you're the same immature idiot (female) or immature jerk (male) you always were and always will be.

The rest of the people who don't pass join the 27 Club, which I don't think really is a thing, statistically. I listened to Kurt Cobain and Kristen Pfaff when I was a kid. *Nevermind* was old by the time my father died, but after I found it I listened to it a lot. I don't remember what I made of it at that age but I knew it was angry, too. I liked Amy Winehouse, didn't much like Basquiat, and didn't know enough about Jimi Hendrix, Jim Morrison, Janis Joplin, and Brian Jones to like them or not, but anyway, they're ancient history. Speaking of ancient history, nobody includes Masaccio, but he died at twenty-seven, though it was in the fifteenth century. I think it's coincidence, that you can pick any age and find hordes of people who died at that age. Schiele died at twenty-eight, Seurat died at thirty-one, Modigliani passed at thirty-five, and van Gogh at thirty-seven. Watteau died at thirty-seven, too, but I always thought he was insipid: too many silvery ladies in sylvan glades. Really, who has ever seen an actual glade, much less danced in one? The thing about the 27 Club is that a bunch of them died within a few years of each other. Which isn't a strange coincidence, either, when you think of all the drugs floating around in the 1960s and how all these people suddenly had money to spend on drugs they knew nothing about. Cobain and Pfaff knew more about drugs than the generation before them but used drugs anyway. I remember reading an interview with Kurt Cobain, who said, and I think I'm quoting here, "opiates are directly linked to Satan."

Apparently, I took my shot at the 27 Club and failed. So I'm twenty-seven and still alive and this is my life now. I get up in the morning, drink a cup of coffee, and have half a cup of oatmeal. I shower and put on the clothes I ironed the night before. Make myself a turkey sandwich on wheat bread. No mayonnaise, no mustard, no tomato, because they all can drip and it's hell to get oil or acid out of a shirt. Lettuce, sometimes. And a banana. Lots of pale foods. If it's not raining or snowing, I walk to work, which is eleven blocks south and two blocks west. I work all morning on descriptions of things that belonged to rich people who are dead and will be bought by rich people who are alive. I generally eat lunch at my desk and I never leave work before my boss. I get home, and sometimes I turn on the news, but since I don't much like what's in the news, I'm more likely to listen to music and pull out a sketch pad until I feel hungry. Then I check the weather and figure out what I'm going to wear the next day, iron what needs to be ironed, hang up the clothes so they won't wrinkle overnight, then do my exercises: sit-ups, push-ups, leg-lifts with ankle weights. I've been doing the same exercises for ten years and I can't say that anything is toned. I still have a little belly, my arms are still as unappetizing as a couple of raw hot dogs, and my thighs still jiggle.

For the past week, I've tried doing meditation at the end of the exercises, but it's not taking. I don't have the kind of brain that can concentrate on my big toe for more than three seconds. I start thinking about other things, like did I have the wrong verb in that last sentence I wrote, or did I turn off my computer before I left, or did my boss give me an annoyed look when he left or was it just kind of an absentminded thing. I start thinking and then I can't stop: one thought leads to another and on and on. Which is unfortunate because I spent good money on that meditation CD.

If one of my roommates is home we might grab dinner somewhere and sometimes I meet a friend for a movie on a Friday or Saturday. Once a month I call my mother. I never minded being alone; I used to think of it as a big relief from the pressure of living with other human beings. Even though the apartment is tiny and my bedroom even tinier, I'd let out a big sigh when I closed the bedroom door behind me, feeling I had all the space in the world to go from the outward-facing me to the inward-facing me. From the me who lived outside her own head, looking and judging and assessing and adjusting after those assessments, to the me who would just be. But then the day would start to catch up and once again I'd be judging everything I did that day.

Hence, the sketch pad and music. I like to read, but reading is iffy because you can't revisit a novel again and again—at least I can't. And when you begin a new novel, you can't be sure that you're going to become engrossed in a story, reluctant to put it down when it's time to go to bed. If you're half-interested or totally uninterested, your mind can wander, and in my experience, it never wanders to anyplace good.

On the weekends I do my grocery shopping, what there is of it. I have to dress for that, too, because of the neighborhood I live in. I don't go to the organic places because, for one thing, I think organic and farm fresh and locally sourced and all that stuff is just crap, no better for you than anything else, and for another thing, I can't afford it anyway. When you don't shop organic you won't run into the mobs of creatures loitering in the organic places but you also can't avoid them entirely. The women with their exercise clothes and their brand new sneakers, their gaudy diamond rings, their hair in identical ponytails and their nails done in the color of the second—in that crowd, if you hesitate a minute you're already out of style. The men with their tans and their identical watches. Their numbers start to dwindle this time of year, as people go away for the weekend, or for the week. By August the neighborhood will be a ghost town. Just as well.

My work friend calls me the Ice Queen. I think Todd has two reasons for that. One is the way I dress; I've never understood why a woman would wear skin-tight pants that show every bit of cellulite. Or pants that end at the ankle, making legs look short and stumpy. I especially loathe clothes cut for a man's body. If a pair of pants ends mid-hip, as they do with men's pants, women have to belt them tightly, which means that half your hip fat is above the belt and half below, and to hide that fat you have to wear a long and loose top, which incidentally minimizes your breasts. So the overall effect is a long torso and short legs: a man's body. Who wants to look like a man, and what man wants a woman who looks like a man? It's not easy to find pants that recognize where a woman's waist actually is. Or clothes that leave a little breathing room. My clothes, I like to think, are flattering without being provocative. Serious-minded. Clothes-as-armor.

The other reason Todd calls me the Ice Queen is that I don't go bar-hopping on the weekends with the office crowd. Even if I could afford it, even if I wouldn't have had to invite myself, I'm not sure I'd want to. Some of that crowd use alcohol to bring them down from whatever brought them up. Cocaine, amphetamines, whatever. When people are high or drunk or drunk and high, they're unpredictable. I don't like that. I'm with Kurt Cobain, except with a broader brush: all reality-altering substances are directly linked to Satan.

I don't think I'm an ice queen. Todd is teasing, but sometimes I think I don't like Todd. Maybe I don't like anybody. Sometimes I wish I didn't have to work and then the world would leave me alone. I wonder if that is what I was thinking that night. I get home, turn on music, and dig out my brushes and paints and try not to think about the things I tend to think about, like whether I meant to join the 27 Club or not. And now I realize that my tiny bedroom isn't the sanctuary I thought it was.

9

He'd gone back to the rectory for his car, and had just switched on the ignition when Megan Marks called to tell him that the principal of the summer CCD school needed to push back their meeting by an hour. Jim checked his watch, recalibrating the day. Scheduling religious education in July meant that some children would be vacationing with their parents, but on Saturdays during the school year, half the children were busy with sports and lessons and the other half were busy on Sundays, even Sunday morning. He was considering a weeknight during the school year; the kids would be tired but they were more likely to be available. He wanted to know who had chosen the workbooks and how long the summer school had been using that series. It wasn't going to be a pleasant interview.

Upper Thames Street had none of the rock-concert blare of lower Thames. Instead, it was a hushed conversation in dappled light. Two-story homes sat quietly, comfortably, their clapboard painted sober colors and adorned with plaques that identified the original eighteenth-century owners. A few had been converted to apartments but most murmured affluence; visitors saw the mansions on Bellevue Avenue and Ocean Drive and thought that's where the money was, and it was true that money lived there, but it also lived quietly throughout the city, in homes like these, million-dollar homes that had been carefully restored and were scrupulously maintained.

That was not the case with the Brennans' house, on a side street off Thames. A handsome two-story, the windows nine-over-nine with the small panes of the eighteenth century and a pinecone lintel above the front door, it needed more than a fresh coat of paint. The house had a decided list that had cracked the lintel and brought the house an inch off the stoop. The practice in the colonial era had been to use beach sand in the mortar and it appeared that nothing had been done to shore up the crumbling foundation.

Maria pulled in behind Jim. “They never lock door even though I tell them,” she said, pushing the door in.

They were halfway down a short hall when Helen Brennan emerged. A sturdy woman in her mid-eighties with a broad, intelligent face. She reminded Jim of the women who volunteered at the hospital: you could see the life in her eyes.

She called over her shoulder, in a voice that was unexpectedly strong, “Peter, it’s Maria—and she’s brought a friend.”

She led them into the living room and Jim crossed a wide plank floor, bruised with age, to shake hands with Helen’s husband, who was rising slowly from a wingback chair. Broad shouldered and bony. Thin, gray hair receding from a wide, rounded forehead. Heavy black brows shot with gray, a long nose, and a jaw that tilted up as if to meet it. His mouth bore the tight look of chronic pain; beside his chair was a walker.

“We’re not getting the last rites, I hope.” A low-pitched voice, attenuated with age.

There had been money but either the money was gone or they’d lost the energy to use it. A Chippendale sofa and wingback chairs flanked the fireplace and a grandfather clock and a Chippendale highboy marked two corners of the room. The clock frozen at 2:07, the sofa particularly exhausted; Jim held his breath as Maria sat, afraid she’d end up on the floor.

“Can I get something for you, Father?" Helen asked. "Iced tea? I could put on a pot of coffee.” And when he said he was just stopping by, “Well, I’m sure you can sit for a minute.” She gestured to the vacant chair. “We don’t have many visitors and we like to hear the news. We take the paper, but it’s not the same, is it, when you’re just reading? No depth,” she said, a little grandly. “No subtleties.”

“What she means is no gossip,” Peter said with a sidelong glance at his wife.

“That’s all the news is today,” she said briskly. “Celebrities and mayhem. Hardly worth looking at the paper anymore.” She turned to Maria, who was perched on the couch. “If it weren’t for Maria we’d never know what’s really going on around town.” Then quickly added, “She’s welcome not just for that, of course.”

“As long as we have a home,” Peter said. And with a little encouragement, explained that they’d been born and raised in Newport and had bought the house shortly after they'd married. Most of Newport's colonial homes had been almost unrecognizable then, the clapboard smothered by asphalt shingles, the roofs crumbling, junk cars breaching like whales from the high weeds in the backyards. "The only reason Newport has all these old homes is that nobody had the money to knock them down, sixty or seventy years ago."

Peter had torn off the shingles, reroofed in slate, and Helen had planted gardens where garbage had been, but sixty years later they could no longer afford the repairs that were needed. A recent offer from Colonial Commission to buy and restore the house meant they'd probably have to move out of Newport, which was an expensive city, but neither wanted to do that. They had no children to help; their nearest relation was a great-niece who was living in Oregon, though they hadn't heard from her in years.

"Oh, we'll figure out something," Peter said. "I tell Helen we always find a way."

"Peter doesn't agree with me," Helen told Jim, "but I think we've found our way, and completely by accident."

"Hardly by accident." Peter said. "Dollars to doughnuts, Taylor's looking to feather his own nest."

Maria caught Jim's eye.

"George Taylor?"

"You know him?" Helen asked. "We've been meaning to visit his store ever since it opened but we'll have to go now, won't we, Peter? It isn't all that far from the last one my father had. Eagan Art Supply. An enormous place. They've chopped it up now to make two stores."

"You couldn't turn around without knocking something over. And I did, often." Peter waited for Helen's smile.

"What I remember is the smell of that store: part linseed oil and part smoke and something else—old wood, I think; it had an earthy odor," Helen said. "Dad didn't make a lot of money at it; during the war I think we barely got by. And I don't think my grandfather did, either. But they did leave a legacy."

Jim had noticed them, of course; impossible not to when they leaned in from every wall. Unframed oil paintings on either side of the fireplace, flanking the entrance to the kitchen, to the dining room, and bracing the small windows. None of them large, but the sheer number of them crowded the room. As the Brennans talked, he'd snuck glances at them and hadn't been impressed with what he'd seen. They were so muted or so dark it was difficult to tell, at a glance, what subjects the artist had chosen.

"My grandfather—well, you could call him a patron," Helen said, "but in some cases I suspect he was more of an abettor. Sometimes the artists couldn't pay, so he'd let them trade a painting for what they needed. I suppose that's why the shop never made a lot of money, even though everyone painted back then. My grandfather should have done well but there were people who couldn't pay and they knew he'd trade supplies for anything they wanted to give him."

"Lousy businessman," Peter said, nodding, "but people did that kind of thing in the old days. People helped one another."

"They still do," Helen said, her eyes resting on Maria.

Maria frowned.

"You haven't heard of the store, Father?" Peter said.

"I'm sorry to say we're carpetbaggers." The word made him grin; it was the word he'd heard used by the old families, people who could rattle off generations of Newport antecedents. "My parents moved here a few years after they were married."

"My grandfather ended up with lots of pictures," Helen said, "and my father added to them, and when they died, Dennis and I split the paintings. It was just the two of us, Dennis and me. Dennis died quite young and then his paintings came to me. I have no idea if they're any good: Dad had a few favorites, but he loved all the artists, good, bad, and middling, and I think my grandfather did, too. I suppose most of them are middling, but there are a few that I like very much."

"Taylor is on the board of the Colonial Commission." Peter sounded as if he liked the group no more than he liked the man. "He came with their offer to buy the house. When he said he had a gallery, Helen asked him if he'd like to see the paintings."

What would he have made of them? Jim didn't imagine they'd look any more promising up close.

"Taylor was going on about Newport's heritage." Peter wore a short-sleeved shirt; the arm nearest Jim bore several bruises, deep red and purple, and scars, mostly small, but one that went nearly from wrist to elbow. He'd been a lobsterman, Jim guessed, and if not, some other labor that could chew up skin when its owner wasn't careful. "I love it when the carpetbaggers come in and lecture the natives about our city. He was winding up about taking care of Newport's priceless treasures—this house, is what he meant—and I got a little heated. The utilities are sky high and on top of that and the cost of food and gas, the property taxes are the straw that broke the camel's back. If Newport really wanted to preserve its priceless treasures, I told him, it ought to take better care of the old Newporters, because we are the priceless treasures he talks so glibly about. That set him back on his heels."

Helen didn't interrupt but she was uncomfortable. The moment her husband paused, she took up the story. "Mr. Taylor thought if he put a few of the paintings in good frames he might be able to get something for them. He wrote a check for the first one, which was very kind of him because he can't know if anyone will buy it."

"He's not doing it for us," Peter declared. "I know you always want to see the best in people, honey, but it couldn't be clearer that he's out for himself. We tell him we won't sell, so he comes up with a way to keep coming back. Maybe he'll sell a painting or two but the main thing is he gets friendly. He'll bide his time for a little while, then try his luck again. If we won't sell, maybe we'll agree to leave the house to the Colonials in our will. Far as I know, they haven't gotten their hands on any new properties in years, so it will be a coup. And at our age, he won't have to wait long. He gets the credit for a new property. Maybe he wants to be board chair or whatever it is, but even if he doesn't, there will be publicity—he'll make sure of that—and publicity's good for business."

"We'll be lucky if he does come back, Father," Helen said. "Though I don't know whether it will make much difference with our bills."

"Oh, he'll turn up again," Peter said. "As long as we have something he wants, he'll be back. No doubt about it."

"So he bought one? Mind if I look?" Up close, the paintings revealed themselves to be landscapes, still lifes, and seascapes rendered, apparently, in shades of brown and black. You would buy one only as an act of charity. Peter was probably right about an ulterior motive: if Taylor resembled his wife at all, he wouldn't deal much in the kinder impulses. Though thinking that without even meeting the man wasn't kind, either. "You said they were traded for supplies?"

"Not all, I think," Helen came to stand beside him and glanced at the canvas Jim was studying. "Hard to see what they actually are under all the dirt and the old varnish but I think some are quite nice, and anyway, my father or grandfather must have thought so, because I believe they actually bought a few. To be perfectly honest," and a smile crept onto her face, "I expect that with many of them, the less you see the better. There were some dismal ones I put in the spare room—I don't have the heart to throw them out and ours wasn't a generation that got rid of things like people do now. You put things in the attic or down cellar and eventually they pass to the next generation. Which now that I think of it is exactly how I got them."

Jim remembered his conversation with Lily Taylor. "Mrs. Brennan, am I right in thinking you hadn't met Mr. Taylor before he came with the offer to buy the house?"

Helen nodded. "It was so unexpected. I told Peter that Mr. Taylor may be an answer to our prayers."

Maria wasn't so sure. "So George Taylor take picture not in this room. Which room?"

"There's more?" Jim hadn't expected that.

"Every room," Maria answered. "Every room have many pictures."

It was Peter who suggested that Helen show him the paintings; in the meantime, he said, Maria and he would take a walk in the backyard and decide whether they wanted to revive an old rose garden.

The first floor had two rooms and a kitchen. Despite the presence of an enormous fireplace, the kitchen was brighter than the living room, the linoleum counters scrubbed spotless, the windows newly cleaned. Maria, he thought, possibly going room by room.

Paintings crowded the walls even here: framed watercolors whose glass also looked to have been recently cleaned, and a few small oils as indistinct as the ones in the living room. Jim looked at the watercolors: Ida Lewis Yacht Club, a regatta on the bay, Green Bridge. The foxing on the mats suggested they were old but at least he could see the watercolors; the glass had protected them.

"Thank you for giving us a nice long visit," Helen said, patting his arm. "Peter's enjoying himself."

Jim shifted slightly, away from the contact. "You don't see many people."

"Well, that's what happens. When you're as old as we are, visits dwindle."

The dining room had a built-in china cabinet and what looked to be a period dining table and chairs. As with the living room, the dining room had exposed beams, wide floorboards that were scuffed and scored, and the air hung heavily, as if it had lingered for years, perfumed by the soft smell of old wood. Jim felt the warmth and odor impressing themselves on the weave of his shirt and slacks.

Helen stopped before a rectangle of rose paint deeper than that of the surrounding wall. "Mr. Taylor bought the one that was here. It was an oil of Trinity Church. The one on the other side of the table was the Quaker Meeting House, I think, but to be perfectly honest, it was hard to tell. He said he'd clean that up a bit and if he thought it would sell, he'd write a check for it."

Jim didn't like to think what he was thinking and he wasn't even sure he had any reason to think it. He didn't know how well the paintings could be cleaned, had no idea whether they'd be worth the effort. Helen's father and grandfather might have liked the artwork but that was no guarantee anyone else would. Possibly, Taylor was being kind. Perhaps Taylor saw that the Brennans needed help and understood that none would be coming from family or friends.

Except that George Taylor had threatened Maria. After that, he'd removed two paintings from the house. Peter might be right: Taylor could be currying favor to advance the sale of the house to the Colonial Commission. Maybe Taylor thought Maria's help would make it easier for them to remain in the house, or maybe he thought she would argue against selling it. But maybe it was simpler than that; possibly, Taylor wanted the art. And if so, Jim thought of two reasons Taylor would want few people to know what he was doing: to discourage competition or to hide dishonesty. Possibly both.

Helen led him from painting to painting, from room to room, almost shyly; clearly she liked all those dark canvases but did not expect that anyone else would. Jim wasn't seeing the canvases; instead, he was taking note of her life: yellowed photos on the refrigerator, old magazines and newspapers on the dining room table, the stillness of the rooms, as if the Brennans were no more substantial than shadows sliding over the centuries-old walls and floors.

She brought him to a large painting in the master bedroom; unlike most of the other oils, this one had been set in an elaborate gesso frame.

"My grandmother had this one over the fireplace in her home. Someone bought it; I don't remember whether she did or my grandfather did. Maybe no one ever told me."

It was as dark as all the others, until Jim realized the painting itself was dark. Black clouds rising from the horizon and advancing toward a beach, the water turgid in the distance, the beach flat and lusterless, the only spot of color the red shirt of the small figure watching the storm come in.

"Peter used to say that our bedroom was the absolute worst place for this painting because it made him want to roll over in bed every morning and pull the covers over his head."

"It is a little gloomy," Jim agreed.

"I don't know what it says about my grandmother," she laughed. "And me. There's another one—I can close my eyes and see her dining room and the one she had over the lowboy. That one's too large for these walls, so I had to put it in the spare room. I thought about leaning it against the far wall in the dining room, but it seems a shame to have one of the few framed ones sitting on the floor. Although it's sitting on the floor in the spare room, where I'm surprised I haven't tripped over it a million times."

Her laugh was warm, encompassing. Jim wished he could do something for them.

"Once, Dennis and I were playing King of the Hill instead of sitting politely, which is what we were supposed to do when we visited my grandparents. Dennis beat me to the top of Grandmother's sofa and promptly knocked one of the pictures off the walls." Her eyes widened, seeing it. "We were horrified. Horrified. We were just little children and we were sure that we'd destroyed it. We hadn't, but as you can imagine, my mother wasn't very happy with us."

Jim smiled. He was pretending not to notice that his leg had begun to itch; the air around them was warm and humid and every time he moved he might as well have been scratching the bites.

"It's hard to let the past go. I've been thinking about that the last few days and I don't know whether it's because I'm afraid I'm losing pieces of myself or losing everyone else. Though maybe they're the same thing. In a way, I think they must be, don't you? But," she said in a stronger voice, "we're here now. Peter is eighty-seven and I'm nearly that and we know we're in trouble. I've thought of what else I can do—I have a good brain—but prospects are a bit limited for someone my age, aren't they?"

She laughed again, and again Jim found himself drawn in. Could he find something for her at St. Patrick? Answering phones, perhaps?

"I don't want Peter to be as worried as he is now. He's always felt it was his job to take good care of me."

He pulled out his phone, not quite sure about the wisdom of what he was doing but determined to do it, anyway. "I have a friend in New York who works at an auction house. Would you mind if I sent a few photos to her? There may be something she'd be interested in selling for you." He was trying to keep the edge from his voice; the itch had become ferocious and he was nearly at the point of shaking.

Helen became indulgent. “That’s a kind thought, Father, but these? I don’t think anyone in New York would be interested in these.”

Jim refused to be less than optimistic. “No harm in finding out, is there?

“This one isn’t too bad but generally, it’s hard to tell what they are, sometimes even when you’re standing right in front of them. Partially, I suppose, it’s the varnish—mastic and all the other natural varnishes yellow and darken over time. Mostly it’s the smoke, though: in my grandfather’s day, everyone burned coal—at one time they mined it on the island. Coal fires are awfully dirty, and my father smoked and my grandfather had a pipe and I imagine that over time, the layers just built up.”

Jim snapped two pictures.

“I’ll show you the one that was over the lowboy. Maybe you will like it, too.”

A few minutes later, he’d sent half a dozen pictures to Emily, including the ones Helen mentioned. Almost immediately, his phone rang.

“What do I think of these? What are they?”

“Emily, sorry to bother you.” Though he wasn’t; he’d made her laugh. “I’m in a house in Newport. Friends of a parishioner.”

“Not collectors.” The smile lingered in her voice, though she must have been jarred to hear from him.

“No, not collectors, exactly.” Belatedly, he worried about the call, about raising the Brennans’ expectations. But now he was into the conversation; there was no hanging up. He explained the situation.

“How much did he pay?” And when Jim told her, “Not much, then. You said there are lots of paintings? When did they have the store?”

Helen had found a seat on the edge of a bed. They were in the guest bedroom. An ironing board had been set up between the bed and the wall, and a small pile of shirts and pants lay on the faded green bedspread. She pulled a pair of pants onto her lap and absently smoothed the legs as she thought. “There was a gap between Dennis and me, and Dad was quite a bit older than Mom—his first wife died in the flu epidemic. His father . . . well, if I had to guess, I’d say he opened it sometime in the 1880s.” She looked up, her eyes meeting Jim’s. “As for the number . . . I’ve never counted the paintings but there must be dozens, don't you think? Maybe tell her that we have a few dozen, anyway. I sometimes worry what will happen if we ever have a fire.”

Silence followed the information Jim repeated into the phone. Helen was looking expectantly at him. Jim shrugged, listening for some indication that Emily remained on the line—or had the call been dropped?

But Emily was still with them. "Dozens," she said. "She actually said she has dozens of nineteenth-century paintings."

"I don't know that they're all—" Jim began.

Emily cut him off. "Wow. Unbelievable. Of course there might be nothing halfway decent, which is the only reason I'm not totally freaking out, but we'd be crazy not to take a look. I'll have to see when one of the experts is available—" She broke off. "You're sure she's on the level?"

Now it was Jim's turn to laugh. "Positive."

"If Todd wants to take a drive up, is she available and okay with it?" Helen was. "I'll call you back. Can you ask her not to sell any more before I get back to you?"

Maria walked out to the car with him. "So what you think? I keep visiting?"

Jim nodded. "I suspect George Taylor doesn't actually believe you've been bringing them cakes."

"Maybe I make a little cake for him—what you think?"

"I think you should stay out of the kitchen."

Maria considered him. "You first man I know don't like cake."

10

Emily and her colleague were coming to Newport on the day Seaside was due to inspect the rectory. He could have given Emily the Brennans' address, but thinking of the couple's disappointment if the visit came to nothing, he'd told her to meet him at the rectory and he would ferry them to the house.

Leo had agreed to let Seaside in, which gave Jim an hour to make the rounds at the hospital. "I will inform them that we are in extremis," Leo said, "though I have little hope that they will complete their work before I dissolve utterly."

When Jim had called Emily, he hadn't considered that his question about the Brennans' art might necessitate her return to Newport. Might, in fact, require her to travel over the bridge that could have been a silent witness to her death. He saw now, much too late, that he hadn't been thinking at all, that he'd given in too easily to impulse.

At the hospital, his first stop was at a room occupied by an old man who turned a vague smile on him. Dementia, Jim thought, or no glasses. Possibly both.

Kit Acker's room was unoccupied and when he walked past it he said a prayer for her soul. Her soul because when he'd made his rounds the day after he'd met her, her bed was empty. Ms. Acker hadn't been discharged, the nurse had told him, nor had she changed rooms. In the pause that followed, he'd finally realized what she meant. "Sometimes it happens that way," the nurse had said.

He didn't agree. Nobody died from bruises and scrapes and broken bones. But maybe the doctors had been right and she did have a heart problem. That could take you abruptly, with no warning. Kit Acker had mentioned an aneurysm. Maybe what she thought was someone watching her was actually something misfiring in her brain because her heart wasn't working correctly. Was that possible?

He had been a little unnerved by it. Still was and who wouldn't be? It had been easy to discount what she said when he thought hers was the voice of the painkillers they were giving her. But it had been harder when she'd died the following day or maybe the same day.

Humidity had crept into Newport. As he walked back to the rectory his pants rubbed against the bites on his leg. Jim was too hot to make the effort to scratch; he just wanted to get to someplace a little cooler, and despite what Leo said, the rectory usually was five degrees cooler than outside. There was no wind; the sea breeze would kick in after noon. Also, no birdsong. He saw a lone sparrow hopping disconsolately at the edge of a lawn.

Was it possible a heart condition caused him to hear what wasn't there? But he'd felt the truck as well, the bridge rising and falling with the weight. Something with the temporoparietal junction, then. He should have talked to Lizzie about that. Maybe he would, the next time he saw her.

Leo stood in the hall, which was gloomy but definitely cooler, squinting at an envelope as if close scrutiny would divulge its contents. When he saw Jim, he touched a manila envelope on the long mahogany table and nodded. "Mail came. Looks like something from Martin Reilly."

The return name and address were unmistakable. Jim wondered how long Leo had been loitering there, waiting for him. "I was talking to him after Father Chace's funeral."

Inside the envelope was a letter wrapped around a smaller envelope.

> I didn't expect to see you at Anselm's funeral or I would have brought this with me. This is the reason I've followed your career with interest. As you can see, I've had it for a good many years and, at times, wondered whether I was doing the wise thing to put it into your hands without knowing what it contained; you can't know completely the mind and heart of another. However, Anselm was a very good friend, and now I have done as he wished me to do.
>
> Yours in Christ,
> Martin Reilly

"Not more bad news, I hope."

Jim looked at the smaller envelope, yellowed and dog-eared, and felt unmoored. "For Rev. James Ennis." He didn't think he'd ever seen Anselm's handwriting. Spidery, tremulous as if he'd written it when he was well into old age. But he couldn't have done it then; he'd been catatonic for twenty years.

His feet carried him to his study. Anselm had known he was a priest? How could Anselm have known, when he'd become catatonic long before Jim had been ordained? Staring at the writing on the envelope, the musty odor of the curtains reached out to him, the remnants of a thousand summer days, a thousand winter nights. Other lives. When you went into them you couldn't know whether some small salvation was waiting or if you were going into an abyss.

"No."

He shoved the letter beneath his laptop, the breathing loud in his ears.

11

It was horrible. A total disaster. Someone else may have managed it gracefully, but I don't see how. You can't pretend something is Fra Angelico when it's clearly Hieronymus Bosch.

I didn't remember what he looked like. Maybe that's what shock does to you, but I didn't even remember that he's young, maybe a few years older than I am. His face gentle as one of the quieter van der Weydens. Pale skin, hair that I thought was black because it was wet when I got a good look at it when we were in the police station; normal people who see him, the kind of people who don't make someone's acquaintance while drowning in Narragansett Bay, would recognize it as a ruddy brown. Maybe all that made it worse, although I suspect it would have been just as bad if he'd looked like a swamp creature.

If it had happened in a movie, the heroine would fall in love with the man who saved her. It's now ridiculously apparent to me that no one writing for the movies ever had a stranger yank them away from the afterlife. Reunion isn't a magical moment. You can't sleep the night before, worrying about it, you sweat from Manhattan to Newport, dreading it so much that by the time you cross from Connecticut to Rhode Island, you're fighting the urge to vomit. When you're finally face to face and you can't escape, it's worse than you thought it would be, because you have no idea what to do or say. It's so godawfully awkward, you both knowing that the only reason one of you is alive is that the other person had to stop you from killing yourself.

I don't know why I said I'd go back to Newport but I was sorry as soon as I said it and then it was too late to change my mind. I planned to brazen it out, to be just the kind of pleased and polite that acquaintances are when they meet again, because that's what I told Todd. We'd chatted while waiting in line at the Second Beach snack bar and I'd mentioned that I worked at Metropolitan. It was a big lie but it had the virtue of being a very short one. The priest must have called Metro and asked for me; no need to tell Todd he had my cell phone number. I don't know how likely the beach scenario was—do priests actually go to the beach?—but I was counting on Todd to know less than I do because he's Jewish. Todd didn't bat an eyelash. I visualized our meeting on the way up, fashioned and refashioned my smile and my greeting because, about halfway there, I realized that Todd wasn't the extra shot of courage I hoped he'd be, because in reality he'd be an unwitting witness.

Despite the practice and preparation, my mind went blank when the priest opened the rectory door.

We avoid people who've seen us at our worst. We dump boyfriends and drop friends and turn down invitations that might lead to a face-to-face with the friend of the friend. We steer clear of the bar and never again set foot in the restaurant. We do, in fact, whatever we can to cling to the idea of ourselves as people who could never sink as low as we actually have. We do whatever we can because that face-to-face would force us to see ourselves through someone else's eyes and to imagine what they thought as they watched us or heard us and also to imagine what they think of us now.

I couldn't even look at the priest. He'd been subjected to the one public meltdown of my adult life—the drunkenness, the coarseness, the anger. And the jump. I honestly don't know why I said what I said to him; it was like being possessed, everything spewing out of your mouth before you've even formed a clear thought. That bothers me nearly as much as the jump, and that's saying something. It was ugly. I was ugly. I had no idea that degree of ugly—which may well be simmering constantly below the surface, who knows?—dwelled somewhere in me. And if I'd known it did, I would have bet my one good piece of jewelry that it would never see the light of day. But obviously it had and I had given it a full airing.

When someone's that ugly to you, the impulse is to retaliate in kind. I didn't think he'd do that, being a priest. He hadn't said anything nasty that night or anytime after. I didn't think he ever would. However, he wouldn't have needed to do it deliberately: he could open his mouth and astonish Todd, my one real friend at Metro, and that would be the end of that relationship. Or he could say something he thought was kind or helpful and completely obliterate what little self-regard I still possessed.

He didn't say a word, though. Didn't refer to our nighttime phone conversations, didn't mention the bridge. He was flustered at first; I could see that even through the fog of self-absorption. Maybe he had to work through it, just as I did, though not exactly from the same perspective. No idea what he was thinking, no idea what he thought of me or what I'd done, but not a word about it. And millimeter by millimeter, I became more confident that he'd say nothing. By the time we were in the car and on our way to the Brennans' house, I could look at him. I could talk about the art, could talk to him. Or at least some version of me could.

— 12 —

"It's broiling in the city. Everyone has totally cleared out of Manhattan and it's not even August. I always wonder why people keep wearing black right through the summer. But I read somewhere that black is no more likely than white to make you hot, as long as you don't wear it skin tight. If you wear black loosely, like people in the desert, convection happens because the heat comes through the cloth and then flows up between the cloth and your skin. It's like being a walking chimney. So I suppose it's not awful to wear black if you wear it loosely, though I don't know how loosely. I don't like the idea of black in summer though; whether or not you actually are hot, you *look* hot."

Her gaze swept around him, past him. Because she wouldn't look at him, Jim was able to look at her, straight on, the first real look he'd taken.

She was dressed for business: a white shirt with the cuffs folded to the elbows; a short, straight skirt in dove gray; gray flats. Patrician, with sharp cheekbones and uncanny eyes—large and a color he'd never seen before, or at least not noticed. The irises nearly clear, and white flecked. Not light blue, but pale, cool gray. A slender neck and a slim, narrow body. She was elegant as a heron, though clearly discomfited, the torrent of words so compulsive that her friend frowned at her, mystified.

Jim was older, had more experience with what people termed "difficult" situations. He'd met with grieving spouses, parents, and children; with college students who didn't know how to come out to their parents; with couples who discovered unpleasant realities about one another during pre-Cana sessions. He'd never saved anyone's life. If he'd carried her from a burning house or wrenched her from a car that had careened off a road and into a river, he'd know how to meet her again: he'd seen that kind of reunion on the news. But someone whose intent would never be certain, although why would anyone be standing on the walkway of a bridge at that hour, drunk, except to kill themselves? There was no template for such a reunion. He knew it, and she did, too.

"So, yeah." She was winding down, her voice a little lower, the words beginning to slow. "I told Todd we should stay overnight but he's absolutely not beachy. He says he has porphyria—the vampire disease—but give me a break. Todd Stein, Father Ennis."

Todd was nearer fifty than forty, balding, and dressed for an outing: blue-striped shirt that was open at the collar, chinos, loafers, and no socks. He had a sharp-featured face: long, thin nose, wide mouth, pointed chin. Handsome, but his color was off—sallow bordering on gray. As Jim leaned in to shake his hand, a strong, sour smell reached his nostrils: alcohol coming through the pores.

"Father Ennis. If anyone is a stellar candidate for excommunication it's my associate, here."

Emily's companion slid a glance at her to see if he'd made her smile. A bit more than a colleague, then, and Jim was pleased to see it. She had friends.

Jim smiled, shrugged. "Emily would have to be a Catholic, but even then . . ."

"I am Catholic." She was willing herself to smile but was too nervous for it to be convincing; she realized it and settled for arch. "Technically. I was baptized but my parents lost interest after that."

"Sometimes that's what happens," Jim said mildly. "A couple will want a church wedding and I'll find out they haven't made their First Communion or been confirmed."

"Todd is one of the nineteenth-century-art experts. Actually," with a glance at her companion, "the big expert in that area."

"American art. My real expertise is somewhat narrower than that."

They were standing just inside the front door. Jim was thinking of the drive up when he asked them if they'd like to freshen up. Todd cast a dubious glance down the dark hallway behind Jim. "We don't want to take too much of your day."

Emily and her colleague had arrived during the fourth wave, the tidal surge of vacationers and day-trippers; the car inched south on Broadway, behind a black SUV with New York plates and a Yankees bumper sticker and in front of a silver convertible with Connecticut plates.

Jim glanced into the rearview mirror at Todd, who was checking his cell phone. "What do you think they have?"

"Not a clue. It was a popular pastime in the Victorian era. The Victorians liked painting landscapes and painting each other painting landscapes. Valleys, lakes, mountains, you name it: it was a golden age for *en plein air*. And consequently, I'm afraid, mediocre art."

"Todd calls it 'the scat of amateurs.' But, Todd, you were interested when I said the artists bartered their work for supplies." Emily, in the passenger seat, translated for Jim. "The amateurs, people who dabbled, were people who had a lot of free time and probably didn't have to work for a living. They wouldn't have had to barter for art supplies. Not that the professional artists were uniformly poor, but some certainly would have resorted to bartering if they couldn't pay for the supplies they needed. So some of the Brennans' paintings were likely done by professional artists, though whether they're actually good artists remains to be seen."

He registered the change in her speech, no longer a cataract of words, sound created to push out the silence and whatever might gather in it. Took a quick glance at her eyes and saw they were calmer.

"I know Gilbert Stuart," he said to keep her talking. "You can't live in Rhode Island without knowing he painted the portrait of Washington that's on the dollar bill. That's about all I know, I'm sorry to say."

Todd had been looking out a window. "Have you heard of John Smibert? Scottish, lived in Newport in the early 1700s. Smibert's considered one of America's earliest portrait painters. Gilbert Stuart was one of his students."

"How about that." Jim was following the progress of a cyclist maneuvering through the traffic. He turned up the air conditioning a notch and cool flowed around his ankles, over his hands.

"Smibert didn't stay in the area. Ended up around Boston. I can't think of any artist born in Newport, but a number of them passed through at one time or another. William Merritt Chase, Edward Bannister, Martin Johnson Heade, John LaFarge—that's off the top of my head. I don't suppose you know any of them? No need to apologize: they're not exactly household names."

Emily turned in the seat, cast an accusing eye at him. "Were you doing research last night?"

"As if I needed to. You wound me, Ems, you really do." Todd fell back against the seat. Then, abruptly sitting up, "I've got one: Edward Malbone. I knew there had to be at least one Newport native. Another portrait painter but Malbone was a miniaturist."

At last, they were on Farewell Street, which cut a path between two cemeteries. On Thames Street, Jim took a left and the traffic vanished. He parked the car but before they got out, he turned so he could see them both. "I'm a little worried because the Brennans are a bit precarious financially. Do you think there's any chance that what they have are reproductions? Because the dealer only paid a thousand dollars and I was thinking that maybe Helen Brennan was right to say he was being kind."

Todd laughed. "A charitable dealer? I don't think so. If he paid a thousand, he thought the piece was worth four, at least."

Helen must have been watching out a window because the front door opened as soon as the car pulled up to the house.

Today, she was dressed for company. Navy and emerald green pants that stopped at her ankles, a button-down shirt that matched the blue of her pants. Gold earrings and a gold charm bracelet.

"Aren't you lovely." Helen took Emily's hands in hers, and Emily's eyes went wide at the compliment. Then, shaking hands with Todd, "I made an orange poppy seed cake. It used to be my specialty. I have iced tea or coffee. Water, of course, if you'd rather have that."

He heard the worry in her voice and wondered how familiar it was to Todd. Or maybe he didn't go to people's homes; Jim didn't know how auction houses worked, whether Emily's colleague usually had contact with the owners. And that made him anxious about the size of the favor Emily was doing for him; at the very least it was taking two people away from their jobs, possibly for nothing. Sitting in a chair that had been brought from the dining room, Jim sent up a prayer as Helen led Todd and Emily from picture to picture in the living room. The veins on her hands were dark, swollen streams running through the delta of skin, and though she maintained a pleasant smile, the thumb of one hand ran lightly across the veins on the other hand, over and over, as if to divert their flow. Jim decided he couldn't watch anymore.

Jim exchanged small talk with Peter as the footsteps retreated from the dining room and sounded on the stairs. He thought he'd hear more conversation and hoped that the lack of it wasn't a bad sign.

To distract himself, he asked Peter about his family.

"Oldest of four and the last one standing; can you believe it? We grew up in the Fifth Ward, which was all Irish then, and I'm the only one who stayed in Newport. Can see why they left, though: Dad was a gardener for one of the big estates and out in all weather. Even as kids we knew we were never going to follow in Dad's footsteps. I was pretty good at math in school and at one time I thought of doing something with it but there was Helen. I knew she wasn't going to leave Newport—she loved the store—so I went to work in construction just so I could stay. Same kind of job as my father's, if you think about it, except we didn't work outdoors in the rain. Did sometimes in the snow."

Peter's hands, resting on the chair's arms, were large and broad, mottled skin covering ropy veins; his knuckles were like burrs on a tree, the skin over them dry and white as plaster.

Jim wasn't a good liar but he'd done this before, so he could bring it out easily. "You mentioned the property taxes the other day. You know, St. Patrick has funds set aside for people who find themselves a little short before their next paycheck. It's something we do all the time; not a big deal. You'd be surprised how many—"

"Oh, we're fine, Father," Peter interrupted, trying to sound affable but there was an edge to his voice. "We do a lot of bellyaching but really we're fine. Don't worry about us."

You couldn't force people; he'd learned that almost as soon as he'd taken the parish. He'd tried to argue about common sense but all some people heard was charity, and they didn't like it. You couldn't go around them, either; he'd already made that mistake, too.

"Dave was the oldest. He moved to Boston and went to work at Sears Roebuck. Betty took a job in a dress shop in New York and was about sixty or so when she married a retired police chief. That was a surprise, I can tell you. And Eddie went into the Navy and ended up in San Diego." He looked at Jim. "They're all gone now, dead and buried. Helen says I'll see them again."

"I believe you will." He pulled up his pant leg to see what it was he'd been itching, and frowned: a large, angry area, a few inches above the ankle, bright red, but no visible bite.

"'Course, Helen's seeing them now, so who's she to say?"

"Seeing who?" Jim let the fabric drop. "Your siblings?"

"Thank God, no," Peter snorted. "I wouldn't want the pack of them snooping around, minding my business. Not that I buy any of it; I believe what I can see." He might have expected a challenge but Jim nodded encouragement. "Helen's her father all over again; what's the word? Fey. Ladies drifting around the house. Even gave her a name: Delia."

"Helen sees a ghost?"

"Beats all, doesn't it? Though to be fair, Helen didn't say she sees anybody. She *senses* Delia. That's what she says, anyway. Helen says she likes to look at the pictures." Peter pushed himself up in the chair and gave him a frank look, man-to-man. "When she came up with this notion, I did wonder about her mind. I thought, 'What's next? Pixies? Aliens?' but so far, nothing else." Peter shrugged. "Just Delia."

When Helen and the others returned, Jim couldn't tell from their faces whether the tour had uncovered anything promising or not; the New Yorkers just looked overheated and Helen wore a businesslike air. "Now let me see. Everyone else wanted iced tea but I don't think I asked you, Father."

When the tea was brought out and the cake was being eaten Todd gathered information; the casual clothing was deceptive. He probed in the guise of small talk, about the store, about Helen's family, about the disposition of the paintings in the years since the store's closure.

Helen couldn't remember exactly when the family had immigrated. "I expect it was somewhere in the 1820s. I know that Fort Adams was rebuilt then and they had to go to Ireland to find master stonemasons. Some of the Irish also came over for the backbreaking jobs, moving the dirt and hauling the stones and things like that. I think my ancestors were the backbreaking workers."

Emily caught Jim watching and included him in the faint smile she'd worn ever since they'd returned from their tour. It was a professional smile, pleasant but promising nothing. And she was professional: sitting erect in the chair, her hands in her lap, he could see nothing of the woman he'd found on the bridge, nothing of the woman who called him. She was composed and the more he looked the more he thought her expression had the set look of habit. Watchful. A bit more than watchful. Wary. As if the conversation might turn against her, somehow. The last time he'd seen that look was on Angelo, the fisherman who'd pulled them from the water and who'd discovered that his part of the narrative was required for the patrolman's report. Angelo didn't necessarily regret his actions but it was plain he wished another boat had been closer to the bridge.

The memory seemed to flip a switch: the motor's growl came out of nowhere, blasting through the gloom of the Brennans' living room. It froze him, his heart thudding painfully against his ribs, his breath held as if any noise, even one soft as a breath, would betray his location, would give it an easy target. But then Helen was asking if he'd like another glass of tea and it was gone again. His imagination. Then and now. Or something worse, synapses misfiring in his brain. The blasted temporoparietal junction.

Emily and Helen returned the plates and glasses to the kitchen while Peter asked a few questions: What kind of sales were the customary fare of Metropolitan Auctions? What was the auction house's commission on sales?

"I don't suppose we have anything big," he said, "but obviously we have something; otherwise you wouldn't be asking all these questions."

Todd didn't deny it. "The dealer didn't see the ones upstairs, did he?"

Helen sat again and brushed a crumb from her pants. "Well, I don't know about 'see.' It was one of those days that suddenly turn stormy. I was rather embarrassed; we only have sixty-watt bulbs. So whether he actually saw them or not . . ."

Emily glanced at Todd. "That larger painting, right? I saw it, too. Should we bring it downstairs?"

"We had a little trouble moving around in the guest room," Helen told Jim. "You'll remember that it's a bit cluttered. I think of it as No Man's Land. It's where the large and the awful ones ended up. And some that are just too dark, even by our admittedly low standards."

"The light could have been better," Emily agreed. "I think we'd have to move a few of the paintings to a brighter room if we really want to get a look at them."

Her voice had become a little breathless and her eyes were fixed on Todd. She didn't notice, as Jim had, that Peter was staring at her. Unabashedly, ever since she'd sat down, admiration on his face.

Helen noticed. "Father Ennis, I was telling Emily that she reminds me of my mother's friend Agnes White. I adored Agnes when I was a girl. She wasn't like the other mothers: she was always perfectly put together and she had exquisite taste in clothes. I thought she was the most elegant woman I'd ever seen."

Emily dismissed it even before the words had a chance to register. "I don't think so, but thank you. You're very kind to say that."

"I've always noticed that women tend to think too little of themselves and men tend to think too much," Helen said conversationally to Jim. "Not all, of course. Just enough to ensure that the species perpetuates itself."

Jim liked that, more so when he saw that the comment had found its mark. Emily opened her mouth to protest again, but then her expression became thoughtful.

Todd brought them back to the paintings. "Mrs. Brennan, I don't suppose your family kept receipts or anything that would help us identify some of the art we've been looking at?"

"Or correspondence?" A note in Emily's voice Jim hadn't heard before: excitement. "Maybe a ledger? We're looking for some way to establish provenance, which can make a great deal of difference in the valuation."

"Funny you should ask. I was just saying the other day that we were sort of a pack-rat generation. We never threw out anything, even when it obviously was nothing but junk. There are trunks in the cellar that have moved from place to place over the years. They came from my father's house and from his father's house and maybe they'll have something useful in them. They haven't been protected from the damp but if you don't mind the mold . . ."

With a soft sound of surprise, she broke off. Her attention focused on something beyond Todd, who was sitting nearest the doorway to the kitchen. The moment stretched and her expression became more concentrated. "A small book," she said at last. "A diary, maybe."

Peter caught Jim's eye: Helen was seeing something, a something that Peter didn't believe in.

"Yes, a diary. From the smallest trunk, I think. It has a name on it: O'Connell. If you find that trunk down cellar, it will have something that might be helpful."

Jim avoided Peter's eyes, unwilling to be complicit. He didn't believe Helen possessed more than a good imagination, but he thought a priest should be neutral in most matters that concerned spouses. He was getting a little anxious about the time, wondering what had transpired between Seaside and Leo, and wishing he kept his calendar on his phone because he knew he had a meeting but couldn't remember when.

The cellar was littered with boxes, as well as an assortment of broken chairs, small tables, floor lamps, a set of wrought-iron patio furniture, three hat racks, ancient typewriters, several sewing machines, snow shovels, rakes, and Jim nearly screamed before he realized he'd put his hand on a stuffed raccoon. It was more than a little disconcerting, squeezing between old, dead things, things someone had sat on, had typed a letter or perhaps a bill with, had used to clear leaves long since dissolved into dust and returned to the earth. The ceiling was low, the walls crumbling, covered with a fine, gray powder. The air was cool but close, dense and smelling of the gray, powdery dirt, as well as mold, and there was no escaping to a patch of fresh air. The breathing seemed louder in his ears, but, Jim thought grimly, the detritus of many lives surrounding him and the gusting breaths in his ears left little room for a ghost. Not even an imaginary one. Though Helen seemed as well-grounded as anyone.

Todd and he waded, slightly bent, through the jumble, which not only was treacherous but also was a fire hazard. It needed to be cleared out. Did he know someone who would haul away the trash but leave the valuables behind?

Jim felt something tickle his ear and stopped to brush away a thick cobweb. "I can't thank you enough for helping us. I don't know how auction houses work but I don't imagine you spend your time poking around in cellars."

"No."

"You must think they have something valuable."

Todd was plucking boxes out of the way, piling them on either side to make a path. "Emily is a good friend."

Todd hefted another box while Jim moved a coatrack between himself and moldering boxes at the bottom of which might be a trunk.

"First time I met her—" A huff that might have been a laugh. "I was coming in one morning and heard someone vomiting in one of the bathrooms. Predictable after lunch but this was a mite early in the day so I was a wee bit curious to see which of my delightful coworkers had gone completely over the top. Ems comes out, sees me and says, 'I think I may need to go to the hospital.' I take one look at her—the sweat's running off her like Niagara Falls and she's up to her eyebrows in jaundice—and I said, 'Cookie, ain't no "may" about it.'"

"What?" Jim straightened so suddenly he knocked over a stack of lampshades. "What was wrong with her?"

"Ruptured gallbladder. She'd been visiting her family in that godforsaken burg and started to feel ill Sunday morning." An empty cardboard box sailed across the cellar. "I asked her why in God's name she didn't go to the hospital then, and she said she didn't want to take the risk that she'd be admitted, because it would give her mother the opportunity not to visit her. That did it," he said, tossing another empty box. "I thought if she's cracking jokes on her way to major surgery, she's got to be a hoot when she's healthy."

Jim was stunned into silence. The obliviousness of it, because he was sure it wasn't callousness: there was warmth in his voice, an obvious affection for Emily.

Jim felt her against him, the sodden dress that was soft as a mushroom cap, her body tense with panic, straining to climb over him, out of the water.

When he'd asked her for help with the art, his first thought had been for the old couple but an almost immediate second thought had been for her. He was trying to keep her close; he felt responsible for her now and even if he persuaded her to talk to a professional, a social worker, or a psychologist, someone who knew how to help people that way, he'd still feel responsible for her. He was the one who'd tried to talk her off the bridge and failing that, had kept her head above the chop until the boat came. Having possibly prevented her death, it had become his job to do the same thing again and again until she didn't need him.

He wished she had someone else, someone better. He heard things. Imagined things. Feared he'd spread darkness to his own niece and nephew if he was careless enough to be alone with them. He clung to saints, to ritual, to the sacraments. Sometimes he thought of himself as an insect, all unknowing on a leaf that was drying up, that was shading into brown before it detached from a stem and fell away.

Eventually, they came across the trunks. If they hadn't been looking specifically for them, Jim doubted they would have found them, shoved into a dark corner, surrounded by soft, mildewed cardboard boxes, half-covered by layers of men's and women's coats.

Jim eyed the smallest one. "Should we carry it upstairs?"

Todd made a face. "Do I want to pick up that thing? Do we even know if it's the right one?"

"It has the right name on it."

"We'd have to clear out half the junk in the basement before we could wrangle the trunk to the stairs."

Helen produced a flashlight, which Emily brought to the bottom step. "Pay dirt?"

"Dirt's the word, all right," Todd muttered.

Emily looked Jim over, grinning. "You're filthy!"

Helen was aghast when she saw them. Todd was sent to the bathroom to clean up while Jim washed his face and hands at the kitchen sink. No amount of brushing was going to improve the look of his shirt and slacks. He felt wretched, grimy, and moldy, and the smell of the cellar clung to his nostrils.

When he gave up on his appearance and returned to the living room, Emily was reading a small leather-bound book they'd taken from the little trunk. They'd removed seven items; the others were clearly ledgers, tall and narrow, the once-handsome leather covers worn at the edges. The books brought the must of the cellar with them; wisely, Emily had put a napkin under the book on her lap.

Todd arrived, looking nearly clean, and Emily glanced up. "We're interested—so, yeah, I'm interested—in two paintings but the more likely one is the big one that was in the master bedroom. I think it might be important."

"It's unsigned, so we can't be sure who it was," Todd said. "No sense getting ahead of ourselves, Ems."

"While you were rooting around in the cellar, I brought both paintings downstairs. You should take a look; they're on the dining room table."

"What do you mean by 'important?'" Helen was standing at the couch, trying to read the book over Emily's shoulder.

Emily turned to look at their hostess. "Was someone in the family named Jack?"

"We really don't want to get ahead of ourselves, Ems." Todd had resumed his seat by the kitchen door and sipped his iced tea. "You can look at a painting and it may remind you of an artist's subject or style, but it's like seeing faces in clouds. If you're looking for something, and you look hard enough, you're going to find it."

"And that sounds just a little patronizing."

"We all do it," he said generously. "I thought I'd found a Glackens at a flea market. I bought it for pennies and all the way home I was terrified that I'd drop it. By the time it and I had arrived safely in my flat, the thrill had worn off a bit. I put it on the sofa and took a good look and I said to myself, 'What the hell was I thinking?' It wasn't by a great artist. It wasn't even a good painting. So, Ems, you wouldn't be the first. Actually, I wouldn't be surprised if everyone at Metro has a story like that."

Emily hadn't really been listening; as soon as Todd finished, she asked again. "Someone named Jack?"

"I think my great-grandfather was John Eagan." Helen had caught Emily's excitement. She came around the couch and sat next to Emily, as if afraid she'd miss a word. "I'm not positive; I don't know much about that generation. But maybe."

"When I brought down the smaller painting I saw the writing on the stretcher. An address and the name: 'Jack.'"

"Really? In all these years, I've never noticed the stretchers. Not very observant, I guess. Even when we took them off the walls to paint or paper. But it couldn't be my great-grandfather because my grandfather was the one who opened the store."

"Maybe it's not John Eagan," Emily said. "Or perhaps John Eagan just liked art."

"I'm too lazy to get up and look." Peter was more animated than he'd been during Jim's first visit to the house. Whether or not this visit was successful, Peter enjoyed having company. "Is it the framed one in the master bedroom? The one of Second Beach?"

"It's Second Beach?" Helen was astonished.

"You didn't know that?" Peter was just as surprised.

"I'm hoping we'll find something definitive in the ledgers," Emily said. "Assuming that it is John Eagan, and that it is a Heade, it probably came into the possession of your family about the time it was painted, which would have been 1860, give or take a year. We know he was working in the area at that time and it fits his subject matter during that period: dark and kind of ominous."

Todd sighed as he looked around the room. "I don't think anybody should get their hopes up. Every once in a while, something is unearthed—from an attic, let's say, or a barn—and it turns out to be an important discovery, but those things are few and far between."

"Is a Heade good?" Peter ventured.

"Mr. and Mrs. Brennan," Emily said, "do you have a lawyer?"

Jim stared.

"We have someone do our taxes."

"He's an accountant, Helen," Peter said indulgently. "Not the same."

Todd sighed again and gave up. "Well, I suppose that's a good point. Good idea for them to have a lawyer no matter what we find at our next stop."

"Todd wants to see what the dealer took," Emily said.

"I made a mistake, didn't I?" Helen asked in a small voice.

The Brennans didn't lock their doors because they couldn't: the house had shifted and while the kitchen door could be secured with a little effort, the lock on the front door no longer met the hardware on the door jamb. Peter didn't see what the fuss was about since they'd lived on the same street without incident for more than sixty years. But the recent activity at the Brennan home, and the idea of people hauling artwork out of the house, didn't sit well with anyone else. Jim thought they might have trouble with a barrel bolt so he volunteered to install a chain door guard, which would be better than nothing but also nothing close to impenetrable.

Todd had explained how the auction house worked, and Helen and Peter said they'd go along with whatever was recommended. When Emily asked if they could borrow the journals, Helen had hesitated.

"I want you to take the picture by Mr. Heade. We have old wiring. If something happened, Peter and I could get out of the house but we wouldn't be able to get the pictures out. The big one that was in the spare bedroom was my mother's favorite painting, so whether or not it's valuable, I'd like you to take that as well." And when Peter protested, Helen had been firm. "I'm trying to be sensible. If there were a fire and we save ourselves but lose our valuables, where are we?"

In the end, Jim agreed to take them to the rectory for safekeeping. After he'd dropped them in the back parlor, checked his messages, left an apology on Victor Belanger's phone for having missed their meeting, taken a hot shower, and changed into blessedly clean clothes, he headed to the book shop.

Michael was smoking, as usual, outside the store. "Don't tell me you've finished it already? I'll have to see if I can find another well-oiled pirate book."

"Actually, I need a recommendation."

Mike raised one eyebrow. "For?"

"A carpenter, I think. Or a handyman. But someone you don't have to pay on the spot. Is there such a thing?"

The other brow went up. "And you think I'd know because . . ."

"It's not for me," he said hurriedly. "It's for an older couple. They need some repairs on their home. Basically, it's crumbling around them and they don't have much money at the moment but they can manage a down payment—" a lie because he didn't intend to ask them for money—"and I'm sure they'll be able to pay the rest by the time the work's done. Some art experts were at their house today. They have a lot of paintings. Dozens. And the experts think at least one is valuable."

Mike took a last long drag on his cigarette, dropped it in the gutter and went into the store. Jim followed, reluctantly. He hated asking people for anything, even recommendations.

Mike went behind the door and flipped the sign to "Closed" before taking out a cigarette and, remembering that he didn't smoke in the shop, replaced it in the pack. He probably smoked at least two packs a day. "So you want a carpenter who'll work gratis for now with the vague prospect that he might get paid later. And why do you think I would know someone like that?"

Jim looked at his hands. "I don't know who else to ask."

Mike snorted. "Big compliment. How did you get involved with these people, anyway?"

"That's a long story."

"Art, huh?" Mike studied him for a moment. "Old couple? It's Peter and Helen Brennan, isn't it?"

"How the heck did you know that?"

Mike never smiled but he didn't have to; he was obviously pleased with himself. "I could make real money if I only knew what do with my deductive prowess. Process of elimination. Who would have lots of art? The Avenue people, who don't need your help, my help, or anyone else's, they think. Some of the billionaires who've been rolling into town for the past ten years or so? I can't see you getting tangled up with that bunch. But I can see you in the scrum with the Brennans. Old, quiet, a little down-at-heel, but living in a two-hundred-fifty-year-old home that, by the way, the Colonial Commission is chomping at the bit to get. She was an Eagan, and the Eagans had art. Anyone who's lived here a while knows that."

"So you know someone who can help?" Jim said hopefully.

"Have to think about that one. Most carpenters I know like to eat." Mike was enjoying himself. "Someone who knows the family, maybe, or someone softhearted. Or softheaded. But that's not the only thing the Brennans need. Maybe even not the main thing. What they really need is a great white shark of a lawyer to keep the crazy Colonials at bay."

"You know a good lawyer?"

Mike wasn't going to be led. He fished a box of cough drops out of his pocket and tapped out two. "Can't imagine why you'd need a name. You have one already—or St. Pat's does."

Stephen Peck was pompous, ponderous, and dim. Unfortunate, but there it was. He'd come with the church and Jim was praying for him to announce his retirement. Steve was somewhere in his late seventies and whenever Jim thought about it, he had the horrible feeling that Steve would outlast him. "I don't think Steve does that kind of work," he said carefully. "I suppose I could ask."

"Just waiting to see what you'd do with that one," Mike said. "Peck's a good soul, but good people can do as much damage as the bad ones, is what I'm saying. You want to fight the Colonials, who have money behind them, you get the biggest shark in our little ocean: Bart Meagher. Knows he is, too, and ain't exactly humble about it. Harvard does that to people, though give him his due, he was a scholarship kid, not one of those legacy babies. Harvard, and Harvard Law. Likes a good fight. Bit of a talker. I've got a feeling he'd like the job: his family was Fifth Ward, too. He can be a little slippery but I think he'd be fine with the Brennans."

Jim was beyond grateful. "I'll give him a call."

"You ought to get some bug spray."

Jim had been scratching one leg with the other. "Yeah, I know."

All day, his mind had been worrying the problem of Anselm's letter, if that's what it was. Could see the spidery handwriting that claimed his name. Lurking now under a blameless laptop like a thing waiting beneath a rock, something that lunged and then scuttled away before you realized the thing had bitten you.

It tugged at him while he'd returned the phone calls, started dinner, was interrupted by a man at the door who wanted Jim to bless his dog, a moth-eaten animal of indeterminate lineage, ate half his dinner, and was interrupted by a parishioner who was selling her home and wanted to know if it was a sacrilege to bury St. Joseph upside down in her backyard, and if not, did he have a small one she could borrow, finished his dinner, and heard Leo's report about the central air. On top of the cost, Jim had a new worry: rats or squirrels in the walls because one of the men heard knocking when he'd rapped against a wall to determine whether it was sheetrock or the old horsehair plaster.

Finally, when he could put it off no longer, he retrieved the envelope and sat with it at the desk.

> Jim,
>
> I am afraid this letter may not be welcome, but I must apologize to you. I should have done so long ago but I am a coward and have put it off too long to do so in person. What you saw that day was consequent of my arrogance and I am afraid to think what it might have done to you.
>
> Just as God exploits our strengths, Darkness finds fertile ground in our weaknesses, separating us from God and all that is good. My pride created what you saw that day. We think we know ourselves but we know even less about ourselves than we

do about the world, and this despite the fact that we spend so much of our lives looking inward.

I hope that you will forgive me, just as I hope God will forgive a sinner who has been blind to his weakness. I struggled for years to understand what God wanted of me and have come too late to that understanding. Lately, I have been praying to God for release. I pray for your soul as well. When you ask God for help, He answers. I hope you will remember that.

Yours in Christ,

Anselm Chace

"Good Lord." Jim balled the letter in his fist and threw it into the wastebasket.

13

The crows awakened him. From the sound of it, three or possibly four, bickering. He opened his eyes. Dark gray walls that had a sickly greenish tinge, darker dresser, a closet door whose varnish had alligatored, creating black lumps where the varnish had congealed and desiccated. The mahogany nightstand beside his bed, also dark, the clock on it showing six o'clock. He closed his eyes, offered up his petitions to sister saints Dymphna and Agrippina.

Breathing. All day, every day. Some mornings it was like being at the bottom of the ocean, the weight of it pressing down like a million tons of water. You had to kick upward with every bit of strength you had until finally you surfaced.

Hot already, the air lifting stale odors from the carpet and the upholstered chair by the bedside table. He wondered if Leo would comment or be satisfied that central air would come soon. He'd turned off the fan before he went to bed; under the sheet his skin felt prickly. His left leg wasn't itchy; it just felt odd. As if insects were crawling over it. He threw back the sheet, sat up, and a wave of heat washed over him.

A few inches above his left ankle was an inch-wide, circular wound, ringed in red. Not exactly a wound: it was as if someone had punched a chunk out, clear to the bone, and then cauterized the flesh, because it wasn't bleeding. He brought his knee up for a better look. The walls were swollen and crimson. A lighter area that he thought was muscle. And bone.

Lightheaded, he closed his eyes. He lay back against the pillows, willing himself not to pass out.

His brain careened from one panicked thought to another. It didn't hurt. Was that good or bad? What was it? Why wasn't it bloody? What exactly did it feel like? Prickly? Crawly? Pins and needles? What was it?

An injury that bad didn't happen without awareness. Did it look like acid dropped on it? Wouldn't he have noticed that? Could he have scratched his way into a large wound? Was that even possible? He'd gone to bed itchy; could he have done it in the night? For God's sake, *what is it*?

Opened his eyes again. Several red lines were beginning to march from the edges of the wound. Infection. Almost a relief because it was something he knew. He lifted his leg and swung both off the bed. Found his phone and dialed Lizzie.

"Aren't you supposed to be getting ready for Mass?"

Surprisingly, a flash of irritation: he didn't tell his sister her business. "It's not even six-thirty. I have . . ." What? What did he have? He felt panic settle in again, squeeze his ribs, force him to take small, gasping breaths. "I've got an infection. Can you give me a prescription for an antibiotic?"

"I'm at the hospital. Come over and I'll take a look."

He didn't want her to examine him. He wasn't sure why but he was very sure he didn't want her to see something that ghastly on his body. He glanced down. The red streaks had advanced.

In the bathroom he found a roll of gauze. Wrapping his leg he became lightheaded once more. He sat on the floor, taped the end of the gauze, and felt a little more normal once he could no longer see the hole.

A few minutes later, he was at the hospital. Lizzie ushered him to a bed and pulled the curtains. She looked exhausted. So bad, in fact, that for a moment he forgot his leg.

"Were you on all night? You look like you haven't slept."

"You'd look just like me if you had my job."

"What's wrong?"

"Nothing." She ducked her head as she lifted his leg, allowing a mass of curls to detach from the mainland and drift over her eyes, effectively hiding her expression. "Anyway, let's see the infection."

Jim pulled up the pant leg. Lizzie began to unwind the gauze. Jim fixed his eyes on the top of her head; he was afraid he'd faint if he let his gaze go lower. He could see the tail end of the part she'd made, most of it obliterated by the disorder of her curls. She'd hated her hair when she was an adolescent; he could still hear the accusatory tone of her complaints, as if someone had forced it on her.

"Jimmy, you're not helping by keeping it bandaged like this. Did you wash it after it happened? Did you put on some antisep—" She grabbed his heel and turned the leg. "What am I supposed to be looking at? Is it on the back?"

Jim lifted his leg from Lizzie's grasp. Nothing. No red streaks, no muscle, no bone because no hole. His skin was unbroken and unblemished. Not even the mosquito bites he thought he'd been scratching for days.

Lizzie frowned, bewildered.

He felt lightheaded again. "It was there when I got up."

"What was there when you got up?"

He knew that look, her lips compressed, the professional, almost predatory light in her eyes. Whatever it was, she would hunt it down, identify it, and decimate it. He dodged the hand that was coming at his forehead. "I don't have a fever."

Her palm smacked against his forehead, anyway. "You having any problem sleeping lately?"

"In this heat?"

"Feeling dizzy?"

"What do you think? You just whacked me in the head."

She wasn't amused. "Have you recently started any new medications?" And, as if he wouldn't understand the word, "Anyone prescribe pills to sleep? Or are you taking antihistamines or any of those supplements like melatonin? Which you shouldn't be taking anyway because there's no FDA scrutiny of them so they could contain anything. You don't take supplements do you?"

He recognized the tone and his panic ebbed a little. She was so ferocious; he almost smiled. "No, no, and no. It must have been a trick of the light."

"You imagined it? You ever do that before?"

The breaths in his ears were long, languorous. And grew loud: her words were coming to him muffled. He slid off the bed, anxiety racing along his veins, though he knew no one ever heard what he did. "I'm not crazy. I need to get ready for Mass. Thanks for looking." And felt her eyes on him as he pushed through the curtains and escaped.

Until the first reading he was celebrating the sacrament through muscle memory; after that, the buzz in his head began to recede.

He wasn't Catholic because he'd been born into the faith; it was something he'd chosen, and continued to choose. The life of Christ, the tenets of the faith, how it was understood by the doctors of the church, how it was practiced by the saints: all of it attracted him. He wanted his religion to be a way of being. He wanted to be ever-conscious of the joy in being, to be aware of the grace inherent in each living moment, to see the world as a gift from God, and every person through the lens of love. Knowing that the sacraments conferred the grace that would strengthen the desire, realizing the great privilege of celebrating the sacraments. And all of it a part of the endless quest to be closer to God.

Sometimes he felt the strength of faith, but more and more he felt weak. Fearful.

It wasn't easy living love. Some days he failed before he'd taken his first sip of coffee. Sometimes words tumbled out before he'd considered their impact. He knew he'd never be perfect; what mattered was the effort. It was why he always said yes if someone wanted his help, whether or not it was congruent with his duties as a priest. Like helping an elderly couple. Like answering a pre-dawn call and driving to the Newport Bridge.

He wished he'd jumped for the right reason, done something selfless, though irrational. He wished the saint of suicides or sailors or water or whatever had abruptly materialized on the bridge, grabbed him by the pants and hurled him over the railing. Anything but the ignominy of panic, the shame that came after.

If the act had been intentional, he would feel better about everything. If he'd felt compelled to rescue her, it might not have been bravery but at least he would be sure that something had pushed him over the railing, because if he hadn't wanted to do it and something had pushed him to do it, that something could have been irrationality but it also could well have been God.

Just now, the breathing, the pounding heat of July, the doubtful look in Lizzie's eyes—they were the only things that seemed real to him. Not the only things: his fear was real, every moment of every waking hour.

His mind wanted to wander during the Liturgy of the Eucharist and he had to keep pulling himself into the present, into the sacrament his congregation and he were celebrating. Looking at their faces, the thick glasses, the deep lines their feelings had etched into flesh. Looking over their bent heads was like gazing into a waning fire: the dark colors of oak bark and walnut, the thick gray of damp ashes, the powdery ash that was dirty white. They struggled to their feet, were careful getting to their knees. Everything was an effort but they came, and many of them came every day. What would they say if they knew their pastor seemed to have had a hallucination? Hallucinations. The truck wasn't real, either, though the sound of it kept coming back to him.

After Mass, he drifted around the rectory kitchen, making a circuit of the table, opening and closing cabinet doors, and finally decided he couldn't eat more than a piece of toast. He knew what he had seen but as he waited for the bread to pop up he didn't pull up his pant leg to check, as afraid that the hole had reappeared as he was that he'd see nothing. His leg felt odd, though. Not the prickling or the pins and needles or whatever it was. Cold, maybe.

Leo ambled into the kitchen and wanted to know what he intended to do about the rats.

"We don't know they're rats. They could be squirrels, could be mice. How hard were the workmen hitting the walls? Maybe they dislodged some plaster."

"Newport may not be a megalopolis like New York or London, but it is in fact a city." This morning Leo chose lemon bundt cake which, strictly speaking, was not considered a breakfast food, but Jim kept this thought to himself. "Newport is a city and cities have rats. And rats carry disease."

"I haven't heard anything."

"I am not a vain man but I would prefer, when I die, that my appearance not have been ravaged by plague. Buboes are quite disfiguring."

Half the time, Jim couldn't tell if Leo said things for effect or because he believed what he said. Didn't matter; Jim wasn't in the mood for it.

"If you die of bubonic plague, I will ask O'Neill-Hayes to touch up your appearance before you're laid in the casket. And then have them keep the lid closed."

"And on the topic of disagreeable things," Leo said, spreading a thick layer of butter on a slice of the cake, "why are two filthy paintings occupying space in the parlor? I suspect but I cannot be sure that they, also, are disease vectors."

Jim explained.

"The bishop would be pleased to know that St. Patrick rectory is being used as a storage shed."

"The bishop can mind his own damn business." Jim snatched up the mug and uneaten toast and left the table. "They'll be gone soon enough."

The cake paused halfway to Leo's mouth. "Feeling a little under the weather this morning?"

Jim escaped before he said anything more.

If he could manage it, Jim tried to do the least pleasant things at the beginning of the day; that way, nothing was hanging over his head, whining like a cloud of gnats. Victor Belanger was sulky. Jim apologized three times for missing the first meeting before he was able to direct the conversation to the summer curriculum. Jim had read the old workbooks, a mix of pop psychology, vague exhortations to be kind, a little Old Testament, and less New Testament. No wonder people were leaving the church; if the workbooks were any indication, few people actually knew what the religion stood for. New workbooks had been ordered, he said, producing samples.

Victor flipped through the books, looking for problems, and objected to the Sermon on the Mount and the sacraments. Speaking as the voice of experience, he said, the teachers wouldn't be able to focus children long enough, distracted as they would be by the summer weather. Jim wondered whether he meant the children or the adults would be distracted, but he kept the thought to himself. For the college students Jim was used to, Victor said, the gospels probably were fine but the readings were too long for high school students, never mind the grammar school children, and the lessons in them too abstract for the teachers to explain.

Sometimes, Jim understood Leo's longing for the Golden Age of Catholicism: parishioners didn't argue with their pastors and certainly didn't condescend to them.

"I know you can work wonders," he said, inwardly wincing. "Everyone tells me you've made the program a success every year. I'm sure you can do it again this year."

Jim went on in this vein for some time and though Belanger was waiting for him to offer a return of the old workbooks if the program wasn't successful, Jim never said it. Raising the possibility would ensure that the program failed; even if it hadn't, Jim would be told that it had.

Jim called Mike Dyer, who'd stopped by the Brennans with a handyman friend. "You're the miracle worker," Mike said. "Peter Brennan *et ux* think you walk on water. And speaking of water, I took a look-see around the house; you know what creek they're going to be up if their art isn't worth the canvas it was painted on."

Late in the morning, Emily rang the rectory bell. "It's just me," she told Jim. "Todd's out of it."

"You mean he's sick?" Though she looked more angry than unhappy.

"He's fine but he's not coming." Today she was dressed casually, her hair pulled back, emphasizing the clean lines of her face. "Metro is officially no longer involved. I'm the errand girl. I'm just supposed to bring back the ledgers and the diary or journal or whatever it is. And give the Brennans our card. Oh, and casually add that they should call us if they somehow wind up with a couple of zillion-dollar paintings, but if the art is worth nothing, well, no harm done. I suppose I get that because auction houses rely on their reputations but still . . ." Her eyes blazed. "They don't give a crap that the Brennans are being swindled. Two old people; how can you rip off two old people? They sold everything for a thousand dollars."

"That can't be true."

But it was.

14

After Jim had driven them back to the rectory, Emily and Todd had eaten a quick lunch and then they'd gone to Taylor's store. They'd browsed a bit, and then Todd had asked if there were any recent acquisitions. They'd been shown the oil that had come from the Brennan home. A small William Trost Richards, and overpriced at nearly nine thousand dollars, a sum that outraged Emily. Todd then told the Taylors he was a friend of the Brennans, and that they had changed their mind about the second painting and wanted it returned.

Taylor had produced a contract. "Todd called it the most duplicitous document he's ever seen."

A short time later, Jim saw the contract for himself. Heavy white paper with the store's letterhead in handsome navy letters. A short declaration midway down the paper: "Art located on the premises of 15 Swinburne Street, paid in full" and below it, three signatures and three names.

Helen said that Taylor had produced it when he made his second visit. The Brennans had understood it to be a sales slip for the first painting.

"So, the receipt for a single work will either name the painting and the artist or, if there's no identification, the receipt will describe the painting." Emily was making an effort to be matter-of-fact. "You wouldn't be asked to sign a receipt."

"I can't believe I was that stupid. I've seen my father's and my grandfather's receipts. I've seen a million of them and I should have realized. It just didn't register. Maybe I thought everyone made their own receipts; I don't know. I should have thought."

Then her eyes filled. "Dad's paintings."

"Take him to court." Emily's words shook with the effort to remain calm. Jim looked at her, surprised by the strength of her emotion. "He cheated you. Filthy swindling vulture. I've seen some nasty stuff at Metro but he takes the cake. Get a lawyer and take him to court."

"We don't have that kind of money. We can barely afford—" her glance slid over her husband and then away.

Peter gripped the sides of his chair and with an effort pushed himself to his feet. "We'll get them back, or by God, I'll wreck every painting in the house."

His expression changed and he suddenly swayed.

Jim moved quickly to take his arm. "I'll get a glass of water," he said, guiding Peter into the chair again.

The watercolors in the kitchen loomed over him as he found a glass and turned the tap. He imagined the kitchen without them, the house stripped bare. The rooms with ghosts of the paintings on the walls, Helen's legacy gathered up and carted away.

He saw Peter's face, bloodless when he'd lurched to his feet, and anger rose again. They seemed to have no good option: lose the paintings or exhaust themselves with a lawsuit. He remembered they were childless. No one but friends to help. He wondered how much time and effort would be required of him; however, there was no decision to be made.

Back in the living room, he handed glasses to Peter and Helen. "Bartholomew Meagher. He's supposed to be the best lawyer in Newport. If he wants money up front, the church can loan it to you."

Helen accepted a glass. "We can't take money from the church."

"A euphemism," Jim admitted. "I meant me. I could lend it to you."

Peter slouched in the chair, looking every minute of his age. "We can't do that. How would we pay you back?"

Emily saved Jim the trouble of a reply. "You'll sell a painting."

"We signed them away."

"Mrs. Brennan, no one's going to believe that's a contract," Emily insisted. "All you have to do is show a judge what an actual contract looks like, and it sure doesn't look like the thing you got from George Taylor. It would be great if we could get some of his other contracts because I'll bet they look nothing like that piece of garbage he gave you. At the very least, he should have included the number of paintings, how many were oils and how many were watercolors. If you're buying a collection, you're very particular because you want to be sure the seller won't hold something back after he signs the contract. Taylor thought you wouldn't know the difference but if you can show the judge a real contract, you can't lose. You have to fight them. You have to."

"Let me pay," Jim said, a little breathless with the risk of it. "I'll be happy to pay for the lawyer so if you don't win, no harm done and if you do win and do sell a painting, you can pay me back."

Peter began to protest but Emily interrupted.

"You have to fight. You cannot let him get those paintings." All eyes on her, Emily seemed to realize how forcefully she'd spoken. She looked a little abashed. "So listen, last time, Todd and I were representing Metro, but today I'm technically just representing myself. I'm supposed to return the books and give you our business card on the way out the door but Metro isn't counting this as a sick day. That means it's a work day, and that says how hot my boss is about pursuing this. So yeah, I showed him the diary."

"The little leather book?"

She fixed her eyes on Helen. "I read the whole thing last night. You were wrong about the business: the store opened in the early 1860s. Your great-grandfather started it."

"My great-grandfather?"

"Jack Eagan. The one whose name was on the stretcher, I think. Actually, I read the diary and the ledgers and I was up until about one-thirty this morning because I couldn't sleep after that. The Eagans used the ledgers to keep track of the business and they also did some buying and trading. There was even a note about one painting that was being held for safekeeping but never retrieved. Sometimes they just recorded the medium and the price so that wasn't much help, and when they did record names, usually I didn't recognize them. I don't know the period all that well but I'm guessing they're generally amateurs. I counted five names I knew, and I checked the web to see whether they were known to have worked in the area. And all of them passed through Newport at one time or another. And two of the artists . . . well." She paused to make sure they were all listening. "You know the paintings Father Ennis has at the rectory? Even one of those will pay for a dozen lawyers if you win a lawsuit."

"You're kidding," Helen breathed.

"No joke." And now Emily was overflowing, and Jim could see what was underneath because she had forgotten herself. It was as if the stiff wrapping paper had been removed to expose something warm and lambent as a brace of hummingbirds. "This never happens. Nobody walks into a house and finds two major artists. Nobody, ever. Metro's playing it cool but the free publicity alone would be worth millions. They aren't going to get involved in an ongoing lawsuit, and they've officially stepped away, but here I am and I suppose I'm unofficial, but in a way I'm not, and of course at this point they can't be one hundred percent positive but I'm the one who read everything and I'm absolutely sure, even before we do a valuation."

Jim looked at the Brennans, who didn't appear to be following Emily any better than he. In a moment, Emily realized it, too.

"So, the art. We told you about Heade. We said he was painting in Newport at the end of the 1850s and into the first year or two of the Civil War. As far as I can tell, that was the first painting anyone in Helen's family—" Her eyes flew wide.

"Helen's fine, dear. Go on."

Emily grimaced but continued on. "It's the first thing they bought, or at least that's the first one documented, but it wasn't bought as part of the business. There wasn't a business then. At least, there were no registers going back that far."

"So it was in the diary?" Jim guessed.

Emily nodded. "A slip of paper was sticking out of it, but I didn't look at it until really late last night because I thought the ledgers would have all the transactions. So I got to the diary last, and when I looked at the paper, it was a list of three paintings, dates, prices, descriptions, and three names. I didn't know what it meant until I actually read the diary. Helen, did you know that your family fought in the Civil War?"

"They did? My grandfather didn't talk much about his parents and I guess I never thought to ask."

"The diary belonged to your great-grandmother. She and Jack Eagan had four sons: Timothy, Owen, James, and John. It seems that Timothy and James were paid to enlist in the Union Army and someone with money paid Owen three hundred dollars to take his place."

"People paid proxies to get out of the service?"

Peter spared him a glance. "They did, Father. Before the days when you could get a doctor to confirm an imaginary ailment, the rich just paid cash to dodge the draft."

"The family thought the money would help the boys get established after the war was over, but all three of them were killed. Everything was in the diary. Two died on the battlefield and the other died in the hospital from an infected wound."

"Oh, my," Helen murmured, setting her fingertips over her lips.

"That left your great-grandmother with one child. She wrote about sending him to relatives in Ireland before he became old enough to be drafted. Fortunately, the war ended before John came of age. There are pages and pages about the money—she didn't want to keep blood money, as she called it, but she thought if she gave the money to charity, it would be as if their deaths didn't matter. She talked it over with your great-grandfather and she did a lot of praying, and she ended up kind of doing the Victorian thing."

"The Victorian thing?" Peter was sipping water; Jim was watching the level, ready to replenish it when the glass was empty. The room was too hot and too close and he was reminded of Leo's complaint that the old didn't regulate well.

"People in those days were a lot more overt about mourning. The men wore armbands, the women dressed in black for a year, and mourning jewelry became very popular. We've actually sold mourning jewelry at Metro. You'd put a lock of your loved one's hair in a pendant, or in earrings, or you'd braid the hair to make a bracelet—that kind of thing. It seems pretty macabre to me and maybe Delia thought so, too, because instead of doing the jewelry thing, she used the boys' money to buy beautiful objects that would remind her of them. That's how she bought the Heade. She must have had a penchant for Luminism because once she got involved with art, she wrote about the artists she admired, and the other two she bought were also Luminists, judging by her descriptions of the paintings."

Helen had been listening intently but the moment Emily finished, she asked, "Did you say Delia?"

Peter looked as astonished as Jim felt.

"Delia O'Connell Eagan," Emily said, nodding. "I got to know her pretty well last night. You didn't know her name?"

"I'm gobsmacked." Helen fell back against the chair. "Absolutely gobsmacked. She's my great-grandmother."

"How she got started is the best part," Emily said. "She actually wrote it all down. It was a gray day and her husband warned her that she was going to be caught in a downpour but she decided to go walking anyway. I got the impression that she was a pretty strong character; she seemed to do what she wanted. Like buying the paintings. That was a lot of money in those days and it's amazing that she spent it, and that her husband let her spend it. Anyway, she liked to walk around Newport and usually she did it alone, which I think was also unusual."

"I'm a big walker, too," Helen said. "Maybe it's genetic."

The two women shared a look. "Maybe it is," Emily agreed. "Anyway, that day she went all the way to Second Beach—miles and miles—because a storm was coming ashore and she wanted to see the surf. Well, Heade was up by the dunes, painting. She went over to see what he was working on and she liked it so much she made an offer then and there. Told him her husband's name and their address so Heade could deliver the painting when it was finished. Can you imagine it? This Victorian lady strolling right up to an unknown man and telling him she wants to buy his painting?"

They considered this. "I'm liking her more and more," Helen said.

"So that pretty much establishes the provenance of the Heade. She wrote his name twice: once, recounting the story, and also on that paper, beside Timothy's name. She had news of him first, and that hit her pretty hard—Owen was fighting by then—and I can see how she'd have an affinity for such a dark landscape. So that's one painting." She glanced around, as if they wouldn't be hanging on every word. "The ledgers helped with the other one."

"The other one is by the same painter?" Peter had finished his water and looked better; when Jim made a motion to get up, he waved Jim to sit down again.

"It was done much later. Different painter and Delia didn't buy it. You don't mind me calling her Delia, do you?"

"I call her Delia," Helen said, "so why shouldn't you?"

Jim was in time to see Peter roll his eyes.

"Todd and I had a big disagreement yesterday about this other one. He thought I shouldn't say anything because it was even less likely than the Heade. Turns out I was right, and I'm going to give him the absolute worst time about that faces-in-the-clouds thing." She took all of them in, prepared to enjoy their reaction. "It's a Hassam."

Three blank faces were turned on her.

"You're kidding, right?"

Jim could have laughed at her expression.

"Wow. Just wow." Emily shrugged theatrically. "I was actually worried that someone might faint. You've never heard the name? Childe Hassam?"

"I've never heard of the other one, either," Peter said. "First time in my life I wished we had a computer."

"We have a few art books in the house," Helen said, "but after you left I checked them. Mr. Heade wasn't in any of them. Are our artists that well known?"

"Well," she conceded, "not like Rembrandt. Martin Johnson Heade. Born around 1820, died in the early 1900s. He did landscapes but is best known for paintings of tropical flowers and birds. Virtually forgotten after his death but now he's considered an important artist."

"You keep saying 'important.' What does that mean, exactly?" Peter said. "Maybe I'm crass for asking but what's he worth?"

Emily hesitated, but only for a moment; she was all in. Jim hadn't missed the look that passed between Emily and the older woman; it was one of affinity, almost affection. "I could get fired for telling you this because they think as soon as you find out what you've got, you'll go to one of the big auction houses. But it's your property and it's dishonest not to tell you what we think we know about something you own. Keep in mind that I'm going to tell you what Heade has sold for, not necessarily what your painting will bring. Also, the auction house gets a commission, so you won't get all of the winning bid. So, keeping all that in mind, Heade's sold for several million."

"Did you say million?" Peter said on a breath, then began to cough.

"I know, right? Pretty great way to start a collection."

Jim was back in the kitchen with Peter's glass. As he turned on the tap, his head was buzzing. It felt too good to be true but why would she invent it?

A few sips of water restored Peter, and meanwhile Helen went to the kitchen for iced tea. Emily followed her and then they were all drinking tea and eating chocolate chip cookies. No one said a word. Jim could hear muffled traffic on Thames Street, a few blocks west. A catbird cried just outside the window. In the kitchen, the refrigerator kicked on. And around them were the paintings, which had kept their secrets for more than a century.

Jim was happy; he'd made the right decision after all. It seemed so, anyway. He'd been feeling a little guilty about judging Lily Taylor without really knowing her, and George Taylor without even meeting him, but it appeared he was right about both Taylors. The Brennans would have been cheated if he hadn't called Emily. Assuming that the paintings were what Emily thought they were, what he hoped they were.

Emily finally broke the silence. "I have to tell you about the Hassam. You may have a few other decent ones, another small Richards, possibly a

Church, which was what Todd expected to find when Father Ennis mentioned the dealer." She looked from Helen to Peter and back again. "I'm actually a little worried about this. I mean, I don't want anyone to pass out."

Peter winked. "We're tougher than we look."

"Childe Hassam—that's with an e on the end—was born in the 1850s, died in the 1930s, and in between became arguably the most celebrated of the American Impressionists. For a short period in 1901, he was painting in Newport. According to the research I did last night, seven Newport paintings are currently known to exist, only one a street scene. The purchase of the one you have is recorded in the ledger. I think Hassam would have been pretty happy with the price because at the time, American art hadn't really penetrated the market; collectors preferred the Europeans. Hassam, actually, is the artist who lobbied hard to change the taste of the museums and collectors, which is why we now have all the American Impressionists here and there around the country. Imagine if the Europeans had bought them all up: we'd have to go to the National Gallery or the Louvre to see them. Hassam was a good marketer for himself and everybody else. Over time, artists wax and wane, but Hassam's stock is pretty high right now."

Helen preferred to hear the rest of the story. "You were talking about the ledgers?"

"Yes. By then there was a store. Actually, your great-grandfather opened it, and not too long after Delia bought the Heade. I think the store was kind of a defensive thing, a way to stop Delia from wandering the island. I think he figured that if he had a store, the artists would come to her. It was an artists' supply shop but they also bought and sold a little art. Delia bought the two other paintings that way. I didn't recognize either artist. The sales were in her diary and the same names appeared in the oldest ledger, which listed everything bought and sold in the shop."

"So why is the other one going to knock us dead?" Peter asked.

"It's going to be a very fine Hassam, I think. In the ledger it's recorded as *Bellevue Avenue in Spring.* Hassam filled the space with carriages in the street and strollers on the sidewalk and when it's restored, it will be gorgeous. You are so lucky!"

Helen cast a worried look at her husband. "We would be if I hadn't given that tour. George Taylor owns everything."

"I'll call the lawyer." Even if the paintings were worthless, Jim was determined that the Brennans would keep them. "I'll call him now; I have his number."

"I don't see how that's going to do us any good." Helen sounded resigned. "We signed the paper."

"No one's going to believe that's an actual agreement to sell dozens of paintings," Emily said reasonably. "All you'd have to do is get a professional dealer to testify that no one sells even a single painting that way."

"But we don't know how," Helen said fretfully.

Peter reached across the coffee table and gripped Helen's hand. "We don't need to know how to do it, sweetheart; that's the lawyer's job."

"It's such an obvious fraud, he doesn't even have to be a great lawyer," Emily said, but she was distracted; her gaze lingered on the hands. Her face wide open, absorbing it.

"He's supposed to be the best. He went to Harvard and Harvard Law School."

Emily came to herself immediately and gave Jim a look. "Whatever. If he has even half a brain I don't know how he could lose. It's pretty clear that Taylor's trying to swindle the Brennans."

"We just leave everything in the lawyer's hands," Peter said. "And when we win the case and sell Mr. Heade's painting, we'll be able to pay all the legal fees. If you don't mind selling that painting, Helen."

"If you want to keep the Heade, you could sell a few of the smaller paintings or the Hassam. Personally, I'd keep the Hassam, but you may not want to."

Peter hadn't forgotten his earlier question. "How much would Mr. Hassam's painting sell for? I know you can't give us an exact number. Ballpark will do."

Emily hesitated again, deciding what she should tell them, perhaps judging the Brennans' stamina. She liked them. Jim saw that she was afraid she would fail them, but stronger than that was a desire to feel their happiness, to feel that she'd contributed to it.

"As I said, you just might have a very, very fine Hassam. And he's sold for as much as eight million."

"My God," Peter breathed. "Eight million. Good God."

"All this time." Helen began to laugh. "I can't believe it. They've been right under our noses all this time."

"Metro hopes that once you establish ownership, you'll want to talk to us about selling one or maybe both and, as I said, the publicity alone is worth millions." Her expression changed. "I kind of worry about that, a little; it's news but do you want to be news? Have your picture taken? Tell the world the story of Delia and her sons? You'll have to think about that."

"Eight million." Peter whistled softly. "I told you, sweetheart, we'd figure out something. New roof, stabilize the house, rewire, new paint job, and we can pay the next ten years of taxes with a single check."

But Helen was thinking of the other possibility. "I don't like to say it, but what if we don't win?"

"Metro's paying me for the day here. My unofficial day here. And they've seen our copy of the alleged contract. They're paying for the car rental and if I wanted to take everyone out for a five-course meal, they'd pay for that, too. The house throws money around all the time but they don't do it for peons like me. They only do it if they see dollar signs."

While Helen was calling Maria to share the news, Jim phoned the lawyer and spoke to the secretary, his mind cataloging all the worst outcomes: they didn't win the lawsuit, one painting wasn't by the artist they thought, neither painting was by the artist they thought, the lawyer didn't want the case and the Brennans ended up being represented by someone like Steve Peck, the church's lawyer.

On the way back to the rectory, Jim worried that the Taylors would confiscate the art before a lawyer was involved. Emily told him that Todd had been thinking several steps ahead. If the Taylors went to the house, the most valuable art they'd find might be worth tens of thousands at best. They wouldn't know that the Hassam was missing because it had been sitting on the floor in the spare room, and if they saw that something was missing from the bedroom, they'd have to come to the rectory for it.

"Todd said they won't do anything before they have a lawyer's advice," Emily said comfortably. "Even if they do, they're not going to appear at your door demanding the missing paintings. Small-town dealers rely on their reputation. And it's one thing to take on an elderly couple and quite another to do battle with a local priest. That's not something they'd want bruited about."

"Your friend has a lot of experience with all this?"

"He's been working for Metro for almost twenty years and before that he worked for a couple of galleries. That's why I was the one who noticed those paintings."

Jim didn't follow.

"Before we even left the city, he was telling me about Kensett and Church and William Merritt Chase. He'd already decided that if we found anything, it was likely to be a small work by someone good but not exceptional. In fact, when he saw the house—well, he didn't expect anything at that point. He'd already decided what wasn't there so he didn't notice what was. So," she concluded, "maybe I was looking for faces in the clouds but he never even glanced up."

She was animated, spilling over with happiness. Jim was thrilled to have even a small part in this moment. The bridge hadn't disappeared but was fading, definitely fading. "I can't tell you how grateful I am."

Emily flashed him a grin.

Emily made a brief stop at the rectory before the drive back to Manhattan. They were at the door, saying goodbye, when she paused, hand on the doorknob.

"You returned my check."

Jim nodded. "My car was fine. In any case, I'd never even heard the word 'detailed' until I saw it in your note. I had to look it up. Usually, my car just gets messier and messier and at some point I notice and clean it out."

He remembered her first call to him, her hesitations making it an awkward, painful exchange. Remembered that he had to convince her of his willingness to listen. He'd thought it was a lingering remnant of shock, of finding herself somewhere she never thought possible. It was something else, though; something deeper. At the Brennans' he'd seen what it was, because he recognized it, or a kin of it.

"If it weren't for you, the Brennans would be in real trouble."

She shrugged. "They still may be."

There was no reason why he should have such confidence in the recommendation of a used-book dealer, but he did. "It will be fine. I'm sure of it."

He remembered the way Emily had bloomed in the warmth of Helen's compliments. "I don't know whether you have the time, and maybe it's something your employers wouldn't want you to be doing . . ."

A rueful grin. "I've already committed a lot of treasonable offenses."

"I think Helen would be pleased to hear from you, now and again."

And just like that, she retreated. "So, yeah, I probably should stop bugging you."

He should have seen that coming. He was horrified. "No, no, that's not what I meant. I didn't mean that at all. I meant in addition." Taking a breath, "In addition," he said firmly. "In addition to me, unless you're too busy. I enjoy your calls; that's why I keep you talking half the night, it seems. But Helen likes you, and I gather they're pretty isolated. I just thought she might like to hear what you're up to, now and again."

She smoothed her shirt, began to hunt in her handbag. "I hardly know her. What makes you think she'd want to talk to me?" The question was delivered offhandedly, but she couldn't even look at him when she asked it.

"If you have the time, it would be a kindness," he said. "Her husband says she loves gossip but what it is, actually, is conversation. I don't think she gets enough of that."

Leo poked his head in. "Thought I heard voices."

Jim introduced them and Leo took a closer look at Emily. His gaze settled on Jim. Opened his mouth and then thought better of it.

Moments later, Emily was on the road.

Despite the fact that Catholics no longer attended Mass, a measure of respect remained, at least among some, for priests. One of the many Newport Sullivans, no relation to Leo, was the handyman Mike had come up with, and when he called Jim, he'd waved away Jim's offer of a down payment.

"You said they'd be paying later, Father. So no problem. Say a prayer for me, will you?"

Surprisingly, Leo hadn't objected to babysitting the paintings a little longer.

"If the Taylors involve the police," Jim assured him, "I'll tell them I allowed the paintings to be moved to the rectory. You had nothing to do with it."

Later on, though, Leo found him in his study. The light was low. Jim had put on a CD but he wasn't really hearing it. He was sitting slumped, staring at nothing, letting the fragments of the day swirl around him. The despair on Helen Brennan's face. The anger in Victor Belanger's voice.

And the morning, which came at him with the force of a night terror. He knew what he had seen; he could never have imagined such a thing: skin and fat and muscle and bone. How had he made it through the day? Lizzie's face, a mixture of impatience and something else. Worry, maybe. Or fear.

"Interesting story about the art." Leo stood in the doorway but did not come in. "Happy news for nearly all concerned."

"I hope they'll be able to keep their home."

"The old couple. They're parishioners, did you say?"

Jim hadn't asked them, but, "I don't think so."

"The young woman, then," Leo said mildly.

"No."

Leo considered. "Perhaps, then, a former parishioner who's now living elsewhere."

"No." Jim turned off the CD player. His back to Leo, he said, "And before you ask, she's not thinking of becoming one, either."

"I didn't think so. You said she lives in New York. Not to incite further defensive outbursts but our vow is to engage with the spiritual lives of our flock. So far I have failed to elicit a response elucidating precisely how that pertains in this situation. I don't object to our holding the paintings, feculent though they are, but it would be good to know why."

Jim turned around. "Leo, let's leave it at this: a corporal work of mercy."

Leo met his eyes. His were watery, the sclera sallow with age, fine veins running along the sides close to the nose. There was nothing in them: no trace of any of the emotions Jim was feeling. "She's a very pretty girl."

Jim refused to react. "She needed my help. That's all."

"I'm not your confessor," Leo said, "but I'd advise care. Especially if she accounts for phone calls at all hours of the night."

Leo stepped back in the hall and was gone.

Jim stood for a while, not moving. Thinking about the assumptions Leo had made and whether his silence confirmed Leo's assumptions. Thinking about what he could have said. On the face of it, the story was preposterous. Two calls from the ether, the eighteen-wheeler that launched two people into the bay. He found it hard to believe and he'd lived it. If he omitted the details that existed beyond belief, there was the fact that Emily had jumped off the bridge and Jim had gone after her. And that was where he came to a stop. Emily wasn't Leo's business, no more than she would have been if Jim's first contact with her had been in a confessional. Let Leo think what he would.

The air hung like crepe in his study; his lungs may have been working hard to extract any oxygen from it. He thought of himself breathing the desiccated cells of scores of priests, released from the rugs, from the upholstery, from the curtains with every stirring of air made by a body moving from place to place in the room. You were never alone; there was always some piece of some body bumping up against you. You might be, in the middle of a desert, but not here, not in this rectory and not in Newport. Newport was old, layers and layers of cells compressed on every flat surface, sunk deep in soft places, clinging to the edges of things.

After a while, he found his place in the breviary but after a few minutes put that aside. Went into his bedroom, removed the Roman collar and dropped it on the bed. Unbuttoned his shirt, shucked it off, letting it fall beside the collar. Unbuckled his belt, unzipped his pants, let them drop.

He sat down hard.

Acid bubbled to the back of his throat and he swallowed it down again.

It's not real.

But it looked real.

He swung his legs onto the bed, shoved himself back against the headboard and closed his eyes to concentrate on what his body felt rather than what his eyes told him. He couldn't go back to the hospital. He couldn't do that again: the odd note in Lizzie's voice, her look, half-irritated and what else? Bemused? Worried? His eyes could not be trusted but perhaps his body could. He tried to calm his mind, breathing slowly. He let the sensations come to him, separate and distinct. His body told him what he'd been feeling all evening: one leg was tingling and the other leg was numb; he couldn't feel his hand resting against his thigh or his fingers moving over the skin.

He opened his eyes again. The numbness was in the left leg, the leg that had first recorded the assault of mosquitoes or some other biting insect, the one in which the hole had appeared that morning. It still had the hole—or had it vanished and reappeared? And now there was another hole, an inch or so closer to the knee. The new hole told him how the first had come to seem so clean; the skin around the edges was ragged, torn, and a dead gray—maybe what it would look like if a bullet had exited there, or something had exploded beneath the skin. Around the wound was an angry red band, but that wasn't what you noticed when you looked at the area.

What you couldn't miss—or mistake—was the activity along the skin shredded at the top of the newer hole, and seemingly all the way down. Maggots were feeding on the flesh, cleaning the wound. Fat, writhing, white and translucent. He squinted at it, just for a moment, and then he couldn't look again.

Lurching to the bathroom, he was sick. He vomited until his stomach was empty and sore, and though there was nothing left to bring up, he continued to vomit until he was gasping, sweating though his body was freezing. He slid down the wall and sat on the floor, his legs out before him on the ugly brown tiles. At this angle, the light was dim with a rancid gray cast, black at the edges. Then he realized it wasn't the light; he was about to faint. He slid further and lay flat, eyes closed, and whether from the chilly tiles or from horror, he began to shake. He curled onto his side and wrapped his arms around himself.

His hands remained under his armpits and he held on tightly. No matter what he told himself, he couldn't bring his hand to touch the deep void in his leg or the ugly ragged thing above it. He knew he should, but he couldn't touch them, couldn't look at them again.

He prayed. To God, to Jesus, to the sister saints who might intervene. Silently, and then he was whispering his prayer, the words running together *helpmehelpmehelpme.*

Time passed.

He had to get himself to his feet. Couldn't lie on the floor forever. If he died and Leo found him there and he was hauled away to the hospital, to Lizzie. Or to the morgue. O'Neill-Hayes dealing with the corpse . . .

Eventually, the shaking subsided and exhaustion overcame every other feeling. He got his legs under him, somehow, and made his way back to the bed.

His leg didn't hurt. Nothing hurt. If what he saw was real, he reasoned, it would hurt. If he could touch the leg, feel smooth skin where the holes were, he would know he was imagining it all. But somehow, he couldn't.

And still, the breathing, as familiar to him as his own heartbeat.

He couldn't call Lizzie again. Not twice in one day. Not ever.

15

At first, I'd been jubilant; you always are when you get your dream job. At least, it was my dream then. Or maybe I just told myself it was my dream. Working at the auction house. Art and artifacts I could touch. Fabulous people. People who were educated and who set the styles in Manhattan. I thought Manhattan was the only place to be in the world.

I was nervous when I interviewed, but I wasn't afraid of what they'd see on my resume, and I didn't worry too much that they'd ask a question I couldn't answer. I've always been confident that my brain was adequate. As for the resume, well, it was a low-level position, so they couldn't have been expecting years of experience, could they?

It was the rest of it that made me vaguely queasy, that made my heart pound as I dressed in clothes that may have been fine but may also have not. I knew I was attempting to pass as someone I wasn't.

Schoharie County. You've never been there, probably. We have an Iroquois museum and a few caves, but if you're not interested in one or the other, you've probably never even heard of it. That part of New York is rolling hills and farmland. Red barns and graceful silos, cows dotting the landscape as if they'd been put there by Turner. Take a closer look and you'll see something different.

Supposedly you don't really see the place you grew up in. Your memories overlay specific locations and so you see where you hit a rock in the road and your bike went airborne, tumbling your nine-year-old self into a ditch. Only you don't see the place, the little hill you'd descended, the wild carrot graceful at the edge of the ditch, the long stretch of road ahead of you; instead, you see yourself on your bike, the cotton shorts you couldn't wear afterwards because you slid over gravel and shredded the side along one thigh, and you hear what your mother said when you came home. I don't know how I saw my home when I was a little kid but by the time I was applying to colleges, I had at least a sense of where I was and could judge the size of the leap I'd have to make to cross to the other side.

Five colleges and I got into four on the strength, I think, of the portfolio I sent. Paintings of my home the way I'd begun to see it. A church, a nineteenth-century spa, and seven houses. I could have included more—there were dozens of places like these in and around Schoharie County, but I chose the grandest ones. They all had the same abandoned air, as if someone had just walked away, in some cases not even bothering to close windows or doors. The grass grown up around them, a few feet high. The paint on them scrubbed off by howling storms and wind-driven snows, the gingerbread broken, the columns listing, rotted. There had been money here, once, and pride proclaiming itself in enormous Greek revival homes with massive Doric columns and elaborate cornices painted to look like stone; Queen Annes with cantilevered gables and elegant towers, fish-scale shingles and iron-railed widows' walks; and wide, solid Federal-style homes that showed orderly rows of tall windows. I would have loved to live in any of them but they weren't habitable and hadn't been for years. In the nineteenth century, the world had marched up to Schoharie County, but then, as it does, the world moved on, leaving those markers of what had once been.

I'd been painting the pictures for years before I realized what it was I was painting. You paint the world around you, and what calls to you from it. Some people would have focused on the barns and the silos, and some would have rendered the soft landscape and the river in gentle tones. I painted buildings. They are what detached themselves from the landscape and focused my attention. And when I was applying to colleges, I was casting around for something that would distinguish me from thousands of other eager applicants and something that would appeal to the elite schools. Finally, I thought of the pictures. I've always been a good draftsman, and looking at the pictures with fresh eyes, or from what I imagined the perspective of those unseen and unknown deciders might be, I saw that I had poured something of myself into them. I loved each building on its own merits but that's not why they called to me, louder than anything else in my world. They called to me because of the people who had inhabited them; I envied the assumption of those inhabitants that life would always be kind to them, would always be good.

When I got to college, one of the Seven Sisters, I saw the contemporary versions of those people. Young women who grew up without thinking about how they lived. Freshman year and we were still getting to know people, making hesitant overtures to our classmates. My roommate and I were going into town and she'd invited a girl at the end of the hall to come with us. The girl—I don't remember her name—wasn't ready; a sunny day but cool, she thought she needed a sweater. I was waiting by the door as she opened up a cedar chest at the end of her bed and I took a curious step closer and was dazzled. There were five piles of sweaters, crammed tightly, thick cashmere in a rainbow of colors. There must have been thirty of them.

More than the luxury cars in the parking lots and the electronic paraphernalia everyone seemed to have, the trunk of cashmere sweaters dazzled and frightened me. I wasn't one of them. I understand now that all those girls knew I wasn't one of them—I didn't own a car, my laptop was out of date, I didn't have the right cell phone, and didn't own a single piece of designer clothing—but for the next four years I devoted myself to their study, as one would a foreign language, so that I could be proficient in them.

There were bad, unavoidable moments during those years. Sitting at the table eating lunch and suddenly my freshman-year roommate says, "Don't bother asking Emily about Europe; she's never even been on a plane." Cornered in a bathroom by a sophomore who'd taken offense at my plain brown hair: "My God, haven't you ever heard of foils?" Freshman year parents' weekend was miserable: my mother wasn't the only widow in attendance, but possibly the only widow whose annual salary was less than what lots of parents earned in a week, and who considered clothing through a purely functional lens.

The admissions office had given me entry to that world but perhaps they never thought how difficult it would be for me to exist in it.

By the time I graduated, the scholarship girl with a part-time job in the dining hall and a mother angry that I'd wasted all that money on a degree that wasn't marketable, I'd changed everything. My hair was right and I had a small horde of the right clothes. I was able to deflect any question and avoid any topic that might lead me to betray myself. But I always suspected that people saw through the façade, and before the job interview I spent more time deciding what I'd wear and what my hair would look like than I spent considering what questions I would be asked and what answers I'd give.

When Metro called to say that I was hired, I was ecstatic. I worked on catalogues and I enjoyed researching and writing notes, proofreading, being involved as a catalog came together and I was proud when it came back from the printer, the photography crisp on the heavy white paper, the text substantial and professional. I did other things, such as answering phones, and hours and hours of grunt work for the experts, but I was also learning the business.

In some ways, the job was college all over again. The group I'd come to Newport with—two coworkers and one's boyfriend—complained about their lack of money but comfortably, because it wasn't really an issue. One, when I'd met her, had asked where my family's homes were. Just like that. Just assuming that I would rattle off a few locations. And while I was pleased that I was able to inspire such assumptions, it bothered me. All the time it bothered me.

No one supplemented my salary, which was small because Metro knew there were lots of trust fund babies happy to take the job if I didn't want it. Most of the money went for the cluttered cell I rented with my roommates on the Upper East Side. Before I met Rob I had five sets of clothes to make it through the week and one good short dress. My wardrobe grew when I was dating; I'd owned the long yellow dress for less than two weeks before I drowned it.

I couldn't ask my mother for money. I wouldn't have asked, in any case. I phoned her once a month—she never called me—and I'd have a store of anecdotes to share with her, and after two or three anecdotes, she'd tell me about the funny thing my sister had said or what interesting thing she had done and then we'd hang up. There was no place in those monthly phone calls for a request, just as there wasn't for confessions. Our phone conversations were a shade less personal than if I'd called in a pizza delivery order. The only thing my mother wanted to know was whether I was still alive.

I've tried for years and years with my mother. All through high school I'd wash the dishes and do the ironing, trim the bushes, weed the rose garden, and vacuum the house. I'd make a cake from scratch for her birthday, try to anticipate her needs the rest of the year. But I eventually realized that my mother wasn't my friend. She could occasionally be charmed by me and if I asked—and throughout my teenage years, I asked and asked—she'd say she loved me. But she didn't. I knew she didn't. I could see it in her face, hear it in her voice as pushed away the question, unwilling to entertain it. She didn't even like me.

My mother did what she saw as her maternal duty by me: I was fed, clothed, and signed up for piano lessons. And, as I passed from childhood to adolescence, she provided what she no doubt thought was guidance. How the pants I was wearing were designed for slender legs. How she'd always held in her stomach so she never had a paunch. Why nail polish never did manage to make short fingers look graceful. And, by the way, men preferred petite women. I could diet, certainly, and did, but I couldn't shrink. In college, she advised me that the arts weren't a career, announced that she didn't like the girls I'd met at school, that college was a dream world and Schoharie the reality that I'd come back to. On and on and on.

I've never known whether my mother was right. Once, she told me I was incapable of loving anyone. Was that an accurate assessment? I don't know.

I've never been sure of my welcome. I think that might be why I've developed a reputation of aloofness. If there's a group of people around someone's desk at work, I never join it. I'll say hello to people but I never make friendly overtures; I wait to see if they come to me. I wait to be asked to join the gang in an after-work drink, even though I can see other people inviting themselves, the group heading to the elevators, gathering up people like a magnet gathers metal shavings. The horrible thing is that after the elevator door closes, after the last bit of laughter disappears down the shaft, I feel empty and sad and I hate myself. I could have attached myself to the group, except that I couldn't because maybe they didn't want me.

In five years, I've moved up a little at Metro, though my salary still barely covers my share of the rent. I'm more comfortable with what I do, and I've made a friend. For Todd, my sense of humor outweighs everything else and as long as I'm bright and witty, my spectacularly dreary beginnings, as Todd calls my formative years, don't matter. I've dated a bit, and the less said about that the better. The one actual relationship, with Rob, was an anomaly in many ways. It went on for nearly five months, for one thing, and he was fifteen years older, for another. He could be good company, but he could also be cutting. Unlike Todd, he preferred that I not be bright and witty, and when we went to a party, he expected me to say as little as possible, as a matter of fact. Truth to tell, he made me nervous, his friends more so, the settings—a penthouse overlooking Central Park, for example—even more so. He'd tell me we were going here or there and I'd be in a frenzy, searching the web to figure out what people wore to such an evening, and panicked if I couldn't find any photos. Sometimes I'd try to calm myself by drinking and halfway into the first glass of wine I'd start babbling about who knows what. I'd get home and relive the evening, lingering on every stupid thing I'd said, wishing I could do it over again, standing outside myself, looking at my fat thighs and the little belly, my stupid face going on and on to someone who doubtless wished to be anywhere else, and I'd hate myself.

There was a time, for a year or two after my father died, that I used to stick common pins in my legs. Near the top of my thighs, where the marks wouldn't be seen. I'd stare at my skin as I pushed in the pin, not all the way, not so far that blood would well up around the metal, but past the bite of the first attack, until it caused a determined throbbing. I don't know why I did that. I don't know why I did a lot of things I did when I was younger. A few years after I stopped, the memory of that became shameful and I never wanted to go back and look at it, to find out why I did it. And, because I don't know the why, I don't know whether or not I really intended to jump from that bridge. Some part of me, though, thinks it may have been where I've been heading all my life.

What I do know is that my ruined dress, blue-tinged body, throbbing brain, and burning lungs were hauled into another world. A little police station, smelling of burnt coffee, and the young cop, plump and baby-faced, exchanging pleasantries with the priest. The priest himself, shivering as he'd cranked up the heat in the car, his face still white with cold and shock, his eyes soft, not the slightest spark of calculation in them. And it only occurred to me later that someone must have retrieved the car and parked it in front of the station, which never would have happened in the city. Anyway, as he drove me home I told him about seeing Rob at the party, and when he questioned me, I could hear the worry in his voice. He was afraid. For me.

And so I started to call him. I was afraid for me, too. I knew I was a mess. I knew I was unhappy and I hated myself and hated my life and I couldn't seem to connect with other people. I didn't feel my friends really cared about me, not even Todd—*how could they?* I thought—and I had never had a normal relationship with a man. People at Metro dated, then they got serious. They had fights and they had great weekends and they took vacations—skiing in South America in midsummer, to a rented villa by Lake Como—and they'd come back engaged. If I had a fight with a man, it meant that after a few dates I'd realized he was a drunk, or the kind of nasty that men are who really don't like women, or obsessed with himself, or just interested in getting me into bed, or just a total asshole, and I was ending it. I took a certain amount of pride in the fact that no man had ever broken up with me. Until Rob, that is.

That first time, I was testing. As I said I'm never sure of my welcome, and though I thought a priest probably had to have at least the appearance of being charitable, still, he was a man the same as other men. But I was so frightened by what I'd done that I couldn't get any food down, and despite the fact that it was July, and July was hot as hell in the city, I felt as cold as I did when he fished me from the bay, a chill that seemed to have settled permanently under my skin.

I called because I needed to talk to someone, which wasn't like me. Usually, when I'm upset I make art. I'll get my sketch pad and do a study of hands or my father's face as I remember it. Or I'll take out the watercolors and see if I can manage subtle textures such as bark in a copse of trees. Once I attempted a still life of cheeses. Oils would be better but the smell would get into my work clothes and probably permeate the apartment. At some point I'll think to look at my phone and I'll see that I should have gone to bed an hour ago. This time, though, art wasn't going to do it, so I tapped in the number he'd given me, my heart pounding because I was risking a cold response, flat out rejection, and I didn't know what I would do if that happened. He'd answered. But when I'd started talking, I caught up with me, and then I tried to end the call before it became apparent that he wished I'd hang up. He interrupted and made it clear, even to me, listening for the slightest cue that indicated I wasn't welcome, that he wanted the conversation to continue.

It was a mistake, asking about Rob. As soon as the words came out, I was horrified. I thought I'd thrown away the opportunity that the priest had made available to me but, miraculously, I hadn't. He was still there, still talking, still listening. Still reassuring and still worried about me.

I don't want to sound pathetic or anything because I realize that by many measures, I lead a pretty good life, but the priest was the first person who'd ever worried about me. Well, my father did, I'm sure, but I was nine when he died. My mother actually said straight out that she never worried about me because I can take care of myself, when anyone can see that I'm a total mess. I don't think she's really looked at me since I was five. I mean, really looked. This sounds self-pitying, I know, but if you know that no one out there worries about you, it can make for a lonesome feeling.

So I called again. And again. He liked my stories. He sometimes asked for details and sometimes just listened, but he always laughed at my jokes. I may have implied that all of the stories were fresh and many were, but some were things that had happened months or even years before.

He was a baritone but when he lost himself in laughter, his voice rose as high as a woman's. It made me smile to hear it. I'd think for days about what I would tell him, would select anecdotes and determine how I would deliver them, how to shape the stories to entertain him. I'd be in the middle of writing a short biography of some artist and a line would suddenly come to me and I'd make a conscious effort to remember it, because if the line made me smile, it would make him laugh.

The priest.

— 16 —

Jim looked out the office window one afternoon and watched an immature robin scuttle behind its sleek parent, which trained an eye on the grass, snatched at something, and gobbled it down. So the babies were on their own. Past the point when vibrating their wings could attract their parents' attention, when their frantic cries would result in food offered from a parent's beak. Nature somehow deemed them ready and if Jim wanted to, he could look online to discover how the parents decided when the fledglings were old enough to fend for themselves. But he didn't need the explanation; he just enjoyed the show.

The feeding station was more work than he'd expected; the sparrows, particularly, were worse than infants, knocking twenty seeds to the ground for every one they ate. Jim had been filling some feeders every day and he raked the ground every other day to clean up the seeds, which otherwise would kill the grass. Nevertheless, Leo believed the feeders were encouraging the rats.

If they did have rats, they would not find the rectory hospitable once the work crew arrived from Seaside; Jim had looked at his bank account and with a sinking feeling had mailed the first check.

Bart Meagher was younger than Jim expected. Not Mike's contemporary, hardly old enough to have earned a reputation. In fact, Meagher was younger than Jim, perhaps no more than thirty. A bit over six feet tall, with a sturdy build and a light tan, he looked like a lot of the affluent crowd that sailed competitively. A good-humored face, small-featured, with a strong jaw. Affable, but observant green eyes.

He was fourth-generation Fifth Ward, he told Jim. "On my mother's side, anyway. Father's side just off the boat. Grew up in the Fifth Ward and as soon as I had the down payment I bought a house there." He shrugged, an oddly delicate movement. "Places get a grip on you, know what I mean? I had a roommate in college who was from Colorado and the poor bastard suffered for four years in Cambridge. As soon as we graduated he shot back to Denver. He missed the mountains. I suppose I'd feel the same if I had to part ways with the bay."

He'd gotten a restraining order against the Taylors. "That will keep their greedy little fingers off the art until we go to court. Justin Wade's their lawyer but we'll see whether the Taylors pull anyone else out of their pocket. Wouldn't surprise me if they did."

The restraining order in place, he'd come to retrieve the art from the rectory. "Better to have it all together. I'm not worried about the wiring; I grew up with knob-and-tube and we never had a problem. Gas, on the other hand: people say it's great for cooking, but every so often a house blows up. I'd rather eat American bland than be blown to bits in the middle of my gourmet dinner. Well, so, I'd also like to have a look at the art; I'm a bit curious."

"Have you talked to the people from the auction house?"

Meagher gave him a narrow look. "She's a friend of yours?"

"Emily? I suppose you could say that."

"If you don't mind me saying so, what the hell planet does she live on?" He began to laugh, enjoying the memory. "She grilled me for a good ten minutes before she was satisfied that I wasn't planning assault and murder before I stole the art and burned down the house. In here?"

Jim nodded and let Meagher precede him into the parlor. "I'm sure she didn't mean to imply anything. She likes the Brennans."

"Well." A noise in the back of his throat suggested that Meagher didn't believe Emily capable of liking anybody. Meagher approached the two paintings, which were leaning against the wall, shrouded by the navy sheets Helen had wrapped them in. "Larger than I thought. Mrs. Brennan will be glad to have them back." He cut a glance at Jim. "She's worried that Delia's missing them."

Jim didn't know whether he was joking. "Helen told you about Delia?"

"She's thrilled to know her own ancestor is what's haunting her." Meagher pulled the sheet from one of the paintings and stood looking at it. "That's what she says, anyway. Can't say I'd feel the same, though. Why would I want Great-Great-Aunt Maeve watching while I unzip to take—" His brows came together. "So we know what this is supposed to be? Looks like they kept it in the smokehouse. Second Beach? Really?"

He let the sheet drop and tugged at the other sheet.

"I've been thinking of getting them a small air conditioner," Jim said. "It can't be comfortable for them in that old house but I wonder if it's allowed in a historic home. You wouldn't know about that, would you?"

"Well, that's a painting. Even with the smokehouse effect." Meagher took a few steps back, cocked his head. Then, "Travers Block, isn't it? Summer—you can just make out the dresses." Suddenly his expression changed. "My God, it does look like a Hassam, doesn't it? I heard all about this one and the other but I just assumed that the odds of having a Hassam . . . but I can see why they think . . . My God. If it's real." He shook his head wonderingly. "Imagine sitting on this all your life and not knowing what it is."

Jim felt it before he identified the mixture of relief and happiness. Until a disinterested party had identified the painting, Jim hadn't entirely believed in the possibility. Now he did. "Da Vinci and Michelangelo are the only names I know. Well, maybe a few more but not enough to field a baseball team."

Meagher was studying the painting. Finally, he picked it up and set it on a chair near a window. Pulled back one of the heavy curtains. Stood for a minute with his hands in his pockets, head cocked to one side. "There's a raft of his stuff at the Museum of Fine Arts in Boston. You've probably seen the one of Boston Common; they market the hell out of it: posters, mugs, calendars, cards, and who knows what else. It really does look like Childe Hassam."

He glanced at Jim. "I took a few art classes in college. I figured it was a good way to meet girls." A smile lit his eyes. "And it was."

He carefully wound the sheet around the painting and picked it up, laughing. "I should be asking you to get this back to the Brennans: the church is better insured than I am. So, the air conditioner? Put it in a rear window, away from the street, and no one will be the wiser."

Jim carried the other painting to Meagher's car, an inexpensive SUV with a rack. "I do some surfing when I can," he said. "Sweeps out the cobwebs."

As Meagher was about to get into the car, Jim decided it was better to speak than not. "Helen seems pretty with it when you talk to her. Doesn't seem to be failing at all."

Meagher looked at him, curious. "Failing? I haven't had more than a conversation or two but I'd say she's rational."

"I have been wondering, just a little . . ."

"About . . ." Meagher prompted when the silence stretched.

Jim couldn't look at him. "The ghost. Delia."

Meagher grinned, then the laugh emerged, full throated. "You think she's losing her marbles because she sees things?"

Jim was mortified. "No, no. I didn't mean . . ."

"I know you didn't, Father."

"I just want to make sure everything goes well," Jim said at last.

Meagher leaned back against the car, shot a speculative look at Jim. "Do you know Seawinds?"

Jim shook his head.

"Southern tip of the island. The one way out on the rocks. I had a little business out there about two years ago and being fourth-generation Fifth Ward, of course I knew the story. When the 1938 hurricane came up the coast, the owners told the servants to stay with the house or they'd lose their jobs. So they stayed. To be fair, no one on the East Coast had any idea it was a hurricane coming their way, but the family must have thought something, because they lit out of town in a hell of a hurry. So the servants were alone in the house, holding down the fort, and probably around the time they realized they needed to get out it was too late to go. The wind must have been howling on the upper stories so they were hunkered down on the first floor, not too much above sea level. Even there it must have been bad, with the wind throwing seaweed and sand and whatever else against the windows. You can imagine them huddled together, listening to the roar of the wind and the sand in the spray smacking against the windows."

He'd been staring into the middle distance, as though he could see the storm in his mind's eye, but now he glanced at Jim. "Do you know much about the 1938 hurricane?"

"A few things," Jim said. "The storm knocked down millions of trees in New England. I think it washed away some houses in South County, didn't it?"

"Yes. It hit at high tide, during an equinox and full moon. Really bad timing. Worst possible timing, as a matter of fact. And it moved a lot faster than hurricanes usually do, and was pushing all that water along with it. So when the storm hit Newport, the ocean swept right through Seawinds and the poor suckers didn't have a chance. I don't remember how many drowned—I heard that story years and years ago from my grandmother." A sudden laugh. "She was still bitter about it. The servants would have been Irish, that's why. Not that she knew them, or even the family, for that matter. Newporters have long memories, though."

"I never heard that story."

Meagher nodded. "And you won't, either, unless you talk to one of the old Fifth Ward families." He swept a hand through his hair, thinking. "I know a few stories, but for what it's worth, here's the rest of the Seawinds one. I went out there because the owners were selling the place. A guy from Virginia was paying close to eleven million for it. Normally, people come to the office but you know the Avenue types: they think the world should come to them—and most of the time it does. I said I'd stop by, thinking I'd get a good look at the house; I like to see how people live. Beautiful day it was, too. Sun shining, no wind, not a cloud in the sky. Lousy for surfing, though; that kind of day always is. So they bring me out to the terrace. Who's sitting there big as life but the buyer himself. Not the usual thing, I thought, when they introduced me, but I figure maybe they're all good friends or something. We have a cup of coffee, exchange nonsense for a bit. Then I dig the contract out of my briefcase and the papers start flapping around like beached fish. Not blowing, like the wind's taking them, just flopping from side to side. I had to hold them down for the family to sign. As I say, it wasn't windy but I didn't think anything about it except Raum—that's the buyer—Raum's watching me with a face like thunder. Then I took out a pen." He smiled reminiscently. "I clicked the ballpoint and it was like someone grabbed the tip of it and just yanked. Once. But I have a pretty good grip."

The hair rose on the back of Jim's neck.

Meagher looked at Jim. "But I still didn't think much about it until I got back to the office and opened the briefcase. Sometimes I can be a little thick, you know?" And now he was laughing. "Soaked. The contract was sopping wet. I had to call them and ask them to come into the office to do the whole thing again. They didn't like that. Not at all. I said there'd been a leak in the ceiling. But ceilings don't usually leak seaweed, do they?"

Jim told Lizzie and Sam the story over coffee and blueberry pie. Triona, who'd been sulky throughout the meal, had disappeared into the house with her new books. The story was a defense; after badgering him about the children becoming altar servers, Lizzie announced that his color was off and he was losing weight. He said he hadn't noticed, and Lizzie was starting to wind up about his eating habits.

He was telling Lizzie the truth, but not all of it. He was having trouble keeping his mind off the leg that had been attacked. Though he wasn't convinced that what he'd seen was real, he nevertheless thought of his left leg as under assault. It had been bitten, and then it was cold and then the flesh had been opened. Now he had periods in which he couldn't feel it at all. That made him worry that it would give out while he was in the hospital, or at the altar, or walking along the street. It hadn't happened but it sat at the back of his brain at all times, like a mass of dark clouds at the mouth of the bay. You knew the wind was keeping the storm to the south but you didn't know whether the winds might shift and hurl it your way.

The Seawinds story was a success. "Meagher took it as a warning. Since then he's steered clear of Mr. Raum." Jim shook his head. "It's like there's something in the water. First it's the Brennans and then, when I expect some sense, it's the lawyer. He looks competent enough."

They were sitting on the patio in the backyard, which was enclosed by a high, wooden fence. Sam's gardens ran along the fence, except for a small rose garden at one edge of the patio. Tea roses, yellow, white, and pink. The first bloom was over; soft petals lay on the ground. The east-facing garden was thick with Solomon seal, gracefully arching over dwarf Shasta daisies, snapdragons, and alyssum. Bumblebees and honeybees, solid and soothing, moved among the flowers. Sam had been deadheading flowers until Lizzie began issuing orders; before Lizzie's orders, Sam had looked relaxed and peaceful.

"The lawyer was recommended by the bookstore guy, wasn't he?" Lizzie herself was an indifferent eater: she liked salad but took barely a tablespoon of everything else, and never finished what she took. While Jim was telling his story, Lizzie set down her dessert plate, a lone bite missing from the small slice of pie she'd given herself.

"Nothing wrong with Mike."

Lizzie reached for her iced tea and Jim knew before she said anything that she was about to make one of her pronouncements. "The guy does drugs," she said flatly. "Ever look at his eyes?"

"Oh, come on," Jim said, outraged.

"Completely bloodshot." Lizzie was unperturbed. "Drugs. I had a guy come into the ER about a month ago who thought he was a condor . . ."

"You didn't tell me that one." Sam had come in from the kitchen, where he'd located Lizzie's missing phone. He'd poured himself two fingers of scotch. Lizzie gave him a quick look then glanced away, but not before Jim saw it.

"I didn't?" Lizzie paused to consider. "Oh, yeah. I think that was the night the drunk guy tried to take out a nurse. I probably told you about that. The condor guy," she said, turning back to Jim, "was flipping out . . ."

"Or flapping out," Willy put in.

". . . because we were preventing him from going back to the nest to feed the babies. Screaming at the top of his lungs that we were killing the chicks."

"Makes you sound like a serial killer," Jim said. "Lizzie the Ripper."

Willy snickered.

Lizzie ignored the comment. "I could have throttled the guy. There was a two-car crash in Middletown, the drunk guy who fell off the back of a powerboat and just missed getting a leg cut off, and something else . . . Maybe a stroke?" She shook her head. "Can't remember, but the drug guy was taking up all this time and I couldn't get to anyone else. He looked and smelled like weed but it had to have been laced with something a lot stronger. Anyway," she concluded, "there's some powerful stuff out there. Your bookstore guy probably sees ghosts every day, and a lot of other things, too."

"Ghosts," Sam said with sudden vehemence. "If people want to be scared, they should watch the news."

Willy looked up from his book. "There are ghosts on the news?"

"Worse," his father said. "Crap happens all over the planet and half the people are too stupid to know it's happening and the other half are too lazy to do anything about it. Desertification is occurring at the rate of twenty-four billion tons of land a year, category five hurricanes are forming at an unprecedented rate, the garbage dump in the Pacific is twice the size of Texas and every year, one or another species is driven to extinction. How many elephants are poached every year? How many marine mammals beach themselves every day? We don't know because we don't care. But let's take drugs and yammer about ghosts: it's a hell of a lot easier than actually doing anything useful."

Surprised by this sudden declaration, Lizzie stole a look at the drink in his hand and frowned. When she was anxious, her eyebrows drifted up and stayed there. She looked tired, too, just as she had when he'd gone to the emergency room. That reminded him why he'd gone, and as the vision of the holes in his leg slammed into his brain, his breath caught.

Sam seemed to come to himself and glanced at his son, who had returned to the pages of his book. "Nevermind. There are enough conscientious people in the world to make up for all the idiots. At least, I hope there are."

"I will invent something to clean the ocean," Willy said. "Like a giant garbage can that we can then shoot into the Andromeda galaxy."

"Said the boy who has a pile of filthy clothes festering on the floor of his bedroom."

"Maybe I am conducting an experiment."

"And maybe you're not," Sam said and, in better humor, was grinning as he turned to Jim. "So your part's done and you're leaving everything up to all the ghost lovers."

Jim thought it better not to mention the air conditioner. "I asked the Brennans if they'd like to receive the Eucharist once a week. Maria is doing everything that needs to be done but I'd still like to keep an eye on them."

He needn't have worried about Lizzie, though; she was scanning the flat surfaces around her. "Sam, did you see my work phone in the kitchen?"

"Maria's the woman from Guatemala?" Sam asked.

Jim nodded.

"She doesn't see ghosts, does she?"

"Not that I know of."

Sam finished his drink in a gulp. "I guess that's one sane person you know." And went into the house to search.

17

Emily called several times a week. At first she'd been diffident, telling him after a few minutes that she'd blathered long enough, or that he probably had something better to do, or that she was boring even herself. He worked hard to impress on her that the calls were welcome and that he enjoyed hearing about her comings and goings. Despite that reassurance, she usually caught herself at least once during a call, and then he'd have to insist, again, that she wasn't interrupting anything.

Jim still felt the blood drain when his phone rang late at night. Though experience had taught him that Emily usually called around ten o'clock, he looked carefully at the number before he answered. He wondered if he would have recognized the number of the unknown caller had he thought to look. Though at two in the morning, when the world was deep into dreams and no hint of the coming sunrise could be found in the chilly air, the habits of sunlight weren't often recalled by brain or muscle.

By ten, the dinner with friends, or the opening of the exhibit, or the new play was over and Emily was home again. She told him about the overwrought entrees, the bits and pieces of odd pairings as "meticulously arranged on a plate as something by Flegel." The exhibits were sometimes fair but she relished the awful ones by artists who were, as she said, "enjoying a moment" in Manhattan. One was "*Curtains*. Silk, cotton, polyester, wool, newspaper, plastic, and rubber. They were hung around the room and the guy had gurneys behind them and on each gurney there were various oddments that were vaguely body-like. It was curtains for them, get it?" She liked to listen to what people said about the exhibits. "Inanities delivered in what the speaker thinks is a thoughtful voice. They're like the people who give this knowing chuckle at just the right time at Lincoln Center: you know they're actually humorless but they've read that the composer put in a musical joke, and they want you to know they get the joke."

He let her talk about whatever came to her but after that first call she never spoke again about anything personal. Once in a while he thought about Leo's cautionary words, and worried whether he would have encouraged the calls had she been male, or much older, or less attractive. But then a sick feeling would settle in his stomach because attractive or not, Emily was a reliable link to an access of mortification and regret. And fear.

He never mentioned the bridge, despite his urge to know what she'd heard that night. Try as he might, he didn't remember her reaction. Instead, what came back to him, losing no vigor as the days and weeks rolled on, was terror so great he felt it would lift him out of his body, pull him up until he dissolved into the endless sky.

For a half hour or so, listening to what she said, he was transported to the world of bad artists, pompous music lovers, and theatergoers who coughed for two hours. But he didn't feel grounded and it seemed more and more likely that no one was, when they felt an unseen presence in their hospital room and then were dead, when their ancestors dropped by from time to time for a chat, when a young lawyer could calmly recount the interference of the dead in his day-to-day business.

And when he was hobbled by one leg that was perpetually numb, its mate prickling as though a thousand ants were crawling on it. The breathing had become louder; all sound was filtered through it, rendering the world more remote than the bottom of the sea. He heard Willy's jokes and saw Lizzie's worry and it was as if he existed on the wrong side of an aquarium, vague entities swirling around him in the dim water while people stopped briefly, their edges softened by the thickness of the glass, their conversations muted, before moving along. Better for them that way, but he would never get closer, never form any kind of bond, and then they would be gone, away from him and into the world, and he would lose forever even the little bit he now had of them.

He'd never been alone with the children, ever, and it had seemed at times an unnecessary precaution because he could never know how much of Blessed Sacrament had been imagination. But now he felt his caution had been justified, had been possibly the wisest thing he'd done in life. More and more he was convinced that something had scuttled across the floor and seized him that day. Better to be a stranger than allow it to reach for the children. He'd been thirteen, after all, when it had taken him. Only a year older than his niece, three years older than his nephew. Innocent, vulnerable and defenseless.

The night he'd seen the maggots, the sister saints, the chieftain's daughter and the Roman princess, had kept their distance despite his frantic prayers. He'd grown so frightened that eventually he'd shut them out, them and their God, shut out everything but the steady pumping of his heart, the rhythmic movement of his chest as his lungs drew in air and pushed it out again.

He'd remembered his conversation with the woman in the hospital, that one malformed or damaged area of the brain could produce things that were seen, heard, and felt. Breathless with terror, he tried to counteract hallucination with things that were solid and real, casting around for something warm and alive, and finally lit on the birds that came to his feeders. The goldfinches, blazing pure yellow, the black on their wings as reflective as enamel. The undulating flight of the titmice, the muted colors, blue-gray and orange, sweet and serene as they traveled between the old maple and the feeder. Carolina wrens small and rounded as if they were meant to be cradled in a hand. Nuthatches, creeping down an oak, examining the bark for bugs. On and on, to cardinals, house finches, jays, starlings, grackles, and sparrows, holding each one in his mind until another flickered at the edge of his brain and he could reach out to it, warm, animate, joyous, and gradually the warmth of the summer night touched his skin again; the pillow, propped behind him, gathered mass and pressed against his back. The smell of old, damp wood, the acid stink of vomit.

He'd taken those sensations—that reality—with him as he'd leaned forward and stretched a hand, finally, down the leg that had been numb. There was the hair and skin of his thigh, covering the strong mass of his quadriceps. The hair was wiry, the flesh warm and a little bumpy under his hand but more importantly, his palm and fingers were cool against his leg. The solid patella, the small scar just below it from a childhood fall, and below that, flesh covering the curved tibialis, running from knee to ankle. He swept his hand from side to side, up and down, and the tibialis ran smooth from knee to ankle.

He still could not open his eyes but he was gaining confidence; no longer lightheaded, and the tingling had vanished, just as the numbness had. The palm of the right hand traveling, questing, and echoing the sensations of the left. He hadn't felt hope; he'd only been too exhausted to entertain fear a moment longer. He'd opened his eyes.

And felt relief wash over him. It was gone. His body was his own again.

After he'd straightened up the bathroom, he got into bed with his breviary. It was nearly four. Less than two hours to sunrise, but clothed in absolute darkness and silence. As on the bridge, the sense that he could be the last person on earth.

And yet, everything but the breathing gone, his first thought was prayer. Whether he believed in it or not, whether he had any hope about anything or had settled permanently into hopelessness, it was habit. So down, the attitude of supplication, the smell of vomit still lingering in the air.

The enemy has pursued my soul; he has crushed my life to the ground. He has made me dwell in darkness like those long dead. My spirit is faint within me; my heart despairs.

The evening prayers had to be said. His mind had drifted for a little, lighting on first one person, then another, as if he needed to bring them to God's attention. And as he was descending, finally, into sleep, a line from the Psalms had come to him.

In peace I will lie down and fall asleep, for you alone, Lord, make me secure.

He sat at his desk on another evening, this one foggy, horns that usually felt companionable sounding doleful notes. Anselm's letter had been retrieved and thrown in the bottom drawer of his desk. He hadn't been able to get rid of it but avoided it as if it were contaminated. Not that he needed to read it again.

"My pride created what you saw . . ."

That was the worst of it. Even in flight from it, as he had been for most of his life, he had doubted that he'd seen anything, had tried to cover it with other scenes, other images. So he *had* seen something then. But if he tried to call it up now, would that make it real? Would that draw it closer?

He thought of Kit Acker, afraid that the unseen presence in her hospital room would discover her awareness of it. Was it possible that such things slithered into the world when God had an inattentive moment? Or was it that the world was wide open to such things because humans had invented a friend and protector?

Anselm, knocking around the rectory, breakfasting in the funhouse kitchen, crossing to the church, companioned.

Lizzie's voice, as clear as if she were standing on the other side of the desk. "Get a grip, will you?"

Her explanation would have been that he'd caught Anselm in mid-hallucination. That he'd been frightened by Anselm talking to empty air and thought he'd seen more than that. Anselm, jittery, jumpy with PTSD, out-piousing the cradle Catholics. And cryptic. The words Anselm had chosen seemed to be deliberately vague, open to a thousand interpretations. Not helpful, and so what was the point of writing them?

But then, he'd nearly forgotten: Anselm, somehow, had known twenty years ago that his altar server would become a priest.

"Just leave me in peace, will you?"

August fourth, feast day of St. John Vianney, patron saint of parish priests. Renowned confessor. Subject to frequent beatings by Satan, who also set the poor man's bed afire. That last was something other people could see, at least; no mistaking smoking sheets and straw or whatever it was they'd stuffed mattresses with in the nineteenth century. Though the priest could have done it himself.

He'd made himself start the day with hope, but the day had taken a file to it. It had been hot, as most August days were in Newport. Now that the air conditioning people were beginning to wrap up, he was glad he'd paid for it; his black pants and shirt absorbed heat and the clerical collar acted like a cork on a wine bottle. The sweat ran under his hair, snaked beneath the collar and trickled down his back. His hands felt swollen and they flexed under protest.

The afternoon had been long, a noisy train of meetings. The sparrows chattered as he crossed from the church, where he'd counted twenties into someone's hand. Groceries, this time, for an old woman who lived alone. You couldn't say no.

He poked his head into Leo's study.

"What time did the Seaside people leave?"

"Nearly seven o'clock." Leo closed his eyes briefly. "I waited for them to finish, you know. I didn't think I'd be able to decently digest anything with all the banging and clattering and their radio blaring what passes for music nowadays. A man should be able to concentrate at dinnertime, and the older one gets, the more important it is to be considerate of the digestive processes. I finally waved the white flag around six and made myself something. Since then, I've been paying the price."

"A good night's sleep should help."

"Oh." Leo sat up straighter. "They're still hearing something behind the walls. We'll want to have someone look into that before the cold weather sets in; if there's an entry somewhere—and I've no doubt there is, and that it's as wide as the Arc de Triomphe—we'll have vermin from the entire island before the first snow. Possibly swimming here from the mainland. They didn't indicate a willingness or ability to do anything about it; they 'wanted us to be aware' they said."

"Okay."

"A lovely thought, wanting us 'to be aware.' Everyone seems to use it and it essentially means nothing. But people do love it."

Jim took a step into the room. "I didn't know Father Chace had served at St. Patrick."

"No?" Leo had returned his attention to the television.

"Martin Reilly said he wasn't here long."

Jim crossed peat-colored carpet until he was beside the chair, looking down at thick white hair, the sharp lines of Leo's cheeks and nose. A forbidding landscape but Jim intended to persist. "You said he spent a lot of time praying but that wouldn't get you transferred to another parish."

"Past history." Leo swept an arm through the air, dismissing him.

Jim positioned himself between Leo and the television. "What did he do?"

Leo acknowledged him, but not happily. "It was a long time ago and it hardly matters now."

"It matters to me."

It was deepest winter on Leo's face. "Why? Why would it matter to you? Prurient interest?"

"It was sexual?"

"Poor choice of words." Leo adjusted his position, looked around Jim to the screen.

Jim held his ground. In the brief standoff that followed, he felt a little foolish, planted between Leo and the television as if he were a stubborn child. Demanding information that might not be useful, might only be disturbing.

"Yes. Yes, yes, yes, if you must know." Leo's scowl was gelid; you could almost feel your face getting frostbit. "From what I heard and that's all it is—hearsay—he was said to have reported another priest to the bishop and subsequently both he and the miscreant went to new parishes. At which point, the story goes, Anselm kept after the bishop. He wouldn't let the matter drop. All I know is that the purported miscreant—and I will not name him—served with Anselm at St. Patrick and a few years later took his own life. And whether that last has anything to do with Anselm I don't know any more than the man in the moon."

Leo's words were clipped but precise as always. "I don't like gossip and I especially don't like malicious gossip. It's ugly. And if one good thing comes from Anselm Chace's death, I hope it's that his death will finally put an end to all the gossip that has been floating around for years. I'm sorry for Anselm and I'm just as sorry for the poor soul who thought he'd be best off dead. It's a terrible thing to be tormented."

— 18 —

Two cars were parked in front of the Brennans' house. One, a silver SUV with a rack, belonged to Bart Meagher. The other was unfamiliar to him and bore New York license plates.

Of all the people he visited, the Brennans felt the most comfortable. No children, for one thing. Or dogs, for another. And the house felt impervious to him, as if the paintings covering the walls acted as a protective layer. Irrational, but his life was anything but rational anyway.

Helen answered the door. When she saw his expression, she grinned and patted her hair. "Maria's sister owns a salon."

He smiled at her, at the change that company had wrought. The first time he'd been at the house, she'd had to rouse herself, solitude having sent her deep inside herself, the polite social habits falling by the wayside on her journey. Now she was relaxed, not the least bit discomposed to find someone at her front door.

"It looks very nice." Because she expected him to say something, and though generally he was unequal to pronouncements on appearance, Helen wasn't really asking for that.

"I would have had a color, too, except that Peter would have fainted if I'd walked in with crimson hair. I've always been partial to red."

"I brought an air conditioner. It's a small unit that should be fine if you have the old knob and tube wiring. We're having central air installed at the rectory so I thought you might like to have this one. I can install it for you, but if you have company I can leave it for another time."

"That's very thoughtful." Helen stood with her hand on the doorknob. "Are you sure you don't need it? You look as if you haven't been sleeping well."

Another change that company had wrought: no barriers to observation now that visitors no longer flustered her.

Behind her, Jim heard voices, low but clearly in opposition.

"Well, what was the point of bringing in an expert if he couldn't tell what he was looking at?"

"It's not that he couldn't tell." Emily, as he'd guessed. "Art is a bit more complicated than law."

A harsh laugh. "Nothing's more complicated than law, let me assure you."

Helen's brows shot up. Her hand fell from the doorknob and she retreated down the short hall to investigate. Jim followed.

"I don't know how it works in law," Emily was saying, "but here's how it works in art if you want to keep your reputation intact. Just to authenticate a piece, an expert has to verify the signature, evaluate the subject, colors, even the brushstrokes against what's already known, and look into its provenance. If necessary, date the paint and the canvas, and even so, a good forger—"

"You think the Brennans are trying to palm off fakes? Christ! The Eagans have been in Newport since the beginning of time! Why in the name of God would they—" He spotted Jim and suddenly heard his own words. "Sorry, Father."

Emily didn't immediately register the presence of spectators. Then the fierce expression evaporated. "Father Ennis?"

"I should have called." Embarrassed; he felt as if he'd walked in on a private conversation. And disconcerted in a way he didn't understand. "I didn't know the Brennans would be busy."

"Mr. Meagher is just telling me what I think. It's kind of him to save me the trouble."

"All I asked was for someone to catalog what's here."

"On the phone, yes. After I rented a car, imposed on a friend who's helping on his day off, and drove all the way to Newport, Mr. Meagher changed his mind." Though she was addressing Jim and Helen, Emily continued to glare at Meagher. "What he really wants is a valuation. Which I can't do because I'm in publications. Which I told him. Which Clay can't do either."

"And which," Meagher said, recovering his good humor, "is my point. Your buddy there is the third person to see these paintings. Including what you say is an expert. So what have we got? If your experts can't provide an expert opinion, what's the point of having experts?"

Emily wasn't dressed for business today; it was a sundress, white, short, showing lightly tanned arms and legs. All of it must have been completely unexpected, Jim guessed, because Meagher, discomposed, was deliberately keeping her off balance.

"You want someone to waltz in and pronounce on a million-dollar painting? An expert? Good luck with that. And especially a painting that's chest high in a lawsuit. Clay can't provide one because he's not recognized by the house as an expert. Neither am I. And if one of us did provide an opinion, it would inevitably involve the company, since we're employees and in what other capacity would our opinion be considered valid?"

Helen moved to Emily's side and took Emily's hand in hers. Giving it a pat, she said, "We're very grateful for everything Emily's done for us. Now, who would like iced tea or lemonade?"

Meagher was too far down the road to turn back. "Miss Bell has rained a lot of words on us, but here it is in a nutshell: she'll save her precious behind while the nastiest white-shoe firm in Boston eats my lunch."

Emily was silent in the center of the small room.

"He doesn't mean that." Helen stroked Emily's arm. "He knows you're doing everything you can do. He's just frustrated, dear, that's all."

"I'm fine. Really." But the words had stuck fast.

Jim realized he was frowning when Meagher glanced at him and scowled.

"Sometimes my mouth gets ahead of my brain."

Which was all the apology Meagher was going to offer, apparently.

Helen bore Emily off to the kitchen. "So the Taylors engaged a Boston law firm?"

Meagher ran one hand through his hair. "That's about the size of it. I had a hunch they'd look a little farther than Justin Wade but I was thinking Providence. The Taylors must have pretty deep pockets."

"Was that why you got the restraining order?"

"No. Wade was the one who claimed that Taylor, by dint of the contract, was now owner of the paintings and therefore should be in possession of them until such time as the court determined whether or not to uphold the contract." Meagher shoved his hands into his pockets and a smile played around his lips. "It was a shot across the bow and a pretty transparent one. After I got the restraining order, Taylor looked north for help, hoping, I expect, that a white-shoe firm from Boston would put the fear of God into two older people and their rube of a lawyer."

A sideways glance at Emily, who was carrying a tray of beverages to the coffee table. "White-shoe firm or no, every last lick of paint stays where it's always stayed."

"I guess that means there's going to be a fight," Helen said unhappily. "I must say, I never expected in old age I'd be going to court with anyone."

Meagher nodded at Jim. "I told the Brennans that our best strategy for the breach of contract suit is to countersue for fraud."

Emily had been redoing her ponytail, twisting the hair to catch the strands that had escaped, distancing herself from the conversation, but now she was drawn in again.

"It's not like they need the money. I saw them: he's wearing a five-thousand-dollar suit and she's got ten thousand in her earlobes and another ten on her finger."

"Could be they're wearing everything they have," Meagher ventured. "Advertising a successful business. Or maybe not. The great unknown is why Taylor thinks it's worth fighting for. Why go to the expense of hiring not the best, but perhaps the second best firm in Boston if the two pieces you've taken are barely worth a few thousand together?"

"He saw at least one of the ones you just brought back," Helen said. "When I gave him the tour, Mr. Heade's painting was hanging on the wall in the bedroom. I thought he'd enjoy seeing some of these old paintings but now I'm sorry I was so foolish. I made an awful mistake."

"You were being hospitable." Peter had made his way into the room, though it must have been difficult to maneuver the walker through the narrow doorway that led from the kitchen. He nodded to Jim. "Didn't hear your car, Father."

He'd been gardening, judging from the bits of dirt still clinging to his pants. "Nothing wrong with being hospitable. Look at it this way: if you hadn't shown Taylor around, he wouldn't have seen the paintings he took, Father Ennis here wouldn't have heard about Taylor and called Emily, and we'd be sitting in the living room worrying how we're going to pay our bills."

He lowered himself to a chair and Helen set the walker to one side. "We're still worrying about that, Peter. A thousand isn't going to carry us very far."

Peter reached out a hand and Helen put hers into it. "But a few million will."

"I can't help being worried," Helen said. "What if the first painting he took turns out to be the only one that's worth anything?"

"It won't," Emily said, but she was distracted, her face peculiarly expressionless as she observed the Brennans.

Meagher gave Emily a look. "The expert speaks. Although you've just been telling me no one can say for sure unless the paintings are x-rayed and tapped for blood and who knows what else. So we think he saw at least one of the big ones. And the so-called experts think it's a Heade, so Taylor would have thought the same thing. The question is this: If Taylor saw something that he thought was worth real money, why did he take the two other paintings, instead?"

"Does it matter?" Jim asked.

"If you're in a fight, Father, everything matters. Or may matter. The only thing that occurs to me is establishing good faith: take the minor ones and pretend you didn't know the major ones exist. But greed doesn't usually take people that way. When people get greedy, they don't tend to play a long game. But no, Father," Meagher said, taking a glass of iced tea, and he might have been boasting a little, "in one way, I suppose it doesn't matter." He raised the glass in a salute. "I still plan to win."

Emily's friend must have been listening because he only appeared when the conversation had given way to the sound of ice rattling in tall glasses. He ducked to get through the doorway and when he had unfolded himself, very little space separated his head from the ceiling. He carried a laptop in one hand and thrust the other hand at Jim.

"Clay Tench." Young, with a body narrow all the way up, as if he were still growing into it, a face that looked a bit dreamy. He repeated the process with Meagher, who did not appear impressed.

"Well, now, if they were cats, you'd be a hoarder, Mrs. Brennan." A Southern accent and if Jim had to guess, he would cross off most of the Deep South as possibilities. "Fifty-three pieces of art. I'm including the dozen or so stacked on the floor in the spare room and also the five I happened to notice in your linen closet."

"You were looking in the closets?"

"The door was open, Mr. Meagher, so as I said, I couldn't help noticing." He turned to Emily. "You didn't mention anyplace else and my mamma taught me not to snoop."

"There's a sketchbook somewhere but I think that belonged to my brother," Helen said.

"So that's it, then," Emily said, satisfied. "We've catalogued everything."

"At least we'll get an accurate count." Meagher looked at Emily over the top of his glass. "Though it would be a deal better if we had what I'm told is a 'valuation.'"

Emily ignored him. "What about identification?"

"I did my section and actually did a sweep of the rooms you were working on. I'm an inveterate note-taker," Clay confided. "Back in college, I had to wear splints every year, starting around Christmas. My problem was that everything seemed important; if it wasn't, I thought, why would the professor be talking about it? My big fear was that my laptop would crash and I'd lose everything I'd written that day. I say 'that day' because I used to back up everything right before I went to bed at night. I had a big old reminder on my desk, and then I'd set an alarm on my cell phone just in case I didn't notice the reminder."

"You made notes, and . . ."

"Emily's always trying to rush me but I've always been methodical and very thorough. It's a vibrant and I think pleasant tension."

"There's tension, all right." Emily's laugh was clear and warm. "But Clay is great at what he does. He's only been with the house for two years but everyone loves him."

Clay rested his eyes on her for a moment.

She was a far cry from the drowned, shivering thing Jim had pulled from the bay a month before. Despite the froth of a dress, she was all sharp edges with Clay, just as she was with Meagher. While her colleague could rest his eyes on her, Jim suspected that was about as far as it went. Meagher, he could see, was trying unsuccessfully to work it out.

"About half of the paintings are signed, and I've got good photos of the signatures, as well as of the front and the back of every piece. It should be fun to see what we can make out when we blow them up."

"It's well past lunch time, and I promised sandwiches and a fruit salad," Helen said briskly, making a quick survey of her visitors, who were wilting, despite the iced tea, in the low, airless room. Peter's face was alarmingly bright with heat. Helen must have thought so, too. "More iced tea. I'll bring that out first."

Jim checked his watch, then his cell phone. If he excused himself, he could pull up a pant leg in the privacy of the Brennans' bathroom. His left leg numb, the right leg feeling so embattled he was beginning to think it would break if he put his full weight on it.

Best not to know. It made him a little sick even to think of it, so why look?

While Helen and Emily were busy in the kitchen, Jim and Meagher wrestled the air conditioner out of the car. "Well, we've got a count, anyway," Meagher said, "but I don't expect a whole lot more from the *amadan* she brought with her."

The unit installed in a rear window, they sipped their drinks while the air grew cooler around them. Jim couldn't eat. While the others chattered about New York and Newport, a hopeless feeling settled on him. He thought of that first assault on his leg, the horror that had driven him to seek Lizzie, and of the revulsion that attended the second assault. It would be like the breathing, with him for life, but unlike the breathing, it would come and go, making him sick every time he had the visitation. And unlike the breathing, it would get worse.

He looked for a distraction. The mob of old paintings, the uneven walls, the windows casting feeble light—it all reminded him of the rectory, dark and airless, which brought him again to his bedroom, the pillows against his back, his eyes clamped shut, willing away what his eyes had seen.

This is your life.

Helen breathed a little easier as Peter's color was restored to its customary pallor, and thanked Jim again. Peter wanted to pay for the air conditioner but Meagher dismissed it before Jim could.

"When Ms. Bell here sells your Hassam," he said easily, "you can buy a brick or a pew or whatever it is St. Patrick is using for fundraising this year."

"So, yeah," Emily said repressively, "I don't do the auctions. But how did you know about the Hassam? Did Father Ennis tell you?"

"You'll be surprised to know I recognized it with my own two eyes. Believe it or not, I happen to know a few more things than law."

"I'm willing to believe a lot of things about you."

Emily walked Jim to his car. "I might bite the bullet the last weekend this month." She put up her hand to shield her eyes from the sun. "I thought Todd hated the beach, but he rented a place here for a week, though I don't know how he managed it; everybody says everything in Newport is gone by the end of January. Gay network, maybe."

Then she stopped short. "You know Todd is gay, don't you?"

"You mean did he mention it to me? No, he didn't."

She gave him a look. "Funny. So yeah, I may come back to wallow in the scene of the crime. I'm actually feeling marginally better about everything. I've never had that much to drink, and believe me, I'll never drink that much again. It was like something else was in control of my body. Including my mouth. I mean, I know I have a mouth on me, but usually no one else knows it. The whole thing was totally bizarre and if I dwell on it I get a little weirded out, but that's normal, right? It might even be healthy, like aversion therapy. Not that I'd ever be tempted again but . . ."

Though she hadn't mentioned the bridge after that first call, he'd known she wasn't done with it—how could she be? She was talking faster and faster and he felt the pressure that had been building inside her.

"That morning when I was driving you home, do you remember what you said?" For a moment he saw her again, damp and disheveled, the torrent of words flowing out of her, the same desperation to dispel the darkness. "You said it was your first time in Newport and you didn't know where you were until you were at the top of the bridge ramp. You weren't looking for that bridge."

"Does it make a difference? Whether I decided to kill myself before I was on the bridge or whether I did when I knew where I was?"

He considered it, standing on the edge of the small yard, in front of a house that was more than two hundred years old, that had been built long before either she or he had been thought of and, with any luck, that would still be present long after they were gone. He thought of the generations that had preserved it, the painting and plastering and repairing and refitting, and imagined what had been in their minds as they were working to make it secure for another day, another month, another year.

"For me," he said, "the greatest gift of the sacrament of penance isn't the relief, knowing that I've been forgiven for the things I've done, but more that I've declared to God a resolution to do better. That resolve; it's hope. Grace in the form of hope."

He leaned against the car, letting it take some weight off his legs. "It's a hard thing, examining your conscience and being truthful about what you discover, and admitting your failings before God. And when you do confess them, you aren't dropping them into some kind of psychic garbage can, never to be thought of again. We don't work that way, unfortunately or not, though much of the time I think it is unfortunate. But when we've forced ourselves to look at our worst actions, when we've admitted they are our worst actions, we also see what we should have said or done and we promise God and ourselves that we will try harder to live up to that better version of ourselves."

He considered the anxious young woman before him; as he expected, she was teary eyed.

"Whether you planned to do it, whether you acted on impulse, or whether you fell because you'd had too much to drink and lost your balance, you don't know what happened, and I don't either, and we'll never know, will we? What matters more is what you do now."

She searched his face. "And that is?"

"Only you know what that is."

When she ran down and was quiet, you saw that look in her eyes. Outside, longing to be in but not knowing how. He didn't know when she'd arrived at that place or what held her there, whether she unintentionally kept people at a distance or was afraid to let them get any closer. And it occurred to him that the two calls that night had been to the right person, after all. Having seen her with Meagher and with her colleagues from the auction house, he thought that for some reason, she dropped her defenses with him. Perhaps it was the Roman collar, perhaps only that he'd seen her at what she said was her worst. He still thought she needed someone professional to draw her out, carefully and artfully, and allow her to take herself apart and put the pieces together again, but he wouldn't suggest it. When he'd mentioned it before, he'd nearly lost her.

"I'll tell you something I do know. I know you can be very funny, and a little ferocious, and I suspect very loving."

"Well." He'd surprised her, surprised and pleased her. "Well," she said again, her smile fading. "Not on the bridge, though. You were there."

"Yes. Technically speaking, you weren't. Unless we're talking corpus only."

Her smile bloomed again. "Sometimes you remind me that you're a priest. This corpus isn't positive I'll come up again this month, but maybe. You don't meet a lot of sweet people in Manhattan. They're just lovely, aren't they? Helen and Peter. So, yeah, I didn't know my grandparents. They died before I was born. I think I told you that my father died when I was a little kid. People tend to die on me. But that sounds like I'm feeling sorry for myself and I'm not, at least not right now, because it's a beautiful day and I'm in a beautiful city. I suppose everyone indulges in a little self-pity now and then. Keeps the blood moving, right?"

Better, he thought, to ignore the last. Instead, he thanked her again for the trouble she was taking for the Brennans.

She nodded. Cocked her head to one side. "Ferocious, huh?"

"Bart Meagher mentioned his phone call with you."

She smiled reminiscently. "Kind of took the wind out of his sails. Harvard and Harvard Law—give me a break. I live in Manhattan: nobody bulldozes me. Do you think he's right, though, about saving my rear end?"

"Not for a minute. He knows you've been an enormous help to the Brennans. Helen said it: he was just frustrated."

"I don't know what else I can do. If I could think of something . . ."

"He really didn't mean it."

"Yeah, well." She was looking at her feet. "I suppose he's a friend of yours?"

"He was recommended by a friend. I'd only met him once before today."

She batted a fly away from her face. Shrugged. "Maybe that's what you want in a lawyer—I hope so, for the Brennans' sake—but wow, what a jerk."

— 19 —

After Mass one morning, Maria approached Jim, her hand held up, an index finger pointed to heaven.

"Last week I lose one job." A second finger joined the first. "Yesterday I lose two job. Now I just clean houses. You know of ladies want someone to clean, you give them my number, okay?"

Maria had been working nearly five years at one of the nursing homes, though her employer refused to acknowledge the vicissitudes of life. A dog could slip the leash during the morning walk and disappear onto Newport's streets, a child could spike a fever in the middle of geometry class, the house could be engulfed in flames; no matter what happened, the housekeeping staff were expected to remain on the job until the end of the workday.

"Boss tell me last week is my last day. I ask why and she have no answer. She do this," she said, shrugging. "Is no answer. Same thing with other place. Other place was better—where Helen was. Boss said I do good job and she sorry but no tell me why. I work there eleven years."

Mid-August: the most popular time for vacations. Newport felt like a city in August, and the citizens under siege. You left your windows open and a fine, gray powder coated the sill, a mixture of dust, soot, smoke, and everything else you didn't want in your lungs. An army of occupation, that toxic air settled on Spring Street and the side streets, to Bellevue and Thames. Every car, SUV, and van, every small and large truck moving through the city and out again, left a trail of invisible exhaust that further concentrated the air, until you felt yourself nearly gasping and still unable to draw in a lungful of oxygen. Heat shimmered off the sidewalks and streets, crept under your collar, and assailed your skin. Little wonder the birds went silent in August and began to contemplate their escape from the city, read the signs, the angle of the sun, and lengthening nights, and understood they needed to gather the will to go. Flowers withered in planters beneath windows. Roses were completing their second bloom; brown-edged petals were beginning to fall on the shriveled remnants of June. Nature was wrapping up, only a few secrets left to show before the first frost, and yet you could look up Broadway and see an invasion, a long line of sedans and SUVs that stretched past the light at One Mile Corner, and you wondered how anyone could see this season as the beginning of anything and especially that the city could hold so many cars.

There were some who, like Jim, could not flee the August city. People who owned the stores, people who ran the bed and breakfasts, the charter boat captains, the organizers of the endless parade of festivals designed to draw people to the city. Of that beleaguered group, the proprietors of the inns and B-and-Bs were the most likely to need cleaning services, and Jim suggested that Maria apply to them. She could take out an ad in the local papers. He would put a notice on the bulletin board at the back of the church, and he promised Maria that he would ask around. That was all he could think of to do for her, but he was troubled.

He didn't know how much the family depended on two incomes, though he guessed that Maria had been paid minimum wage at both nursing homes. The fact was, he didn't know the most basic information about a lot of the people who filled the pews on weekday mornings, Saturday nights, and Sunday mornings. Unless they came to him, and most didn't, he didn't know whether the octogenarians at morning Mass saved money by only eating two meals every day and cutting their pills in half, whether they got themselves dressed and to church for daily Mass because the phone never rang, whether their calculus did not accommodate any risk to themselves because they could not relinquish driving, a proof of their vigor and independence. Although he was among the first to know about the signal events—the hospitalization of a child, the death of a spouse, or the move from a house to a nursing home—the small shifts of life were recondite, despite the fact that those small shifts could produce the same overwhelming despair. Sometimes after Mass his parishioners would reveal things to him without knowing: a quality of eagerness that accompanied the information that a son or daughter was coming for a visit would open his mind to the long loneliness of a life. But that didn't happen often enough.

He knew that his enemy, to be scrupulously watched for and to be fought with all the passion and intelligence he could muster, was despair, which corroded the desire for life and love that was the inheritance of every human being. A death, especially of a spouse or child, was a battle cry. He'd learned to position himself on the front line, to march beside a survivor in the days before a funeral and in the months thereafter, until that pull of life and love became stronger. But what of the sly attacks—the chronic illness, the job loss, the drug addiction, the alcohol dependence—that did not announce themselves with a clarion call but just as thoroughly deadened the heart to the sweetness of love, the soul to the joy of life? How could he fight the enemy if the field of battle was hidden from him?

Maria was a fighter. He knew where she had come from, the small house with the dirt floor, the village where no one progressed beyond an elementary school education, and he imagined he knew something of the tenacity and strength required to move north, to find work and walk to the job in all kinds of weather. Maria and Jorge now owned a house, drove two SUVs as pristine as if they'd just left the dealership. Their children played in the marching band, ran for student council, belonged to school clubs, and took tennis lessons. Was each day a fresh challenge to prove they belonged in the country, in Newport, or was it vengeance on the country they'd come from, that had withheld all these things from them? Or was it just a determination to rise and continue to rise? Maria's strength of will wasn't easy to defeat but it didn't mean that the family didn't need help despite it. It didn't mean that Jim could remain a spectator.

And then he wondered whether he believed in everything he was thinking or was it all a show for the listening ear of God. If there was a God. One leg seemed to be permanently numb, the other could freeze him suddenly, in the midst of Mass, at the hospital, meeting with parishioners. Walking through the door to one of the classrooms in the summer session, he'd nearly fainted with pain that was like a chainsaw chewing through the bones just below his right knee. These compassionate thoughts and noble resolves were the worst kind of hypocrisy, not because he was trying to fool anyone in particular, or even himself, but because he was trying to fool a deity who seemed less plausible every day.

"What I'm saying is there's slim pickings here." Mike Dyer flicked his cigarette into the street, pushed himself off the lamppost he'd been leaning against, and turned into his shop. "I'll tack it up somewhere but who do you think is going to want a house cleaner? The summer crowd who thoughtfully oil the books before they try to unload them? The crackpots who hoard all the dollar books they buy? I think the only shot she's got here is the crowd that's a half-step above those people wandering the beaches with their metal detectors, hoping to find doubloons. I get a few regulars who come waltzing in, casual as you please, but as soon as they're within sight of the new arrivals box they become as rigid as hunting dogs; you can practically hear them baying. Maybe there's a first edition of a rare book from the eighteenth century and that idiot Dyer didn't notice the goatskin covers or that Thomas Effing Jefferson signed it."

Mike's grin revealed two rows of uneven yellow teeth, a few nearly sideways in his mouth. "Someone might want a housecleaner. I wouldn't bet money on it, though."

Mike taped the notice at the edge of the counter. "Looks a little lonely but I never had room for a billboard."

"Barely enough room for you."

"Why I spend my time on the street. Why you should buy more books."

"Not because they're great books?"

"That too. Matter of fact . . ." He brought a small stack of books from under the counter. "Book for one kid. Book for another kid. And three for you. You wanted psych."

Jim looked at the titles.

"You got your survey, your PTSD, and I threw in some Jung. Personally, I recommend the Jung; it's like watching cartoons. I'll put them in a bag for you if you want to look at the new stuff. I didn't see anything come in but you never know."

"I think I might have read Jung, years ago."

"You'd remember," Mike said, searching his pockets for cough drops. "Big dream guy. Must have done a lot of peyote in his time."

"Funny you say that. Lizzie said—" And then he looked at Mike's eyes which were, as his sister had noted, bloodshot. Very bloodshot. It could have been the result of tobacco smoke, but, "well, never mind. How much for the psych?"

Mike was looking at him appraisingly. "New parish keeping you busy or are you on some kind of diet?" Then he shook his head. "My private stock. Long time ago I thought I'd try to figure out why the hell people do the crap they do. Consider them a loan. Figure I can trust a priest not to keep them."

Jim knew he was losing weight; he wished people would stop telling him. "I'm reasonably honest."

They talked about the Brennans, who'd had another visit from the Colonial Commission, though not in the person of George Taylor. Coached by Bart Meagher, the old couple said they would consider the group's interest in their home. No need to tell the Colonials, Meagher said, that they expected to be able to afford the renovations the house needed.

"Meagher's working out, then."

"They like him. I do, too. He doesn't miss much. Although he doesn't do much for my friend at the auction house."

"He doesn't have to make friends with the world. Just do a good job. But the cleaning lady—"

"Maria."

"Yeah. Odd that she would lose both jobs in a week."

"I suspect it's not a coincidence. Did I tell you that's how I met the Brennans? George Taylor accused Maria of stealing from them and she asked me to contact Taylor and vouch for her. Taylor could have called the two nursing homes and gotten her fired. I don't like to think anyone would be that spiteful but you never know."

"Maybe." Mike picked up the coffee mug, saw it was empty, and with a look of disgust replaced it on the counter.

"If not the Taylors, who? Someone must have gotten her fired. Other than the Taylors, I can't imagine the Estradas have any enemies. They're quiet, hardworking people."

Mike hesitated but in the end he just shrugged. "Yeah, maybe so."

Jim found nothing in the boxes of new arrivals. After ringing up Jim's purchase, Mike looked over the handles of the cloth bag he held out for Jim. "Did you get your central air yet?"

Jim nodded. "And may have stirred up a family of rats."

"That's it, then. Some people eat when they're worried, others stop. Hope you figure out the rat situation. You ain't looking too good these days."

Jim took the bag. "Thanks. I know."

20

The English sparrows hadn't been the first to find his feeding station, but once they'd found it they'd rarely left, attacking it in groups of four or five, bickering and feinting and scattering seeds from sunrise to sunset. He knew he couldn't avoid them in the city but they weren't native: in 1851, eight pairs had been released in Brooklyn, and when they didn't thrive one hundred more were carted from England by Europeans longing to bring a bit of their homeland to America. His were the many-times descendants, he supposed, and wished the Europeans had longed for cheeses or wines. Anything but the jabbering, fecund birds.

Nevertheless, he was now bringing his morning coffee to the yard, enjoying the birds for a few minutes before he showered and dressed for Mass; it also prevented him from breaking with charity at the sight of Leo's breakfast. Later in the day, he'd spend time in the back parlor, the air hissing through the new ducts that had been cut into the floor, dazzled by the colors flying around his yard. House finches, the males vibrant red when the sun struck them, a pale cherry when the clouds scudded by. Goldfinches, breasts and backs glowing, the black-and-white stripes on the wings crisp and sharp.

Surprisingly, Leo enjoyed them nearly as much as Jim, though he speculated aloud about the diseases they might harbor. Not surprisingly, he preferred to watch from a comfortable seat in the parlor, which was nearly twenty degrees cooler than it was outside.

"A good hobby for a priest," he said one afternoon. Jim had just returned from an unpleasant interview with the summer school principal. With the summer sessions over, the principal customarily met with the pastor to discuss the level of attendance, the success of the curriculum, and the suggestions for improvement that had been tendered by the faculty.

Belanger wasn't a very good actor, although perhaps it was that Jim could warm to him no more successfully than he could to the sparrows. Belanger was openly contemptuous of the staff; because they were teachers or because they were women? Viewed the children as irritants. And as he talked it became clearer that he had little respect for Jim.

Before the meeting Jim had been swatting his right leg, which felt as if it were beneath the needle of a sewing machine, stabbing pains running from ankle to knee. The whoosh in his ears, the numb left leg.

He gave Belanger fifteen minutes to complain that the books weren't age-appropriate, that the teachers hadn't enough time to prepare lessons around the new books, and that the children had been more distracted this year as a result. Jim had been trying to master his anger but then Belanger began a long-winded critique of the decision to abruptly abandon the old curriculum. Never saying it was Jim's decision, though they both knew that's what it was.

Jim had taken up one of the old books, *Our World*. "I understand the new books are harder, and the children probably prefer the old books, but they're supposed to be learning their religion, not a lot of pop psychology. *Our World*," brandishing the book as if it were evidence of a crime. "It's God's world. God's."

"It has the imprimatur," in a voice that could have frozen the bay. "We wouldn't have used it, otherwise."

"I don't care if it was handed down on Mount Sinai. I had to hunt to find God's name. In this book I finally found the name of Jesus Christ on page twenty. Of a thirty-page book!"

If Belanger had spoken, perhaps he would have stopped, but the principal sat stiffly, straight-backed with righteousness. Perhaps he would have stopped if Belanger hadn't presented him with an opportunity to voice the fury that writhed like a pit of vipers. Whatever it was, Jim didn't try to stop, and possibly he couldn't have.

"Maybe they can't absorb everything. Maybe they won't understand everything. Maybe they'll never learn the difference between Aquinas and Augustine, or be able to give a dissertation on the mystery of transubstantiation, but at least they'll learn the name of their savior, which is a lot better than the nothing we were teaching them before." His voice was loud, shaking with sudden rage. He heard himself but he still couldn't stop. "Why not call it what it was? Babysitting! All that was happening every summer was nothing more than babysitting, and I don't care if the kids liked it better or it was easier. We're not doing that again. Absolutely not. We're not going back to the old books."

Belanger was white-lipped. He would have a lot to say, but none of it would be to Jim. Seeing his face, Jim's rage had evaporated as quickly as it had come and he sat back, deflated, his voice echoing in his ears. Horror engulfed him. *Defender of the Faith.* He'd completely lost control.

Silence between them for a long moment as Jim pulled himself together. "I shouldn't have . . . I'm so sorry. I didn't mean to go off on you."

Belanger was rising to his feet. "I wish you good luck with the program. Please accept my resignation."

Jim had let him go. Mortification pricked his skin, his face went hot and then every follicle on his head seemed to jangle. He put his arms on the desk and dropped his head on them. He didn't care if Belanger complained to the bishop. He didn't even like the bishop. But he was losing control of himself. As if something was taking over, one sense at a time. Hearing what wasn't there. Seeing what didn't exist. Losing all feeling in one leg. Every day he lost a little ground.

He'd gone to the back parlor to be soothed by the birds. Belanger could say what he liked to whom he liked; Jim had apologized and that was all he could do. At least the teachers would be pleased by the departure of their condescending principal. He wasn't worried about the bishop, whose range of options was constrained by the priest shortage. At worst, he'd get a reprimand. But he had lost control.

Leo was contemplative on the sofa Jim had pushed close to French doors that offered a view of the feeders. His shirt looked like a light snowfall on muddy ground; he was eating homemade cookies dusted with confectioner's sugar.

"Victor Belanger resigned this afternoon."

"This is cause for regret, or were you the agent of his departure?"

"I didn't expect he would do it today."

Jim let himself fall heavily at the other end of the sofa, which thirty or forty years before might have shown a navy-and-white-striped pattern, but which now was brown and tan; at some point, he had to hire someone to clean the furniture and the rugs.

"Ah," Leo said, following the flight of a chickadee. "He objected to the new curriculum?"

"He objected to me," Jim said. "And the curriculum. Mostly me, I think: I lost my temper."

A ghost of a smile. "It's obviously within your purview, the religious studies program."

They sat for a while as a pair of titmice scribed garlands on the air between the feeder and the cherry trees. A Carolina wren, head hunched into its shoulders, a long, white streak dashed over its eye, stabbed at the suet. Jim had counted; sometimes as many as two dozen birds were at the feeders or on the ground. The last to leave, usually, were the mourning doves, their blue-lidded eyes uncanny in the fading light.

Leo pushed the last of the cookies into his mouth and dusted off his fingers. "I'm assuming you will do something about the rats. Surely you've been hearing them."

"Actually, no," Jim said absently. He had noticed a bird at the edge of the crowd of sparrows. It looked to have patches of blue. Reaching for the guide that was kept on the little table beside the couch, he began to page through it, quiet excitement working up his body.

"You must be a sound sleeper." Leo sighed. "The young never appreciate the sleep they get. They never, actually, appreciate any of the blessings of youth. Eyesight. Hearing. Hair. Point is, I'm a light sleeper now and I hear them in the walls. They may as well be moving furniture about."

Jim frowned. "I'll buy a few traps."

Leo sighed again. "Well, I suppose one must start somewhere."

The maple's leaves were browning at the edges, curling as if they'd been scorched. A few had fallen onto the bare earth beneath the tree. Looking for worms, a robin poked at them, tilted his head and eyed the ground before stabbing the soil. A shake of its head and the bird skittered deeper into the shade.

"I wonder if there's anything like a Roquefort in the refrigerator," Leo said consideringly. "I do like the veiny cheeses."

"I don't know what's left." Jim was paging through the book. "Maria tossed a lot of stuff when she cleaned the fridge."

"There is such a thing as being overscrupulous. Cheeses improve with age."

Maria had been on the job for a week. The rectory's previous housekeeper, who'd been employed by the church for nearly twenty years, had been making unhappy noises of late. Still, he was surprised when he arrived at the rectory after making his rounds at the hospital and found her waiting for him by the side door.

She was a small, heavyset woman with an aggrieved air, given to frequent muttering that was best left unexplored. "I'm sorry, Father, to be bothering you right now, but I'm not going to be able to come back."

"Is something wrong?"

"I could take the ants," she declared. "Although everyone could have made my life a lot easier if they wrapped things up and stuck them in the fridge instead of leaving everything wide-open on the table, and a trail of crumbs all over the kitchen. And the bedroom. But I said I wasn't going to say anything about that, and I won't, though why grown men should be eating cherry pie in bed, I don't know."

A little stunned by the unexpectedness of the complaint, Jim didn't know what response to tender.

"Them ants have been a scourge but I put up with them. They're dirty but at least you can see them. Besides which, you know what they do. Ants, bees, hornets—you know what they do. Mosquitoes. I hate mosquitoes but you know what they do: a mosquito's going to bite you."

"Well, yes," he said mildly.

Somewhere in her early fifties, she had a husband and thirty-year-old son at home, two daughters, both married, who lived on the other side of the bay. Her small brown eyes, perpetually narrowed, must have terrified her children. "I told my husband when I first heard them, and he told me I better tell you because it could be a big problem."

"I'm sorry but I'm not sure what you're talking about." But she had prepared her speech and was unwilling to get to the point too soon.

"My husband says they'll chew anything: clothes, furniture, wood, plasterboard, you name it. Says if they really get going, they'll eat through every beam in a house. Have to tear the whole place down and start all over again. Says he's seen it happen. Ron said if they chew through the wires they could start a fire. The whole place would go up—you got a lot of wood in here and you'd be dead in your bed before you knew it."

"What will?" Although now he knew.

"Rats. Soon as them guys came in and started tearing up the place. Rats don't like disturbance; soon as you start messing with things, they're rocking and rolling. Didn't see you and I didn't like to bother Father Sullivan, so I told the A/C people there to tell you that something had to be done about them."

Jim was a little irritated that she'd wanted to spare Leo, the Hansel and Gretel of pastry crumbs. "Yes, I do know about the problem."

"Well, that was last time I came. Today I go in and I'm down on my hands and knees, scraping something off the rug in the sitting room. It looked like marmalade. My kids do something like that and they'd never do it again, believe me. You just can't vacuum it up, like it's dust or something. Marmalade, jam, anything like that, soaks into the fibers of the rug and you have to go at it with a wet sponge, and then wring out the sponge and go at it again."

"I'm sorry; it sounds like a lot of work," Jim said with a sympathy he did not feel. He understood that cleaning must be an unpleasant occupation and thought she was the sort of person who took out the accumulated aggravation on whatever couldn't fight back: the floor, the furniture, him.

"I had three kids." Having got what she wanted, she waved it away. "No big deal. But I hear this bang and it nearly gave me a heart attack it was so loud. I thought the A/C people were back so I got up and took a look out the window. I didn't see the van but I know how old places settle. So I'm back at the stain and as soon as I start scrubbing it happens again. Sounded like it was right behind me, in the wall."

She took a breath. "I live in Fall River with a husband who works nights. I'm used to doing a lot of things myself and not much bothers me. So my next thought was that the A/C people screwed up and put the ducts in too close to the paneling. Can't say I was surprised: it's hard to get anyone who does things the right way. Or maybe they don't care. Nobody takes pride in their work anymore. So when the A/C kicks on and starts blowing air at the paneling, it dries the wood and then you get this cracking noise."

Jim was nodding, wishing fervently to be inside near the air conditioning. The sun was beating on his clerical clothing, a black polyester shirt and pants, and his skin felt prickly with heat and sweat. He could smell the dirt in the air, he thought, the exhalations of thousands of cars, mixed with road dust and the effluvia of the pizza place at the end of the block. Cicadas roared their stuttering call. And there was the breathing; he wondered how he could still hear it over the sputter of a motorcycle, the rap pouring out of one car and jostling with what sounded like forty electric guitars emanating from the jeep behind it.

"I got up and felt the wood. Figured I'd tell you about the problem because if that goes on all year, the panels are going to split and it's going to cost the church a lot of money to fix it. And I was right; the panel felt colder than I thought it should. So then I knocked a few places, just to see how much air there was between the panels and the plaster. And something was knocking back."

"As you said, it's an old building," he began, but she cut right through it.

"I said knocking back, Father. Like I knock once and it knocks back. I knock twice and it knocks twice. See what I mean? It's doing the same knocks I'm doing. I grabbed my sponge and got out of there. There's something in the walls. I don't know what it is but it's something. I can deal with ants. No way am I dealing with something I don't know. I'm sorry to be leaving, Father. I know you've been sick and when you're sick you don't like a lot of disruption."

Jim rocked back on his heels. "Who told you I was sick?"

For the first time in memory, her look softened. "Nobody had to tell me, Father. I know it's not my business to ask, and you have the sister who's the doctor and all and I'm sure she's taking good care of you. Whatever it is, I hope you get better."

21

He had begun to look at pieces of himself. His jawline when he was shaving in the morning; his feet, white as poached fish, when he put on his socks; his shoulders, thankfully covered, when he adjusted the alb and chasuble. He didn't want to see the whole; he'd been told often enough that his appearance wouldn't please him. His pants bagged and shirts ballooned around him, as if his clothes were trying to escape his body, put as much distance as possible between them and his skin. He cataloged the parts that he allowed himself to look at, then wondered how much of what he did each day was done to distract himself. Sometimes his right leg was crawling, prickling, and stinging, and at other times it was fine. Sometimes the left leg would be so numb he was afraid to stand on it. If both legs were involved, a sick feeling would go through him and he would fight the fear that it would creep up his body, the stinging and the cold; at such times, he would freeze for a few moments, in the middle of the hospital, saying Mass on Sunday, or even sitting with the birds.

At night, he undressed in the dark, the lights off and the shades drawn, his eyes closed as he peeled the clothes from his body and dropped them on the floor, slid between the sheets and pulled the top sheet to his waist. It was safe then to open his eyes; nothing to look at and nothing to be frightened by. The breathing he could deal with.

And yet. One evening he'd forgotten. Not forgotten exactly; he'd been distracted. Lizzie had stopped coming to morning Mass. He'd looked for her every morning for a week, and when he was certain she was avoiding him, he'd called.

She was never willing to volunteer much, and he disliked the position that put him in. He felt like Torquemada, felt he was brutalizing her, though his questions were prompted by concern for her and were no more insistent than the inquisitions to which she occasionally subjected him. They had gone back and forth for about ten minutes before Jim decided to probe one suspicion he'd been entertaining.

"I don't want to talk about it. Anyway, he's going to be a full-time drunk unless he gets a grip on his drinking. He used to have a drink or two on the weekends but now he's coming home drunk—actually drunk—on Friday nights and usually one or two other weekdays. That's three days a week. If he hates his new job that much he should just quit. I'm thinking I'll yank Sam and the kids to England for a week before he gets into some kind of disgusting habit. Triona won't be happy because she'll miss the beach but she'll be really unhappy if her father turns into a lush and his esophagus has to be ripped out because he has cancer."

Jim suggested that a conversation would be easier and possibly more effective, but he knew Lizzie would do what she wanted to do. She always did.

Jim loved his sister but he could never have lived with her and he didn't quite understand how Sam managed it. Lizzie not only did what she wanted to do, she also decided what everyone else would do. The Clarke family was a dictatorship; benign, certainly, but absolute rule nevertheless.

Sometimes, Jim wanted Sam to speak up, to refuse whatever it was that Lizzie intended him to do. To ask why Sam didn't deny Lizzie in anything, large or small. Perhaps Jim wanted it so much because he never spoke up to Lizzie, either, and wished to see someone, just once, take her down a peg. Sometimes he seethed for an hour after contact with his sister. Had to talk himself down, sing to himself the old song that Lizzie meant well, she really did, that she didn't stop to consider her words before she said them, didn't notice the tone in which she said them.

He admired Sam, possibly more than anyone he knew. At least, some days he did, and usually at a distance, because of all the noble virtues, forbearance was the hardest to admire, and easily mistaken for weakness. It wasn't weakness, though, because Sam was agreeable without being malleable. You could see that Lizzie's directives didn't penetrate farther than the surface; other people might think that Sam was diminished by them, but Sam knew he wasn't and if it bothered him that other people might think differently, he didn't show it.

Jim had never seen his brother-in-law direct a single hostile word at Lizzie. Sam could appear mildly irritated but the feeling remained unvoiced, vanishing as soon as it appeared. His was, Jim thought, a larger spirit, a wiser one, possessing a discernment that enabled him to see precisely what he sacrificed and what he retained by keeping peace in the family. Lizzie, Jim felt sure, didn't recognize any of this. And that was why he pushed Lizzie so hard during that phone call: Sam's drinking worried him.

Lost in thought, he'd unbuckled the belt, let the pants drop and as he'd done thousands of times before, bent to pick the discarded pants off the floor. Which had brought him face to face with his lower legs.

With the holes and the maggots on one leg, and on the other leg, the mound, which had movement. He dropped heavily on the bed, and as he watched, the skin at the top of the mound broke, the pain small but sharp as a mosquito bite, and an earwig emerged from the mound, pincers high and furiously working. A dull glint to the body, the abdomen striped like a wasp, the small head with antennae twirling, it crawled down the mound, scrambled around the hair on his leg, and dropped onto the sheet, as if it knew precisely where it was going.

This time, he didn't vomit. Didn't faint. He wasn't exactly sure what had happened. He only knew that when he checked the clock, four hours had passed. He was sitting in the same position, and evidently had been for all that lost time because his neck hurt as he'd turned his head to see the clock. His limbs protested as he stood up, as if the muscles had been locked. Knowing before he looked that his legs would be unmarked, unblemished.

He understood. His mind pushed the words away before they could coalesce but they kept swirling around his brain and finally wouldn't be denied any longer. Now he knew what had happened to Anselm.

The room around him receded as if he'd been pulled out of his life and was viewing it through a telescope on the moon. He saw himself, a small, bony figure, shoulders hunched, head down, alone in a dark room, no more able to help himself than a nestling fallen from a tree. Every moment weakened him, enfeebled him, until he succumbed completely: a few minutes gone, a few hours, and then time would stop forever for him while the world went on around him.

Since that night, the world had receded a little, as if he were feverish. He was encased in fear, every moment of every waking day. As he said Mass in the morning and on Saturday and Sunday. Visiting the sick at the hospital. Meeting with the organist, who wanted to begin a children's choir, talking with the pastoral assistant, meeting with the parish council. Taking the phone calls that came with a petition for help. Writing his homilies, reading his breviary, comforting the families of the recently deceased, in the midst of a funeral or nuptial Mass or a baptism. He was afraid all the time because he knew something was eating him alive.

One night he was sitting in the chair by his bed, the Jung in his lap, and he realized he'd been picturing the drop from the bridge, estimating how high he would have to go to ensure death rather than paralysis. The flat stretch of the east span, where he'd found Emily Bell, obviously not high enough to ensure damage but the bridge rose to twenty stories at its apex. A fall from that height wouldn't be the same as hitting pavement, but not much different, either, the water only slightly more yielding. He'd looked it up: internal organs would be dislodged and hemorrhage, ribs might break and, depending on the angle of impact, other bones would shatter. Face-first and the water would split and peel the skin from the nose and chin. Still, though, you might not die on impact. You could be flailing in the bay for minutes, battered and every breath agony until your heart quit. Then the question: If you didn't manage to kill yourself instantly, was it better to die over minutes than to die by inches? Better to make a brutal end to yourself than to be entombed with nothing but horror for company? It could almost be seen as a victory over whatever it was—his brain? Or something malevolent that accompanied him through the days, that hated breathing reminding him every waking moment that it was there?—because by ending his life he would stop it.

Although.

God forgave those whose mental disorders drove them to destroy themselves. If an untreated imbalance of chemicals in the brain, a blow to the temporoparietal junction, or a mental illness that resisted pills and therapy and everything else medical science could throw at you made life an endless agony of pain and despair, God, in his goodness, forgave the sufferer for killing himself to escape that unremitting torture. A merciful God recognized that such an act wasn't coldly rational, that the individual was no more culpable than the child who points Dad's gun at a playmate and goes *Bang*! But Jesus had talked of the unquenchable fire, the eternal fire, Gehenna, reserved for those who refused to believe in God's goodness, in his forgiveness, in his mercy. And if he wasn't mentally ill, was slipping off a bridge a renunciation of God's mercy, of God's ability to heal all manner of affliction?

He still had Anselm's letter. He'd meant to throw it out a hundred times, but he couldn't seem to stop reading it, as though it would reveal something on the hundredth examination that it hadn't on the first. Why couldn't people say what they meant? Why couldn't people say straight out why they were firing someone from a nursing home job or had stopped coming to morning Mass? He thought he was pretty straightforward, though he did have lapses, just like anyone else, but those were for good reasons. For example, you couldn't tell your sister that you may or may not be hallucinating because she'd worry. He wasn't going to tell Mike that he wanted psych books to figure out why he was hallucinating, if that's what was happening; that wasn't Mike's business.

If Anselm had been straightforward, he'd know whether or not he was crazy, whether something was wrong with his brain, or an early shock had made his brain go haywire, or whether the source of his troubles could be found outside himself. Instead, Anselm had paraded his little host of sins in front of the reader, mixed the procession with a few cryptic remarks, and Jim knew no more than he did before. No clue whether Anselm was tormented by something evil or was descending rapidly into madness. If Anselm's letter had said plainly what was happening, it would have been more help than Mike's books had been. He'd flipped through the survey book, read the chapter on psychosis. He'd browsed schizophrenia. And he'd gone right through the book on PTSD. He could be having psychotic episodes. He could have PTSD. The problem was that he couldn't be sure. All the books in the world wouldn't tell him absolutely what had happened at Blessed Sacrament, whether he imagined himself to be witness to something that had stirred the chemicals in his brain or lit an area that in other people lay dormant, or whether something malign really had come sliding over the floor of the church and fastened onto him for all eternity.

Lizzie had mentioned Anselm's limp. Something he might have remembered if he hadn't shoved Anselm and Blessed Sacrament to the back of his brain. He could see Anselm now, shrunken in the green chasuble of Ordinary Time, crossing from the altar to the pulpit, one foot coming down deliberately, his body rocking slightly to one side so that the other leg could swing forward, as if the knee were locked. An injury? Perhaps from war? Or had Anselm been beset by some horror that attacked with pinpricks, with cold, with nightmare visions? The only link he had to Anselm was Martin Reilly.

The phone rang and rang, and just when Jim thought it would go to voicemail, Reilly picked up.

"Father Reilly?"

A pause. "Man of the Island. Unless someone happens to have filched his phone, which given the world as it is today doesn't seem much of a stretch."

"I'm sorry. Yes, it's Jim Ennis."

"Ah, now, I thought so. How are you then?"

Jim had no idea how to answer that. He was standing on one leg that was afire, another leg that was completely numb. Over the hiss of the central air, disembodied breathing was steady in his ears. He was tired of reminding himself not to talk over it; no one could hear it but himself. He was exhausted from lack of sleep. Weak from lack of food. His stomach was permanently tied in knots. How was he?

"I've been better."

"Sorry for your troubles," Reilly said politely. "How can I help?"

He should have thought this through because he had no idea where to begin. In the distance, the wail of an ambulance on its way to the hospital. He went into his bedroom, closed the door behind him. "I wanted to thank you for sending that letter from Father Chace," he said, stalling for time. "You must have had it awhile."

"It was no trouble." But now the voice had become wary.

"I was wondering . . ." How to get the information he wanted without giving himself away? Once you asked a question, you couldn't take it back. Reilly was breathing on the other end, an old man's whistling breath.

"You were good friends," he said at last. "Do you know if he served in the military?"

A grunt of surprise. "The military? As a chaplain, do you mean? Did he tell you he did?"

"No." The wrong tactic, he realized; the origin of Anselm's limp wouldn't have told him anything. "I was wondering if he changed in the time you knew him."

"Ah, that's the question, is it? Did he change at all? Sad to say, we all change. Shrinking and liver-spotted and wrinkled as an old paper bag. Everything goes, you know." It was a stage voice, not an ounce of sincerity in it. "Although I can't say I'm willing to rush the alternative, heaven notwithstanding."

"True enough." Jim forced a laugh.

His head was throbbing and muzzy, and through the pain he realized he'd passed the point where the decision was in his hands. It was like having an infection: you watched the wound and at first you thought it might heal cleanly, then you saw the infection beginning to snake away from the jagged flesh and you thought your body still might heal on its own and, finally, as the infection crept over new territory, you knew your body wasn't enough, that it couldn't fight the infection without help, that you had to seek the agent of help outside your body.

He sat in the chair, one hand with the phone at his ear, the other resting on the breviary he'd left that morning on the side table. Prepared to withstand whatever might come. "Did he ever complain of pain or any other problems? With his hearing, maybe?"

"And why would you be wanting to know that? It hardly matters now." Reilly's voice was wary once more, forbidding, and sudden fear sprang up, that Reilly would find an excuse to end the call, and he would know no more than he already did.

"I'm in sort of a bad place." He pushed the words through the engulfing fear and immediately the breathing in his ears became louder. "I'm afraid I'll end up like him."

A long silence. That whistling breath. When Reilly finally spoke, it was without a trace of the brogue. "A man can't help what he is but he can help what he does."

True again. "That's why I called you."

"Me?" Reilly sounded genuinely surprised.

"He gave you the letter to give to me. He obviously considered you a good friend."

"I was but I don't know anything about the letter. He didn't tell me what he'd written and I didn't ask." Reilly became emphatic. "It wasn't my concern."

He should hang up. Before he revealed anything more. He hated asking for help. It had been hard to ask Mike to recommend a handyman, and this was infinitely worse. Some last bit of lingering pride tickled him, telling him that it was better to go on as he had been, alone, that if he said more he'd hate his weakness, would never be able to look himself in the mirror again.

"He was trying to tell me something but I think he didn't know how much he should say." He closed his eyes against what he would say, willingly or not. "He wasn't sure what I saw."

"I'm sorry." And it seemed to Jim that Reilly was about to end the call. "Sorry but I can't help you."

Jim talked over him, in a rush now to let the words out. "When I was an altar server at Blessed Sacrament. My mother used to wash the altar server vestments every week." And behind his lids he saw her, bent over the ironing board, steam, starch-sweetened, innocent, rising from beneath the iron. Her hair, soft brown, curled haphazardly on the back of her head, more orderly along the sides where she could see it. Driving him to the church, where he'd run in, cassocks and albs flapping behind him and, faster, out again, unencumbered and uncommitted for the rest of the day. "I would bring them to the church on Saturdays and one time I walked in on something I wasn't supposed to see."

"Dear God," Reilly said, low.

Despite the breathing, a hurricane that was powering along the nerves in his body, it only took Jim a moment to understand. He almost laughed when he realized what Reilly meant. Of course it would be the first thing to come to mind. And now Reilly's wariness became clearer. "He wasn't a pedophile. I don't think he was, anyway. Neither am I. That's not it."

Reilly let out a breath. "*Deo Gratias.* Thanks be to God. You never really know people but still, he's the last man I would have thought . . . I'm glad it's not that. Very glad it's not. But if not that, what? What was it, then? What did you see? A woman? Not another man."

Ordinary things. They were all ordinary suppositions. And that was about the limit of the rational world. He hadn't yet walked Reilly past the boundary of that and he hesitated, not knowing if his hesitation was on Reilly's behalf or on his own.

He was propelled into speech by the thought of the lost hours, the fear that if he didn't talk now, he might never be able to again. "I came into the church and he was in front of the altar. It was dim. There were a few lights on but not in the sanctuary. I could see him, though. He was arguing. I think it was arguing, anyway; I remember thinking that's how my parents argued after my sister and I went to bed. Quiet but intense."

"That's it? You called me about that?" A gust of air that was relief. "You weren't supposed to see him arguing with someone? That's all? Anselm wasn't perfect but he didn't set himself up as a saint, either."

It was like trying to talk when there was a jackhammer right beside you. It scrambled your thoughts, whirled them until you didn't know what you were saying. He'd have to gather the words together and hurl them past a wall of noise if he wanted to get them out. "He was arguing with some *thing.* Not a person, a thing." Then realized he was shouting.

A sharp intake of breath.

"I'm sorry. I didn't mean to yell. I know what this must sound like." But now that he'd started he would finish. "I thought I saw something, but I was thirteen and I was frightened and maybe I imagined it. The church wasn't well lit, and so it was hard to see anything, even though I thought I could, but later I thought I imagined it all, despite the breathing. Breathing can be your own, right? Something with the eardrum, maybe, some kind of fault in the mechanics of the ear where you hear yourself breathing. Someone told me recently about a certain kind of brain malfunction and it might be that, because it can produce things like breathing that you know aren't real." A thought drifted at the edge of his brain and then he had it: Emily, spinning out words to keep the darkness away. "I mean, I have held my breath and still heard breathing, but it could have been my imagination. But then you sent Father Chace's letter and I knew; well, I'm not sure I knew, but I didn't want to open it. I wasn't ready for it. I was afraid and it took me a while to open it. And when I finally did read it, I thought at first it didn't say much of anything, but then things got worse and I'm wondering if maybe Anselm's letter validates what I saw." He heard Leo's voice in his head: *validate, another one of those words they sling around nowadays and it means nothing.*

He wasn't sure Reilly was still on the line. "You said you were the one who found him. You'd come down to the island to have dinner with him. So I thought if he was—bothered, I guess—he might have mentioned it to you. I thought maybe you could tell me. Did he ever say anything about hearing breathing? Or pain that didn't have any cause? Did he ever say he saw things that weren't real? Or did he—" His voice shook a little. "Did he lose time?"

For a minute, Jim was convinced that Reilly had hung up. In a way, he wouldn't have blamed Reilly.

"Holy Mother of God."

The sound of that voice wasn't the crack of ice beneath your feet; it was the shock of the water that told you that you'd truly fallen in, left the world on the other side. He didn't regret it because he'd understood, finally, that the purpose of the breathing was to keep the words locked in. Maybe Reilly couldn't help, but Jim felt he'd claimed some kind of victory just by telling another human being that he was tormented. And if Reilly could help . . . "If Father Chace said something, it would probably have been to you. You were his friend; he might have confided in you."

"Sweet Jesus." A pause. "I can hear that you're troubled. And I don't want to make it worse, but have you seen a doctor at all?"

The way you'd speak to a child. And now he knew how that woman in the hospital must have felt. Her name wouldn't come to him but he couldn't forget the face, swollen and bruised as if it had been trampled. Talking herself into rationality. He must sound mad. Knew he did.

And now he knew how it felt to be dismissed.

What difference did it make whether Anselm had been tormented by his own brain or something uncanny? It wouldn't tell him anything. A small boy's horror, whether or not he'd actually seen anything, could have triggered all the rest of it, the breathing, the wounds.

Psychosis, Lizzie had said.

He saw himself going down the obvious road: the visit to a psychologist or maybe psychiatrist, the tests, the drugs. They would take his parish away. If he were depressed, they wouldn't, but hallucinating? Despite the shortage of priests, the bishop couldn't take a risk on someone so unstable.

People would come to the church and he wouldn't be there to listen. To baptize them, marry them, and bury them. To help them with their bills. If he were heavily medicated, he wouldn't care whether the Brennans were turned out of their house or not. Wouldn't know whether Emily found someone else to talk to, whether someone more talented than he had helped her. He wouldn't recognize himself. A man under the care of a psychiatrist—he wouldn't know who that was. He'd have to start all over again. Would he have to leave the priesthood? Never again celebrate a Mass? Could he live without that?

Desperate, he threw down his last card. "He knew I was a priest. Father Chace knew it. The letter was addressed to Reverend James Ennis. How would he have known I was a priest? He was catatonic by the time I entered the seminary."

A long pause. "I did notice that." Another pause. "You didn't express an intention then? I thought perhaps you'd discussed it."

"I was thirteen years old when he was at Blessed Sacrament." So alien now; those years might have belonged to a different person. But he felt a stirring of relief because Reilly was with him, still. Perhaps out of curiosity or morbid fascination; whatever the reason, Jim was grateful that the old priest was listening, and behaving once again as if Jim were rational. "I wanted to be a Major League Baseball player."

"I was curious about the contents of the letter," Reilly said. "But no, that's not quite right. I was apprehensive. When I saw you at the funeral,

I considered whether I'd be compounding damage done if I gave you that letter. I'd brought it with me, you see. Can you tell me what was in it?"

Jim read it.

"Yes, you saw something you weren't supposed to see. That's what you said. And it's in the letter. If you don't mind me asking, what was it you saw? You said it wasn't human. If it wasn't human, what was it at all?"

Up the concrete walk to the stairs, eleven steps to the wide oak doors in front, over the dark stone floor in the vestibule to the second set of doors. The rows of stained glass windows casting muted colors on the pews in the nave. Thick smell of wax candles and old wood. The small red glow of the sanctuary lamp. The life-size wooden cross overlooking the marble altar.

Standing in the sanctuary, in front of the pulpit, his back to Jim, was the pastor. Wrists no bigger than Jim's, hands as delicate as petals as he lifted the Host during the consecration.

"Father Chace? I've brought the vestments."

The silence outside: no low hum of traffic, no sound of birds in the maples that surrounded the church. Stillness, as if when he walked into the church he'd walked out of the day. No sound outside but something in. Breathing. And oddly below that, because wasn't breathing the softest sound, the murmur of a single voice. Praying, it must be, but odd for that, because you knew what praying sounded like, without thinking about it. It was all in one tone, not the up and down of this.

"Father Chace?" He didn't want to interrupt but he couldn't stay where he was and he was reluctant to take another step because that would bring him further into the church and closer to it.

Father Chace didn't stir. And now he thought there were two voices. No one there but Father Chace, but he clearly heard two voices, low, continuing without a break. Father Chace's and a deeper voice. The voices seemed to crawl to him over the floor, and up his ordinary jeans and the t-shirt that smelled of laundry detergent, though he couldn't make out a word or even a clear syllable. Not coming through his ears, but wrapping its arms around him, enveloping him, going right through the skin and sitting in his head.

Dreamed a thousand times, felt a million more. The words like an army—crabs, maybe, or beetles—scuttling along the floor and up his body. A thousand times, he'd leaped out of the dream, heart pounding, before it was too late. And when that feeling of something crawling up his legs came over him—which happened at odd times, any time, so that he existed in a state of constant apprehension—he pushed it away before it could fully envelop him. He pushed it away now, whether or not it was the right choice. He wouldn't look at it. Couldn't.

"I don't know," he said firmly. "It was dark."

"Too dark to see but you know it wasn't human?"

"I mean the thing was dark. What was in the sanctuary was dark. Most of the church lights weren't on, so the sanctuary was dim, but it wasn't dark. The thing I saw was dark. He was arguing with it and all I know is that it had no feet. I remember that. I could see that. Then Father Chace turned and I saw it behind him. Just a flash of it. You know how you see something and only afterwards you realize what it was you saw? I was a kid. I was thirteen. I was frightened half out of my wits—" wincing at the choice of words.

He suddenly recalled the hot, sweet smell of urine when he got in the car. Mortified when he realized what he'd done and braced himself to hold his body away from the seat so that he wouldn't leave a telltale stain on the fabric. That's what had muscled to the back of his brain anything he had seen: the car couldn't go fast enough not because he wanted to get away from the church but because he needed to be out of the car before his mother found out he'd peed in his pants. At thirteen years old. If anyone found out, he'd never get over it. "I don't know whether I can pull that image up after all these years but I'm a coward. I don't want to try."

"I'm so sorry. To be so troubled in mind. I've always thought it worse than bodily pain."

"Yes, well." He had that, too. "I'd be foolish to ask you to take the word of a thirteen-year-old boy."

"I don't know," he said, musing. "He did know you would be a priest, and that may be a guess but it strikes me as odd. If you just called to tell me you saw something—what did you say? Not human?—I doubt I'd believe you. But there's that letter. And I did find Anselm; I told you how that was. I expect it was the biggest jolt I've had in life."

Jim forced himself to wait.

"There was the limp. Anselm didn't have it before he went to Blessed Sacrament. I asked him about it and he brushed it off. He wasn't one to spend much time thinking about himself, you know."

"That could have been a fall. Or surgery."

"Not sure about that and the time's well past when I could ask."

"My sister remembers him as high-strung. She's an emergency room physician. She thought he had what she called an exaggerated startle. Said it was a symptom of PTSD."

"I don't know about that, either." Reilly seemed to hesitate, then Jim heard a small sound, sort of a grunt; he'd made a decision. "You said we were friends and I thought we were but I saw Anselm only twice after he went to Blessed Sacrament. I'd call him and he wouldn't ring back, or if he did he said he'd be away, had another engagement; always something, it was always something. He was avoiding me. Maybe everyone, for all I know. The first time I went down on my own and he wasn't glad to see me. He'd lost more than two stone and he wasn't a big man to start. So off we went to dinner, whether he wanted to or not, and I can't say he heard much of what I was saying: he was only half there. I don't know that he was hearing the breathing you say you hear but he was distracted by something. That I am sure about.

"The second time I went down because I'd received his letter to you. To be held until he asked for it and if he didn't, to be sent on his death. I thought—well, it doesn't matter now what I thought—but I drove to the church the day it came and that's how I was the one to find him. I told you how that was. The look of him. Whatever it was took him quickly, I think, but that letter—whatever it was, he obviously knew it was coming."

22

My stock had risen after that weekend, as my late-night swim in Narragansett Bay was retailed here and there through the house. People thought I must be a madcap, like something out of a Depression-era movie. I was invited to a weekend in the Hamptons and to two parties whose existence everyone else had probably known about for months.

I wasn't a madcap. I was still my same screwed-up self. I knew that I was just as screwed up because I should have been thrilled by the invitations, but I wasn't. Even though party invites were infinitely better than casual offers to join the usual group for an after-work drink. Even though I had never received even a single offer to join the usual group. Maybe I wasn't excited because I didn't know what to expect, what to bring, or what to wear. Maybe I wasn't thrilled because I knew I wasn't adept at small talk, and I assumed that's what conversation was at such parties.

So I skipped the Hamptons thing but went to the two parties because transportation wasn't involved, so the only expense attached to each event was a bottle of halfway decent wine. The first one was at a condo on the Upper East Side. An elevator with wood polished to a high sheen, a short hall with nineteenth-century oil paintings of hunting dogs, and when the door opened, a beautiful marble foyer, wide rooms with huge windows and ornate crown molding. It took my breath away. I could imagine the original owners occupying it three seasons a year, decamping when the weather turned hot, passing the summer at their homes in Schoharie County and visiting the caves, entertaining their friends, and sketching the landscape.

The current owners, one of the much-higher-ups and his husband, had furnished the rooms in white: white marble tables, white upholstery, white curtains. German Expressionism, not a particular favorite of mine, glowered at us from the walls. Lots of people I didn't know, and a few

I did, the latter insisting I repeat the tale of my late-night swim for the former, until I began to see why I'd been invited. A glass of wine in hand, I wandered, pretending to look at the art, and I ended up by the windows, watching the city many stories below me. Hoping no one else would ask to hear the tale of my ruined dress. Figuring out how long I should stay before I could excuse myself and go home. And when I judged that sufficient time had passed, I slipped away.

A younger crowd was present at the second party, including the group that went drinking on Friday nights. For the most part, I liked them, but thanks to the higher-ups party, I suspected that it was the madcap who'd been invited. No one asked me to tell the story; everyone seemed to know it. Listening to the chatter, much of it Metro gossip, I began to feel like an imposter, feigning an interest in who was sleeping with whom, who'd had a bad lift, who was showing too many drug-fueled nights.

When I went home that night, I opened my closet and really looked at the collection I'd amassed. The good skirts and pants and jackets and tops. All the gray because Rob thought I looked good in gray. I was tempted, just for a moment, to take a pair of scissors to everything. I could feel my fingers closing around them, could hear the businesslike sound as they cut through cotton, silk, wool, and linen. I couldn't afford to do it, but every bit of clothing in that closet, without exception, abraded me. Together, they nearly obliterated me. And yet.

And yet that's what I'd wanted as far back as Schoharie.

Then I thought of the priest's world. The world with the chubby cop who knew the priest's sister and joked about how tough she was before he thought to ask you why you were dripping on the station's linoleum floor. With the old people who didn't size you up as you were shaking their hand, guessing your worth. With the priest with the van der Weyden face, who had been frightened for you and perhaps still was.

Grace in the form of hope, he'd said.

I did call Helen, as he'd suggested. Generally, I stuck to the comings and goings of my day and I asked her about the shop. Things would come to her between one call and the next, artists who'd stopped by, sometimes to buy supplies but also, she thought, to be in a place that was familiar. One of her regular patrons was a man who lived on Ocean Drive; he might be still alive, she said, though very old at this point. A surprising number of her patrons were musicians performing at the jazz or folk festival. I knew a few of the names she remembered and I could even picture one or two while she was talking.

Otherwise, she'd keep me abreast of doings in the backyard garden or what she'd seen when she took her daily walk. Often she was asked for directions or to recommend sights to see or places for lunch or dinner; I had the impression that tourists were thick on the ground. Sometimes she'd had a call from the lawyer, and I don't know whether he was being nice or egotistical but it appeared he was always upbeat. I'd talked to him, as well. After that charming encounter at the Brennans' he called one evening full of questions. I was asked to recount my call from Father Ennis, how I'd involved Todd, the first visit to the Brennans' and what had happened when we went to Taylor's gallery. I didn't much feel like talking to him and I had to remind myself that I wasn't helping him, I was helping Helen and Peter.

He was as bad on the phone as he was in person. I'd get out a sentence or two and then he'd interrupt. Could I clarify, could I say specifically, was I sure about . . .? I knew he was doing his job but, frankly, he irritated me. All that male energy coming through the phone, like the shock wave from cannon fire. Father Ennis had called him in, I told myself, so the lawyer couldn't be all bad. Helen had confidence in him and Helen's no fool. So I answered the questions and clarified and specified and assured, but when he said he might be getting back to me I thought: not in this lifetime, cookie.

I told myself that I called Helen because I'd been asked, because they were lonely, but I was glad that Father Ennis had suggested it. She was part of that other world, the priest's world.

There was a little church, a block north and east. I'd lived in the same lousy building for years and never noticed it was there until I went hunting for it one Friday after work. St. Joseph Church, with a Saturday Mass and two Sunday mornings. I went to the later Sunday morning one and sat in the last pew. A small church, with delicate chandeliers of pale yellow glass that looked to be Murano. The Stations of the Cross marching around the church in carved birch. A tidy-looking sanctuary with a rood screen painted in a vaguely Byzantine style, in which the four evangelists were portrayed in colloquy. People filtered in: couples, families, older people, a few that may have been homeless.

I was technically Catholic, baptized into the faith, but that was the last time I was in a Catholic church until people started getting married. I was always surprised to see the name of a Catholic church on a wedding invitation; no one I knew gave the slightest hint of a spiritual life and, in fact, their behavior strongly suggested the opposite. When I attended these weddings, the feeling of a sacramental celebration tended to be subsumed by the drama of the dress, the bridesmaids' attire, and so on.

St. Joseph was something different. At first I was hesitant, knowing I was a stranger to the church, thinking I might stick out as someone who did not belong. The building itself was a little grand, but as people came in I began to relax. They were ordinary people, a few dressed up but most in casual clothes, who found a pew, genuflected quickly, and just as quickly made the sign of the cross, knelt to pray, and then relaxed in the pews and waited. No checking cell phones or watches; they just sat waiting for the priest to emerge from the sacristy and the Mass to begin. Not completely silent, of course, because people never are: some shifting, coughing, a brief whispered conversation, a child commenting or questioning in a bright voice. But while the superficial feeling was of expectation, there was a deeper, powerful sense of quietude. It was like a still day in October, brilliant leaves floating gently down and then settling gently on the ground.

I sat in my pew, amid the stirrings and rustlings, and watched people setting down the burdens of the week, letting their shoulders drop and their backs relax and their breathing become quiet and slow.

It didn't feel like the city. Manhattan is many things, but it is never still. It didn't feel like Schoharie County either, abandoned and bereft. St. Joseph could have been a quiet island in the roiling sea of Manhattan, or an oasis in Schoharie amid the ruined, desiccated, nineteenth-century buildings, but it wasn't. The priest came in, the Mass began, I found my place in the book, and I joined in only because I didn't want to call attention to myself. Most people went to communion, but I didn't, and I felt a little awkward as the pews around me emptied. But then they came back to the pews and it was fine.

I was a spectator. And I was following some sort of compulsion, though I couldn't put into words what that urge was. But I recognized the people around me as one small stream that flowed into the wide river of all congregations over all the years, here and over all the world, and the source of that wide river traced to a trickle two thousand years ago, and it was a peaceful thought.

The following Sunday saw me in the pew once again.

23

Lizzie had been at morning Mass, but when it was over, she'd hurried by him. She rarely left without saying hello, but more tellingly, he'd seen her face.

He debated with himself the rest of the morning. He was in no shape to help anyone. If Lizzie could manage a hospital's emergency room she was well equipped to handle any crisis. The closer he drew to Lizzie's family, the more likely it was that whatever had poisoned his life would reach out and poison Lizzie or Sam. Or one of the children. God knew, it liked children. Nevertheless, it nagged at him and that afternoon he called her.

"Nothing's the matter, Jimmy." She'd sounded irritated, but he had pressed, knowing that she was more than forthright by nature; in fact, she held rigid ideas about the truth. She would never lie, not even a white one. She reminded him of some of the nuns he'd had in grammar school: no shades of gray. If he continued to press, and if he got the question right, she'd have no choice but to tell him.

"Kids okay?"

"They're fine."

"Still planning to go to England?"

"Look, I have to go."

"How's Sam?"

"I don't have time for this. I really, really don't."

"Sam's still drinking," he said, ruthless. "Is his drinking worse? Or did something happen? Did something happen to Sam?"

Lizzie was exasperated. "All right: he didn't come home until three o'clock this morning."

"Did you talk to him?"

"When was I going to do that? I had to get lunch, turn the house upside down because Triona lost her front-door key, drop her off at Sarah's, locate Willy's trunks and take him to the Raffertys', and then get to work."

He thought of Sam, drinking until closing at one of the locals' bars and, after that, what? Invited to someone's place for another round? While Lizzie was lying in bed, eyes open, the stress running in lines across her forehead, worrying.

"I'm sorry."

Another long breath. "Not as sorry as he's going to be when he gets pancreatitis. Or stomach cancer."

Some emotion transferred itself to Jim: the world paused while his heart stopped and then it began to beat slowly, painfully. As if it knew his thoughts, the breathing became a roar. He would not be silenced, though he felt sick with what he was about to do.

"Why don't I take the kids out for dinner tonight, so you and Sam have time to talk?"

He could feel her surprise and it saddened him. He registered a bite on one leg, sharp as a stiletto. Felt movement below his knee but it wasn't real. It wasn't.

A pause while she was deliberating. Then, "That would be good. I need to tell him I'm pregnant."

He smiled to himself when he replayed her voice: exasperated, as if pregnancy were the last straw of the indignities inflicted on her by an uncaring universe. Other people would have been flattened, a pregnancy added to a husband who was drinking heavily, a stressful workplace, an incompetent coworker, and possibly more he wasn't aware of. Not Lizzie. Well, he thought, at least that's another bedroom that would be occupied. Jim wouldn't say that to her, of course, but the thought returned to him off and on during the day. Most of his day was out: at the hospital, visiting the homebound, another funeral, a meeting with the organist who had managed to corral four children for a choir, phone calls, and when he was at the rectory, drop-ins. All the time his mind telling him he'd made a mistake.

Lizzie's children weren't used to him, and they picked up a current from him, jangly nerves and fear and a dull horror of what he was doing. He wasn't supposed to be here. He wasn't supposed to be with them.

Nothing good would happen; he knew that. Willy was fidgety, Triona was mulish. He knew he had crossed some kind of line but he could not go back. He had made an offer, and his sister, who never accepted help, had taken it. The stress and worry; you couldn't pretend you didn't see.

In one way, he was glad he had an excuse to be out of the rectory, away from the hiss of the central air and whatever it was that was battering the walls, away from the dim rooms and oppressive furniture, the ghost of Anselm, the letter from Anselm. He couldn't escape the numbness, though, or the pain, or the breathing, or the conversation with Reilly, who said Anselm had known it was coming. In the moments between, all day, when his brain wasn't occupied with listening or talking or writing checks or making plans, he felt he was at the edge of some great hole and could easily plunge into a darkness so thick and deep he would never climb out.

He stood in Lizzie's foyer, sweat beading on his face, waiting for the evening to be resolved. Triona wasn't quite a teenager but she also wasn't a child; they went nowhere with Jim and his niece wasn't leaving the house until she knew why. She turned a stubborn face to her mother, waiting for an explanation.

Lizzie had been trying to hustle the children out the door but abandoned the effort with a shrug. Afraid that she would feel compelled to tell the truth, Jim produced a gift certificate from his wallet.

"A thank you from a parishioner," he said. "I thought you'd like to eat by the waterfront."

Ignoring her uncle, Triona glared at her mother. "I want to finish *Quo Vadis*."

"You can finish that any time," Lizzie said.

"Maybe Triona is afraid of tourists," Willy offered.

Triona turned the glare on her brother.

Lizzie was looking at him oddly, frowning. Jim managed a smile through a sheen of sweat, thinking that would persuade her not to ask how he was feeling, which was always a precursor to a million invasive questions. "How about this," glancing from Triona to Willy and back again. "We have dinner and then do something fun after. Your choice. And Willy's, of course."

Still mulish, but something flickered in her eyes. "Ghost tour." She slapped it down, reminding him of Lizzie, defying them to challenge her.

"Ghost tour?" It wasn't what he expected. Although he didn't know what he'd expected. A movie, maybe.

Triona proffered an explanation. "It's a tour, with a tour guide."

"Do you mean the guide is a ghost?" Jim wondered if his nephew's voice cracked because he was trying not to laugh at his own jokes.

Accustomed to such sallies, Triona shot him a look.

"Triona, we don't believe in ghosts." Even Jim recognized that Lizzie's tone was likely to make any twelve-year-old dig in her heels. "The church says there's no such thing. Right, Jimmy?"

As far as he knew, the church had never pronounced on that topic. "I've never seen a ghost," he said consideringly. "Bigfoot, maybe. Pukwudgies, definitely."

Triona's expression changed; she'd scented an ally.

"Pukwudgies sounds like something you hit with a stick," Willy said.

"Or something barely edible. An oat cake," Jim agreed. "'Try a little pukwudgie with a bit of butter on it? Or would you prefer to have it with our special haggis jam?' Actually, they're the little people of the Wampanoag. About knee high and tricky little beggars."

"Sarah did it when her cousins were here." Triona was now making a direct appeal to her uncle. "You go to one of the hotels to get your ticket and that's where the tour starts. Sarah says you go to graveyards."

"It would be better if a ghost gave the tour." But Willy was beginning to think about the thrill of wandering around the city after dark, listening to tales of the dead but not-quite-gone.

It was a measure of his sister's distraction that she was leaving the choice to him. Her eyes were troubled but inward looking. "If we find a ghost," he told her, "we'll invite it back for a cup of coffee."

Jim didn't get to the waterfront much during the summer; like most locals, he stayed away from Memorial Day to Labor Day, leaving the shops and restaurants to the tourists and the college kids. But he did have the gift card and he guessed that if they went early enough, a table would be open.

They made their way from the Mary Street parking lot to Thames Street, where the meaty miasma of burgers was inescapable. Oily, so thick it could have attached to the sweat, which had clung stubbornly, despite the air conditioning in the car. He thought he felt calmer, now that he was no longer closed in with the children, but his heart told him otherwise, thumping madly.

Thames Street was the interior of an ant hill, cars flowing south, bumper to bumper, people streaming out of shops to join the currents crowding the sidewalk. And like ants, cars and people appeared oblivious to all but their own mandate: searching for parking spaces, drivers slammed on their brakes and narrowly avoided being rear-ended; the pedestrian flow pushed people off the sidewalk and perilously close to moving cars; and focused on their destination, couples with small children darted without warning across the street. His eyes remained on his niece and nephew, though Willy's neon green t-shirt, sizes too big for him, made him hard to miss. Willy did have to be monitored at intersections, as he rarely looked ahead; he preferred the sky, the buildings and, especially, the dogs. Triona, dressed exactly like every other pubescent girl, tanned arms sprouting from a v-neck of some semi-sheer synthetic, slim legs emerging from skimpy shorts, was more challenging to spot in a crowd. Triona was dazzled by any teenage girl who passed them on the sidewalk, studying their hair, their clothes, their shoes, and apparently how they held themselves: he saw her audition a slouch, a slink, and squared shoulders within the space of a block.

He was sorry about it. Triona was the intrepid child who began surfing with Sam when she was eight, who'd been skateboarding since she was six and bore scrapes and bruises throughout the warm months, and who for several years had unsuccessfully petitioned Santa for a boa constrictor. Those were what society called rough edges and he hoped society wouldn't smooth them all as she grew into adolescence. Although it hadn't with Lizzie, and Triona was nearly as outspoken.

The Black Pearl was dark, a long room with a low ceiling, and heavy tables that were too close together. It also was hot despite the fact that it squatted halfway down a wharf. A few families were apparently finishing very late lunches, and several older couples were well into early dinners. Jim recognized no one, but hadn't expected to; any place that was popular with tourists was bound to be proportionately unpopular, in summer, with locals.

Lizzie wasn't everyone's cup of tea. She said what she was thinking—and if you didn't know she wasn't motivated by anything but a desire to be helpful, you would think she was rude. Jim loved her, but even he wasn't always ready for her: she could barrage you with questions and opinions, the latter coming hard upon the former. He'd seen her with her friends, with Sam's family, with the children, and she was invariably the same. Sometimes, Jim could see clearly what she was thinking, and he would wait for the action or the observation that came a moment later. If Willy was reaching for a third brownie, she'd swoop in and whisk the plate away, telling him that it took twenty minutes for his brain to learn that his stomach was full and no one was vomiting on her watch. He didn't understand why she hadn't spoken to Sam.

If she couldn't bring herself to do it, was there another way he could help? He couldn't imagine having a conversation with his brother-in-law; in the time he'd known Sam, they'd always talked across Lizzie or the children. A few sentences while Lizzie was on the phone with the hospital, or putting candles on a birthday cake, but that wasn't a conversation; more a punctuation to the easy, familiar silence that could drop gently on members of a family. He prayed that Lizzie would make a conversation unnecessary.

And meanwhile, there were the children who, when they'd finished perusing the menu, would expect entertainment. He was terrified of them, both as innocent as he'd been at Blessed Sacrament. Beneath the table, something could be moving now, slithering across the scarred floor to attach itself to one or another of them, the way it had attached to him. Abruptly he pushed his chair away from the table, sat sideways so he could see both feet. One leg was numb and the other was conveying something new to his brain, a sense that it was being roasted slowly, an agonizing pain that came steadily and sank so deeply it made his hands shake. He breathed slowly and deeply, while Triona walked the table nearly page-by-page through *Quo Vadis*, which took them through dinner.

They had an hour before the ghost tour began, so Jim suggested ice cream. They wandered past the shops and the outdoor bar to the marina, which at this time of year was packed with million-dollar yachts, their fiberglass hulls sleek in the declining sun. A small gate bore a sign forbidding trespass to all except yacht owners, but nearby was a bench, and Jim was relieved to sit again.

Willy spotted a gull, gray-and-white coloring as sober as a Pilgrim, sturdy as a bowling pin, sitting atop a piling, and went to investigate.

That left him with Triona, who sat beside him, put her tongue to the pistachio finial, and rotated the cone. "Mom's mad at me," she said matter-of-factly. "She hates me."

"What?" Jim took a good look at his niece. "Your mother doesn't hate anybody. As far as I can see, she doesn't even dislike anybody."

Glancing up at him, her expression was accusing. "She made you take us to dinner so she could get away from me."

"That's not true." He couldn't imagine how she'd arrived at that idea. "I was the one who suggested dinner, not your mother. I had the gift certificate."

"You never take us anywhere."

The air had grown a little cooler, blowing clean off the water. The sun gilded the picket fence, the gulls, and lit his niece's hair like a halo. As he searched for a response he tracked idly among the throngs of tourists, the bright t-shirts and shorts or jeans, the inescapable flip flops, then felt a jolt: his nephew wasn't where he had been a moment before.

In the milling crowd of tourists, anything could have happened quietly, without attracting attention. Clambering around the sea of people he could have tripped and fallen into the water. Could have been marched away by someone who'd been prowling for young boys.

"Willy—" Jim said, but as soon as he'd launched himself to a vertical position he spotted his nephew at the edge of a sightseeing clot, trying, apparently, to sneak up on the gull. He kept his eyes fixed on his nephew, determined not to lose sight of him again.

Triona's need to talk was ferocious, blowing past her adolescent self-consciousness and even the oddness of her companion, a priest who was with them so infrequently that he may have been a casual friend rather than a close relative. "I don't care what she thinks, anyway. It wasn't my fault. How was I supposed to know he could tell?"

He sat carefully, shifting his weight when pain shot through his hip. Keeping his eye on his nephew, trying to listen to his niece, to talk through the breathing that was like a November gale, to ignore the fire of one leg and the ice of the other. "I'm sorry. I don't know what you're trying to tell me."

"I poured Dad's scotch down the drain. Not all of it, just half, and then I filled the bottle with water."

Startled, his gaze slid to his niece. He kept his voice neutral. "And your father found out."

She was still puzzling it out as she licked the cone, determined not to look at him. "It looked the same and smelled the same."

"Probably didn't taste the same, though."

The cone was forgotten. One arm of the v-neck was sliding down her shoulder, the skin over her collarbone so pale it was nearly blue where the strap of her bathing suit hid her skin from the sun, freckled where the sun's rays had found the flesh. "How would I know that? I'm too young to drink."

His godchild. Lizzie said Triona resembled him; the sharply arched eyebrows, the broad cheekbones, and the wide mouth were kin to what he saw in the mirror, and, as their eyes met, the light blue irises, orange-flecked. Her fingers wrapped around the cone were so fine he nearly could see through them; and her body was as sweetly made as the sandpipers that skittered before the waves at Second Beach. He knew her face and Willy's as well as he knew his own, greeted their images every morning, said goodnight to them every night while he was on his knees. His was a selfish love: when he prayed, he never asked that the children be healthy, or even happy. He only prayed that they continue to live, because even though he didn't know them, and they didn't know him, he would be hollowed out if he lost either of them.

He needed to say the right thing. The right words would reassure her but the wrong ones would flatten her—though it possibly wasn't the words but how he said them that would help her. But which were the right words and how could he know how to say them?

He was an adult and she needed the comfort of an adult, and perhaps it was propinquity, that she would have turned to anyone, but perhaps she felt that he was family, felt the bond, slight though he'd fashioned it, that existed between them.

A small part of him, the selfish part, was glad of the moment and he had the decency to be ashamed of it.

"I don't care what she thinks, anyway," she said again. Waiting to be contradicted. "Maybe she wants to get rid of me."

He knew what he couldn't say. He couldn't explain to Triona that her mother wasn't angry at her, that she was angry because her husband's behavior was now affecting one of her children. And possibly angry at herself, because she hadn't acted before now. And might not have, in fact, if Jim hadn't offered to take the children to dinner. And maybe, a little bit, angry at Triona because Triona had brought the matter to a head. But he couldn't say any of that.

"She loves you. If anything ever happened to you . . ." He knew that wasn't the right path and tried another. "Do you think your mother can switch love on and off like a lamp? Do you think love really works that way?"

After a moment he saw the slow, almost imperceptible nod.

He had no idea she was that young. His longing to reach for her, to hold her until she knew that she was loved, was a new pain.

"Your mother is a pretty determined woman but that's beyond even her. When you really love someone, you can't turn it off: it's like trying to turn off the sun. You can like someone and then not like them, but love is bigger than that. Stronger. The most powerful thing in the world, I think."

He considered her for a moment, how deep her unhappiness must be to have confided in him. "Maybe it doesn't feel that way right now. Sometimes you can feel love, like you're at the beach and there's not a cloud in the sky, and the water's cold so you run out of the water and the sun hits your skin and you feel heat right to your bones."

He was watching closely; otherwise, he might have missed the subtle shift of her body that told him she was listening.

"Other times, maybe it feels like night and you can't feel the warmth. You can't see the sun and you can't feel it, but you don't for a minute think it's not there, do you? You know the sun is right there where it's always been, burning just the same as it always does. Your mother's love is just like that. Whether or not you feel it, it's always there."

Voices swept into the silence, people and gulls and, mixed with the dull roar of a power boat somewhere on the bay, the clatter of dishes from the nearby restaurant.

"How do you know? You don't love anybody."

He knew she was a child but the accusation stung. "You think I don't love you and Willy?"

Her silence was a prod: he couldn't seem to stop himself.

"Every morning, every single morning, you and your family are the first things I see when I wake up. I put photos in my bedroom just so you'll be the first thing I see. Before I even get out of bed. I have a picture of you running into the water, and one of Willy feeding a gull and the two of you making a snowman with your dad and every single day those pictures warm my heart. Every single day."

Too late, he understood her silence. And saw himself as he was: blasted, sweat-stained clothes sticking to his skin. Alien. How stupid he'd been to think the books might be enough. Maybe he had known they'd never be enough; perhaps he'd just hoped they'd be something. They might have been something but clearly, not something that mattered.

He was quiet for a minute, absorbing it.

"Never mind," he said, fighting an urge to weep. "Not important. But listen, I do know your mother. She's my sister, and whether I like it or not, I've been on the receiving end of her love my whole life. She's just about as bossy as any human being can be—ah, you recognize that, do you?"

Because finally, finally, he'd gotten a response. He'd bent his head to watch her face and it wasn't a smile, just the suggestion of one, but it was encouragement enough.

"And she can be a real nag; heaven knows that's true. But it's because she loves me." Corrected himself: "Loves *us*. Your mom might get mad, and believe me, she's been mad at me more times than I can count, but she doesn't stay mad long. It's like clouds passing in front of the sun."

Triona remembered her cone, turning it slowly on her tongue until she'd cleaned up all the drips. Her attention strayed to a pair of teenage girls who were too young to be wearing tank tops that were too tight and cotton shorts that were too short.

"Mom wants you see a doctor. She said she thinks there's something systemic going on."

The same flat tone in which Lizzie delivered all her pronouncements. Though here it was meant to be dismissive, the words a barricade between him and her family.

He stood. "We should get going; it'll take a few minutes to get to the hotel, then we need to figure out where the tour group meets."

Wracked as he was, he could still feel the distance she'd put between them, her family clustered together, her uncle safely far away. That is what he'd wanted; hadn't he always told himself that? He was the one who made himself the occasional visitor, the bringer of books, though Lizzie had invited him to be more.

He felt wretched. On a hot August evening, tourists wandering America's Cup Avenue, a young couple, arms around the other's waist, an older couple holding hands. A mother pushing a stroller as she laughed with a friend. A toddler whining until his father picked him up. Three young women, close as petals on a flower, interrupting each other as they chatted to an unseen someone on a phone.

He forced himself to focus on the children and to concentrate on the movement of muscles, willing them to work. Though he wouldn't meet anyone's eyes, knowing how he appeared, even without the limp. At the edge of his hearing, beyond the crowds on the sidewalk and the never ending screech of seagulls he thought he heard an engine start up.

Their tour guide announced that he was eighth-generation Newport.

"Bill Reed, and please call me Bill." Jim recognized the name: Reed taught history at the high school and occasionally contributed history op-eds to the local paper. "I grew up with all the stories and tonight I'm going to share some of them with you. How many of you believe in ghosts?"

Reed's gaze slowly panned the group. They were sober-looking couples in their sixties, parents with pre-teen children, and several young couples, one of whom, they told Jim, were on their honeymoon. Reed's gaze had alighted briefly on him and swerved back again; Jim knew he didn't look well but surely, he thought, he looked fit enough for a two-hour ramble around the city. Triona and Willy kept their hands down and though Willy raised his when the guide asked if any of the crowd weren't certain, his eyes glinted with poorly concealed mirth.

They left the hotel and crossed America's Cup Avenue and Thames Street. At the bottom of Washington Square he stopped and beckoned them to draw close. All around, throngs of tourists passed, some pausing when they noticed Reed, who wore a black cape that rose high on his neck and swept to his ankles, and held an old-fashioned brass lantern in which a candle flickered wanly. Coming down Broadway, cars slowed, crawling to the end of the street while the occupants decided whether the gathering was a crowd or a mob. While tour groups were a familiar feature of Newport's summer landscape, few were nocturnal; however, the cape and lantern, those artifacts of the eerie, had the opposite effect on passersby, reassuring them that no sinister activity was in the offing.

Reed brought the lantern high, illuminating his head and upper body. "You can find nearly four hundred years of Newport history if you look for it. The history before that has melted away like morning mist; little remains of people such as the Wampanoags and the Narragansetts other than the name of a place, the word spooling out long from the mouth. The colonists were differently minded, building solid testaments to their existence: these houses, these churches, the carved stones in Island Cemetery. Those early settlers meant to be felt down the ages. And each generation after them knocked wood together to build more houses and taverns, piled brick upon brick to make the Colony House you see before you and the Brick Market you see behind you."

He had a rich, deep voice and the measured cadence that came with long practice. The voice was soothing as a lullaby but then his tone began to shift.

"There are other things the colonists and their descendants left behind, other places that have escaped the memory of this town's inhabitants, all but disappearing in the welcome fog of time.

"The weeping trees on Farewell Street, at the southwest corner of the cemetery, were planted where the workhouse once stood. The workhouse is long gone but the documents remain, establishing in 1723 the American colonies' first warehouse for the poor, and later decreeing that the residents of that domicile should either be worked harder or removed from that residence and exiled from the town. And duly noting when town laws were properly executed by the administration of . . . fifteen . . . twenty . . . or thirty lashes upon the intractable poor."

Reed turned to sweep the lantern in an arc behind him.

"The hanging trees of Washington Square are testimony to an amoral practicality that was overtaken by a transparent piety. Welcomed early in the city's history for the money they brought to Newport, privateers were punished when sentiment turned against them. A speedy trial, a quick hanging, and a long time swinging in the sea breeze and dripping in the rain as warnings to others who'd taken up lawlessness."

Triona had been edging closer to Jim; Willy, he discovered, was already at his side.

"The docks that witnessed Newport's determination to become preeminent in a miserable trade and where, by the mid-eighteenth century, more than half the country's slave traders moored their ships. The marketplace where a portion of the ships' shivering cargo—my ancestors, among them—were sold. God's Little Acre, the remote corner of Island Cemetery, where the small, rounded stones were carved with a single name that harkened back to ancient Greece or Rome, though those poor souls captured on the western shores of Africa had little to do with Ptolemy or Caesar or Cassius."

Jim hazarded a look around him. Spellbound, he thought. Reed had a preacher's mastery of the tightly reined drama; perhaps he could be found behind a pulpit on Sundays.

"The buildings that housed Newport's twenty-two rum factories, where sugar cane from the South was turned into liquid gold that was transported to Africa and traded for human lives. The floorboards in centuries-old buildings along Thames Street, now creaking beneath the weight of shoppers, but once trod by men willing to pay for a simulacrum of passion or for oblivion through alcohol and opium.

"What lingers in the yellowed town records, and whispers between the floorboards of Thames Street shops and behind the walls of colonial homes on Spring Street, what can be heard in the rustle of leaves in Washington Square and the restive waves that pound the rocks below the mansions of Ocean Drive, is the echo of violence: the greed that led to hanging, the fury that led to imprisonment, the sting of the whip, and murder. Violence may be the force on which many cities were founded. Newport, this small city in the smallest of states, deciding that it could not survive without it, encouraged it, and had been doing so from the earliest days of the English settlers.

"Tonight, we will walk the byways of this town and discover that some inhabitants of this place have never left, fearing the judgment on their lives. Many others were taken too suddenly, too unexpectedly, to hear the call to come home. And if we encounter these restless souls, we may do well to turn over in our minds the reckoning that will come to us all . . . for I assure every one of you that it will come."

The cars continued along Broadway; tourists ambled across Washington Square. Reed's group was silent as stones. Jim looked from one child to the other. Triona and Willy were barely breathing. Even when the group began to move, the children remained affixed to him.

Willy recovered first. He turned his face to his uncle, his expression solemn. "I think that man might be crazy."

Jim laughed. He had no idea how his nephew had happened. Taken altogether, Willy could well have come directly from God, something to charm and delight the universe.

"I think it may not be wise to follow someone who believes he is in a horror movie."

"Sarah didn't tell me about that." Triona was coming to herself, dismissing it in her own way. "That was creepy." She increased her pace, glancing over her shoulder to make sure her brother and uncle were behind her. "Hurry up or we'll miss something."

The tour included tales of violent deaths and subsequent hauntings, as well as ghost hunting. As Reed brought them to each location, he instructed those with cell phones to take photos and indicated where they were most likely to capture ghosts. Willy and Triona were assiduous, but when it came time to inspect the photos, brother and sister looked hard but saw none of the small white lights that according to Reed were spirits who lingered in the city.

They meandered up the middle of Washington Square, the elm trees towering overhead, moonlight flickering through the leaves of a Norway maple. They aimed their phones at a beech, the elms, and at a linden; these, Reed said, were kin to those from which pirates had swung, gasping their last breaths on earth. Arrested by the caped figure, small knots of people lingered at the edges of the group, listening for a minute or two or perhaps perusing the faces of the credulous.

By their third stop, Triona was positioning herself close to Reed and avidly sweeping the location for apparitions. Jim was pleased that the tour seemed to have pushed her mother temporarily to the back of her mind.

They wandered through an alley as Reed told them of smugglers, and the young boy who'd drowned in a drain pipe when the tide found him waiting to intercept a privateer's illicit cargo. A half hour later, they'd left Thames Street and the crowds. The air was cool; the lowing of two horns heralded fog coming up the bay. A muted glow came from the period street lights, just enough to ensure they wouldn't trip on the brick sidewalks. Their group crossed paths with couples heading to the restaurants and bars, but more often they were alone, drifting from place to place, following the brass lantern that rocked gently before them.

An odd smell here, sour, but not food, not any of the smells he recognized emanating from the many restaurants in the area. His legs were worse. He feared he would lose control of his left leg because his skin no longer registered the cotton pants that covered it, the sock that went midway up his calf, his fingers when they slid across the fabric or pinched desperately, hoping the lost sense would somehow return. He thought his toes were moving because he had the sense he was wriggling them, but he felt nothing when he tried to bring his toes up against his shoe. His right leg more than compensated: walking a little behind the group, the leg felt it had been plunged into fire; though no one would see him, he had been patting his pants surreptitiously, to make sure they weren't wet with blood.

He no longer heard the engine, though.

On a short, narrow street, colonial homes sat nearly on the sidewalk and their interiors were warmly lit behind curtains and shades. He'd let the group get ahead of him, the children's voices excited, the adults chatting, enjoying the evening.

"Hey." Willy suddenly materialized beside him. "You are supposed to be taking pictures."

"I'm the chaperone," Jim answered. "You're the ghost hunters."

"If there are any ghosts lurking nearby, maybe they will show up for a priest. You are probably the last person a lot of people see when they are dying."

"That's a morbid thought."

Willy's voice was carrying; abruptly, Jim became the show.

"Did I hear we have a priest with us tonight?" The crowd, busily snapping a moment before, paused to look around.

"Here." Triona held up a hand.

The crowd parted for Reed, who approached with a thoughtful expression. "We don't have many men of the cloth on our tours. What denomination?"

The words emerged thinner; Reed's customary speaking voice.

"We are Catholic," Willy said. "Except my father who is supposed to be Episcopalian but he is at home."

"Catholic. From one of the churches around here or are you visiting?"

"He's from St. Patrick," Triona said. Apparently, the children had decided to speak for him.

"He does not live in the church," Willy clarified.

The swinging lamp came close. "You."

"Yes." Though Jim didn't know precisely what he was affirming.

"You have an interest in the spirit world?"

"I'm chaperoning my niece and nephew," Jim said, resisting the urge to step back, away from the lamp.

Reed's voice deepened as he half-turned to the crowd. "But you acknowledge it. God, 'maker of all that is seen and unseen' is there in the Roman Catholic confessions, and of course in those of many other faiths."

The group had collected around them. The fog was bringing cold and damp that should have brought relief to the leg that smoldered, but didn't. He longed to return to the rectory and collapse on his bed, but the children needed to be delivered safely to their home, and Jim couldn't do that until they'd completed the tour. His first real outing with them could not be a failure. Would not.

"What I acknowledge," he said, trying to make joke of it, "is that it's getting late and that children get cranky if they stay up past their bedtime."

Someone laughed behind him. Reed wasn't amused; it was his show, not Jim's. He brought his lamp higher and studied Jim's face. Smoke from the lantern tickled Jim's nose, but he did not look away.

Reed's eyes glittered in the lantern's light. A flash of fear, replaced by something harder, willed. His voice was low, intended only for Jim, who recognized John's gospel. "'The whole world is under the power of the evil one.'" And even lower: "Get behind me, Satan."

Reed resumed his place at the front of the wraith hunters. "Many people think they're too sophisticated to believe in what they can't see. To them, I repeat these words of the Good Book: 'Blessed are those who have not seen and have believed.' Just because you've never seen something, don't be sure it isn't there."

The group moved on to the next location. With an effort, Jim got himself moving. His heart was pounding, each beat telling him to get the children home.

He wouldn't do it. Despite his panic, he wouldn't do it. His first outing with his niece and nephew and very likely his only outing with them. They were having a good time wandering the city at night, hearing Reed's stories of dark deeds and sudden death, but mostly they were thrilled by the possibility that they might photograph a spirit. They'd be disappointed if their uncle dragged them away. Despite everything, he wouldn't do it.

"Scolded by a spirit stalker," he muttered.

"Who thinks he is Dracula," Willy said, watching the cape swirl as Reed led them on.

Jim laughed. "You are a wonderful child."

"That is not what my mother says."

"Take some pictures," Triona urged.

Reluctantly, he pulled out his cell. "I don't even know if I can take pictures on this." Willy took the phone from him and located the camera.

Jim swept one hundred eighty degrees in six shots and flipped through them. "Nothing."

"You weren't really trying," Triona said. "When we get to the next place, take a lot."

At most locations at least one person captured a pinprick of white light, which Reed assured the crowd was a spirit. In light-dense New England and tree-dense Newport, with the sea breeze stirring the leaves, it was hard not to capture a small light here and there. It was a good way to keep the crowd engaged, though.

The last stop was Trinity Church, a latecomer to colonial Newport's religious landscape, Reed said, built in 1726. A clapboard building solid as a battleship, the wood painted cream, black shutters on the staid rows of windows. The upper half of the clock tower was bathed in misted light; the rest of the church glowed faintly in the gloom. They walked through the gate on the northwest side of the church and stopped on large flagstones that were surrounded by several sarcophagi and rows of graves, some marble and grand; others small, slate, and so old they were sinking unevenly into the earth.

Willy nudged him. "Take the graves."

Triona had left them and was wandering among the stones, trying to read the names and dates. Now that his occupation had been announced to the group, Jim felt it was inappropriate to ghost hunt but he took out his cell phone anyway, lest his relatives call attention to him again. He shot a few pictures of the graves but more of his niece and nephew. The guide directed people to a particular window on the second story and he snapped several more. All the while, the breathing was steady, not gusting as it had been earlier, but too loud to ignore.

The fog was thickening the air, basting the flagstones, the living and the graves. It tickled the hairs on the backs of his hands and made him shiver. The sour smell had returned, gathering around him as he watched his niece and nephew roam among the stones. It was the smell of decay, harsh and thick, flowing up his nostrils and into his mouth, taking up residence at the back of his throat. He coughed, snapped a few pictures, and stopped to cough again.

"What did you get?"

"Nothing." Jim flipped through the pictures and handed the phone to Willy.

"This is not nothing." Willy enlarged one photo and handed it to his uncle.

It was the window they'd been directed to photograph. Two faces were distinct in the grainy photograph, one with deep-set eyes, screaming, the other not quite in profile, with a hawk-like nose and an agonized grimace.

"Did he get a ghost?" Triona was scrolling through her own photos. "A zillion graves and nothing." She looked up. "Did you, Uncle Jim?"

Jim hardly knew what to say. He enlarged the photo and the faces came close.

Willy took Jim's phone and gave it to his sister. "Look," he said with some satisfaction. "I knew he would get a ghost."

He wasn't the only one to have captured apparitions. Around them were gratified murmurs and much sharing of phones.

"Everyone see something?" Reed was walking among the group, glancing at phones. "Most people do. If you take photos of that particular window, at a certain angle, you'll see something." He was again speaking conversationally; the tour was ending. "Maybe you've seen stories of the Virgin Mary's image appearing on a tree, or viewed a photo of what appears to be phantoms lurking in the darkness of a forest. It's called matrixing, which is our tendency to impose an order, particularly something human such as a figure or a face, on something that's random. At Trinity Church, the play of light and darkness, combined with flaws in the old glass and our tendency to make sense of what we're seeing, results in the faces we see."

"Not Dad," Willy said. "Dad would see glass. Then he would tell you how old the glass is and then he would tell you exactly how glass was made three hundred years ago and how hot the fire would be and why it had to be that hot and why the glass has flaws. And he would tell you how it is made today and where it is made, even though you are not interested."

Jim laughed, realizing how frightened he'd been a moment before, then noticed that the excitement had faded from Triona's face.

The tour ended, the group ambled in the direction of the hotel, chatting and joking. Willy a few yards ahead while Jim tried not to limp, tried to breathe through the stench. Seeing Reed's eyes, the fear unmistakable in them. Wishing with all his heart for even an hour without fear, without pain. Which reminded him. A glance over his shoulder told him that his niece was falling farther behind.

He knew what dread was. He'd lived with some form of it for twenty-three years. He'd carried it alone, and for most of that time he'd done so as an adult. It stung, no matter what age you were. Not the fear so much as the loneliness. No one to hear your jabbering mind, no one to relieve your worry. He knew his sister loved his niece, knew that his brother-in-law did, but Triona didn't know that.

He paused under a lamp in Queen Anne Square and waited for Triona to catch up. The rest of the tour group beginning to scatter, some headed to the waterfront, others walking in the direction of the hotel. Around him families wandering on the paths, over the grass, eating ice cream cones, pushing strollers, walking dogs, groups of college kids on their way to the bars on lower Thames.

Triona did not believe in his love and even if she did, it wasn't what she wanted, but he could offer her something. Less, admittedly, but something. He wanted to do it, and maybe because the urge arose from something closer to need than to desire, he thought for this once he could risk it, thought maybe that's why the day had worked out the way it had. The early dinner, the hour before the tour began that gave her time to confide in him. Even the gift certificate, which he'd had for nearly a year.

The image he'd carried with him: Sam holding the glass to the back of Willy's neck. Maybe he could rest a hand there, briefly, just that slight human contact, his palm warm against Triona's skin. Letting her know that she had his support, even if she didn't believe in his love. She could easily walk out of it, if she chose. A few seconds of contact, while he said a few reassuring words.

Propelled by a gathering wind, the fog crossed Thames Street and entered Queen Anne Square, swirling around the lampposts and over the cobblestone walk, crept around the low walls that were designed to suggest house foundations, and circled inside the walls, gathering, massing. The figures in the little park grew pallid and indistinct as the fog closed around them. As he waited for his niece, fog drifted past him as if directed, moving east and swallowing up the city as it went.

The ground beneath his feet trembled once, twice, hesitant at first, then more steadily beneath the weight of something approaching. It shuddered through his shoes, up the bones of his legs, the numb leg going colder with it, the other leg defiantly burning. Then he could hear it. It was what he'd heard that night on the bridge.

His mind insisted that it was imagination but the shuddering ground was a potent argument. Habit kicked in: prayer and petition and plea. Though as he called to them—the sister saints, the protectors—they were no more real to him than the faces in the Trinity windows, a trick of the brain, a manifestation of human credulity and the desire for the extraordinary in the endless plodding of days. What would it hurt, though? He remembered Anselm's letter: *When you ask God for help, He answers.* Except that no help had been coming so far, and he'd been asking God for twenty-three years. Trying to hide in God's shadow. On his knees by the narrow bed in the room he'd painted blue, whispering in the round church at the Abbey, in the Belgian library, at Salve, at St. Patrick, every night and morning and in between. Hours and hours of it, when he was exhausted, cold, desperate, frightened, despairing. No help had come from God. His only help had been from Reilly, and that only a warning that he'd know when it was coming.

It was coming now. And just as Reilly said, it was coming quickly, the earth juddering with the concussive force of what was approaching. He felt rather than saw the space he was in, the saplings, the faux foundations, the lampposts, the only hiding place a fireplace and chimney, false as the phony foundations, and no better as a shelter. No place to hide, hoping it would be carried past him by its own momentum. No water to hurl himself into. And he could not run, his sweating, broken-down blot of flesh stubbornly rooted to the brick walkway. He was dizzy with fear as the roar of the motor rose in his ears. He thought of how shaken

Reilly must have been, finding Anselm Chace, and Reilly was an adult; the children would be horribly traumatized.

The children.

Triona a few steps behind him or maybe more, still dragging her feet, his nephew somewhere ahead in the fog, though he'd sworn he wouldn't lose sight of Willy. Their faces the first thing he saw in the morning because he yearned for hope. He should have thought of them first, put them first because that's how love thinks, but he hadn't, though he knew how it could crawl up the innocent bones of a child. Though he knew how it inflicted its sly torture day after day. He sucked fog into his lungs to be heard over the roar and he shouted.

Triona was hurrying, but toward him, when he meant for her to run away. Inches between them when she stopped. He staggered back, out of her reach.

The world fell away.

— 24 —

Maria did a good job; I was surprised and I wasn't. I was because Jimmy had recommended her. Actually, it was more like he implored me to take her. She'd lost her job, he said, and the family depended on the money she brought in. Jimmy is a pushover. I can see him as a kid, standing in front of the concession stand at Second Beach, skinny, white as Antarctica, ears big as cake plates, sand frosting his legs up to the knees, waiting his turn to order. Except there was no taking turns: you had to be aggressive and muscle your way to the front of the mob and make yourself known to the kids who worked on the other side of the counter. Otherwise, you'd starve to death. Sometimes I'd wait to see what would happen and usually nothing did, so I'd get behind my little brother and give him a whack between the shoulder blades until he started moving. I figured Maria was some sad parishioner who was too feckless to keep a job and threw herself on Jimmy's mercy. It sounded just like Jimmy, I thought.

Anyway, Maria came to the door with her bucket of supplies and we looked at one another, each of us sizing up the other. That kind of surprised me. Not that she was sizing me up; it was that she didn't bother to hide it. I liked that. Most people will take you in little sips, a quick glance here and there, so you can't be sure they're doing it. Not Maria. She looked me over in what seemed to be a disapproving appraisal. I like someone who's straightforward like that and I readjusted my thinking. So, not feckless, then. She'd do a decent job at least once.

She's smart. I'm not philosophical—Jimmy's the thoughtful one of the family, or maybe he's just the agonizer of the family and anyway he has the time for it—but I always feel kind of sorry about immigrants. They come to this country from someplace worse, and if they weren't educated in their original country they never catch up in this one. Even if they were educated: I've worked with a couple of people who had been doctors in their own country and one was a CNA in this country and the other was an orderly going to night school at fifty. I feel bad because what a waste of a brain. Especially since it takes guts to leave your home and go to a country where you don't know anyone and you probably don't even speak the language. So you've got someone who's smart and dynamic and they're emptying bedpans and bathing patients. Some of them move up the food chain but no one, or almost no one, ends up in the same place they were in their original country.

Anyway, I could see right away that Maria was smart and she also had that kind of edge I like. As I explained where everything was, you could see that she was impatient to get going on the work. It wasn't exactly that she was frowning, listening to me, but she wasn't happy, either. She looked like I feel when I think I'm wasting time. She knew she was supposed to be paying attention to me, but she was also drinking the house in more of those big gulps, figuring out how large the house was, how much junk we had in it and how dirty it was. I kept my instructions short and let her at it. I had to get to the hospital, anyway. When I got home late that afternoon, I walked in and could smell the whole house from the foyer. Lemon oil, window cleaner, the ammonia smell of the bathroom cleaner, the chemical stink of the pine-scented all-purpose cleaner, a kind of dry and dusty smell underneath, which happens when you vacuum. I could have hired her full time just to have the house smell like that whenever I walked into it.

I like a clean house but I don't like to clean and anyway the house is ridiculous. I'd been thinking I'd never be able to clean it by the time nine months came around and, after the baby, I wouldn't do the job well. Babies take time, and anyway, I don't think I'd want to be running the vacuum downstairs and have the baby upstairs choking to death or quietly spiking a fever of 106 and frying his brain. Anyway, I won't have the energy for it. I'm not exactly twenty anymore, and I remember being bone tired after Caitriona and William. Babies take a lot out of you and I'm not going to bounce back as fast as I did with the first two.

Who were planned.

You could have knocked me over with a feather but I suppose it's what God wants. Or maybe it's God's idea of a joke. Sometimes I think God throws us a curve ball every now and then just to give himself a laugh. I remember the nuns saying God tests us but I don't think that's right, when he knows better than we do how we screw up everything and would flunk even the easiest tests he could fling our way. I think they're jokes, not tests, and that's how he gets himself through the eons. Not that I'd ever tell Jimmy that; he'd be horrified. Anyway, I'm really looking forward to the backache and the varicose veins and twenty-four-hours-a-day reflux.

The house is five bedrooms and two baths, a double parlor, a library, big dining room, and a huge kitchen. It's a beautiful house, the kind of place I used to admire when I was a kid. It was built around 1890 and most of the original details are intact: parquet floors, dentil molding, built-ins, gorgeous fireplaces and tile surrounds. Some idiot knocked out the pantry to expand the kitchen like they were planning to prepare state dinners for the White House, and when Sam wanted to turn the side porch into a sunroom I told him I wasn't going to destroy anything else. He didn't argue with me because he knew I wasn't keen about buying the place to begin with. I told him it was too large but he wanted it. It didn't seem like such a big thing—we could afford it—so I kind of shrugged and gave in.

And now, Sam isn't coming home. To the house he wanted. Swell.

I put up with a lot of nonsense at work. I'm an emergency medicine physician. In Newport. We have island crazy for half the year and it's a special kind of crazy. Some of the locals never cross the bridges and they make their own fun, right here on Aquidneck Island. They shoot themselves hunting illegally. They strap on their skates in January and promptly fall through the ice in whatever pond happens to be nearest them. They fish off Brenton Point in November and get swept off the rocks through a combination of big waves, which they should have noticed, and the slippery bladder wrack and that bright green seaweed that cover the rocks they're standing on, which they definitely should have noticed. Couples get into fights and throw things. Parents and kids get into fights and throw things. They eat mussels they've gathered on the rocks and are clobbered by projectile vomiting. Their knives slip when they're overhauling their lobster pots. They join the frostbite fleet and capsize in thirty-seven-degree water. When someone arrives hobbling or staggering or gasping or is ferried in on a stretcher as a result of island crazy, I stabilize them and then, if they're halfway alert, I let them know just how stupid they were. You have to do it then because that's the only time they're going to listen to reason. Sometimes it works. And sometimes you know it's not going to work because they just aren't that bright. Though even when it's obvious their brains are about the size of a squirrel's, I let them know just how stupid they were to do whatever it was they did to land them in the hospital. You have to try.

The rest of the year, we get the kind of crazy you can find anywhere, except we get more of it than we should. I mean, the island isn't that big. Someone told me that Newport has loads more bars than it's zoned for. I believe it. There are the locals' bars, the kids' bars, the upscale bars, and every weekend in the summer we get people from each kind. They get into fights, they smash their vehicles into parked cars and everything else that is or isn't moving, they push their motorcycles past the point of control and are tossed into the median, they fall down and split their heads on the cobblestones, they trip and tumble off piers and gulp a gallon of water before they're hauled out of the bay, they go for a 2 a.m. stroll along the Cliff Walk and accidentally take a dive onto the rocks below. Anyway, they end up in the ER and I or someone else patches them up, or stabilizes them to be transferred to Rhode Island Hospital. Usually, I don't tell them what they did was stupid because who thinks it's smart to drink until you can't see straight? And even if I did tell them, I'd have to scream: a lot of people don't seem to know that alcohol affects your hearing and the more alcohol you consume, the greater the hearing loss. That's why drunks are so loud.

I told the kids their father's new job had later hours, but I don't think either of them believed me. When Sam came home, he was loud, and he didn't know he was loud. Once in a while he'd arrive home at the end of dinner but usually it was much later. Which meant that I'd have to figure out what to do with the kids when I had the evening or overnight shift. Triona told me she was old enough to babysit Willy, but she wasn't, and Willy insisted he was too old to need a babysitter, which also wasn't true. If I was home, I'd hear Sam throw his keys on the table in the foyer, and then his steps in the hall, heavy and deliberate, as if he could sober up by the time he reached the kitchen. He'd drop his lunch bag on the counter and if he saw the dishes had been washed, which meant that dinner had been over for a long time, he'd stay in the kitchen. I'd leave him there. Better than asking where he'd been; I'd have to be blind, deaf, and anosmic to not know where he'd been.

One night we were in the middle of a late dinner and he came wandering in, pretending he was sober until he fell against the dining room table. Willy's milk went flying, half of it immediately sucked up by the rug under the table, some of it soaking into the tablecloth, the rest of it pooling in Willy's plate. I'd made chicken, potatoes, and corn on the cob and Willy had just finished his corn; Willy said the plate was a study in white. Triona wasn't amused and, under the table with a sponge and a bucket, neither was I.

There were a lot of smart people at Harvard and a lot of morons, too. Medical school was different; you wouldn't have survived if you couldn't memorize vast blocks of information, and you wouldn't do well if you couldn't think quickly under stress. Anyway, I met a lot of smart guys in college and med school but Sam was the smartest man I've ever met. We used to walk in the Sachuest Wildlife Refuge when the kids were little, and Sam would bore them to irritation and outrage, telling them about the plants and the ocean and the birds, how the island was formed, how North America was created gradually over billions of years, all about the glaciers and the inland seas and so on. He'd do the same thing when we traveled; a year ago, we went to Spain, and the only thing the kids actually listened to was his discourse on the Spanish Inquisition. When we took the kids fishing, they got a long lesson they didn't want about the bay. It was interesting to me; it's a large estuary that's on the Gulf Stream, which brings up fish and other marine life from the mid-Atlantic region and the south, including tropical fish like crevalle, butterflyfish, and burrfish. The kids did like the seal-spotting tour we took, although Sam supplemented the guide's knowledge at length. Sometimes I wonder if Sam would have preferred to be an oceanographer or geologist. But then he can get started on the Peloponnesian War or the physics of space flight and I think maybe he would have preferred to be a historian or an astronaut. I always wanted to practice emergency medicine. I like not knowing what's coming in from minute to minute, having to figure out quickly what's wrong and then treating it before the patient crashes completely.

When the kids were little, Sam acted as if he thought they'd disappear at any moment. He'd hunt them down when he came home from work, as if to assure himself that they hadn't vanished during the day. Usually there was no hunting Willy, who even as a toddler had an uncanny sense of time and would be waiting by the side door for his father. Sam would scoop up Willy and run around the dining room squawking, pretending Willy was a bird, and Willy would throw his arms out and scream with laughter. Sam was constantly touching them, putting a hand on someone's head as he passed through a room, bumping into them where they were standing in the kitchen, holding them up to his face and rubbing their cheeks against his five o'clock shadow, placing a cold palm against the back of someone's neck when he came in from shoveling snow. He read to them every night; when Triona was small, he'd carry Willy into her room and she'd snuggle beneath the covers, head in one hand as she lay on her side, looking at the pictures, Willy tucked into the curve of Sam's body, preternaturally alert for a toddler. Sam used to read with all kinds of voices and accents; the kids loved it. Later, they congregated in Willy's bedroom, Sam letting Triona decide when she was too old for bedtime stories. On my way down the hall with a load of laundry, I'd pause in the doorway, looking at the three heads bent in concentration, and I'd wish that I could stop time.

Sam realized what she'd done before I had worked it out. He poured himself a scotch and soda, took a good sip and his face went blank and then puzzled, as if he'd heard a noise he couldn't identify. He dumped the rest of the glass, then poured another shot and tried it neat. Looked at me with creeping irritation. I asked him what was wrong and he knew, then, that Triona had done it; Willy wouldn't have thought of it because he's always in some kind of happy world where everyone loves everyone else and that's all that's important. In a way, he's not wrong, when I think about it. Anyway, I hate conflict but Sam hates it more than I do; I don't think we've ever had a real fight in our marriage. When he told me that someone had watered down his scotch, I said that I would talk to Triona.

I spoke calmly, because I knew I had to do it, but when I found my daughter in her room the following day, I got as far as telling her I wanted to talk to her and then my mind went blank. She'd been halfway into her closet, rummaging around, and she started to say something and then read my face. I just wanted to get it over with. I was due at the hospital, and probably I should have spoken to her earlier but I didn't get around to it until there was no time left. So all I had time to say was not to do it again.

I'm not like Jimmy. I see a problem, identify it, and fix it if I can. I don't know, though, how we got to where we are. I don't know exactly when Sam went from liking a drink to needing a drink but it's been that way for a while. If he had been one of my patients, I wouldn't have hesitated to say something. But I didn't. I never said anything to him. I don't know why I didn't, but I didn't.

I told Triona she had to apologize to her father and—reluctantly—she did. Sam went to work the next day and then he didn't come home. Ten o'clock, eleven, midnight came and he still wasn't home.

The bars close at one o'clock and I gave him a half hour to get to his car and drive home from wherever he was. I lay in bed with the lights on, trying to read the latest *New England Journal of Medicine*, but I could see him in a million different places: car gone off the road on Ocean Drive, him passed out over the steering wheel as his car, dangling from the rocks, was slapped by waves; or his car sideways against a tree in Portsmouth, the gas spilling onto the grass and Sam half in and half out of the car, held in place by his seatbelt. When you practice emergency medicine, you learn to focus on what's in front of you but I couldn't focus on the article; I'd seen what happened to flesh and bone, eyes penetrated, ears sheared off, half a face torn away. Sam had beautiful hands. Anyway, I don't think I remember a single word of that article. Eventually, I must have dozed a little because I didn't hear his car, and didn't hear him until he started up the stairs, lugubriously, shoes knocking against the risers.

They call them "after parties" but it just means that a lot of hard-core drunks need to keep on drinking, so they move to a place where they can continue to suck down alcohol. I assumed that's where Sam had been and my guess was that it was another guy's house, maybe someone Sam works with.

I sat up in bed but didn't say anything when he came in. He was startled to see that I was awake, and hesitated, but then crossed the room, sat on the edge of the bed, and kicked off his shoes. His skin glistened with sweat that I could smell as soon as he came into the room. His body's musk and the sour smell of alcohol coming through the pores; it made me queasy. I turned off the light and slid down the sheets to escape it. Turned my back on him and closed my eyes.

I could have told him that Willy hadn't wanted to turn off the bedside light at ten o'clock; he wanted to wait for Dad. Could have told him that Triona hovered around me all evening, my anxiety feeding into her unhappiness. Could have said that both kids were quiet all night. But I was too angry to say anything then and, frankly, I didn't know what to do. I didn't sleep. Sam lay beside me, adenoidal gusts, reeking of alcohol, pushing into the room and driving out the chilly night air. My head ached from exhaustion, hurt so much that I could feel every single hair sticking out of its follicle. I was so tense that I was nauseated. I had to go to work in a few hours and I didn't know how I was going to be able to do that. And I thought, how could I do my job when I was so upset and distracted?

He was asleep when we left the house the next morning. Slept right through all the chaos of breakfast and wrangling kids and their belongings into the car so I could take them where they needed to be. They knew he was home; his car was parked beside mine and I suspected that Triona had looked into our bedroom right after she awakened. It was a little more chaotic than usual, but as soon as I was alone I started worrying about the end of the day, and would it be a repeat of last night. I worried right through Mass, though it usually settles me, and around the time Jimmy was at the consecration I added a small worry to the larger ones: I needed to avoid Jimmy but make it seem only that I was in a hurry, not that I was avoiding him. All I wanted to do was get to the hospital and turn on that part of my brain, and hope it would work, and that I'd get so involved that the previous evening would feel as remote as Mars.

Jimmy doesn't often call. That was a surprise. My little brother, who hesitates and beats around the bush and can't tell the bishop that another priest in Newport has Jimmy running day and night, doing his work. Who lets himself be bullied by just about anyone who cares to do it. My little brother. He drives me nuts much of the time but when he called me the next day, he just made me sad.

"Why don't I take the kids out for dinner tonight, so you and Sam have time to talk?"

I was shocked when he picked up the kids. He hadn't been at the house in weeks, which would have been the last time I'd seen him without the chasuble and the alb. He was wearing a short-sleeved shirt and his arms were tendon over bone, the fat and muscle burned away, and his pants were sizes too big. His color was beyond bad. I should have noticed that before. Usually he's pale; he's never had a tan, even when we were kids and spent half the summer at the beach. He was gray, with a sheen of cold sweat that told me he was in pain. But what disturbed me most was that thousand-yard stare; it's what people get when they've got terminal cancer. I felt sick looking at him.

The kids didn't notice; they were yammering about the ghost tour. That idiot tour. If I had been in my right mind, I never would have agreed to it. I'm sure the church says they don't exist and I don't want my kids caught up in a lot of paranormal nonsense. But Jimmy knocked the wind out of me.

I know what's wrong with him; it's not like I'd forget that my little brother came flying into the ER because he saw something on his leg that wasn't there. I'm not so stupid that I can't put that together with all the questions about narcolepsy and catatonia and the weird priest we had when we were kids. Jimmy has had some kind of psychotic episode. I'm not a psychiatrist but I've seen enough people in my career to recognize mental illness. My guess is that it was a single event but it freaked him out. It would have freaked out anyone, I suppose, seeing something that wasn't there. Anyway, I expect that Jimmy needs to be talked down because he obviously hasn't been eating or sleeping well. I can't do that; he needs a psychologist or a psychiatrist.

So now I have a husband who's a drunk, a brother who's mentally ill, one kid who's miserable, and the other kid who would be miserable if he hadn't been born with an extra dose of endorphins or something. Plus, I'm pregnant at thirty-nine. Swell.

I prayed Sam wouldn't stay out all night but part of me hoped he would, because then I wouldn't have to talk to him. But then I'd also have to tell Jimmy that I hadn't had a heart-to-heart with Sam, after all the trouble Jimmy had gone to and the effort he was making despite the fact that he's basically crashing mentally and physically. Which I think he recognizes and which has to frighten him. Anyway I would have to talk to Sam eventually, so why postpone it? So I called, but Sam never answered.

He came home around six. Dropped his keys on the hall table and came into the kitchen to see whether we'd had dinner. I was waiting for him, and by that time, I didn't care whether he was drunk or not. I'd been thinking about my brother, and the kids, and about the family I thought we had six months ago, and when he walked into the kitchen I saw the tie he'd worn that day, sticking out of his pocket. It was silk, green anchors embroidered on a navy background. He didn't like cute ties—small polka dots was about as wild as he usually got—but I'd liked the green, and anchors are part of the state's seal and anyway were small, so I bought it and Santa had left it under the tree last Christmas. I saw myself, standing in the clothing store on Bellevue Avenue, tie in hand and happily thinking through the reasons why he might or might not like it and it was all I could do to stop myself from crying.

"No dinner? Are you putting us all on a diet?" He was making a joke of it. Then he saw my face and his mind went immediately to where mine goes. "What's wrong? Where are the kids? Liz?"

He didn't give me a chance to answer. "Lizzie?" He crossed the floor and stopped in front of me. "What's happened?"

I got myself under control. "They're fine," I said. "They're out with Jimmy."

"Jesus." He sat down heavily in the chair nearest mine, putting his hand over his heart. "Jesus. You scared the crap out of me."

He wasn't drunk; I couldn't even smell alcohol on him. For once, he must have come home straight from work.

"Jim?" The name came out slowly, disbelievingly. "The kids are with Jim? Really?"

"He had a gift certificate to the Black Pearl."

"Yeah, but Jim?"

Then I saw it. Jim never offered to take the kids to the beach, or a movie, or for ice cream. He'd never volunteered to babysit the kids even for an hour. I don't know how I never noticed that.

I wasn't a crier. It hurt me, physically, to cry, as if I were forcing my body do something it wasn't made to do. It made my nasal mucosa swell and then I'd be coughing from postnasal drip, the tickling in my trachea too strong to ignore. My eyes were leaking but before I launched into full-blown weeping I got myself under control. I wiped my eyes and took a swipe at my nose. Saw my hands clasp together, reddened from all the handwashing you have to do at the hospital. Nothing ever came of crying, at least not if you were an adult. If you cried for the dead, they didn't feel pity and come back to life. You couldn't mend an injury or cure an illness by crying. I knew that. Situations didn't resolve because someone cried. I blamed it on hormones. Better that than thinking you've completely lost it.

I pulled myself together and faced the fact squarely, without any emotion attached to it: I'd failed my own brother. Whatever was wrong with him, it wasn't anything new. It didn't begin the day he flew into the hospital, gripped by some nightmarish hallucination. Whatever it was, and I suspected psychosis, Jimmy had been suffering it for years. I remember Jimmy leaping away when I tried to put my first baby into his arms. I'd thought it was the typical reaction of an unmarried male and I'd laughed. But the memory sparked a new worry: Was Jimmy afraid he'd hurt the kids?

Sam was slumped in the chair, watching me fearfully, not knowing what to do because I never cried. But I was thinking of my poor brother, the pushover. Suffering for years on end when I should have noticed but never had. Of course he wouldn't hurt the children, but what kind of agony was he living with to make him think he could?

"He wants us to talk," I said when I'd pulled myself together.

Sam didn't particularly like that, but he didn't say anything.

I wasn't sure how to begin. I hadn't had time to think about it and I suppose I'd thought I could figure it out while I was waiting for him to come home. I hadn't expected him to come straight from work. I also hadn't expected him to be sober.

I can deal with lots of things. The million ways the body breaks down and the millions of causative agents like amoebae, spirochetes, and bacilli. Compound fractures and bad puncture wounds don't bother me a bit. Gashes. Near amputations. Overdoses. But feelings drive me nuts. Dealing with them just isn't in my genes. And my genes are supported by learned behavior: no one in my family ever talked about feelings. We never said we were angry or upset or that we loved one another, though of course we did love one another. Anyway, I had no precedent for the conversation I was supposed to be having with Sam, and as a result I had no language for it. I couldn't figure out how to ask if Sam had fallen out of love with me. Even if I did know how to ask, I didn't want to ask. I never thought of myself as a coward but maybe I am.

Sam relieved me of the necessity of speech. "I dropped a dime."

And then the story came out. His promotion had brought him to a different building and the first week he'd been there, he'd noticed a narrow room with a small window. It was near his new boss's office and held little more than a desk, a chair, and a computer. He'd asked his boss about it and was told that it was off limits. "'Even to me,' he said, the liar." Whenever he met with his boss, the room was empty but he noticed that the chair was sometimes pushed into the desk and sometimes not, so someone was using it.

He heard people talking at lunch. They'd say something was going to make it onto the DILLIGAF list.

So far the story sounded improbable and it also sounded like the Navy. "What's the DILLIGAF list?"

"Frank Whiston, guy who's been there awhile, said he didn't know a thing about it. Same thing with Don Petit, even though he was one of the guys joking about it. Asked a couple of other guys and only one would tell me. Al Sousa. Only honest one of the bunch. Said it's Does It Look Like I Give A Fuck. Military's alphabet soup. I hate that crap."

That's all he got but in the next few months he'd heard the DILLIGAF mentioned now and then, usually accompanied by a shrug, although once he'd heard someone intone in response, "the wages of war is death," which caused Sousa to leave the lunch table abruptly, before he'd finished his sandwich.

I didn't want to interrupt but I couldn't help myself. "Actually, it's the wages of sin, not war."

"Not a lot of Bible thumpers in my division," Sam said.

The week of July Fourth, it finally clicked. He'd been listening to the news on his way into work and almost as soon as he got in, he heard someone mention the DILLIGAF list.

He'd tried the door surreptitiously and had found it was locked. He assumed it was always locked, so he started to go out with the gang after work, and when they'd had a few and decided to pack it in and go home, he'd swing by the office. He'd go to his desk, turn on the computer, hang around for a few minutes pretending to work and when he was sure he was alone, he'd go down the corridor and try the door.

"That's why you were coming home drunk?"

"I don't have much of a tolerance for alcohol but I wouldn't say 'drunk.'"

"I would."

Last night, someone had left the door unlocked. The computer was on. All he had to do was hit the keyboard to bring the screen up, revealing months of data.

"The thing about the military," Sam said, "is that everything is by the book. They test something, they record it; they deploy, they record that. What, when, where, and how. Scrupulously, as if precision and comprehensiveness are equivalent to competence. They want everything because they have no idea what's important, and that's because half the time, they don't know what the hell they're doing. You gather every last bit of data, whether or not it's useful, and log it, so it can go into someone's nice, fat report, showing how hard everyone's working and how successful their group is. That report gets sent higher and higher up the ladder, and nobody really looks at it. Nobody looks at the data. Not really. They look at the summary, where everything is nice and rosy, and then they approve it and move on. All the reports and that goddamn paperwork just so someone can get a pat on the head and a service award or a promotion."

Sam found himself in a narrative eddy; with an effort, he picked up his story. "It was a death roll: seals, dolphins, whales. Where, when, and how many. Every time there's a test of the new sonar system, everything within miles dies or strands itself and dies. That's why the computer is off limits."

"Oh, my God." I thought back to what I'd seen on the news. There had been a story about dolphins beaching in Connecticut. A whale was found on Second Beach, but that was a solitary animal. I remembered stories about scores of fish dying, but that had to do with algae blooms that sometimes affected parts of the upper bay; the algae took oxygen from the water and when fish were deprived of a sufficient amount, they could die by the hundreds. That didn't have anything to do with sonar, I thought.

"No," Sam said. "We're only indirectly responsible for fish kills at the top of the bay. Those usually are pollution, runoff from the streets. The public wouldn't know about most of the marine mammal kills. If they happen well past our territorial waters, the animals will be eaten before oceanic currents carry them to shore. Maybe the fishing fleet are bringing up dead marine life but maybe not enough to know something's wrong. Or if they do think something's wrong, are they going to say anything?" Sam shook his head. "Not a chance. Not if there's a possibility their catch is tainted, or that the government will call a moratorium on fishing while it studies the cause."

"So the kills and strandings happened every time the new system was tested? I can see why they'd keep it a secret, but why would they even record it?"

"The reports have been coming in from different locations, so the only one who knows the enormity of the kills is the person putting together all the disparate bits of data. My boss, probably. For the guys monitoring the strength of the sonar, the fact that it's destructive is old news. We've known for the past fifty years that sonar is a hazard to marine life. It generates low- or mid-frequency sound waves at more than two hundred decibels. Know how high that is? We talk at about fifty decibels. A lawn mower is about one hundred decibels. A chainsaw is twenty or so decibels above that. The loudest head-banger bands are a hundred thirty decibels."

"Which is why Triona and Willy will never be going to a rock concert," I said. "I won't be party to their noise-induced hearing loss."

"The pain threshold for humans is one hundred ten decibels—think of what it's like if you're standing next to someone using a chainsaw. Now imagine two hundred decibels coming at you. You don't even have to be near the sonar. It can travel hundreds of miles, and even three hundred miles away it will come at you at one hundred forty decibels. Whales will dive so fast to get away from it that their eyes and ears bleed. They can get a lethal case of the bends. Imagine something so painful that you'll throw yourself on land—that you'll die—to get away from it."

It was a lot to absorb. "How can we be letting that happen? Why isn't anyone trying to stop it?"

Sam didn't get angry very often, but when he did, his words came faster and despite that, were more carefully enunciated, as if he wanted every letter to be soaked in fury. "This new system is sonar on steroids. Something that approaches two hundred sixty decibels, can be felt nearly a thousand miles away, and happens to be at a frequency to do maximum violence to every goddamn marine mammal unlucky enough to be hit. No wonder the information is on a single, high-fucking-security computer. If anyone had half a brain, they would have destroyed the reports as they came in, but that's the government for you."

"They would never deploy something that awful," I said. "Would they?"

"We all get the testing summaries. I've seen phases one, two, and three. All successful. As far as the government's concerned, full steam ahead. When the final phase wraps up, the system will be green-lit to manufacture and deploy. Then we'll be able to kill massive amounts of marine life all over the world."

Sam was red from the neck up. Bright red. Practically glowing. "If I could shoot every short-sighted fucker on the planet I'd do it in a heartbeat."

He was making me nervous; I'd never seen him incandescent and I started worrying about stroke. "Why didn't you tell me? I had no idea what was going on. You should have said something."

Sam's anger is like water in a sieve: he just can't hang onto it. I often think Willy got a double dose of Sam genes, or maybe some kind of mutated version because Willy never even gets mad.

"I had a couple of options." He went to the fridge, located the pitcher of ice water, and poured himself a glass. "I could be a good soldier and send the information higher up the chain of command, where it would disappear. Alert the Fish and Wildlife Service, who might study it for a year or ten. Send it to Oceana or Greenpeace or one of those groups that couldn't prevent their lawsuit from dragging on and on while a species or two vanishes from the planet." His eyes met mine and his smile was rueful. "Not much choice, really, but whistleblowers generally don't fare well. The kids aren't going to be too happy if I spend the rest of my life in prison."

That shook me. "Prison?"

Sam downed half the glass and rejoined me at the table. "The Whistleblower Protection Act doesn't cover unauthorized access to a computer or giving classified information to someone who isn't entitled to it. What they're doing is a clear violation of the Marine Mammal Protection Act, but I don't know if that helps my case, especially since the government's the one breaking the law. Even if I submitted the information confidentially, the press can be required to reveal the source. On the other hand, very few people have been prosecuted for whistleblowing, so there's that. All in all, I think it's lucky that I'm married to a doctor: you can afford to pay the mortgage while I'm doing time."

I took a look around the kitchen, the old-fashioned, glass-front cabinets, the wavy glass in the big window that overlooks the backyard, the red oak floor, glasses and plates on the counter, most likely from one of the kids' afternoon snack, and felt I was seeing it all for the last time. "You said you dropped a dime. You've already done it."

"Last night I spent nearly six hours collecting all the data and emailing all those fucking reports to Becky at the *Boston Globe*."

Becky was a college friend and the only person we knew who worked in the media, but she was a financial reporter.

"She can write a story as well as anyone else. Whatever she wants I'll give her. Including the use of my name."

Newport is a city, but it's a small city and, more to the point, a lot of people around here work for the military and its contractors. If the *Globe* report shut down the project, a lot of people probably would be affected—not just the people in Sam's department but also people who work with me, and whose kids go to school with our kids. We could become pariahs.

"You should have told me instead of springing it on me now, when the damage is done."

Sam had been sitting back in the chair, waiting for me to process everything, and now his eyes met mine. "You think I should have called last night to discuss it with you? Risk getting caught before I'd sent a word to the media?"

"This is a huge decision. It's not like picking out wallpaper or something. You should have told me about it so we could have figured out what to do."

My brain kicked into problem-solving mode as I began to think about our options if Sam was fired, if the kids got harassed at school, if I started getting heat at the hospital.

If Sam went to prison.

Maybe I could call Becky and have her promise to keep Sam's name out of the story. If she couldn't, I could tell her not to do the story, and then we could send the information anonymously to someone at the Providence newspaper. My brain was firing away and my mouth was, too.

"The reports needed to go to a national paper, not a regional one. In any case, you're not going to call Becky."

"There's no way she's running the story before we have a chance to think about what we're doing."

"I've already thought about it."

"Well I haven't!"

"And that's the point, isn't it?"

It sounded like criticism. I played it back in my brain because I didn't quite believe it. But yes, despite the fact that it was said quietly, it was unmistakable. Sam was criticizing me.

"What exactly do you mean by that?"

"Would you do nothing if you knew the government planned to manufacture a killing machine?" Sam said calmly. "Something that will destroy hundreds of thousands of marine mammals?"

"Of course not."

"Would you have thought of an option better than sending the information to the media?"

"I'm not sure. That's what I mean: I have to think about it."

"I think you'd have made the same decisions I made if you'd been sitting at that computer, seeing all that data. And having decided, you'd have acted without a second thought. If the decision had been yours. But it wasn't. Not this time."

I'm really not good with emotion. I admit it. And my job doesn't encourage it. I have to be dispassionate even if someone's shrieking in agony, because the more you get distracted by someone's emotion, the more likely it is that you'll miss a diagnosis. You have to be sympathetic, of course, especially when you're taking a history, but you also have to keep plowing along until you get every bit of information they can give you.

I had no idea what was going on and I couldn't get a clue by the tone of Sam's voice or by reading his face. He wasn't happy; I knew that much. Was he accusing? Angry? Smug? Condescending? I had no clue. And somehow that infuriated me.

"If you're trying to tell me something, just say it, will you? Just spit it out. I'm not going to waste my time guessing."

Then I threw myself out of the chair and started picking things up and shoving them here and there. The dishes from the drainer, the plates and glasses the kids left on the counter after they'd had lunch.

"I'm not accusing you of anything." That was Sam's reasonable voice. Or maybe he was just tired. "Just saying that in nearly fourteen years of marriage, I've made one decision and you've been grousing about it ever since."

Well. Yes, that clarified it. And of course I knew what he was referring to. "The house is too large. It's way too large." Then I caught myself because with another child on the way, it wouldn't be quite as outsized as it had been. "Anyway, that's ridiculous. You make as many decisions as I do."

"Public or private school for the kids. Where we set up our joint account and how much we contribute. Who does our taxes, what cars we buy. What we named the kids, though I had some involvement in creating them. Admittedly my involvement was more limited than yours, but even so."

"You're kidding. You think I spent all that time doing car research because I was mad about the house? Mad for fourteen years?" I'd run out of things to put away. Or maybe I wasn't noticing them anymore. "Do you actually think I am that petty? That I even care whether our guy or someone else does our taxes?"

"If you're not blaming me for the house, then why am I still hearing about it after all this time?"

God spare me from sensitive people, I thought. Because he was. Apparently. Apparently it was my fate to be surrounded by them. Jimmy, for the first part of my life. Sam, for the rest of it. This must be another of God's little jokes. "I complain about everything. That's just the way I am. Usually no one's listening. Anyway, it's not like I mean anything by it."

"I see."

That noncommittal sentence, blandly delivered, told me nothing. Or maybe it did say something and I was just too thickheaded to understand. Maybe it was like some kind of code and I was too obtuse to figure it out. If I had all the time in the world maybe I'd figure it out but who has all the time in the world? "I'm a take-charge kind of person. I see something that needs to be done and I do it. Anyway. Anyway, you knew that. You knew how I am before you married me."

I dropped onto the chair beside Sam. I couldn't think of one more thing to say. I blinked furiously as my eyes filled again. I had this horrible, hopeless feeling, like all the world was on one wavelength and I was on another and I didn't know how that had happened.

Sam didn't say anything for a minute. Then he got to his feet. "Lizzie." He took my hands and pulled me up and against him and he put his arms around me. "Poor Lizzie," he said softly.

His cheek lay against the top of my head and I could feel him smiling. At that point I just gave up trying to figure it out.

We did a lot of talking after that. I'd say it was a frank discussion but nobody ever has a frank discussion. You're always holding back a few things because you don't want to sound too harsh about the other person, and you don't want to reveal too much about yourself, like maybe you aren't quite the perfect person you thought you were.

"Anyway, you didn't have to get drunk. You could have come home and gone back to the office later."

"If I'd come home I'd have had no way of knowing if someone was working late. Going out with them I'd also be sure they weren't going back to the office because they'd forgotten their keys or their wallet or something else. It worked out pretty well. But I don't think I was actually ever drunk."

"Believe me, you wouldn't have passed a field sobriety test."

Sam opened the refrigerator again. "Alcohol is no substitute for a good turkey sandwich," he said. "With pickles. Do we have pickles?"

"On the door."

He methodically assembled his sandwich, just as if it were any other day. I'd be able to recognize him from the back of his head, I thought, the way his hair curled a little at the nape. I'd know his hands: the backs of both were virtually hairless and there was a light-colored freckle on the index finger of his left hand. I knew everything about him that didn't count, and nothing that did.

Actually I did know a few things. I knew he was a good man. A man of strong convictions. I just hadn't realized he was so brave about them.

Then I wondered if he'd committed an act of treason.

Sam laughed at the last thought, the first true laugh I'd heard from him in weeks. "Only if marine mammals have declared war on us. Which actually would be a reasonable thing to do, given the present circumstances."

"What if the paper doesn't want to do an article about it? Will you send the information somewhere else?"

"Let's hope they do." He was washing up his few dishes and turned to me, a sponge in one hand and a knife in the other. And now I saw a glint in his eye, an expression that looked at once familiar and reassuring. "Plan B involves nuclear weapons."

— 25 —

Cold. His toes felt as if they might snap off and shatter like icicles. A chemical smell that was laundered cotton, alcohol, and plastic, and that got into the lungs and held on. The loathed breathing, and over it a cacophony: the steady, high beat of alarms, and distant conversations, and moaning, a woman screaming. He was alive. He wasn't frozen. He knew where he was.

And opened his eyes.

Lizzie may have heard him; she had been turned away, talking to a nurse, but whirled around and stood over him like grim death.

"What the hell happened to you?"

Red curls boiling out of her head, her blue eyes stormy, her wide mouth fierce. Familiar with that look all his life, he smiled even as he became aware that every inch of him hurt, including his lips. "Aren't you supposed to be the one telling me that?"

She came closer and leaned in, inches from his face. Her freckles blurred together; he felt the warmth of her breath. "You went down like a sack of potatoes in the middle of Queen Anne Square. How about that for funny, Jimmy."

"I've never seen a sack of potatoes in Queen Anne Square." He tried to sit up and his arm collapsed with the weight, throwing him down again. Confused, he tried to discover why but as soon as he moved his head a wave of nausea washed over him.

"You scared the hell out of the kids. You don't remember?"

He tried.

"You did the stupid tour and you were going back to the car. Triona said you yelled at her to hurry up and when she tripped on the bricks you fainted."

Nothing, still. "Is she okay?"

"Willy called me." There was no mistaking the fury in her voice. "He thought you were dead."

He was alive but on a distant planet: cold, gray, lifeless. A jumble of images in his head: Willy chasing a gull, the windows of Trinity Church, the cozy homes on a dimly lit, quiet street. *The whole world is under the power of the evil one.* The final few minutes came back to him and he felt the horror run the length of his body. "Oh, God. Triona and Willy."

"Fine. They're fine."

"Are they really?" Realized he was weeping. Couldn't stop it. "God, I'm so sorry, Liz."

"Don't worry about it." She dismissed it, as if she'd expected nothing better of him. That made him feel worse. "Triona has a few scrapes; she'll heal. But you . . ." The anger flashed again and for the next ten minutes she barraged him with questions. What he'd eaten that day, how much he'd drunk, did he have any pain and if so, what kind, how often, what duration, in what context. About hearing problems and vision problems. He answered all of them, though not completely.

"Sounds like a vasovagal reaction to me. You were sweating like a pig when you picked up the kids." She saw his expression. "Yeah, I noticed. I'm not surprised you're drawing a blank: it can wipe out your short-term memory." She stepped back and glanced at the monitor. "Your blood pressure is coming up but it's still way below where it should be, and you're still tachycardic. You were really dehydrated; we've been pushing fluids for the past hour."

He eased a little, comforted by the professional language. He'd always had confidence in her abilities. And she loved him—there was that, too. Took a breath and tried to recover. "Lucky you were on."

"I wasn't." She looked at him narrowly. "I was home. Remember?" And seeing the knowledge come into his eyes, her expression hardened. "Don't even ask; we're talking about you. Willy's not the only one who thought you were dying."

"Thanks for coming in."

She gave him a what-did-you-expect-me-to-do look. "Do you mind telling me what the hell is going on?"

"I guess I fainted."

"Yes, and in case you didn't notice, you fell on your hand and broke two fingers." She snorted. "Your other hand. The left one. Can't you feel it?"

"Well," he said a little sheepishly, "everything hurts."

"I'll bet it does. I don't know how you managed to inflict so much damage on yourself. It looks like somebody threw you off a cliff. Anyway, you must have gone down sideways, smacked your cheek against something—one of those stupid lampposts, probably, and it's a miracle, by the way, that your cheek's not broken although it looks pretty awful—grazed something else or maybe the same thing with your shoulder, then hit the stones. Nothing else is broken, although I suspect from the way you're acting that you've bruised a rib. You've taken some skin off here and there and there's a huge hematoma along your right thigh."

"It doesn't sound too bad," he said hopefully.

"Jimmy." She looked him up and down. "You're skin and bones. And your legs—"

His heart started to pound. Could she see it, then? Again, he tried to sit up, and the broken hand made itself known. A roaring in his ears as black swirled from the edges of his vision. He fought it back. "Lizzie . . ." he said, struggling.

She adjusted the bed after he assured her that he wouldn't faint again. She put a hand on his back and held him in place while she shoved pillows behind him. He reached down with his good hand and tugged the sheet.

His legs were afire from knee to ankle. No holes, no mounds. Nothing crawling, thank God. "It looks like I've been scalded."

"It's petechiae. It's like every last capillary in your legs exploded. Petechiae is pretty common but I've never seen anything like this. Combined with the weight loss it's not good. I didn't feel anything when I palpated your spleen, and your lymph nodes felt fine when I checked your armpits and your groin."

"You checked my groin?"

"Oh, for God's sake, Jimmy, I do it all the time."

"Not on me, you don't."

"You've got nothing I haven't seen a million times before." But now she was fighting a smile. "Anyway, you were still out of it." She stopped, thinking. "You were out for nearly three hours. That's not normal, either. I thought concussion but you're pretty with it, or about as with it as you ever are."

Three hours. Recalling the four he'd lost, he shrank from the thought.

Lizzie had a few more questions. Odd ones: Was he tired, did he get any exercise, was he worried about anything. At last she said, "Your leucocytes look okay, so no sign of infection. Your hematocrit is low but still within normal range. I'm going to admit you."

"No!" He could hear Kit Acker's oddly detached voice declaring that she was being watched. "I don't need to be admitted."

Lizzie came in close, again, and her expression broke his heart. "Jimmy, something's wrong with you. I don't know what it is. You could have anything from Rocky Mountain spotted fever to mono to leukemia. The only way I'm going to know is if we run more tests."

He was so tired. He remembered the thing they'd called Indian sunburn, one of those things passed from generation to generation of kids. You put your hands on the unsuspecting arm of another kid and twisted as if you were wringing out a rag. A nasty thing that hurt like hell. He felt as if that had been done to every limb and every organ in his body. He longed for his own bed and for relief.

The tears came to his eyes again and he closed them quickly, so Lizzie wouldn't see. He felt hounded, harassed, persecuted on all sides. Felt the injustice of it. "No," he said again.

"Sorry, Jimmy, but you don't have a choice. Your blood pressure's still so low I doubt you could stand up without fainting again. You're still tachycardic. We did a CAT scan to make sure you didn't throw a clot when you hit your head but the fact remains that you didn't wake up for three hours. That's not good. Anyway," she said, satisfied and maybe a little smug, "you can't go anywhere before we splint your fingers."

It was a cheerless space, comprising nothing that couldn't be disinfected. The monitor by his bed, tracking heartbeats, blood pressure. A saline bag dripping liquid into him. The sheets and blanket coarsened by some harsh detergent. Lizzie had come by after her shift, glancing at the monitor, clicking through his chart, her expression worried, though she told him his numbers were improving.

"Did you talk to Sam?"

"Everything's fine."

"What did he say?"

"Never mind about that. Are you going to tell me what's going on or what?"

He'd closed his eyes, said something about being too tired, and though she tried, she wasn't able to get anything out of him.

He was tired, but he hadn't slept, or, if he had, only in small patches of time. Most of the night he stared at the ceiling, shame so powerful it oozed from every pore. At least, he thought, he hadn't disappointed anyone, because no one expected anything from him. He had no close friends, no friends at all, though perhaps Mike Dyer was a friend. But that got him thinking of Emily, of all the stupid things he'd said to her on the bridge, the gratitude he should have corrected but hadn't because he was always thinking of himself, though he had a thousand ways of pretending that he wasn't doing so.

No friends and no connections at all except Lizzie and her family, who would not expect anything from him because he'd given them no reason to. He listened to Lizzie after Mass, impatient for her to rush off to her day and relieved when she did. Refused to let the children be altar servers, used the excuse about the formal training, when she knew he could have trained them himself. He hurt her, over and over, and though she'd kept coming back, he had been relentless. He'd pushed her away, kept the children at a safe distance, and never explained because he couldn't. It was for their own benefit, so that none of them would ever feel a presence sinister and malign slithering to them, wrapping around them.

He replayed the thing coming at him through the fog. The same thing that had come at him on the bridge. The same vibration, the same roar, the same cold terror.

And then he had a new thought. What if Anselm Chace's catatonia or whatever it was wasn't a defeat but instead a defense? What if his mind had chosen a recoil that had lasted more than twenty years? In a way, it was better to think he'd willed what he was during those two decades, hiding himself rather than being overcome and trapped with that thing roaring in his ears and eating him alive invisibly.

In one of the psychology books was a section on disassociation, how the mind can retreat to a corner of the brain, away from horror or unpleasant thoughts. Perhaps that was what Anselm had done initially, during the months or years he avoided contact with Reilly and probably all his friends. And then, perhaps, Anselm discovered that it wasn't enough, that the thing could find him there, and at that point had erected walls, sheltered in a small place, the walls between it and him.

He didn't know and couldn't find out since there was no one to ask. No one could know what had been happening inside Anselm's brain. Just as no one knew what was happening in his as his ears conveyed steady breaths that belonged to nothing seen, as his sense grew that something was watching him.

The devil is prowling around like a roaring lion looking for someone to devour.

And his brain, as it always seemed to do, immediately supplied a response: *Fear not, for I am with you.*

Words. They slid over you and did not give you what you needed. All those words to Triona, when she needed to be wrapped up in her mother's arms, feeling her mother's love.

Lying in bed, drifting on some kind of painkiller, his chattering mind slowed. A geyser that was at full throttle the moment he became conscious each morning, telling him what he needed to do, what he was thinking, and never shut off until his brain started dreaming, began to lose energy, as if the water supply slowly was being turned off. Died by half, then half again, then was a trickle. Then nothing. He drifted for a while, lost to the commotion of the hospital, the rain outside his window. His breathing and the other like warp and weft.

He felt it before he identified it: sorrow, a longing for God to walk through the days with him, watch over him as he slept. Sorrow and regret because he wished with all his heart he could believe. Poked lazily through his brain, peered into dark corners. Nothing: not the smallest speck of matter, not a single cell, believed. No reason to believe, nothing in his life on which belief could be founded. He didn't know how anyone did believe, whether it was an effort of will or just a letting go of rationality.

His unbelief didn't bother him at this moment because if it didn't make life any better, it certainly didn't make life worse. Once he was out of the hospital, though, how would he function? He was a bad liar. How could he say Mass? Write homilies? Bring comfort to the sick and the love of God to the dying if he believed God was a kind of metaphysical matrixing?

He lay in darkness—covered by the thin blanket, someone moaning in a room down the hall, the muted conversation at the nurses' station—drifting, four stories above the streets of Newport, and cast his mind back but couldn't find the moment or the day he had stopped believing.

Sam brought the children in the following afternoon. Triona, knees skinned below the cotton shorts, stood as far away as the room permitted, wide eyes never leaving him, as if she thought he'd suddenly reach out and grab her. He felt sad about that; she would never again confide in her uncle because relatives should be predictable, reliable, safe. His niece knew now that he wasn't any of those things.

Willy, though. He brought himself right up to the bed, his arms as white as January, smelling faintly of sunblock. Looked his uncle over, and a lightness came to his eyes. Feigning wonder, he declared, "You are more bruise than man."

The deep voice, the precision of each word as funny as anything else. Jim huffed. "Don't make me laugh; I've got a cracked rib."

But felt something lift off him.

After a while, Sam making small talk and Jim nodding as well as he was able, Triona grew more accustomed to the sight of her battered uncle, becoming more interested as she became more detached; Jim wasn't part of her immediate family and therefore Triona saw no imminent threat to herself.

Jim, too, felt detached, swaddled tightly in pain. He'd been taken off the painkiller, and shortly after, every variety of misery had bloomed into existence. His cheek burned and the throbbing in his hand kept time with his heartbeat. He was icy from the hips down, felt he had been beaten internally; unless he took small sips of air, a stabbing pain in his side took the breath from him. Through it all was the endless, hated breathing.

He pretended to be surprised when Triona announced that a baby was on the way; even that small motion hurt. Sam gave him a sympathetic look and kidded the children about another mouth to feed.

"I will give Charlie my vegetables," Willy said. "I will just eat hamburger and fries."

"You don't know it's a boy, does he, Dad?"

"Charlie can be the name of a boy or a girl," Willy said. "That is the great appeal of the name. But Charlie is going to be a boy."

Sam stepped in before the argument could escalate. "Tell your uncle what we're going to do to the bedroom."

And just like that they forgot Jim was there, lost in preparations for the baby, which discussion included Willy's petition for a dog; he reasoned that a dog would be good company when his mother was up at midnight feeding the baby. Whenever Jim smiled, pain swatted him, but that didn't stop him.

Sam brought them back to their uncle, trying to normalize the experience for the children. "You made quite a splash on the ghost tour."

"That's what happens when you don't drink enough water," Jim said, grateful for the kindness. "Next time I do a ghost tour I'll drink gallons before I leave the rectory."

"Mom and Dad got there before the ambulance," Willy said.

"You can thank Triona for that." Sam set a hand on the back of his daughter's neck. "Her cell phone broke when she fell so she had Willy call us. Triona thinks fast on her feet."

Triona glowed with pleasure.

"Actually, on her bum," Willy said. "There were a zillion people looking at Uncle Jim. I thought they were going to get trampled by the ambulance guys. Mom was crying and Triona was, too, but I knew you were going to be okay, even though Dracula man said you were dead. You were hardly bleeding, and anyway, Mom was there."

"I wasn't crying," Triona said.

Willy ignored that. "The Dracula guy was pretty random. First we take pictures and the only thing we see in the photos is a bunch of little white lights, and he tells us the little white lights are ghosts. Then we go to the church and we take pictures and this time we see faces, but he tells us it is not ghosts, it is matrixing."

"Trinity Church," Jim told Sam. "There's one window that has flawed glass and when you take a picture, the flaws make you think you see faces."

"How does he know that what looks like ordinary lights are ghosts and what actually looks like ghosts are not ghosts? If everybody sees lights, it makes sense to say they are lights and if everyone sees ghosts, it makes sense to say they are ghosts."

Sam shrugged. "Hard to argue with that."

The night was turning to day, the light creeping gradually through the blinds. He could see three quarters of the room without turning: there was the blue faux-leather chair, there was the half-open door to the bathroom. Beside him was a table with a urinal, a small box of tissues, the paper Sam had brought but Jim hadn't read because he didn't want to move his arms.

Which is why he tried not to look down. Despite the fact that his throbbing left hand was lost under the bandages, every time he noticed it he recalled the two fingers bent grotesquely, the nails flat against the back of his hand. His right arm was attached to the drip and he couldn't look at that, either. Beneath his skin was a bit of plastic tubing that Lizzie said was too flexible to break but what if it did, a small piece sucked away by the mad pumping of blood, carried to somewhere that spelled an instantaneous death. He had been aware of the arm as soon as he'd awakened and held it rigid for hours, even though it ached and he longed to move it. When he'd been forced to do so, he felt the world spinning. He hated needles.

He closed his eyes and listened, felt his way around the room. Heard the breathing in his ears. He had no sense of being watched, no unseen presence lurking in a corner or anywhere in the room. Maybe it would come later.

Or not. He was being a big baby.

"Rather large for a baby, I think." Leo ambled into the room and dropped a white paper bag onto the over-bed table. "Cupcakes," he explained, with a measure of satisfaction.

Leo rarely smiled, finding very little in the world to please him. However, he was making an effort. Something twitched at the edges of his lips but then collapsed for lack of conviction. "How are you feeling?"

"I'll live. Thanks for coming in. Lizzie said they'd let me out today but probably not until early afternoon. Oh, God," he said, as the thought struck him. "What happened to the Masses?"

"Celebrated without a hitch. I enlisted Kevin's aid. Quite naturally, he was willing to renounce a little pleasure on the golf course when informed that you were indisposed." Leo pushed the chair to Jim's bed and sat.

"I'm sorry, Leo. I didn't want to be admitted. I've left you a mess to clean up."

"Have a cupcake. You'll feel better." Another attempt at a smile.

"Can't hurt more than it already does," Jim made a like effort, and pain shot up the side of his cheek. He hadn't actually seen his face but he could guess. Bruising and scrapes, maybe a black eye because the skin around his eye felt tight.

"Or look worse than it is. You bring to mind Saint Sebastian, clubbed to death, though the masses of ignorant humanity believe he was killed by a grisly bouquet of arrows."

"Interesting image. You haven't seen my legs. They look like they've been parboiled. Lizzie said it's broken capillaries."

"What's the tally?"

"Two broken fingers." He lifted the hand. "Black and blue all over. Bruised ribs. I did a really good job of it. Weird stuff going on with my heart but not heart disease; Lizzie tells me we don't have that in the family and she's not going to do a cardiac catheterization, thank heaven. She's testing for this and that; I couldn't stop her. She's like a human bulldozer. But she won't find anything."

"She won't?" Leo sat back in the chair, elbows on the fake leather arms, fingers steepled together.

"No. No, she won't. Lizzie was . . ." Jim saw her face again, anxious, despairing, afraid that someone she loved was slipping away from her. ". . . upset. She really wanted to do the tests. But I don't have leukemia or mono or anything else." If he were honest with himself, he was glad to be under Lizzie's care for the time being. Aggravating and stubborn as she was, Lizzie was his sister, his blood, unwaveringly loyal and always on his side, and he was comforted by her presence. He felt less alone, even though the brutally rational part of his brain insisted that he was. "I told her that if I agreed to be admitted, she had to promise she'd get me out of here today unless she finds something major. But she won't."

"You're sure of that." The steepled forefingers tapped together.

Jim looked at it. Considered the odd note in Leo's voice. "Yes," he said at last.

Though he was always disheveled and usually sprinkled with stains or crumbs from the assorted cakes, pastries, pies, or cookies he loved, Leo nevertheless had a certain presence. His face maintained its accustomed wintry expression, but as Leo's eyes rested on him, Jim saw that they weren't cold, they were kind.

"Had enough?" he asked mildly.

Jim snorted, then winced; even that hurt. "Any more and I'd be dead."

Leo said nothing. Still watching, the fingers tapping, patient.

As the silence stretched, a thought pushed itself up through the pain. It came out low, almost inaudible. "What?"

The fingers tapped together again. Still that direct gaze, kindness in it. "I had a call from Martin Reilly."

Heat flushed up from his toes, torching every nerve as it swept up his body. He'd been stupid to involve Reilly. A moment before he'd only been helpless. Now he was exposed. "What did he tell you?"

"Point is, the care of a parish isn't for everyone. There are many ways to serve God."

The world lurched violently. Moving more quickly than Jim had thought possible, Leo was up with the small pan that was on the bedside table. Jim retched in wracking spasms, bringing up clear fluid; he'd eaten nothing all day, had been in too much pain to even look at the food. His eyes felt like they were going to explode but he couldn't stop. It was as if his body were trying to turn itself inside out.

Finally, he was done. His stomach throbbed and his throat was raw; he hadn't noticed that these two things had survived the fall. His arm ached around the IV needle; he'd been leaning on it as he was vomiting; the thought of it made him sweat. Sliding down the pillows, he repositioned the arm. Turned his head to wipe his mouth on the pillow.

Leo brought the tray into the bathroom and was back a moment later. He looked remarkably the same. Shirt a little tight over his old man's belly, a grease stain where he might have swiped the crumbs from a buttered muffin. The slight look of distaste with which he met the world. But his eyes were fathomless now.

"You want me to go under my own steam before they have to haul me away to the nuns? Is that it?"

Leo didn't pretend to misunderstand him. He sank heavily into the chair and folded his hands in his lap. Long-fingered, waxen in the way of the old, and delicate; if his hands had ever known manual labor, all traces were gone. "Ah, well. I told you the converts are generally a bit loony. Point being that Anselm waited too long."

"And that's why Martin Reilly called?" Snarling at Leo wasn't going to change things but he couldn't help his feelings. "To make sure someone gets me to a sanitarium in time?"

"Actually, he sees the matter differently, and we'll leave it there."

He listened to the phlebotomist's cart rolling from room to room, muted conversation at the nurses' station, the beeps of the machines monitoring his blood pressure, his temperature, recording how much oxygen his body was receiving. "Have you called the bishop?"

Leo looked away. "I believe the bishop to be a decent man but I've never thought of him as a discerning individual."

"What does that mean?"

Leo returned to him. "No. I have not called the bishop."

Jim relaxed a little. "Thank you."

Leo nodded. "Well," he said, reaching for the bag of cupcakes, "if you won't, someone must."

Leo peeled the paper from a cupcake and bit. Chocolate, with raspberry frosting. Crumbs rained down.

"What happens if I decide to take a leave?"

"You go, perhaps, to the sisters. Probably to the sisters; they're very good and they have some experience. Point is, they'll do what they can and please God, they'll succeed."

Leo was giving him time to think. After all, it actually was kindness.

Whether his stay with the nuns was temporary or not, he'd probably lose his parish. Who did they have to put in his place? That had become a perennial problem: there just weren't enough priests for any diocese. But even if he recovered, somehow, he wouldn't return to St. Patrick.

And that made him think again about the bishop. Who would decide that he was a liability. The bishop was a vain man, pompous, and none too bright, enamored of the trappings and the power of his office, concerned primarily with the appearance of things. He had known of a priest who'd clashed with the bishop frequently, until the priest had been loaned to a mission parish in Alaska. If the bishop allowed him to retain the clerical collar, it was likely he'd be sent away, too.

His life was here. He believed that who you are is based on love, of how well and in what way you loved other people, but a smaller part was the love of a place, and that could be just as strong. The geography, the topography, the way the wind smelled, the way the seasons painted and repainted the landscape, the sounds of a place. He was, in fact, a man of the island; Reilly was right about that. He fell asleep to the rich notes of foghorns, rose to the intimate chatter of birds and the traffic on Broadway. For him, nothing was more beautiful than the sight of Narragansett Bay from the top of the Newport Bridge, looking out to blue that stretched beyond Aquidneck and Conanicut islands and widened to occupy all of the southern horizon. He could look at that forever and never grow tired of it. He loved the sharp air of a fog, the massing of clouds as a storm came over the water. Loved the way the rain was a gray curtain as storm clouds came up the bay. Loved the way people rushed to the shore after a big storm, to see for themselves where the waves had hurled sand and seaweed, tossed rocks and lifted roads. He loved the way people brought folding chairs to Brenton Point, at the southern tip of the island, set them up on the rocks, and watched the ocean as avidly as if it were a movie. Loved the bay in all seasons, the smell thick and sweet, the water a sunny green-blue in summer, a deeper hue in autumn, and dark blue, nearly black, in winter.

He loved walking along Spring Street, two centuries of houses pressing against the sidewalk. Loved the solid, homely lines of the eighteenth-century designs. And that reminded him of the Brennans and their need.

Meagher had asked him whether he would testify if it came to that, and he'd agreed.

All the people to whom he brought communion, the weddings that were booked, the people who came to the rectory door or called at all hours because there wasn't enough money to pay the rent or the grocery bill. Emily, who trusted him. What would happen if she called once, three times and he never answered, never returned her calls? And Lizzie. Who was going to have a baby. Caitriona and William.

Everything would go away.

It came to him suddenly: the breathing had stopped.

He held his own breath to hear, but no, it wasn't there. No gusting, sighing, or languorous respirations. No huffing or blowing. As if someone had removed the hands that covered his ears, the world was coming to him unfiltered: the squeak as Leo shifted in the chair, footsteps in the hall, the hum of conversation at the nurses' station.

It was listening.

His gaze flew to Leo, who was waiting, not unsympathetically. Of course Leo wouldn't know; he'd never heard the breathing. He managed a single word.

"When?"

"Well, that's up to you. As people say in this era of atrocious euphemisms, 'whatever you're comfortable with.' Though most often, when people say that, they know perfectly well the situation is not comfortable in the least, as pertains here, come to think of it. You can speak to the bishop, or I can, and everything will follow after that. It's up to you to decide."

A last question, the one he was afraid to ask. "What do you think is happening?"

Leo was ready for it. "The pertinent question, actually, is what do you think?"

Jim could have laughed; wasn't that the question he'd been asking without end? If he was truly psychotic, he wouldn't be able to function at all. If he was truly tormented by something unseen, the unseen would have to exist. "If I knew, would I be asking you?"

"I think you know," Leo said quietly.

"It would help to have a second opinion." Finding that irritation worked just as well as anger.

"It wouldn't change anything."

It was hard to think through pain. He could catalog that, anyway, and easily. His body had been sending unvarnished reports to his brain. What was throbbing dully, what was furiously aching, what felt like it was being flensed, what was pounding, what felt like a horde that was crawling beneath his skin and chewing flesh as it moved. He thought he could almost reach in and lift the bones out of the fiery cauldron that was his muscles and organs, arteries and veins, just go in with pincers and lift out white bone.

And hard to follow a single line of thought when despair was overwhelming. What would be the point of life if everyone and everything you loved were taken away?

Anselm Chace had been alone. Not even his closest friend had known that he was fighting a war that was killing him by increments. Anselm had blamed it on pride. Jim could hear his voice in the church, low and angry. PTSD, Lizzie had said, and Jim wondered if his former pastor had become the shell of something human, insentient and unresponsive, because there was no one at his side, no one to help or at least share the burden. For whatever reason, and certainly it could have been pride, Anselm had decided to fight alone.

He wasn't Anselm Chace. He wasn't alone. He'd called Reilly. Reilly had talked to Leo. He didn't see how that could help but at least it was more than Anselm had done. And somehow he had Lizzie and Sam, Triona and Willy, and, yes, Leo: more people to love than he had any right to expect. He had the Brennans and Emily and Maria and her family, the people who filled the pews, the people who came to the rectory door. He kept them all at a safe distance, but still, he couldn't help loving them. And now he felt a deep sorrow at the thought of Anselm, rattling around the rectory at Blessed Sacrament. He had been so alone.

"I've been thinking," he said, not quite having made up his mind, even though for once his thoughts had followed a straight path. He had tallied up everything he would lose but had given no thought to what it might cost him to keep what he had, even for a short time. The agony was almost past bearing now and his mind would not go beyond that, would not even hope that the worst had arrived. Like trying to encompass one's own death, there were limits to imagination, places the mind could not or would not go. His heart sank as he spoke the words.

"I know I need help. But I'm thinking I might wait a bit."

Leo looked impassive.

With a small sigh, the breathing began again.

— 26 —

Bedridden. Some poor soul, wracked by ague, cholera, or the myriad other ills that were the medieval's lot, must have come up with the word after being pricked and pummeled by the straw upon which he lay, and tormented by the fleas and lice and bedbugs and all manner of assorted multi-legged creatures bred by the straw. Jim's mattress was cleaner, certainly, and he was thankful for that, but it was also cheap, and because it was cheap, it was thin. The bed also was reasonably clean but it was old and the slats deeply bowed, a fact to which he had been indifferent until one side of his body had become a throbbing purple bruise. On her last visit to his hospital room, Lizzie had unofficially but no less forcefully prescribed a day of rest and delivered an impassioned encomium on sleep, but his bed rode him, pushing into every sore spot from head to feet, forcing his muscles to a constant resistance that made them ache, taking him to some place far from the Land of Nod. All night he'd start to drift, exhausted, and immediately his body would begin to roll down a gentle declivity to the center of the bed. Any movement was like being sprayed with buckshot, painful in so many places it was impossible to say what hurt most.

He'd been discharged the previous day, as Lizzie had promised, and Sam had hauled him into a car. His brother-in-law had half-carried him through the back door, the kitchen, and hall, holding him under the arm, although Jim felt less stable for it. He'd carted Jim up the stairs and set him on the bed. Jim had assured Sam that he would take it from there and while Sam looked dubious, Jim thought he was relieved to be released.

The next morning, he'd come to consciousness bone-weary from lack of sleep but with no thought about what had happened; that quickly changed when he tried to sit up and swing his legs off the bed. It hadn't helped that he got in and out of bed on his left side. Fire shot up his left arm and someone took a sander to his thigh. He fell back, panting.

"You can't give me five minutes of peace, can you?" he said to the breathing. "No, of course you can't."

Someone had closed the drapes at the two windows, which faced north and in consequence normally brought in as little light as could be managed. The room was subterranean, cool with air hissing through the vent in the floor. He guessed it was no later than eight. Leo would be just beginning the Mass. That meant he was alone in the rectory. Well, he amended, not exactly alone; he hadn't been alone since Blessed Sacrament, but it was doubtful that his companion was likely to assist him in any way. He wasn't hungry but his brain was starting to signal that it would inflict a migraine on him unless he supplied it with caffeine. He would have to make his way to the kitchen, and fairly soon.

The major thing was that he badly needed to pee. No wonder, he thought, with the intravenous drip thinning his blood for countless hours. And no, he wasn't going to look at the bandage they'd taped inside his elbow when they took the drip out. He'd rip it off at some point without looking; why make himself nauseated if he didn't have to?

His gaze traveled over the photos, as it always did, and he let himself sink into them: the excitement tinged with fear as Willy offered a slice of bread to a gull; the shivering ecstasy of two small children peeking over their snow fort. But then he thought of the thing coming at him on Queen Anne Square and he sought the crucifix over the door. Walnut, with Christ carved most likely in ivory. Suffering, but not depicted with the grotesque voyeurism of the German artists. Acknowledged, or not, by generations of priests who'd occupied this room, but always there. Comforting in a way that was different from the photos of the children. More than a century of pastors and priests, believers or willing to act as if they were. He could do that, too. And out of habit, he said a prayer for the souls of all those priests and promised that as soon as he'd seen to his body's immediate needs, he would read the morning prayers.

He sat up and a small heap of clothes swung into his vision. Then he remembered.

Three in the morning or thereabouts. He'd rolled on his hand and was ripped from dreams. In pain, fearing he had reinjured the fingers. He'd lain with his eyes closed, attempting to will himself to sleep, but eventually he'd abandoned the effort and opened his eyes. Stared up, he supposed, at the ceiling, which appeared to him only as a thicker darkness in the dark room.

Newport was quiet. The bars long since closed and the after parties, if there had been any, over; the streets were empty. No foghorns calling to ships in the bay. At this hour, had the wind been blowing from the west, he might have heard the rhythmic sound of tires passing over the expansion joints on the bridge. Perhaps the wind was blowing from a different direction. Or perhaps no wind because no rustle of leaves came to him. He heard his own breaths in a slow waltz with that of his companion.

The air around him was tainted with the stink of the hospital, which had gotten into his hair; he hadn't showered since the accident. The darkness felt heavier, somehow, for it. And as he lay in bed, teasing out the mix of odors that constituted the smell, an image slowly came into focus; depths of light and darkness, then shapes and, finally, light illuminating the shapes. Staring into the night, he saw them clearly.

He saw himself in a small room, strapped with old sheets to a narrow bed, his eyes closed, mouth gaping, his body recoiling from an unseen battering. He saw nuns coming and going, stripping and bathing him and putting him into clean clothes while he shuddered and twitched, his face a mask of agony. Saw his sister leaning over him, showing him a newborn, its head and arms poking out of a soft, blue, baby blanket. His nephew, she said, James. Saw a tall, slender young man sitting by the bed, talking to him in the deep, thin voice that still cracked in places.

Of all the things inflicted on him, this he was sure about. Miserable though he was, his brain was very clear about this: he did not believe it. Would not believe it. Would not believe it because it was so transparently a lie, so obviously the product of a wracked body and brain that had circled around and around itself for endless weeks now, poring over the damage to his flesh, poking into every part of his mind, seeking signs of disorder, faulty synapses, damage from a long-forgotten trauma, a malfunctioning temporoparietal junction.

"Show me something I couldn't imagine," he said to the room. His voice a croak, as if pain had scored his vocal cords. "If you're so set on scaring me, show me where you come from. Show me the godforsaken pit you crawled out of. Go ahead—or go away."

And now he heard murmuring. In the hush of sleeping Newport, in the deep darkness of his bedroom, sounds that might have been speech but were too muted to understand. Steady enough to be a chant. Every hair on his body stood on end.

Something was in the room with him.

At last.

He'd pushed himself up, got his shoulders against the headboard. He was panting with the shock of it. Or not with shock; in fact, he'd expected this. Instead, he was gearing up for a fight. His eyes registered nothing more than shapes. There was the dresser, the chest of drawers, but his eyes couldn't tell him anything beyond that. He might have been miles underground, all light sucked out of the air, the air itself weighted, nearly liquid. He couldn't see but he felt a presence, muttering as if to itself, and the words were indistinguishable, though close to his ear. He thought of Teresa of Avila. No form is seen but the object is known to be there.

Had he been in less pain, he would have been terrified, but pain, he was surprised to discover, was a barrier to fear; his throbbing hand, a thousand pinpricks where he'd scraped his face, the ache of his bruised ribs, were more real to him than anything else.

He knew a moment's satisfaction. "You fucked up," he told the room. "You should have stopped with your army of insects. You should have stuck with the mosquitoes and the maggots and the earwigs. But it's too late. You've racked me and boiled me and grilled me and now I'm in too much pain to care whether you're here or not."

But the murmuring went on and his mind replayed the images: the bed, the body on it silent but eloquent, crackling like electricity.

"You can't kill me; there wouldn't be any point to it. And I don't think you can, anyway. I don't think you have the power to do that."

No response beyond the murmuring. Low, as deeply pitched as distant thunder. Not in a corner of the room, not in any particular location, it seemed to exist in the room like air, all around him. It teased him, made him think that if he strained he might discern words, but if there were words, they weren't in a language he recognized, nor could he tell where one word began and another ended. And then he realized it didn't matter if he understood because it wasn't directed to him. Whatever was in the room with him was communicating with something else, and the communication involved him.

He refocused on what was real, something undeniable, and now he was chronicling his misery, pinpointing the sources of pain, analyzing the variety, from stabbing and burning to aching and gnawing and throbbing.

Still the murmuring, insistent, seeking a way in.

This is your life. Forever.

There were noises among noises. The small creaks around the rectory as wood cooled and contracted in the night air. The exhalations as his lungs exchanged air. The thud of his heart as it pumped blood. Gradually, even the worst of the pain began to recede and he floated, as if in an underground pool. His breath in his ears and silence beyond that. Warm, supported, worry and pain leached out by the black water. His body weightless in the water, arms drifting out, the muscles of his legs relaxed, not needed because the water cradled him. The water and the air the same temperature, which was the temperature of his body. His mind drifting, each thought attenuated, the time between thoughts stretching as his mind wound down. Finally stopping. His mind was nowhere, emptied of thought. His brain superfluous in the womb. This is what it is like to be dead.

Hidden among the thick branches of the venerable maple in the rectory yard, a small disturbance, a rustling, too insignificant to be noticed from the ground, large enough to rouse the sleeping inhabitant of a nest. Sound pierced the damp air, burst into the room. The loud, harsh cry of a blue jay. Two sharp, descending notes of warning: predator.

Jim abruptly came to himself. He was standing by the rectory's side door, his pants on, his arm halfway into his shirt. What had he meant to do?

— 27 —

He needed a plan to get through the next few months. He needed to be a witness for the Brennans, needed to get the religious education program to align with the school year. Needed to sort out the rat problem, pay the balance of the air conditioning. And somehow he had to figure a way to care for those who needed money; maybe he could talk to Bart Meagher about establishing a fund. Needed to perform September and October weddings, couldn't remember but didn't think there was anything in November. He wanted to baptize the new baby, Lizzie's baby. And Lizzie's baby was many months away. He didn't know how he could do it but he wanted to try.

Leo would be watching him. *What do you think?* he'd asked. There was no good answer to that: if he said what he now firmly believed, it would seem he was on the road to madness, and if he said mental illness, the end result was just the same. He didn't need to ask Leo's opinion; Jim didn't imagine the nuns exorcised demons from the patients at the facility they ran in Massachusetts. Reilly, though . . .

The person in the bathroom mirror was almost unrecognizable because a fair amount of the saline appeared to have gone to his face. His left cheek was swollen and lumpy, as if it had been packed with rags; the eye, bloodshot, was a malignant-looking thing lurking at the bottom of a well. A good bit of skin above and below his cheek had been shredded and around the scabs the skin was deep violet and red. He'd have to explain himself for a few days, especially before Mass, because people would be horrified by his appearance. Though now that he thought of it, how was he going to say Mass with only one working hand?

A few minutes later, he was in the kitchen, drinking bitter coffee he'd poured from the pot Leo had made at least an hour before, and trying to make his way through a bowl of cereal. The front door buzzer sounded and was immediately followed by the door opening and a shout.

"In the kitchen," he said. "On your left."

Mike Dyer appeared in the doorway. "Holy Mother of God. Don't tell me one of your parishioners did that."

"What are you doing here?"

"Nice welcome." Mike set a few books on the kitchen table. He might have slept in his clothes; the chinos were wrinkled and gray along the cuffs, and the button-down shirt, which could have been white at one time, was nearly as sallow as Mike's complexion.

"Sorry. I wasn't expecting visitors. It's not that I don't welcome the company."

"Yeah, I know." Mike looked around. "Figured it would be a little cheerier than it is. Inspirational, like all the stained glass at the church. Who did the decorating? Victoria, just after Albert passed? Got any coffee?"

"I meant how did you know?"

"Saw Newport rescue haul you away." He saw Jim's surprise. "Me and about half the tourist population. Thought I'd bring you some reading to pass the time but the hospital said you were discharged. So here I am."

He brought his mug of coffee to the table and sat opposite Jim. The acrid odor of cigarette smoke swept across the table. The urge to cough was strong but Jim didn't think he could manage it without passing out.

"How long you going to be out of commission?"

"Just today, I think."

Mike's laugh turned into a wheeze. "You plan to conduct your priestly duties looking like that?"

Jim knew he shouldn't feel insulted, but he was. In some ways, Mike was worse than Lizzie. "Once word gets around, maybe Mass attendance will pick up."

"Not likely, but possible." Mike was surveying the room. "We are getting into the slow season. Kids going back to college, the music festivals wrapped up. No more big parties on the horizon. Except for the cruise ships, you might be the only game in town."

"Lizzie wouldn't agree with you there. About a slow season in Newport, I mean." A shame because life wouldn't be easy when Lizzie was carrying an extra thirty pounds, much of it in an enormous ball below her chest.

"Suppose so. Emergency room's always rocking. Did you hear about the kayaker they fished out of the Sakonnet River yesterday? Eighty-five years old and paddling solo. You wonder how some people live as long as they do."

"How do you know every single thing that happens in Newport County? Do you own a fleet of drones or something?"

Mike shrugged. "All you have to do is listen. Two or three guys sitting around Cappy's having a beer, people in line at the drug store. We are a yappy species, Jim. Heard two guys yesterday at the Y while I was doing the weights—"

Jim couldn't stop himself. "You work out?"

Mike shot him a look. "Three times a week. Religiously." The word seemed to entertain him. "One of them upgrading the electrical system and the other one rebuilding chimneys at that pile at the south end of the island. Big thing now is buying up one of those piles and turning back the clock so it looks just like it did when Mr. and Mrs. Snoot lived there. New Gilded Age crowd trying to bring back the old Gilded Age. Like there was something worth bringing back."

For once, Jim thought he knew something about Newport's comings and goings. "Is that Seawinds?"

Mike was studying his options on the table: coffee cake, pound cake, a tin of homemade fudge, a bag of saltwater taffy, a plate of molasses cookies, and another of chocolate chip. He finally cut a large piece of coffee cake. "Seawinds, Seabreeze, Seasick, Cecil B. DeMille. Whatever. Henry James called Newport a breeding ground for white elephants. That was 1907. Now we're into reanimation of centenarian pachyderms."

"It's on an outcropping. A lot of chimneys."

"Could be." He took a bite and washed it down with coffee. "When did you make this coffee? 1915? Mason said it was his fourth chimney and was pissed because he didn't get the job until July and it's windy as hell this time of year. You ought to have napkins out, but I'll make do. What's it called?"

"Seawinds. Bart Meagher was telling me about it. He worked on the sale."

"Oh, yeah." Another large bite. "Speaking of yappers. How's that going?"

Jim had to think; it felt so remote that it all could have happened years ago. "So far there's been a restraining order, a suit for breach of contract and a countersuit, and last I heard they were in the discovery phase.

I think that's what he called it." Jim suddenly remembered the battle he'd interrupted in the Brennans' home when he'd brought the air conditioner. "He suspects there's money behind the Taylors because they've hired a Boston firm. I'm a little concerned that will make a difference."

"Dark money, huh?"

"The Brennans are worried, too, but they have a lot of confidence in Meagher. I hope he'll be okay. You did say he was the best."

"He tell you which dark pockets he thinks the money's coming from?"

Jim shrugged, and pain shot up his left side. "Last I heard, he didn't know."

The slice of coffee cake eaten, Mike eyed the pound cake but decided against it. "If the money's coming from a local, it won't be a secret for long. Like I say, people are yappy as little dogs."

Jim was beginning to feel that he wouldn't have the strength to climb the stairs again. If he closed his eyes, he'd fall asleep where he was. But then he brightened. "Meagher thinks it's haunted."

Mike was brushing crumbs off his shirt but looked up, scowling. "Thinks what's haunted?"

"Seawinds."

"Meagher sees spooks? I wouldn't have figured Meagher for one of that crowd. Well, in any case, good luck to Casper. According to the yappers, the owner's a real son-of-a-bitch. Some big contractor for the Navy. Talks like new money: wants everything done yesterday, real short fuse, and a bully. Raum: that's the name. I pity the poor wretch who has to haunt him."

Leo meandered into the kitchen and was more startled to see Jim vertical than he was to find a visitor.

"Your sister told me you'd better be in bed when she comes by." One eyebrow lifted eloquently. "The tone in which the statement was delivered was, I believe, somewhat menacing."

Jim rolled his eyes—which also hurt—but was grateful for Leo's timing, though he wasn't sure he had the energy to stand up.

"I'm throwing myself out of here." Mike tossed back the last of his coffee. "Nearly nine, anyway; gotta get ready to open the store. Feel better."

Leo contemplated the bookseller's retreating form. "And that's odd, too," he said. "Feeling better. Better to wish the afflicted to feel worse, to be less capable of feeling. That would mitigate the pain."

Jim got his legs under himself and looked anxiously at the books.

"Just go to bed. I'll bring the books up later." Leo was eyeing the various offerings on the table. "After breakfast."

The challenge presented by the stairs made him lightheaded. Each muscle protested in turn, as did every bone. Halfway up the stairs black spots danced before his eyes but when he closed them, he could feel his body sliding out of control. Grabbing the railing with both hands, he hauled himself up, step by step.

He'd been half awake earlier, when Leo had poked his head in the bedroom before Mass. Lingered for a minute—Jim could feel him, although he hadn't opened his eyes—and then was gone.

Lying in bed again, the covers up to his chin, he tried to remember. The searing pain in his leg, the cold sweat. The smell a miasma rising to him, sweet and caustic. His hand going to his pant leg, checking for sticky blood. He shifted into what was a vaguely more comfortable position and his gaze wandered to the crucifix again.

He understood none of it. What he knew was that disembodied breathing didn't accompany people through their lives. Something unseen didn't lay siege to one leg and numb the other. People who fell didn't normally sustain the number of injuries he had. He felt as if he'd been beaten by a mob wielding baseball bats. Every organ hurt, every bone ached, the skin all over his body felt raw and his brain throbbed.

First there had been the breathing, years of it. Then the bites that weren't bites on one leg. Then the crater and then the lump and the maggots. The earwig, although was that before or after the numbness? The hole in time—time that had passed without him knowing or remembering. The stench that felt like it was swallowing him. The beating. More time lost. Last night. A vision and visitation.

He sought a pattern, hoping to predict what would come next, but instead of logic, his emotions chattered. Why him? The pastor of a church in the littlest state, on an island in that small state, and not even the plum parish of the island. Was it coincidence that Anselm Chace had served at St. Patrick? Was it chance that he'd been an altar server at Blessed Sacrament? Was it a completely random thing? And if not, why would anything be bothered with him?

He didn't want to dwell on what had happened in the small hours before dawn. Let the past remain past. It was hours ago, receding second by second, and he wouldn't revisit it. He had obligations to fulfill, things to do in the next few months to ensure that St. Pat's would pass to the next pastor in good order. He needed a month, maybe two. He'd like to hang on until Lizzie had her baby but that might not be possible.

His parents smiled at him from the chest of drawers, his father sporting wide sideburns and the Ennis ears, his mother's hair straightened and pulled back with a clip. They looked comfortingly ordinary and that was the way he remembered the house he grew up in, with light green wall-to-wall carpeting, an overstuffed sofa and chairs. His bedroom had been deep blue—he'd chosen the color when he was six—and he remembered his father standing on a chair, fluorescent stars and planets in hand, a large book on the bed and opened to a map of the night sky that showed him how to arrange the constellations and planets on the ceiling. Lizzie's bedroom had been white, the counterpane pink until Lizzie announced that she hated pink; thereafter, it too had been white. Lizzie could sometimes make him mad when they were kids; he didn't see why she opened her mouth as often as she did, why she couldn't let things lie. He thought that was the way she was made, that their mother knew it and didn't try to suppress it; both parents believed in letting their children be who they were.

His father had taken him to Fenway Park. The air had been cool but the sun warm; they'd sat only about ten rows behind first base. He knew all the players, had pictures and posters in his room at home. He was looking forward to seeing his favorites that year: Boggs and Clemens and Evans and Burks. But as they settled into the seats, their franks and fries in brown boxes on their laps, he'd looked around the ballpark, familiar to him from other days, other games, but never as bright as it seemed then. *This*, he thought, *is when summer really begins*. And he'd glanced at his father, who saw something in his expression and echoed it. They watched in silence, side by side, as the players ran onto the field and went through their warm-up routines, and without a word being spoken, he'd felt his father's joy in him, and something warm bloomed, suffusing him with happiness.

He hadn't thought about his childhood in years, but even so, other things were easy to find. Christmas morning and their mother unwrapping the sweater Lizzie and he had bought for her, pretending to be surprised, though Lizzie and he didn't know it then. Going to Bellevue Avenue with their father, who gently steered them away from the harsh colors that caught their eye to the softer colors their mother preferred. Driving down to a clam shack in South County, their father whistling along with the radio. And even earlier, their mother wrapping him in a towel as he emerged shivering and blue-lipped from the ocean, pulling the rough cloth around his shoulders and rubbing up and down his arms to get the circulation going, she told him, while he danced on the sand to warm up. Making a fort out of sofa cushions and two blankets, hiding there in semi-darkness with Lizzie.

Lizzie. He hadn't wanted to hurt the people he loved. And despite everything, he had.

Leo came slowly down the hall, stopped in the doorway. "Where do you want me to put these?"

"Thanks for taking Mass this morning."

Leo set the books on the table beside the bed and looked down at him. He had crumbs on one side of his mouth. Coffee cake, probably. And possibly a cookie or three. "You could hardly have done it yourself. You must be feeling better, though, or at least well enough to want breakfast, but you look even more ghastly than you did last night. The bruising is rather lighter in color but has revealed the infinite variety of the spectrum."

"I saw it in the mirror this morning," Jim said. "Egg-yolk yellow, a mossy green. If it's a spectrum it's a grisly one."

"That was the bookseller? Reminds me a bit of my father. Chain-smoker. Dead before his sixtieth birthday. I often think I should go in but why buy when we have a perfectly good public library?"

"I'm going to take tomorrow's Mass," he said firmly. "Our Lady of Sorrows."

"Oh, I don't know. It may be a bit premature." Leo nodded to Jim's left. "Your hand, after all."

"I can manage with one. And people will just have to get used to my face."

Leo considered it. "We'll see what tomorrow brings."

He turned to leave.

"Thanks for coming to the hospital," Jim said.

"No trouble," Leo said absently, and then left.

And that was as odd as anything else. The ordinariness of it.

He listened to rain spitting against the windows; it was the kind of day that couldn't decide what it was, overcast one minute, brighter the next, the air heavy with moisture, then spilling a few drops. He looked at the small stack Mike had brought. He'd have to roll onto his left side to pick them up. Or haul himself to a sitting position. Either one did not seem appealing. And at this point, when he'd finally admitted the truth, neither was worth the effort.

He was dozing when he heard the voice. His eyes flew open.

"Willy."

His nephew stood in the doorway. The wide mouth like Lizzie's, his father's Roman nose. Scrawny arms protruding from another neon t-shirt, orange this time. Baggy cargo shorts. Black sneakers. Large black sneakers; his feet were sizes too big for his body.

"I have come to cheer you up." The deep, cracked voice. Just the voice could make you smile.

"Does your mother know you're here?"

"Mom is at the hospital, yelling at people."

He should have been frightened for his nephew, should have insisted that he leave. Instead, he told himself he had gained ground after his late-night battle; today the breathing was a soft sigh, a gentle breeze on an early summer day. The truth was, though, that he was pleased. More than pleased; he was thrilled that one of the children had come to visit him. He pushed up in bed and braced himself with a pillow. "Does anyone know you're here?"

"Yes." The word drawn out, indicating that Jim should have known. "I called Dad. It is too rainy for the beach and I am too young to babysit myself. I told Dad you were going to babysit me until lunch. Triona will be home at lunch, although I do not think she is a capable babysitter. I brought a chessboard."

"Your father was okay with it?"

"Why should Dad have an objection to chess?"

Jim was grinning. "How did you get in?"

"Through the door." Nothing gave him away unless you watched his eyes, which were ready for the next ridiculous question, anticipating his answer.

Jim gave up. "I don't know how to play chess."

Willy set the chess set on the bed. "I am glad to hear that. Dad has been teaching me and I never win. You will be performing a small service for humankind, preventing one child from becoming permanently disheartened."

Lizzie arrived late in the day, bearing a large bowl of macaroni and cheese. "Eat it all. You need to gain weight. And here's a slice of pecan pie. Pecan pie is calorie-dense."

He had been dozing again and sleep was slow to leave him. His mouth was dry but at least it was one part of his body that didn't hurt. "What time is it?"

"Six. Leo says you've been in bed all day. Sit up." She yanked the pillows from under him and punched to flatten them as he levered himself to approximate a vertical position. "After eating this you should do some walking so you don't get clots. Eat."

The bowl in his lap had blue flowers on a white background. He thought he remembered it from childhood. "I never feel hungry when I first wake up."

Lizzie put her face close to his. "I'll give you a choice, Jimmy: either eat or I'm going to make you pull down your pants so I can see what your legs are doing."

Jim picked up the fork.

"Everything was negative," she said, watching him carve a lump out of the mountain of macaroni; it was overdone and he could picture it dropping like a weight down a well, splashing when it hit his stomach. "No concussion, no heart disease, no malignancies anywhere, nothing bacterial or viral."

"You thought I had cancer?"

"I'm still not sure you don't," she said bluntly. "We didn't pick up anything on the tests but you have lost a lot of weight. I haven't been thinking of zebras but maybe I should."

He was contemplating the glutinous clump on his fork, wondering how much he was required to eat before Lizzie would go away. "Zebras?"

"Yeah. When you're in medical school you learn about all these weird diseases like nocardiosis and kuru. They're so rare that you'll probably never see a case but when you first start your practice, you hope to see something exciting so when a patient comes in, you look for something exotic. Anyway, one of the things they tell you is that when you're examining the patient and taking a history, you should be trying to rule out the most common stuff, not the exotic stuff. Your patient is a lot more likely to have the flu than he is to have dengue fever; in other words, your patient probably is a horse rather than a zebra. Get it?"

"I just fainted, that's all."

Her gaze traveled over him. "Yeah, that's why you're skeletal. When I first saw you I thought you were dead."

Lizzie never intended to shock; she just couldn't help it.

"Did Willy tell you he came to see me?"

Her expression softened marginally. "Sam told me."

Once you got past the idea that a ten-year-old boy had decided to visit his ailing uncle, a priest who lived in a rectory, it had been a perfectly normal morning. They played chess. They chatted. Rather, Jim asked questions and his nephew answered. Jim listened through the breathing. No ratcheting up of pain, no untoward noise: nothing disturbed the first real conversation he'd ever had with Willy. He kept telling himself that he and his nephew were talking, imprinting the idea of it on his brain, the thrill of it on his heart.

He maneuvered the yellow lump to one side of his mouth. "He is one amazing kid."

"Yeah. We don't know where we got him."

"Well, wherever he came from, don't give him back. So." He swallowed, and broke another chunk off the Everest of food to show that he intended to follow directions. "Triona still upset? I didn't mean to scare her."

"Sam took the kids to Frosty Freez after dinner." She was up now, looking at the photos on the dresser, folding the spread that he'd kicked off the end of the bed. "I don't remember this one of Triona at the beach."

"You gave it to me."

"Well, anyway, she's fine."

He took a deep breath. "She thinks you don't love her anymore."

She dropped the spread on the bed. "What? For the love of God, why would she think that?"

He explained.

"All I did was tell her not to do it again. That's it. That's all I said. Why would she totally freak out about that?"

She was genuinely mystified; that was the amazing part of it. "Just talk to her. She needs some reassurance. But don't tell her I told you what she said."

"I won't say anything: I'm not an idiot, Jimmy." She was up again, folding the clothes he'd dropped on a chair, pulling the curtains wider. Agitated. Angry, actually.

"Everybody thinks I'm the reincarnation of Genghis Khan or something, laying waste to all before me. Just because I see something that needs to be done and I do it. I can't help it if people take it the wrong way." She stood by the window, looking out. Glancing over her shoulder at him, "Anyway, we can't all be as hypersensitive as you are."

He listened to the rain hitting the windows and studied her figure, the slender, freckled arms, the narrow shoulders. She'd never been good with subtlety, the thousand little cues in speech and manner that most people began to read before they could even walk. He suspected that Triona wasn't the only reason she felt bruised but he wouldn't ask about her conversation with Sam; she'd told him that things were fine and he didn't need to know the details. But for the first time in his life he felt sorry for his sister.

"How are you feeling? Any morning sickness?"

"I never had it with Triona or Willy and I don't have it now." She crossed to his bed again. "In any case, I'm too old to be having another kid. Women my age are at higher risk of hypertension and gestational diabetes. There's also an elevated risk that the kid will have some kind of chromosomal defect. I'm praying that everything will be okay but I'm not going to worry about it." She moved to the blanket, pulling it up nearly over his head, then folding it back so it lay neatly from his waist to the end of the bed. "No point worrying. I leave it in God's hands. What's going to happen will happen whether I worry or not."

"Does Sam know about the risks?"

"Keep eating." She sat once more in the chair but her eyes were roaming, searching for disorder. "You think I'm going to tell him that? It would freak him out. Maybe he looked it up online; I don't know. Or maybe he didn't." Coming back to him, her eyes had softened. "You should have seen his face when I told him: I thought he was getting an MI and I'd have to whip out the defibrillator. Anyway, he loves kids. If I popped out another twenty, he'd be thrilled."

"I'm glad that all's well."

She fixed him through narrowed eyes. "Jimmy, despite what everyone thinks, I'm not an idiot. I know you keep trying to change the subject. Are you deliberately starving yourself to death? And no, that's not a rhetorical question."

"I've been busy."

"I saw you naked." She put up a hand to forestall him. "I've seen a million penises, okay? They're not that interesting, believe me. Anyway, you've got significant wasting and you don't get to that extreme just by being busy. So are you going to tell me what's going on or not?" She stared, letting him feel her determination.

He stared back at her, his mind going blank. Not a hard thing to do with the ever-present breathing; if you didn't think about what it was, it could be as soothing as waves breaking on a beach.

"All right," she said at last. "We'll just chat about other things." She glanced around and spotted the books. "What are you reading these days? The pope? Lives of the saints?"

"Some of them are for Triona. Willy took his. Maybe you can take Triona's with you?"

"She's probably about a dozen books behind but I'll take them home. What's this other pile?" She picked up a book and read the title: "*Living with PTSD*." Dropped the book on the table and gave him a look. "*Psychosis and its Evaluation*. Lovely." She read the title of the next book and then the next. He watched the flush bloom on her cheeks. "What is this?"

"Mike brought them. I thought I was interested in abnormal psychology a few weeks ago but it's pretty dull. I have to tell Mike I've moved on. I couldn't understand any of it, anyway."

She was silent but he could feel her watching him as he ate. "So first you come to the hospital totally freaked out about your leg but there's nothing there. Right after that you were asking me about catatonia. And that PTSD guy. Father Muldoon."

"Chace," he said automatically.

"You start telling me about seeing ghosts—"

"I don't see them."

"And who knows what else you're seeing. Anyway, you've lost all this weight and you look like there's something systemic happening, but I can't find anything."

She was working up to something and even though he knew it was futile, he made an effort to stop her. "So that means there's nothing wrong."

"For God's sake, Jimmy, have you looked in the mirror?" Exasperation shot her out of the chair. She seemed to tower over him, a roman candle about to explode.

He shut his eyes. "I don't want to argue with you."

"You don't need the books: I'll tell you what's wrong. You're having psychotic episodes. You need a psychiatrist; I don't do that stuff."

He knew she was a great diagnostician. Knew that she could put her finger right on a problem that other physicians couldn't have detected without the help of scans and blood tests.

"Believe me, there's nothing wrong with my mind."

"You've got all these pictures of the kids but you've never offered to babysit them until this week. You won't let them be altar servers. You didn't want to go near them when they were babies. I kept telling you they wouldn't break if you held them but that wasn't it, was it? You weren't afraid you'd drop them; you were afraid you'd freak out on them. That's it, isn't it?"

"I wasn't wrong, was I? The one time I babysat I went down like a sack of potatoes." He was hoping for a smile, which did not come. "Maybe I have the gift of prophecy."

She sat on the bed beside him.

And took his hand. Her skin lightly freckled, the fingers long and graceful, nails trimmed short and neat.

The hospital room was white in his memory: white walls, white pillows, white sheets and blanket. Their mother nearly so, a gray pallor on her cheeks, her lips blue-tinged. Her breath coming at long intervals. He hadn't recognized death when it came. Lizzie had, though. And when she had, his sister became someone else in that moment, as if her essence had departed with their mother: her expression gone slack, emptied of emotion, as if she didn't know how to feel. On the other side of the bed, Jim had fought every good instinct, had conquered compassion, sympathy. Love. Instead of holding her, giving her warmth and comfort, he'd given her prayers. Words. Endless words.

How could she still love him when he had given her so little cause?

"Don't worry," he said and gently removed his hand. "Father Chace just kind of threw me for a loop."

"Don't worry? Do you have any idea how sick you are? Do you actually want to die?" He could see her searching for something, her brain working faster than his could. "Jimmy, psychosis can be caused by lots of things. Medication, stress—and I'm thinking it probably is stress. You've always been too sensitive. I know a woman in Providence who's really smart. Nupur Balakrishnan. We were in medical school together. I called her when you were in the hospital and she can make time for you this week. You probably just need some meds."

That was the flip side of a strong will: Lizzie made plans for you and then pushed you to follow through. He remembered nearly drowning at the beach one summer, Lizzie deciding she would tow him on a boogie board, bullying him onto it, his hands gripping the sides in terror because he knew she'd go out too far. Their mother must have been reading her book because she didn't notice when the wave knocked Lizzie over and threw him off the board and into the roiling spume. The burn of salt water in his nostrils as he was slammed to the bottom. His scalp scraping against a quahog shell, his body rolling over and over. He didn't die. Someone pulled him out of the water, but it wasn't Lizzie, who hadn't known the wave was coming; there hadn't been big waves before that. Lizzie took charge and, mostly, things went right, but not always. Even at four or five, he knew that.

"I'm not going to a psychiatrist."

"You want to freak out in the middle of Mass? You want to have some kind of psychotic episode in the middle of a wedding and think something's attacking you?"

He took a breath. "Maybe something *is* attacking me."

"Look, if you want me to, I'll take a day off and go with you."

There had been a freshman at Salve who sometimes dropped by for chats. Unusual in itself; when they got to college, most kids ran wild for a year or two, at least. Average height, a little thick around the middle, wavy, black hair that was greasy, a few days' growth of beard standing in little patches. He'd lean against the office door and ramble, most times making sense and sometimes not. Jim had tried to help in all the ways available to him but the boy had resisted. Sophomore year, no more visits, and he'd run into the boy one day; he seemed to be walking through water, pushing slowly through it. A few halting sentences delivered in a flat voice. The boy lasted a semester, then disappeared from campus.

"I'm not taking medication. There's nothing wrong with my brain. Besides, I need to be to be vigilant."

"Vigilant?" A shriek that penetrated every corner of the rectory. "Holy Moses, you actually think something's attacking you?"

He knew what he knew. Nevertheless, there was a problem with his logic. If God did not exist, neither did God's adversary. He set the bowl on the nightstand and closed his eyes. Everything hurt, every last cell pained him.

"You really think you're being attacked?"

"Yes."

Lizzie was incredulous. "By what? Monsters? Zombies? Succubi? Demons? Satan himself? You really think that?" Judging by the volume of his television, Leo's hearing wasn't what it once had been, but the old priest wasn't deaf. Jim refused to imagine what Leo must be thinking. "Why for the love of God would anything torment you?"

The breathing, steadier than his own, carried him along for a few beats while he wished himself anywhere else. "I don't know."

He knew Lizzie wouldn't believe him, no matter what he said. No one would. He knew that he was a weak man, faithless to God, faithless to his own flesh and blood, and therefore not worth the effort it took to torment him. But hearing her dismiss him so easily, so confident in her assessments and opinions, never a moment of self-doubt. At eight years old, at twenty, at nearly forty. He hated her for a moment. Just for a moment. He couldn't help it; if the situation were reversed, he would have believed her.

He opened his eyes and the room looked gray; Lizzie, too, part of a world he couldn't access. "This isn't normal," he insisted. "You don't know the half of it," and seeing that look come into her eyes, "and I'm not going to tell you, so don't bother asking. I've got a million things wrong with me and you've run every test you can think of and the best you can do is say what it's not."

"Jimmy, listen to me. Listen, will you? If the obvious diagnosis is staring you in the face, you don't go hunting for something exotic. You had a psychotic episode. More than one. Probably caused by stress."

"And that caused the weird thing with my legs, and the tachycardia and all the rest of it?" he said stubbornly.

"There are a million bizarre little viruses out there. I think that's what's going on with your legs; we ruled out pretty much everything else. If you had some strange virus, it could have run its course over a few days and by the time we ran the blood tests it was no longer live. You probably had a mild fever and didn't notice it. The fainting and all the rest of it is probably diet-related. That's the way you've always reacted. Everything goes to your stomach: when we were kids, any time you were sick or upset about something you stopped eating. Not to this degree, but you didn't have psychotic episodes when you were a kid."

"I am not having psychotic episodes."

"I'm going to make an appointment with Nupur and you're going to go. Even if I have drag you there myself."

He didn't remember ever lying all day in bed; certainly he hadn't as an adult. He suffered through colds and staggered through everything else, going early to bed early now and again when he hadn't needed a thermometer to tell him he had a fever. After Lizzie left, he listened to the birds and thought briefly about checking the feeder, worried that he wouldn't make it to the feeders and back again, heard the traffic on Broadway, fell asleep, and awakened again to the birds and the traffic and the voices on the sidewalk, and he had a feeling of life rushing past him, as if he stood on the side of a highway from present to future, and all the world except him were on their way to something better or merely more.

He realized he was listening for knocking. He'd put down a handful of traps and hadn't caught anything. He had walked around the rectory, checking to see if the foundation had holes large enough to admit a rat. If there were holes, he didn't find them. He also didn't hear knocking.

Anselm rattling around the rectory. Had anything visited him while he was at St. Patrick? Or was it just the issue with the other priest? It could have been child abuse but Anselm would have taken exception to a lover, as well, of either gender. Or it could have been nothing related to sex, though that seemed unlikely. St. Patrick, apparently, the beginning of the end for Anselm. A good reason to haunt it, if you believed in ghosts.

Jim did not. Nothing his eyes couldn't see: not God, not the saints, not ghosts.

He read his breviary. Recalled his conversation with Triona and skittered away from it, embarrassed by words and more words, choosing instead to think about Willy's visit. And then, because he didn't have the energy to get out of bed, he pulled himself to a half-seated position and reached for one of the books on the nightstand. Psychosis, apparently, was a symptom, not a diagnosis. It could be the first manifestation of schizophrenia or some other psychotic disorder, or it could be an isolated incident. Psychosis was thought to be the product of genetics and psychological stress that happened early in life, while the brain was still developing. Illness, lack of sleep, drug use, a brain injury, or mental trauma, like the death of a loved one, could trigger psychosis, and adolescents were more likely to experience it, possibly because of the hormonal changes that happened in the brain during puberty.

He couldn't pretend that it didn't fit. Psychological stress early in life, and mental trauma later, could trigger an unmooring from reality. Psychosis was a brief, recurrent, or permanent severing of the ties that anchored you to reality. You heard things that weren't there, saw things that didn't exist, believed things that weren't true. You could be depressed or anxious, could have trouble sleeping and struggle through the day. You could become paranoid.

Psychotic disorders comprised a host of illnesses with frightening names. He went to the chapter on schizophrenia, which was something he'd at least heard of. He saw the list of behavioral changes and didn't recognize any of them. He didn't think he had any compulsions or repetitive movements, or at least not more than he had observed in others. He didn't have aggression or hostility. Then he came to the cognitive and psychological changes, which included hearing voices, having hallucinations, feelings of persecution, religious delusion, fear, memory loss. He'd never met anyone who had schizophrenia. He didn't know but he suspected that someone who had the illness would be unable to do exactly what he was doing now, wouldn't be able to do a little reading, immediately apply that reading to oneself, and then talk oneself down from terrifying certainty. But, of course, he couldn't be sure. He'd never encountered anyone who had the disease.

He didn't think he was ill. Had been absolutely certain until Lizzie stormed into the bedroom—he hadn't been awake when she'd entered but he knew his sister: rather than walking into a room, she took it by force. What if Lizzie was right? He had no experience with demons but she had plenty of experience with illness. One of her great talents was as a diagnostician. Everything he experienced, all the things he thought of as torments, could as easily be products of his own mind rather than of an outside force. A little more than one percent of Americans had schizophrenia, but that was more than two and a half million people. There were no numbers for demonic torment but he knew it would be a zebra in Lizzie's universe.

Lizzie wasn't always right. But this time, what if she were?

— 28 —

When I started dating Rob I was a twenty-seven-year-old virgin. I expect that's uncommon but I never did any research and so I don't know how uncommon it is. Maybe I'm in the tenth percentile, maybe the fifth or possibly the second. At one time, it mattered to me. I thought the rest of the world, the non-virgin world that is, was in on some sort of grown-up secret and that I was on the outside looking in. In college I knew a few girls who were unusually self-possessed and at Metro pretty much everyone was skipping from self-confidence into just plain arrogance. And sophisticated and so blasé you'd imagine that if a bomb went off beside them, they'd do nothing more than raise an eyebrow before they dived back into their martini. I believed that everyone had something that I lacked, some deep knowledge that was the spring from which all that urbanity flowed. When I was in college, and throughout my twenties, I thought that what I lacked, one important difference between me and all the people I knew, was sexual experience.

I'd dated men before Rob. Not many, and none for long. You'd think for the first few dates a person would be on his best behavior but they weren't. They'd down one drink after another, they'd boast about what they owned or who they knew, they'd tell you where they were now and how far they would go in life, they'd complain about their last girlfriend and women in general, they'd enumerate the parts of you that appealed to them. They'd try to grope you throughout dinner and then leave you to find your own cab. Or they'd want to "move on to the next part of the evening." I don't know how any woman would want to have a second or third date with any of them. I certainly didn't. When I declined to have sex on a first date, one guy accused me of being a lesbian, threw the word at me with all the savagery he could muster. I'm not a lesbian or a ballbuster or a man-hater or anything else they hurl at you when they're disappointed.

Men can get mean if you don't want to have sex after a few dates. And why would you want to have sex with a guy like that?

The fact is, sex frightened me. Women have a little power when they have their clothes on. Not nearly as much as a man does, of course, but some. When women have sex with a man, they lose whatever power they have. You're naked, for one thing, and you lose power being naked because you can't immediately run out the door if things go south. And in my experience, they can go south very quickly. So yeah, you're there with not a stitch on and the man is bigger than you and outweighs you by a good seventy pounds and their strength is in their back and arms. Once you've shed your clothes, you've got nothing other than your wits between whatever the man wants and you don't, and I never liked the idea of that.

I never saw what women got out of sex, anyway. The vast majority of women don't get orgasms from sex. I've read that at least seventy-five percent don't have an orgasm unless they are manually stimulated, so the point of intercourse as physical pleasure eluded me there. And I never could see myself having babies, unlike some women I knew in college, the "ring by spring" seniors whose life plan was to get engaged before graduation. I'm not kidding: that was their entire life plan. Two of my college friends married men who were miserable, immature and oafish and vaguely misogynistic, and that was the bargain they made with themselves because they wanted babies. As I say, the idea of being pregnant and giving birth wasn't something I ever pictured for myself. So that eliminated the other reason that I'd yearn to be, as the saying goes, deflowered.

Women like romance. They like Hollywood's romantic comedies and romance novels. Not all women, of course; there are the mystery lovers and the literature lovers, and the women who would rather go shopping or play tennis. But a lot of women like romances and I think if they didn't, they'd never have sex. Instead of looking at the world the way it is, romances describe a world the way women wish it to be, with alpha males who fall under the spell of a certain woman and become completely devoted to her, fighting off threats real and imagined while talking about their feelings as frequently and openly as women do. The message is that a woman needn't have reservations about a man who's aggressive and ruthless because he'll turn into Mr. Forever Devoted to You when he falls in love, and the only thing he'll ask of you is that you get orgasms before he does. I think women eat up romances because if they didn't, if they really looked at the world, they'd never want to have sex because what's in it for them?

The flip side of this is the male romance. Romance is never the point of stories written for men; usually they're hunting down some criminal or trying to save the world from asteroids or aliens and romance happens as a nice perk. Romance for men is nothing more involved than sex with a beautiful woman with a spectacular body and the libido of an eighteen-year-old boy. Women in these stories tend not to talk much, or wear much, either. Some of them run around with no underpants. How many actual real, living women run around with no underpants? It's unhygienic.

What these two kinds of romance have in common is that all the women belong to that elusive twenty-five percent of women who have an orgasm during intercourse, and just before (women's romances) or at the same time (men's romances) the men do. Talk about a willing suspension of disbelief.

I shouldn't have to tell you that these passionate encounters never result in a diagnosis of something nasty. In the world of fantasy, by which I mean the whole of publishing and all of Hollywood, no one ever gets syphilis or gonorrhea or HIV or even herpes, though twenty-five percent of Americans have genital herpes. There are no trips to the doctor because you've developed sores or a rash or a drip or an itch. That doesn't happen in the world of make-believe.

Maybe I overthink things.

I didn't date in high school and I did very little in college. I saw college as a kind of paradise, with brilliant professors, fascinating courses, smart students, and profound discussions late into the night; in other words, everything home hadn't been. And for the most part, it was. I graduated *summa cum laude* and was proud of myself (no one else was), especially because I never took a course because it was easy and would boost my GPA; instead, I pored over the offerings each semester and selected the ones that seemed the most interesting. I majored in art history and did some studio art, but I also took some biology, some chemistry courses, a couple of foreign languages, a little literature, and a little history.

The first party I went to was my freshman year, and it was at Harvard. It was crowded and hot and there was a lot of alcohol and noise. Some guy came up to me and started talking about himself; he was related to someone famous, though I don't remember who, exactly. He was about two inches shorter and had drunk much more than I. I remember being glad that already I had someone to talk to, although I wasn't doing much talking. My fear had been that everyone would know I was a hick and I'd end up standing around watching my friends make a splash. I was a little bored by the guy, who droned on and on, and I think I wasn't particularly paying attention because it seemed a little abrupt when he suddenly leaned in to kiss me. And in the second I was deciding whether I wanted to kiss him back, he shoved his hand under my belt and into my pants.

For a moment I had no idea what to do. Then I was out of the building and on the lawn, shaking like I'd stepped on a live wire, and panicked that someone I knew might have seen it. I don't remember how I got back to school, and I don't remember his face. I do remember how I felt, though. I didn't go to another party for three years.

I didn't meet many men in college; I went to a women's college so you'd have to leave campus to find them and I rarely did. In college, I had two main areas of study and I became proficient in both. The first was art history; the other, as I've said before, was how to simulate a privileged upbringing. In my case, the latter meant avoiding topics like my hometown, my summer jobs, my scholarship, and focusing on visual clues like hair, makeup, and clothing. By the time I graduated, I knew what kind of job I should have, how to dress to get the kind of job I wanted, where to live in Manhattan, and which blocks were perfectly acceptable if you couldn't afford to live on one of the best blocks in the city.

I had friends in the city. I went to alumni events in Manhattan and met more people. I didn't realize it then, but I'd set myself on a certain track without knowing what it would mean. To an elite college, to art history, to New York and the right address in Manhattan and to Metropolitan. I thought it would be a secure world, a world where the sun beamed down every day. So, yeah, it was a very small world. My college friends had jobs in art galleries, or in publishing, or they worked at various nice nonprofits and they earned almost nothing but it didn't matter because their parents had bought their condo and given them an allowance. The men I knew through them were lawyers or worked on Wall Street and the money they made allowed them to buy a summer place somewhere, or a boat, or to go skiing in the Andes in July.

I made a rich girl's salary—peanuts—and I was supposed to be happy about it because it was a glamorous job and other people would have jumped at it. The thrill wore off fairly quickly and I began to feel I was just moving stuff around, from dead rich people to living rich people. There was some decent art, but also truckloads of things I didn't care about: necklaces and sports memorabilia, furniture and Chinese vases, rugs and eighteenth-century guns. While I was helping people sell all the junk they'd inherited I started to see my college friends pair off with the men in the crowd. You'd be meeting them regularly for a movie or Sunday brunch and then they wouldn't be available anymore; they'd have disappeared into coupledom and eventually you'd get a save-the-date for their wedding. In the first few years after graduation, there were a lot of weddings, which wreaked havoc on my bank account. I'd look at the groom and if he were marrying one of the ring-by-spring women, I'd wonder what it was about him that convinced my friend that she wanted to spend the rest of her life with him. A few years out of college the next rash of weddings happened and I'd look at the groom, and he'd be a little beefy but would have a cloudless brow and a sweet face and I'd wonder how my friend found someone like that in the city.

I had two nice male friends. Todd was gay, but the other one was definitely straight, and at one point or another I'd think his suggestion for dinner or a play might actually be a date but it never was. The men who asked me out tended to be arrogant and aggressive, men who took you to the restaurant of the moment and then expected you to shed your clothes as payment for an expensive meal. Or the ones who invited you to a party and looked you over carefully when they came to the door, deciding whether your appearance reflected well on them. They were the ones who'd put you in a cab at the end of the night and good luck to you if the guy behind the wheel was a psychopath. The one nice guy who asked me out took me to dinner, and then to a bar where he drank one beer after another and told me about his dead mother, his brutal father, and his awful childhood, and then never called me again.

I'm pretty sure there is something wrong with me.

Rob was fun at the beginning. He met me for lunch, took me to dinner, and we went to exhibit openings and the opera. We went to lavish fundraisers. People knew who he was; politicians would come over to us and talk, and I would stand beside Rob, smiling because no one ever expected me to open my mouth. My only job was to look interested, which is more difficult than you'd think it would be. The big stress was finding the appropriate clothes.

For a while, Rob didn't push for sex and I thought that must be because he was in his early forties and past the age in which men see everything as a prelude to sex. It was a surprise and a relief. At the end of the evening he'd give me a kiss in the car and I'd go to my building, giving him a little wave as he drove off.

Rob never asked questions, not even how my day or week had been. He usually called on a Tuesday or Wednesday to remind me of a Friday or Saturday date. After a spectacular party one evening and a nightcap at a chic bar, he invited himself to my apartment. Thank God the roommates weren't in. All I'll tell you about that is that it was mortifying because when Rob encountered an obstacle, I knew he was mystified because he grunted an interrogative but kept on pushing. Perhaps he'd never had sex with a virgin.

After that night, I didn't feel like I'd crossed to the other side or that I was in on any secret. Sex was something, but it was something like a deep facial, more painful than you expected it to be, leaving you raw afterward, and of dubious benefit, but all the women you knew did it and now you'd done it, once. It wasn't at all like graduating *summa cum laude*.

Then he dumped me.

We were supposed to spend the weekend in Newport; we were going to a party at one of the mansions. I knew very little about Newport, even though some of my coworkers preferred it to the Hamptons. It felt exotic, I don't know why, like Shangri-la. I did some research, as earnestly as if I were gleaning bits of information for a Metro catalogue. I scoured the stores for the right dress and what I ended up with looked as expensive as it was. I liked that. So when he called to say the weekend was off—he said he had to work—I felt as if all those hours of hunting had been wasted. And when my other friend at work mentioned a mini-vacation in Newport, I felt that the gods had smiled on me. I'd get to wear my dress after all. Rob had paid for the tickets, so all I had to worry about was cab fare and not spilling anything on the dress because it was silk. Or getting a heel caught in the hem and ripping it. It was a dress that was good for a season or two, and if Rob and I went somewhere else, I'd be ready.

I spotted him before he saw me. With a pretty girl, possibly twenty-one or twenty-two. If I ever happened to run into him again, I'd ask him why. Was it because I was too inexperienced for him? Was it because he'd been repelled by my fat thighs? Was it because he'd seen the cramped quarters of the apartment, and a view of the battered furnishings in my room made him realize I wasn't who he thought I was? Or was it none of those things, only that he'd suddenly seen me through my mother's eyes?

Then I ended up on that bridge.

When I saw that younger and better version of me I'd realized two things: my hair and my clothes weren't fooling anyone—it was obvious that I was a nobody from nowhere. And that there was something wrong with me. I had shot myself straight from Schoharie to the very small world I now inhabited because I thought that's where life was kind, where the sun shone every day. I thought by entering that world, I'd find someone to love me, but why had I ever expected that to happen when even my own mother didn't love me?

There are no drunken geniuses, Dylan Thomas notwithstanding. For every glass of alcohol, your IQ drops about twenty points. Out goes your ability to be objective and your ability to reason. I'd had two glasses of wine by the time I left the mansion and what I knew was that I was wearing a thousand-dollar dress that I hadn't yet paid for and couldn't return, that I'd looked like a total fool, and that no one could ever love a total fool. I wandered up the street and then went west simply because it was downhill, found a bar on one of the wharves and had two more glasses of wine. At that point the room became untethered and whirled around me when I looked up from my glass, and I thought I didn't like Manhattan, didn't like where I worked, I had almost no real friends, no boyfriend, and I couldn't find a single aspect of my life that made it worth enduring. My life was destined to be more of the same and then one day it would cease to be more of the same because I'd be dead.

Marcel Proust—at least I think was Proust—said that he knew that shared loves existed but he didn't know their secret. That thought has always haunted me. It did when I was in college and watched my friends with their boyfriends. It did during that second spate of weddings, the pleasant-faced men standing stolidly by the brides, about to launch into shared lives. I may have been dubious about sex, but I wasn't in any doubt about love. I'd made myself over, invented a new person, because the old one wasn't loved and I wanted someone to love and someone to love me. When I saw Rob with that woman, I felt that no one ever would, because everyone knew what I knew about myself: no matter what guise I wear, there is something fundamentally wrong with me.

So I walked around Newport, through waves of couples laughing their way down the sidewalk, and I sat for a while on a bench, the cold drifting in over the water, and when I finally got up again I headed away from the couples and the bars. The laughter and the little shrieks that some women emit to show the world they're there. The neighborhood I walked into was quiet and dark. It must have been foggy because the cold came down in wet drops from the branches that stretched over the sidewalk. I don't remember whether I heard foghorns; I don't remember hearing anything. I stumbled along a small bridge, came to a larger road, walked past a gas station and, in front of me, though I didn't realize it at the time, was the off-ramp of the bridge.

If a car had come down that ramp as I was going up it I probably wouldn't have survived, but no car did. I walked up the ramp and met a walkway and stepped onto that. I felt the wind raise goosebumps and lift my hair. I had no idea where I was going but I kept on walking.

Then the priest came.

One thing I like about Newport is the trees. I grew up in farm country, and farmers aren't partial to trees: they block the sun, drink water, and eat nutrients. You'll see cattle grazing or endless rows of corn grown for feed, but surrounding those domesticated acres of earth, trees are massed like a malign army waiting for the signal to attack. Scrub oaks invade the yards of abandoned houses, fast-growing birches, shedding their skin like snakes, press up against the windows and doors, silently and persistently demanding entry to claim what once was theirs.

Manhattan has a few trees outside Central Park. They're hard to look at. You see a pallid, spindly trunk growing out of a small plot in a sidewalk, and someone's put low fencing around the plot to keep the dogs away or a tall fence meant to protect it from errant cars or the destructive whims of young idiots, but the real threats are bad air and a surfeit of shade. You see these trees with scraggly branches adorned with a few exhausted leaves and they're struggling toward the sun but you know they'll never get high enough because they're surrounded by twenty-story buildings. There's never enough dirt around them, and even if there were, the dirt is awful, gray as ash and barren because a century's worth of car exhaust has fallen on it and what kind of plant loves lead? In college, there were trees all over the campus but they seemed less like living things than art exhibits; I sensed they had been planted in the same way people furnish a room, with the expectation that they would confer grace and elegance. In Newport, they're all around you, and I've since learned that a lot of the old ones were planted with hope rather than with expectation.

I think I felt them before I noticed them. Stumbling along in what I now know was the Point neighborhood, and sunk in my own misery,

I still felt the trees on every block, trunks solid and thick with age and holding up a canopy dark against the sky, the smaller trees sending tentative branches toward the sidewalk, the multitude of them evidence of some kind of homely, arboreal pride.

When I went back to Newport with Todd, they cast cool, green shade where they hung over the streets. They reached their branches wide to embrace the sky, towering in some places, spreading their skirts over others, and showed a whole world of greens and habits. You get a different feeling when you're walking among trees, even those of a small city like Newport. In Manhattan, you're alone in the dense block of air, parting it and pushing through it. In Newport, you're walking around and under something that is shaping the air for you, taking in particulate heat and delivering something cleaner and cooler for you to breathe.

It may be that I was looking for distractions and it certainly was true that I had plenty of free time after Rob unfettered me, but when I went back to New York after that second trip I looked into Newport's trees, to see whether I had invented them because I wanted to find something positive about the whole horrific weekend.

And discovered that Newport's arboretum was unique in America. The island had been fully forested when the first Europeans arrived and immediately started hacking away at the trunks and ripping out the stumps to clear the land for farming and grazing and to build houses and ships. By the time of the Revolutionary War, Newport had become a horticultural wasteland and when the British evacuated, they tried to destroy the few trees that remained. Newport had a change of heart in the 1840s and 1850s, when some summer colonists, college professors from the million universities in New England, brought seeds and saplings from their travels in Europe and Asia to see what would thrive in the temperate climate. Horticultural fever struck again in the 1880s, when one of the wealthy summer colonists encouraged her friend, the director of the Arnold Arboretum, to ferry more botanical exotica to Newport. There later was a kind of competition among the Gilded Age set to cultivate the most spectacular specimens—I suppose they wanted appropriate adornments for their mansions.

From these generations of enthusiasts came the Newport arboretum: London plane trees, European beeches, tulip trees, saucer magnolias, Mongolian oaks, Turkey oaks, Wych elms, white ash, Siberian elms, Atlas cedars, ginkos, dawn redwoods, weeping hornbeams, weeping beeches, blue atlas cedars, Yeddo spruce, Japanese zelkova, sassafras trees, horse chestnuts, Camperdown elms, and maidenhair trees, many rare, some stretching one hundred feet into the sky, some as wide as one of Manhattan's pocket parks. One American elm in Newport managed to survive the Dutch elm disease epidemic. America's first fernleaf beech supposedly was conveyed to Newport in a bottle carried by a young girl who crossed the Atlantic from England in 1835. There were tree societies in Newport and tree experts.

I didn't go back to Newport in August because by that time Todd had a boyfriend and while I wasn't explicitly uninvited, Newport just dropped off our conversational radar, as if it had never existed. I didn't fault him for it because who wants to tell a new boyfriend that his swell summer house comes with an unattached female? I finally got back to Newport in late September, when I had enough money to afford a car rental and two nights at a bed and breakfast. I thought I'd spend the first afternoon wandering around, looking at the trees, and the second day I'd do a historic home walk. I wouldn't see everything I wanted to see in those two days but it didn't matter because I knew I would return again and again. Once you looked past the beach and the bars and all the cheesy little shops, Newport was a dazzling horticultural and architectural experiment, the product of generations who indulged their quirks and their eccentricities and their obsessions, fervently, unselfconsciously, and without a trace of postmodern irony, that killer of passion.

Saturday morning, I was standing at the front door of the Brennans' home, intending to ask Helen who had been working on the house: the lintel was repaired and a new lock affixed to the door.

I confess that I took an immediate liking to Helen because she flattered me. When Todd and I went to her house that first time, she was a little flustered by a lot of company but when I shook her hand, she looked into my face, her eyes warm, reminding me a little of the cop, and said I was lovely. Some people throw a compliment at a mirror: your words are meant to reflect well on you. Or it's a boomerang that goes whistling around the other person, who may not be beautiful or brilliant or whatever, but it makes the other person notice the compliment applies perfectly to you. Helen's compliment was artless; you could see it in her face. She said what she was thinking and you can't not be charmed by that.

When we went to her kitchen that time, to bring food and drink to the men who just sat there waiting, as men do, for women to take care of them, she directed me to the plates and glasses, and while she was transferring things from the refrigerator to the counter, she talked.

About what the house was like when they first moved in, about the things Peter had done because Helen preferred wood to carpeting, pale colors to white walls, gardens to moth-eaten grass.

She said Peter could do anything. And then paused in what she was doing and looked at me, a little smile on her face. I thought she was trying to counteract the immediate impression you had when you saw the house, the exterior paint that was peeling away in strips. Only later I understood that she wasn't talking about the house at all; she was welcoming me in.

I had never encountered it before but that doesn't mean I didn't recognize it when I saw it. And I was embarrassed because it made me feel like an imposter or a fraud. She might welcome me now, I thought, but as soon as she figured out that something was wrong with me, she'd shut the door and lock it. I almost felt like I was a danger to her and her happy world where people had problems, certainly, but weren't messed up. Eventually it would be apparent to her that I carried twice my weight in baggage. She'd see whatever it was my mother saw in me. And that would be the end of that.

Before I met the priest I'd poured my thoughts, wittily phrased, into the emails I wrote my mother. I discovered that she saved them to a folder on her computer, though she hadn't saved the sweater I knitted for her when I was in college or the watercolor of our house that I'd done during my first year in New York. It is understating the case to say that she wasn't sentimental, so I figured my emails had some value, either as observations or as humor. And for a while, I was doing the same with Father Ennis but that was a little different. I was trying to keep him on the phone because if I sat quietly with myself for any length of time, my head would explode.

It was different with Helen. I didn't try to entertain her and I made no effort to prolong the conversation. The opposite, in fact, because I was trying to hide my real self from her. I couldn't stop calling her, though. She always sounded so happy to hear from me.

When I'd left the third time, glad to be out of the company of the lawyer, Helen had taken my hand in both of hers and invited me to visit. She meant me. Just me. So I did. Anxious when I arrived at the door, afraid she'd forgotten the invitation or changed her mind, having had enough of me after my phone calls. I had a question handy if it appeared that I wasn't welcome: I'd tell her that I'd just wanted to check a certain painting for a signature.

She greeted me in khaki pants, a red-and-white-striped shirt and red cotton sweater, clothes that looked like they had gone out of style and then come back again. She also wore red canvas sneakers. "I'm a great fan of red," she told me, "and too old to consider any but my own tastes." And without looking me over, smiled into my eyes and said, "How delightful it is to be young and beautiful."

When she said things like that, every muscle in my body relaxed, like I was floating, supported on a warm wind. "I brought a few things," I said, and held up the bags.

It was pathetic, I knew. Too much. My first thought had been books on Hassam and Heade, but then I worried that maybe Todd was right and the paintings were copies, or that Bart Harvard-and-Harvard-Law Meagher would totally screw up the lawsuit and Helen's paintings would end up in the hands of the greedy bastard art dealer. So instead I bought fresh bagels, a small box of chocolates, and a tea towel with New York icons like the Statue of Liberty and the Chrysler Building emblazoned across it. I'd also come across hand-dipped bayberry candles, which I thought would be right at home in an eighteenth-century house. I'd had to stop myself from buying more because it was making me crazy. As soon as I bought something, I'd think maybe she wouldn't like it. Maybe she didn't eat bagels. Maybe she was allergic to chocolate. Maybe she thought souvenir tea towels were tacky (which was true but they were also fun if you only bought one). Maybe she'd think I was a sad case, attempting to bribe her with Big Apple swag.

"This is all for us?" she said, mystified, as I unpacked the bags in her kitchen.

I'd also bought a pair of gardening gloves for Peter. "I wasn't sure what you'd like so I got a little of everything." It looked stupid, this odd collection I'd laid on her counter. "Maybe I overdid it a little."

"Well. Maybe just a little." Helen tried to keep the amusement from her voice. "You don't want to spoil us too much; we might faint from the shock of it."

I'd worried about leaving Peter alone; he was in the little yard behind the house, deadheading plants. He had a pair of pruning shears and a purple, plastic bucket that hung from a rope attached to his walker. Maria Estrada had done the planting, he said, and some of the watering, and the least he could do was to keep the plants blooming until the first frost. "We still have a good month before that happens. I used to lose interest around Labor Day but this is the first real garden we've had in years."

"He's fine on his own," Helen told me once we'd left the house. "I try to take a walk every day for about an hour. It gets the blood moving and it's good for my hip, which I broke about a year ago. They patched me up and packed me off to a nursing home for rehab. That's how we met Maria. I'm very proud that I recovered completely; people my age often don't. I'm a pretty good walker, but I hope I can keep up; you have long legs."

"Before I moved to Manhattan," I said, "I strolled."

Helen looked frightened. "You aren't one of those power walkers, are you?"

"Not in a million years. I'm not the most coordinated person on the planet; I doubt I'd make it more than a block before I tripped over something and fell flat on my face." That reassured her. "I do a lot of walking because it's cheaper than the subway and a whole lot cheaper than cab fare."

Helen was, in fact, a brisk walker. She had a few stories to tell me as we went south on Thames Street, past stolid eighteenth-century houses with dainty windows and clapboard painted in powerful colors that would have overwhelmed twentieth-century capes and colonials but seemed muted when they were massed. I read the plaques as we passed, neat little rectangles that told who'd built the home and when.

A wind was blowing in from the water and you knew how cool it was when you emerged from the shelter of the houses. Across Washington Square, autumnal gusts pushed us along. Helen buttoned her sweater but shook her head when I asked if it was too chilly for her.

Washington Square had been named for the president but was actually given to the city in 1660 by the English king. The Colony House, at the top of the square, was built in 1739; the Brick Market, at the bottom of the square, dated from 1762. The statue of Oliver Hazard Perry was erected in 1885 and faced Perry's home, next to the movie theater. "He was the big hero of the 1812 War," she said. "A miserable affair: lots of dead, no undisputed winner. He's the one who said, 'We have met the enemy and they are ours.'"

For some reason, that reminded her of the lawsuit. "Bart calls a few times a week."

"Is that much happening?" I could hear him on the phone, badgering them for information, relentless as a nor'easter.

"Oh, no." Helen was watching a young couple who were holding their toddler's hands and swinging him along between them as they walked. "He just calls because we're old."

"What?" I looked around to see who'd heard me—the question had been part shriek, part squawk, and entirely unattractive—but realized it hardly mattered since I knew almost no one in Newport.

"All right," she said, laughing. "He calls because we're old and he's a considerate young man. I think he feels responsible for us, though he needn't; we're perfectly capable day-to-day. It's the year-to-year things, like the house, that defeat us. He's very sweet. I would never say that to him, of course; men don't like to think of themselves that way, and especially not young men, but that's what the best ones are."

I had an image of him standing in Helen's living room: the tan, the ease, haranguing me about appraisals. I didn't pretend, after two phone calls and one encounter, to know Bart Meagher, but what I'd seen of him was as familiar to me as New York cabbies: aggression with a latent element of violence, every contact with the world abrasive.

"I should know the family, but I don't. It's funny to say, but in Newport terms, where we live is a world away from the Fifth Ward. It might as well be Outer Mongolia."

"The Fifth Ward is where all the mansions are?"

"Good heavens, no. They're just modest homes."

"He grew up working-class?" I found this hard to believe.

"I don't know when that expression came into being but I've never liked it. Peter was a construction worker; I was a salesperson in my father's store and then I was a teller in a bank: Did either one of us not work for a living? The whole concept of classes is ridiculous and demeaning; didn't our ancestors flee their homelands to get away from that?"

"I'm sorry. Really. I didn't mean anything by it."

She patted my hand. "I know, dear. Some things just wind me up."

We passed a Japanese maple that rose from several graceful trunks and paused under a copper beech that spread over the sidewalk, shading the street. We'd been walking uphill, and perspiration beaded on Helen's forehead. Watching her unbutton her sweater, I asked if she thought it was time to turn back.

"I wanted to show you where our store was, but perhaps another day."

"What happened to the store?"

"The short answer is that Dennis died," she said, "but we hadn't been doing well before that. For a long time, things were pretty bleak in town. I hung on for a few years and then—" She shrugged. "I hated to do it. I really did, but I had to face reality. I closed the shop and a dear friend found me the job at a bank."

"The tourists and the summer people weren't interested?"

"The tourists didn't start coming until the late 1970s. Or not many, anyway. And we didn't have many summer people, either. I remember when those houses along Ocean Drive went begging for buyers. You wouldn't have recognized Newport then."

I thought of Schoharie County, the empty houses and decaying churches. "Are you sorry you closed the shop when you did? I've only been here twice, but Newport seems pretty affluent now."

"It might have done well today if you could pry people away from their phones and video games. You can't imagine how many times I see tourists who are glued to their phones. Why do they bother traveling if they're just going to stare at their phones? Never mind, I'll save that particular rant for another day." She paused, having momentarily forgotten the question. "The shop. The store wasn't doing well and there wasn't much construction going on in town. Peter was out of work for months at a time. So am I sorry? No. Not really. I don't regret closing it."

I thought I understood. "The bank job was a regular income."

"That wasn't an easy thing for Peter to accept." She tugged on her sweater, and began to button it. "Time to turn back, I think. The problem is that my mind doesn't know my body isn't twenty anymore, so I sometimes keep going until my body insists that I stop. It's a very odd feeling and you'd think I'd be used to it because it happens just about every day. I start to do something and then I'm in the middle of it and I catch myself thinking I'll take a rest after I finish the job. It's as if my old body is communicating covertly with my much younger brain."

"Do you miss twenty?"

The sun lit Helen's hair as she emerged from the shade, picked out glinting silver strands among the flat white. The skin over her cheekbones was dry, and soft around her mouth; I tried to imagine what she'd looked like then.

"It depends on the time of day," she said. Something gathered behind her eyes. "Generally speaking, no." Her voice was stronger, brisk. "I was raped when I was nineteen and I still had the horrors a year later."

Helen had always been a walker. Every day, she walked to her father's store in the morning, stocked the shelves, swept the floors, polished the counters, walked home for lunch, and then returned to the shop for the afternoon. When the store closed, she walked home with her father.

"Newport was a different place then. Bellevue Avenue was always nice but the closer you got to the waterfront, the rougher it was. Spring Street was better than Thames, but that wasn't saying much, not then. He was in the military and it was just a few years after the war, and when he fell into step beside me, I saw the uniform and just started chattering away. Even when he took my arm and pulled me off the street I wasn't alarmed. I thought he was going to steal a kiss. I don't know whether you've been down Spring Street but there are all these little side streets, some narrow enough to be called alleys." She'd stopped walking and I had a bad feeling she was reliving it, but then she shook herself and resumed her steps. "It's always easier walking downhill, isn't it?"

I asked if she needed to rest, though I didn't know what I'd do if she did. There were no benches to sit on and I didn't have a car. I could have called a cab, though.

But she was fine. "For a long time, I wouldn't step foot outside the house unless I absolutely had to. No one talked about it in my family. It wasn't as if it never happened; it was more that it happened to us all, and we were just trying to get back to normal. You don't, of course." She stopped, thinking.

I wished I could take back my question. She was old, she wasn't strong, I'd wanted to have a pleasant chat and instead I'd led her to this. "You don't have to talk about it."

"I know. It's all right. And as a matter of fact," she said, walking again, "I was just getting to happier memories: Peter. I almost said 'no' the first time he asked me out. And even though we had a bite and saw a picture and it was a lovely evening and I liked him, I almost turned him down when he asked again. The first time I told myself I was just testing the water, to see how I would do on a date. I said the same thing the second time but that's not what was happening."

I could hear it in her voice: "You were falling in love?"

Helen laughed. "More like being swept down a river. When it's not the right person, you're looking to get out of the water practically as soon as you wade in, but with Peter, I was carried along and not thinking about a destination, but then all of a sudden I wanted to swim, so I'd get there faster."

I'd done a lot of scrambling out of the water. Pretty much no swimming. "That must be wonderful."

"You've never been in love?"

"So, yeah," I said, "I'm the Two-Dates Queen. Once in a while I'll get to three but generally two is more than enough."

She stopped again and I felt the air cool around me, the sun warm on my face, heard the cars coming down Touro Street singly rather than the solid stream of summer. "I do this all through the fall," she said, buttoning her sweater to the top. "First I'm too hot, then I'm too cold, then I'm too hot again, fuss, fuss, fuss; that's what old ladies do, don't they?" She pulled the sleeves down, nearly to her knuckles. "That's better. I've always thought love isn't as easy for us as it is for them. Women spend altogether too much time thinking. Peter is like a lot of men: the first look is also the last look. They see you before they know you, they decide they want you, and that first idea of you stays with them, even when you get old."

This was news to me. "Sort of a willed blindness?"

"Oh, I don't think it's conscious; it's just the way some people are. Though," she said, laughing again, "it could be that some men just don't want to admit they've made a mistake."

She slowed a little. "The sidewalk in this area is bad. Frost and tree roots kick it up and it's never really fixed. I always have to go carefully; I don't want another broken hip."

You couldn't miss that she was old, but her voice was strong and so animated you could almost forget her age until comments like that brought home the difference between us.

"Maybe you should take my arm? I know you manage it all the time without me but as long as I'm here, why not? I'm not the most graceful person in the world but four legs are better than two, right?"

"That's very thoughtful. I think I will, just for a bit."

It was a small gesture, but when she looked up at me, I could see her feeling for me had deepened without my awareness of it. Maybe I should have recognized it earlier, because you don't talk about rape to an acquaintance. I hadn't though. And I didn't know how it had happened, whether it was the visits or the phone calls or maybe the sad collection of stupid gifts. I thought I was pretty good at reading people but usually I was looking for signs that said I wasn't welcome or that I'd stayed too long. I knew those signs in all their many manifestations but probably didn't know anything else nearly as well. Maybe it wasn't that I saw it, exactly. I think maybe I felt it as much as I saw it—something about me spoke to something in her. I didn't know what that something was, but her expression warmed me.

More than that. It felt like she'd seen right through the surface and found me somewhere, hiding, and that's what spoke to her.

We'd covered a few blocks when she spoke again. "I was in such a bad way. Telling my parents, going to the doctor . . . my mother took me and I couldn't look at him. I didn't raise my head the whole time. I was very, very young and, well, it was awful. A few months later, my father closed the original store and opened another one on the other side of Memorial Boulevard, much closer to home." Her steps slowed. "Shall I tell you what helped me?"

"Sure."

"You'll think I've lost my marbles. You'll think I'm just a crazy old lady."

"I would never think that," I said, curious now. "You have more marbles than most. A surfeit of marbles, in fact."

"Well, it was Delia. That's who helped me."

"Delia?" That wasn't what I was expecting. I'd been thinking some trite piece of wisdom that she'd taken to heart. "Your great-grandmother? That's not crazy. Wow: she must have been really old."

"She wasn't old," Helen said, a smile playing around the edges of her lips. "She was dead. When she came to talk to me she'd been dead for years."

We came to an abrupt stop and my arm fell to my side. "Seriously?"

"You can see why I don't share this story very often," she said, enjoying my reaction. "Or at all, really. It does sound nutty. I didn't believe it myself. After the shock of it wore off, I thought I must have dreamed it. Oh, I've felt her from time to time. At least, I think I've felt her. A few years ago, I told Peter that I felt a presence in the house, just to test his reaction. Not so good," she said, rolling her eyes. "You should have seen his face. So I clammed up. Didn't say I'd ever talked to her or that she'd talked to me."

I wasn't surprised by Peter's reaction; I expect I was wearing the same look. Nevertheless, Helen pressed on with her story.

"I should have guessed that she was a relative but I never did; isn't that funny? Even when she told me where the diary was—I should have guessed but I wasn't thinking. When I saw her that time, when you and your friend from the auction company were here, I was gobsmacked. There she was, practically flesh and blood. All I could think was that I hadn't dreamed her after all, because here she was again."

I don't know how you can tell that someone is demented. Her face looked normal, the milky blue eyes full of humor. "So your great-grandmother came back from the dead to talk to you after you were . . ." I stopped, realized I couldn't say that brutal word. ". . . and she's been with you ever since."

"You don't want to believe all those stories about haunted houses," she said scornfully. "People don't come back because of *things*. People bring them back. Love brings them back." And, thoughtfully, "Maybe, too, it was the force of her will. She did what she wanted to when she was alive, so why would death stop her? She must have seen that I was in such a state that I couldn't find my way without help. So she came."

"Like a ghost, you mean? Floating along in a long, white dress?"

Helen laughed. "Oh, my dear." She took my hand and gave it a shake. "I probably shouldn't have started this story. You're never going to believe me."

She was creeping me out a bit but it was also disorienting: her appearance and her words just didn't go together. I looked around at the colonial buildings and the massive trees, both sturdy and becoming a little more familiar each time I came to Newport. I could imagine the people who first occupied those houses, people as ordinary as me. I couldn't imagine those people, drawing water from their wells, weaving their own cloth, eating what they grew or raised, I couldn't imagine those people, so rooted to the earth, lingering after they'd been lowered into the grave. "I don't know," I said truthfully.

"Well, believe me or not but let me get to my point." We were at the bottom of Washington Square. Helen moved a little closer to a wide brick building to escape the wind. "And no, not like a ghost. I remember that I was getting ready for bed, and I was feeling so low. I thought my life was over. It was the oddest thing; one minute I was upset and the next minute I felt calmer, as though someone had put their arms around me. I didn't mind when she came into the room because I knew she'd brought that feeling with her. She sat at the end of the bed and she was as real as you are. She was more vivid than life, even. Chestnut hair and a long jacket with lace at the neck. The jacket was a deep blue; it looked so pretty with her hair. A pin with seed pearls held the lace together. She had hazel eyes. A strong face; you wouldn't call it beautiful. She looked just like anybody else, except for her clothes, of course. She told me that she'd buried three children. One of them used to sing for her; she loved *Moore's Irish Melodies* and she said he sang like an angel. The oldest was serious, like his father, but also, like his father, he was a great reader; she wondered what he would have become if he'd had the chance. And the other—I remember how quiet her voice was when she mentioned him. He was softhearted, she said."

I wasn't convinced that she wasn't inventing, though I couldn't imagine why she'd make it up. "Did you guess they were your great uncles?"

"I didn't know who *she* was! And she wasn't exactly the kind of person you'd interrogate. She was a formidable presence; sympathetic but also quite bracing. 'You're grieving a loss, too,' she told me, 'but we're made resilient and we're made that way because we're meant to live.' She said she could have spent the rest of her years in mourning. People did. They never took off their mourning clothes, she said, never took their eye off what they lost. But that's not living: life goes forward, not backward. She said you have to make yourself go forward, and if you can keep moving forward, you'll come to yourself again." She paused reminiscently. "Put bluntly, she was saying that I'd grieved long enough. And so I went back to work in my father's store. Not that I had much of a choice: when someone comes back from the dead to tell you to do something, you do it!"

It sounded very unlikely to me. "So does she talk to you all the time?"

"If you had the choice between heaven and earth, which would you choose? I believe I've felt her presence from time to time, but the only other time I've actually seen her was when you asked about the diary. You know, people talk about guardian angels, but I wonder if they have it wrong. Maybe the spirits who watch over us aren't angels. Maybe they're the spirits of people who love us, whether they knew us in life or not."

I tucked that away to think about later. "So Delia told you where to find the diary."

Helen nodded. "That started me wondering what they know. The dead, I mean. Did she come that first time just because I'd been sad for so long, or was there another reason? It was a month to the day after that visit that Peter invited me to a movie. Can you imagine? I couldn't look at myself in a mirror—couldn't bear it. I've no idea whether Delia's timing was deliberate but I do know I was thinking of her when I said yes: I was afraid she'd scold me if I turned him down. She was in my mind later, too, when Peter asked me to go steady—I don't know what people say now but that's what we called it then."

"Exclusive. We say it's an exclusive relationship. Or a committed one. Or maybe monogamous."

"Really?" A smile. "I doubt I'll ever get to use any of those, but it's nice to be in the know."

"So, you were thinking of Delia . . ."

She nodded. "After the rape, I didn't feel the same about myself. You're no longer the inviolate entity you believed yourself to be and that's a shattering realization. You feel broken and defiled and you begin to think everyone else sees you that way. Newport was such a small town then; it was a stretch to imagine someone didn't know I'd been raped, but I'd been telling myself that Peter didn't, somehow. It made it easier for me to be with him. When he asked me to go steady, though, I had to make sure he knew what had happened; it would have felt wrong not to."

"I don't think I could have done it."

Helen laughed. "You would have if you'd feared the wrath of your long-dead great-grandmother!"

"He must have known, already. Right?"

"His heart had already settled on me. And there it's stayed."

We were at the top of Thames Street by then, enclosed by homes that had been old before Helen's relative had been born. Their very existence, despite hurricanes, blizzards, and enemy occupation, was miraculous in a way. I didn't know what to say so I said nothing.

"It amazes me to think how many years ago all that was. I'm eighty-six and I can't do all the things I'd like to do, and I miss Dennis, and my parents, and the friends I used to know. But I have Peter. I have love. And—" patting my hand, "I'm still making friends, even at my age. Lovely friends. Delia was right: if you're always looking backward, you'll miss what's ahead."

A few minutes later, we were inside the Brennans' house and Helen was calling for Peter. We found him in the yard, spent flowers scattered like a halo around his head.

— 29 —

The college kids who staffed the bars, restaurants, and hotels were gone by late September. The new crop of freshmen at Salve Regina had checked into their dorms and started classes and could be seen, now and again, stocking up at the supermarket or wandering downtown. During the weekends students came east over the bridge from the state university, came south from the colleges in Providence, but lower Thames Street, whose summer sidewalks were nearly impassable with the crush of college kids, was finally navigable.

Honeymooners journeyed to Newport in September. Families made the trip on the weekends. On a Saturday, Broadway could still become choked with cars, but fewer of the license plates read New York, New Jersey, or Connecticut. Newport was in the midst of the slow wind-down.

Throughout September night had moved in as inexorably as a fog coming up the bay. The daylight that had begun to disappear in unnoticed seconds during July and early August now was departing minutes at a time and, as it went, it took summer's warmth with it. The nights came on harder, cooler, the air sharp as a warning.

The birds knew it. You could hear the geese, flying late over the city, their voices louder in the dark and the cold of the September sky. You could see it at the feeders: one day a strange bird would be gulping the mixed seeds, and the shape and colors of it would make you hesitate, irresolute, torn between remaining in place, drinking it in before it flew off, or running to the guide books in search of the name. A fat grosbeak, or a northern flicker, looking large and out of place, its back a rich blend of black and mocha, cheeks bisected by a brilliant slash of red, a black quarter-moon bib below a long beak. And the next day that traveler would be gone. Many of the summer's birds would stay, the house sparrows and the jays and the cardinals, arguing and battling right through the winter.

They would risk the long freezes and heavy snows, having acquired the habit of bird feeders. But when you thought of that you were anticipating what was to come.

He knew he made people stare; who could help themselves? His face bruised and swollen, limping when he walked. If that weren't enough to focus the attention of even the most distracted, the clerical collar, added to the rest of it, made him, he told Lizzie, the cynosure of Newport. At least for a few weeks. He heard his mother's voice, her eyes taking in some guest at a long-ago Christmas party: "He's making a spectacle of himself." He wasn't drunk, though, nor was he oblivious. He was, however, a spectacle.

Lizzie didn't try to find the humor in it. She had returned to daily Mass, planting herself in the front row, near the center aisle, and her expression told him that her thoughts weren't on Eternity. She tracked him from entrance hymn to final blessing, her eyes narrowed in appraisal, crawling over the bruises, which had gone from purple and black to red and yellow, cataloging every bead of sweat that bloomed on his face, waiting for disaster. He had bought a scale and watched it as closely as Lizzie studied him, hoping every day that he'd gained a pound or two, but pain and anxiety gnawed at him and swallowed his appetite. At least, he told himself, he wasn't losing any more weight. He couldn't banish the limp, though; a spike had been rammed through his foot, and every step drove it higher through stringy, traumatized flesh, almost to the knee.

Despite that, he wasn't going to the psychiatrist. No doubt an indicator of failing mental health, but still, he wasn't going. He didn't want a final diagnosis, didn't want drugs, didn't want to go to a place that would monitor his every move. He wasn't going, and please God, he could hang on until the baby came.

Leo was more discreet than Lizzie. A quick sweep when they met in the kitchen each morning, and Jim thought Leo was infinitesimally surprised that Jim had made it through another night. He was tempted to ask Leo which signs would compel him to call the bishop. But then, any answer would have been frightening, so what was the point?

He tried not to alarm people more than he had to: he wore long-sleeved shirts, and with the collar he was hidden from chin to toes. He did what he was supposed to do: masses, Saturday afternoon confession, visiting the homebound, burying the dead, organizing the religious education program, dealing with the business of running a church, listening in on the new youth choir, returning phone calls, and answering the doorbell. Worried that he would have a sudden break, that he'd walk through the door of an elderly parishioner and scream at a surge of pain, or that he'd be in the middle of a conversation and realize the choirmaster or the pastoral assistant wore a look of horror, which would tell him that he had become incoherent.

However, he missed nothing. No one could fault him because, crazy or not, he was performing every function expected of him, fulfilling every duty. Not fulfilling, though; that would require a sincerity or piety he didn't possess. That worried him, too, the thought that it was apparent in what he did and that his hopelessness might shake someone's faith. But he continued anyway because there wasn't another option. Maybe he looked odd, maybe he limped, and maybe people thought, as Reilly had with Anselm Chace, that he was listening to something only he could hear, but he was functioning, though he was burning through every ounce of energy.

Nights were the most difficult. He'd hear the roar of Leo's television, and, more than ever, the world seemed to be on the other side of thick glass. He prayed without any expectation that his petitions would be taken up. And he had the sense of the world closing in, as the night drank more and more of the day, felt darkness gathering around him and out of it coming that loathed breathing.

The bridge pulled at him. It would be the focus of his thoughts long before he realized he was thinking of it. What time of night was quietest on the bridge, the bars closed, the night shift arrived at the workplace. How late the truckers rolled, how early they began. An abandoned car could cause an accident, better to walk along the deck, the breeze gusting as you ascended to the top, the smell of the bay pushing into your nostrils, the damp air cloaking you. It would be peaceful, looking out to the mouth of the bay, the land dark and quiescent, a sleeping animal, the blinking lights of the Castle Hill lighthouse and that of Beavertail and maybe Point Judith in the distance. He'd be slouched in the chair in his bedroom, dreamy, mind floating along like driftwood, and then he'd suddenly pull up, frightened by his thoughts.

Sometimes he was not alone in his office, in his bedroom, in the otherwise-empty church as he was putting things away after Mass. As soon as the awareness came to him, he shut it out. Whether or not it was a product of his imagination, acknowledge it and he was Kit Acker. Speak to it and he was Anselm Chace. Listen to what it might tell him and he was, perhaps, Emily Bell, walking to the bridge, her instincts suppressed by alcohol.

His guiding star was the baptism. If he could struggle along until Lizzie's baby was born, he would be satisfied that he'd held it off as long as he needed to, though not as long as he wanted to. Bench trials were scheduled sooner than jury trials, Meagher said, but the Boston lawyers had filed a motion to postpone.

"Well, so, there are two possibilities. You have an old couple, a sweet old couple, and it's like having Bambi on trial; no one who has an ounce of compassion is going to take Taylor's side. Taylor's crew might be panning for gold: a recent history of late payment or nonpayment of bills would suggest the Brennans needed the money more than they needed the art."

"They wouldn't sell their paintings."

"Why not? People sell their wedding rings, so why not a heap of old paintings?"

"Helen would sell her wedding band before she'd sell those paintings. Those paintings mean a lot to her."

"Which brings me to the second and more likely possibility: if you screw around long enough, a defendant could run out of money or run out of time."

"Run out of time?"

"Meaning no offense but . . ." Meagher hesitated. "So they attenuate the process, drag it out as long as possible. Peter and Helen are in their eighties. They're stressed. Peter is recovering from a stroke. I don't like to say it, and I wouldn't say it to anyone but you, but I think the calculus is this: delay and delay, outlast them, and then see who's in charge of their estate. As far as I know, they have no close relatives, and the lawyers probably have done a little research to see whether there's anyone waiting in the wings. They win by attrition."

Jim knew he couldn't hang on indefinitely. He was barely getting through the day. Psychosis or torment, it hardly mattered. Either way, he was dying.

If he hadn't known it before he collapsed in Queen Anne Square, he knew it now. Sometimes, death felt like a friend, waiting just outside the door. Sometimes it was a voice, calm and peaceful as moonlight, beckoning him. Often, it felt like stepping off the world, nothing finished and nothing to mark his time on the planet. More and more, especially late at night, it was just pure loss, everything sucked out of him: the parish, his sister, the children. Unexpectedly, Leo, too. The wintry expression, the careful diction, the compassion behind it. He felt embarrassed that he'd ever been distracted by the animal part of Leo, his reaction to Leo's love of food a nasty bit of enculturation. Had seen him at best as a slight help, at worst as an enormous irritation.

"Would you need me in a bench trial?" he'd asked Meagher.

Meagher had taken a long time to answer; more than anything, even Lizzie's daily assessment, it told him how bad he looked. "I'd planned to call you, the so-called experts, and keep Maria Estrada in my back pocket." The green eyes flickered briefly to Jim's and then deliberately looked away. "But if you think you might be unavailable . . ."

Though irrational when, after all, he'd asked the question, he'd been offended by Meagher's answer. He didn't want kindness and if he were honest about it, which he hadn't been in that moment, he would have realized that he'd been more upset than offended. People were kind to the dying; he thought he was dying, but he didn't want anyone else to think it.

"Did I say anything about not being available?" Heard the edge in his voice but ignored it. "I just asked the question. I think I have a right to know whether you'll need me."

Meagher slowly shook his head, as if to dislodge an unwelcome thought. A slight shrug, broad shoulders pushing against an expensive-looking shirt. "I'll let you know when we get a date."

Jim later revisited the conversation and decided to apologize the next time he saw Meagher. A week later, Meagher's secretary called him. Could he meet with the lawyer that day or the next?

When Jim saw Meagher, the apology died on his lips. Meagher had three monitors on his desk, as well as a fat pile of folders; one lay open before him. His shirt was as rumpled as if he'd slept in it, the sleeves rolled back to the elbows, and as Jim entered the office he rolled the sleeves down, becoming instantly businesslike. He nodded at the chair. When Jim sank into it, facing Meagher across the desk, the lawyer went right to it.

"So here's what we've got. My clients: an old couple, one impaired by a stroke, and the other who speaks to ghosts. My witnesses: number one, a woman who says that George Taylor accused her of stealing but who was recently fired from not one but two jobs and no one cares to go on the record to say why. Theft, perhaps?"

"Maria's the last person—" Jim began, but Meagher glared at him and held up a hand.

"Let me finish. Second witness: a priest, a bit of a tippler, who passes out in the middle of Queen Anne Square."

Jim wasn't going to be interrupted this time. "I didn't pass out. I fainted."

The hand went up again. "Third witness: a so-called expert from a New York auction house. Totally unreliable because she's totally unsound, having jumped off the bridge earlier this summer."

A blast in his ear that may have been the breathing or the shout of denial.

"Oh, yes. Our friend Emily Bell has a few problems, doesn't she?" His voice was low, but the green eyes were glittering with fury. "And how is it that you happened to be on the Newport Bridge at two o'clock one summer morning? Are you an insomniac? Were you stargazing? Night-fishing illegally from the bridge? At the dog-end of a bender? Is there something else I should know? That line you fed the police about the phone call I appreciated as a piece of pure fiction. No one calls a random priest when the cops and fire department are just three digits away. Excuse my language, but how the fuck am I supposed to win this if everyone involved is keeping me in the fucking dark? Don't you think I should know what the fuck is going on before I put any of you on the witness stand? Or maybe you have such a lot of confidence in me that you think I can wave a magic wand and keep our Boston friends from doing their homework?"

Pain coursing along one leg, the broken fingers throbbing but louder still was his heart, smashing against his ribs. "You know that isn't true."

"Which part?" Meagher said evenly, his smile a rictus. "Which part isn't true? You tell me because I don't know whether any of it is true or not."

"None of it. I don't drink. Ask Leo Sullivan. Ask my sister."

"Can they also confirm that you didn't have a fight with your girlfriend the week of July Fourth?"

The breath went out of him. He'd forgotten. He'd thought of it, briefly, but had dismissed it when he discovered the cop knew Lizzie. Didn't think there would be gossip and once he'd decided that, he'd never visited it again. But here it was and he'd made it worse. All the phone calls he'd encouraged. The length of those calls. The hours when the calls were placed. No one would believe they weren't involved. "That's what you think?"

"Frankly, I don't know what to think. Because I don't know. If I don't get any information, I draw my conclusions from whatever I do have. Just as a judge would. Well, so now Taylor's motion makes sense; the deeper you dig, the worse it gets. You have a woman who can't keep a job. You've got a priest who's so hard-core he literally can't take a walk in the park without landing flat on his face. You've got the same priest fucking around with a beautiful girl, who happens to be the so-called art expert and who is so fucked up herself that she tosses herself off a bridge. By the time Boston is finished, the judge isn't going to give a damn about the paintings. They're small potatoes compared to the rest of it. It's a fucking three-ring circus."

Meagher was winding himself tighter and tighter. "And where does that leave me? Who's left to testify? Can't call the priest, can't use the testimony of the expert, can't cast shade on the Taylors by calling the thief, and so I'm reduced to the Brennans. At this point, if you told me the two of them were running a meth lab, I wouldn't bat an eyelash. The only thing that wouldn't come to light is Helen and her pet ghost, although I'll have to make damn sure she doesn't talk about it. I'm totally, totally fucked."

Jim had never been so angry. Blind, deaf, about-to-explode angry. Meagher was white fury glaring at him. Jim found himself on his feet and headed to the door.

"That's disgusting. She's just a little kid . . ."

"She's closing in on thirty and she looks like a fucking model," Meagher shot back.

"I don't care if she looks like Black Death!" Jim was shouting now. "I'm a friend!"

Meagher came halfway out of his chair, as if he meant to launch himself at Jim. "You want to know what that is? You really want to know? That's the oldest one in the fucking book."

This was the world he was fighting to stay alive in. This was the world that Triona and Willy were growing up in. No wonder Emily wasn't sure whether she'd intended to leave it: it was brutal. Coarse and brutal and he was sick to death of it.

The chair screamed against the floorboards as he yanked it from the desk and threw himself in it. "Listen to me," he snarled. "Just listen. Believe it or not, someone did call me. Someone called to tell me there was a woman on the bridge. That's what they said. Did I think she was young? No. Did I think she might be pretty? No. Did I think I'd be having some sort of illicit rendezvous in the middle of the night on the east span of the Newport Bridge? No. I thought there'd been an accident. I thought someone was *dying*. That's why you call a priest. Because someone is dying."

Meagher was impassive.

"For the record, I have no idea what she was doing on that bridge. She was drunk. Just to be clear—to be very clear—she was so drunk she could hardly walk. She wasn't doing anything deliberately—her brain had switched off well before I got there. Whether she intended to jump or not I don't know. I'm not even sure she actually jumped. She just went over."

He didn't think he could be any angrier but it had become something he no longer could contain. It was stretching, growing, clawing its way out of him. "And if she did jump, who could blame her? It's the middle of the night and she's alone and a man comes along and wants her to get into his car. Do you have any idea what she could have been imagining?" He only realized that now. *Sweet Jesus.* He could see her face, the terror in it. "If you had the choice of dying by your own hand and dying after some . . . some freak that crawled up from the bowels of hell had finished with you, what would you choose?"

He heard his own words and stopped, stunned by them. Not because of what he said but because he hadn't had to reach for them. They were what, consciously or not, had been rolling around his brain for weeks, perhaps months. He pulled himself back, as if from a distance. Saw the cluttered room, Meagher behind the desk. Beheld something moving in the lawyer's eyes and realized how he must sound.

He tried to pull his thoughts together. "One of the fishing boats called 911 and after we were finished with the police I gave her a ride home. She called later to thank me. So," he continued, "it was sheer fucking coincidence—" and seeing Meagher raise his eyebrows at the word, "yeah, I know that word, too. It was sheer fucking coincidence I had her number when I went to the Brennans' house. I was trying to help an old couple who are afraid they'll spend their final years on the streets. Just like I was trying to help when I went to the bridge that night."

He couldn't tell if Meagher believed him or not but it didn't matter. "Just for the record, Emily's been calling me. She needs to talk and I let her. Maybe that doesn't look good but I don't give a damn how it looks: if she wants to call me every day of the week, I'll talk to her. I'll be a friend to her. That's my fucking job."

Meagher said nothing for a minute. Then he reached for a pen and made a few notes on the pad he had before him. Looked up at Jim, who was trying to calm himself. "I only use that word for effect."

Jim was still steaming. "What?"

"Fuck," Meagher clarified. "I only use it to see if it gets someone a little exercised—hotted up, my grandmother used to say. I'm a lawyer by profession but also by inclination. I try not to let my emotions affect my ability to articulate my thoughts."

Jim struggled to maintain an even tone. “What exactly are you talking about?”

Meagher sat back in the chair and crossed his arms over his chest. Despite the pose, he didn’t appear relaxed. “I figured if you got exercised, you’d defend your lady love’s honor.”

“Despite what you believe, I never laid eyes on her until I found her on the bridge.”

“I didn’t say what I believed. I just said what it might look like.”

“So you do believe me?”

“Well,” Meagher began, green eyes alive with humor, “I might have thought a few things until you called her a ‘kid’ and then went on to defend your own honor. I wish I’d thought to take a video.”

With a sigh, Meagher acknowledged Jim’s expression. “I’m just trying to do my job, here. If you’re taking someone to court and you’re worried you’ll lose on the bare facts of the case, you try to make the case about something else. No one’s going to side against an old couple who signed a contract that was so vague as to be meaningless. If I were working for the Taylors, I’d try to turn the tables. So they’ve got a poor old couple, and Taylor wants to help them out by buying a lot of worthless art from them. But then you and the ‘kid’ swoop in, realize it’s worth a bit more than nothing, and convince the Brennans to cry fraud because if they lose in court, no harm done but if they win, you wouldn’t turn down a token of gratitude for your trouble. Someone has to pay for that expensive air conditioning you’ve just installed in the rectory. You couldn’t accept the Hassam or the Heade of course. But as long as the old couple insist, maybe you would agree to one or two of the smaller ones that you’ve admired. They’ve been catalogued by experts; you’ve figured out which ones will make it worth your while.”

“That’s ridiculous. I’m a priest. No one’s going to think a young woman in New York is in league with a priest in Rhode Island. Even if they did believe it, there’s the contract. You said it yourself: who’s going to believe it was for all the art?”

“The Brennans believed it, until you got involved,” Meagher pointed out. “They would have honored it if you hadn’t put ideas in their heads. You got the Brennans to scream foul. After seeing your performance, I’m not too worried about most of it. I don’t know what we do with the cleaning lady, though.”

Jim stared, his heart hammering against his ribs, every muscle so tense it ached. He’d been tricked. It had been a performance, an act.

Meagher was writing on the pad, the gold pen the kind of thing that parents would give a college graduate, possibly inscribed with a name or initials. Meagher didn't look up. Was waiting, possibly, to see whether Jim accepted Meagher's explanation as an apology or viewed it as an excuse.

Maybe it was neither. Maybe it was misdirection.

Jim was a connoisseur of raw emotion. It wasn't something he'd wanted to be and in fact it was something he'd never thought about in the seminary. Priests were fed a rich diet of joy and grief and the in-between emotions, frustration and incomprehension among them. Anything, even joy, could flip so quickly into despair that you had to watch carefully to make sure you intervened before it happened because it was harder to pull someone back from that depth.

So Jim knew, watching the busy hand of the lawyer, that no one could manufacture a flash that wasn't heat but instead was as pure and cold as sunlight on snow. For a moment, when Meagher surged up from his chair, Jim had been in the presence of rage so elemental he thought his next breath would be his last.

Jim almost laughed; he could have told the young lawyer how badly he was mistaken. Nothing deadened the appetites like pain.

"The call." Meagher looked up. "I didn't believe it and neither will the Boston crew. As I said, I don't know why someone would call you instead of 911. It's a lot more likely that you were in the car with her and she either tried to jump out or you stopped because you were having an argument. Either that or she called you because she was drunk and wanted you to pick her up. But if you've got proof that the call came in from a third party . . ."

"Two calls. Actually, there were two." The calls had seemed the least important part of that evening. "The first time I thought it was a wrong number and I ended the call. He phoned again right after that. I hate to say it but there's no record of either call."

"Ah, well, Father, you don't have to keep a log; the phone does that for you."

"That's what I mean. Neither call showed up in my phone log. I did look. In fact, I did everything I could think of. I checked my phone, went to my provider's website and searched that way. I even had their tech people search and I must have spent forty-five minutes with them. They swore up and down there had been no calls."

"That's really what they said?" Meagher leaned back in his chair, considering. "If Taylor's crew asks for your phone records, and I expect they will, they won't see anything to back up your claim about a call, though they'll discover all those incoming calls from New York."

"It's bad, isn't it."

"Don't look so stricken." Meagher was making notes on the pad. "One missing call is a glitch. The universe hiccupped. The fact remains that someone called you for whatever reason but you'd never met her before. Two missing calls, though; that's more problematic. Unlikely. Stick with the one call, okay? No need to mention the other one. We'll work around it. Hope they don't ask for those records but plan as if it's a given. Give me a day or two to strategize about it, and absorb the rest of it. If that is the rest of it." He cocked his head, eyes narrowed. "That is the rest of it, isn't it?"

Jim asked his own question.

"How did I know about the bridge?" Meagher put down the pen and sat back. "The plaintiff had a cop on their list of witnesses. So I took myself down to the police station and read the report. Nicely detailed it was. What time the call came in, reporting people on the walkway, the time the unit was dispatched to the bridge, at which point I imagine you were already flopping around in the bay. Who said what when questioned by the officer, including the fairy tale about Jamestown. In all seriousness, it took some kind of balls to jump in after her."

Jim ignored that in favor of another part of the night. "Did you say someone called before Emily fell in?"

"I have a copy of the report if you want to see it." He dug down into the folder and produced a sheet of paper. "On the face of it, it's pretty damning. According to the report, a call came in at 2:27 a.m. about two people arguing on the walkway on the east span of the bridge. Newport's finest arrived on the scene to find a male and a female had gone into the water and had been pulled out by the time the unit arrived."

Jim tried to keep the dread from his voice. "Does it say who called it in?"

Meagher gave him an odd look but glanced at the paper. "A long-haul trucker driving west over the bridge. Man, I wouldn't want those hours." Shaking his head, he saw Jim's face. "Not someone you know, is it?"

"No." Jim's voice was faint; he was listening to laughter.

30

Columbus Day weekend is the last hurrah for Newport. I always think of Eliot: not with a bang but a whimper. Fewer acute intoxications, car crashes, and drunken fisticuffs, no boating mishaps and little water-related hypothermia. The emergency department is almost quiet and that gives me a chance to think.

I have a few theories about the "why" of the weekend. The obvious explanation is that ninety percent of the college kids are gone but I also think it's a vibe. Summer makes you think the world is warm and forgiving and that you are invincible and immortal. That's why people get too close to waves pounding the rocks around Brenton Point: they think if they lose their footing on the rocks, the sea will give them a hug and a pat on the head and deposit them gently back on terra firma, instead of doing its best to pulverize them before spitting them out. I get people who are dropped here by Newport rescue and they've got broken arms and legs and cracked skulls and chunks taken out of them and they're shocked that their friend the ocean could do this to them.

There's less of that in autumn and I think it's because the wind is wilder and the air is colder and the days are shorter: winter is coming and people believe in winter in a way they don't in summer. People know you can freeze to death in winter, that ice can flip your car or hurl it into a ravine. You can get frostbite in winter and anyway, if you're out in ten-degree weather, you can feel your face and your fingers getting numb so you know, with that little taste, that frostbite happens. Nothing like that in summer. You're out there and you're hot but no one ever thinks the summer air will kill you. Sunstroke and third-degree burns don't make the headlines. People think that the only thing you have to be careful about is keeping kids and animals out of cars.

Anyway, I was glad that it was a pretty slow weekend. I don't want people to fall off the Cliff Walk or anything like that but normally I like to be busy. Now, though, I was tired when I awakened, even if I'd slept through the night, and I had a bad case of heartburn. The baby was making itself known at odd times; I'd be getting a patient's history and I'd feel like someone had taken a feather to my skin from the inside. I'd have a stethoscope to a patient's back, listening for rales, and I'd recoil at a small movement in my womb. I'd think of how many more weeks it would be and I knew what I'd feel like, and I'd wish it were all over and little what's-its-name was out and about and I was myself again.

Actually, I tended to think of it as Charlie. That was Willy's name for it and whenever I remembered his explanation of his choice, I found myself grinning. If Charlie turned out to be just like Willy, it would be a good thing. Willy is a sunny child who makes me laugh hard at least once a day. He's a straight-A student; the difficult work involved in rearing Willy is figuring out what to give him so he'll continue to be interested, because he really isn't learning anything in school and though we were tempted to get him bumped up a grade or two, we were advised to keep him with children his own age. It was Sam's idea to buy the books the high school freshman were reading. That and the sophomore curriculum kept him busy last year so this year we moved on to the junior and senior curricula. So far, it's working out. He's interested in the books and as for school, he's an entertained observer. He has a lot of friends and his teachers like him, which tells us he's probably not showing off in class. Not that I think he would; he's as laid back as his father.

Triona is more like me, expecting the worst and surprised when the worst doesn't happen. She isn't as easy as Willy and I don't think girls ever are as easy as boys. In my experience, girls are more complicated beings at every stage in life. Girls have to test everything they see and hear, run it through their minds and make sense of it. Boys often let things flow here and there while they're involved in whatever obsession they have at the moment, and for Willy, the obsessions were Legos, then bivalves—which I'm glad has passed because it meant a hundred fall and winter trips to the beach so that Willy could creep along the high water line looking for shells, which he would take home and exhaustively research—then cooking and now it's science fiction and volcanology. Girls do latch onto things, and for Triona it was snakes and reptiles in general, then skateboarding, then the Nobel laureates and for the past month it seems to be concertinas: two months before Christmas she's already told me twice that's what she wants beneath the tree. I'm going to have to do a little research to see how loud and painful they can be in the hands of an amateur.

Charlie's a perfect example of the difference between my kids: Willy named the baby and he knows that Mom has been cranky but it's water off a duck's back and except for nagging me about getting a dog, that's the end of it. Triona is wondering when we're going to get baby clothes and if so what color since we don't know the baby's gender, and how long is Mom staying home, and who will watch the baby when Mom goes back to work? I have a suspicion that Triona's afraid she'll be taken out of school and perhaps the concertina is something for her to do while Charlie naps.

Partly, this is just Triona. Not all girls think their parents are incapable of acting rationally and barely competent at child-rearing. Triona's always been that way. She's the one who dumped Sam's scotch down the drain because, in her mind, neither Sam nor I were doing anything about his drinking. She's too young to understand, but I give her credit for doing what she thought she should do, even if it was the wrong thing. Even if she hadn't needed to: Sam has returned to his former habit of a drink on Friday night and two on Saturday.

I don't know what we're going to tell the kids. Not about the sonar thing; that was easy enough. They both think their father's a hero. Triona of course had a million questions and Sam had as many answers. When she asked if he'd broken any laws, he told her he was covered by the Whistleblower Protection Act. That seemed to satisfy her.

Jimmy wasn't so easy to explain to the children. After the kids went to bed, Sam and I spent hours talking about it. We always seemed to drift into the library to talk. Sam gravitated to one leather chair and I'd take the other. We'd discuss arguments to convince Jimmy to get help. What to do if he didn't go on his own. What to tell the children. How much to tell them. How they would react. Sam suggested that we not force the issue with Jimmy before Thanksgiving. He thought the kids would be excited to see their cousins and we wouldn't dilute the pleasure of Triona and Willy announcing that Charlie was on the way. After Thanksgiving, we'd swing into action because Christmas, otherwise, might be a disaster: who knew what might happen with Jimmy at midnight Mass and Christmas Day Masses? Anyway, I thought Sam's idea made a lot of sense.

I didn't anticipate how it would feel to hash out things with Sam. Usually I figure that I'll just waste precious time if I'm drawn into a discussion and, at the hospital, it's true, most of the time. You can't have a long chat if someone presents with chest pain or stroke symptoms. You have to make your best guess and act on it. And we were talking about my brother. It was hard to voice what I was thinking, to actually say the words. I had to get over the urge to shut Sam out. But Sam has a different perspective and it was good to hear it. Anyway, he's the smartest man I've ever met. We're a little awkward together: I'm too polite and Sam's more deferential than I know he actually is. I guess we'll get over that; with two kids and another on the way, you don't have much time for the delicate emotions.

I had no confidence that Jimmy would go anywhere willingly so getting him to a doctor or a clinic or a hospital wasn't going to be easy. And there was the second issue, still under discussion: If we had to force Jimmy into a psychiatric hospital, what should we tell the children?

Just thinking about my brother makes me want to weep. He's skeletal. His clothes drop from him like they're on a hanger, not a person. The last fat to go on the body is around the eyes, and Jimmy's eyes are two febrile orbs banging against his sphenoid bones. I had my suspicions before he took the kids that night but when he collapsed I doubted myself. For one thing, his legs were like nothing I'd ever seen before, the petechiae so severe his skin was practically glowing. It was as if he were having a severe allergic reaction except it abruptly stopped around his groin. That was weird, too. Just to be sure, I ran some antihistamine through him and then I ran every test I could think of. Nothing happened with the antihistamine and nothing came up on the test results.

I sifted through assorted bacterial, viral, and parasitic possibilities, and even threw in a few zebras, because after all, Newport gets a million tourists and maybe Jimmy picked up something; it would be just like him. Then I started thinking oncology. Scans, x-rays—I had plenty of time to use just about every piece of diagnostic equipment we have because Jimmy was out of it and wasn't about to object. No cancer, at least none we could see, and when a patient looks like Jimmy does it's usually pretty advanced by that time and easy to spot.

When I finally went home the night Jimmy was admitted to the hospital, I was back to psychosis. I was pretty sure he had hallucinated the laceration or whatever it was on his leg. Next time we saw him he had all those questions about mental illness. Even before Jimmy started talking about being tormented by demons or whatever it was, Sam's comment had supported my diagnosis. He was right: Jimmy was never alone with the children, like he was afraid he'd hurt them. That broke my heart because when you have something psychiatric going on, you're all alone with it, and Jimmy must have been alone with it for years because the thing with the kids wasn't new; he'd never been alone with them.

Mental illness doesn't run in my family but that doesn't mean anything. I did one psychiatric rotation years ago and what I remember would just about fill a thimble. I recognize it when I see it because I've seen a fair amount of it but that's the beginning and end of what I know. Nupur Balakrishnan was great. The day after Jimmy was admitted, I called her and told her everything I could think of and she was a big help. She's really smart and I thought Jimmy would be in great hands.

Except Jimmy wouldn't go. That's the exasperating thing about psych patients: they believe they know better than anyone so they don't do what they're told. Not that other patients do. I can tell a guy with gout to ditch the red meat and jettison the beer and I can see from his expression he's not going to do it, even though he came in screaming in pain and wearing cut-up sneakers because his toes are so swollen he can't get shoes on. If that kind of thing doesn't put you on the straight and narrow, I haven't a clue what will.

The day after Jimmy slammed himself against the concrete, I called Leo Sullivan. He was not happy to hear from me; maybe he doesn't like doctors or something. I told him that I'm going to manage Jimmy's treatment, so if Jimmy has another break on Leo's watch to call me before he calls anyone else, and in the meantime, I'm going to make him see Nupur.

"Psychosis?" Leo Sullivan said.

I started to explain but he interrupted in an arctic voice. "I am aware of the condition. And you have confidence in your diagnosis?"

I always do.

"Not a possibility that your diagnosis may be informed by your vocation?"

I don't know Leo Sullivan, except what I've heard from Jimmy, so about all I knew is that he loves dessert. I was adding pompous to my little store of information. "Do I think he's crazy because I'm a doctor? No. I think he's crazy because he's psychotic. Don't tell me you think he's being tormented by demons."

"Ah. So he does think that. It wouldn't be unprecedented, you know."

Holy Moses. "Psychosis isn't unprecedented, either. In fact it's a lot more precedented." Which I wasn't sure was actually a word.

Unbelievable. Generally, I have a lot of respect for old people. Also for priests. But it sounded to me like Father Sullivan had boarded the bus to Crazy Town, too. Anyway, I understood, as Leo Sullivan obviously didn't, that Jimmy's body wasn't going to take much more abuse. "Unless you're qualified to diagnose demonic torment, my diagnosis is a lot more likely. Even if you are. Anyway, Jimmy has the classic symptoms of psychosis. He needs to get to a psychiatrist before he goes down like a sack of potatoes again. So call me if it looks like he's having another break and I'll haul him off bodily to Nupur."

"I don't see why—" he began, but I cut him off.

"Call me. Just call me, will you?"

During the next few weeks, I took a soft approach, not pushing too hard because we were going to try to get through Thanksgiving, but making sure that he wasn't waiting for a little shove to get him moving in the right direction. It was like talking to Stonehenge. My brother the pushover wouldn't be pushed. He still looked bad but at least he was no worse and, anyway, the bruises faded on his face and his fingers were healing—I didn't think he'd take the splints off before they'd healed completely but you never know.

I also talked to Nupur about committing him involuntarily and she told me that I'd have to demonstrate to a court that he was a danger to himself or others. I hated the idea of parading Jimmy's problems in front of the public. But then I worried that he was parading them himself and I just didn't know it. About then, I'd realize I was twisting myself into knots and I'd do something to distract myself, because all that anxiety couldn't be good for Charlie.

Friday of Columbus Day weekend, Sam got a call from one of Betsy's colleagues at the *Globe*. The day before, there had been a stranding on Cape Cod.

Ever since Sam told me about the sonar, I'd been scanning the news every day and not just the local or national news. There were three strandings in September, two in August, and when I did some research, I found clusters in June, May, and February. Forty sea lions in Southern California, thirty-two Minke whales along the Eastern seaboard from Maine to North Carolina, nine beaked whales in New Zealand, seventeen dolphins in Australia, harbor porpoises and killer whales in Ireland, seals in Cornwall. It was sickening. Maybe they weren't all related to the sonar system—I can't imagine why anyone would be testing it near Auckland but who knows? The day before the call, seven right whales had beached themselves in Provincetown.

Right whales are one of the most endangered species on the planet. Sam said we nearly hunted them to extinction in the nineteenth century. They can grow to fifty feet and sixty tons, which is amazing considering that their diet consists of things like sea slugs and krill, which look like tiny shrimp. They are filter feeders, which means they take in a lot of water and filter their food as they expel the water again. They can eat about twenty-five hundred pounds of food a day. They can live sixty years or more. They are docile mammals, live close to shore and move slowly, which means that some are killed every year by boats.

It's thrilling to see a whale. Sam and I have taken the kids on a few whale watches, including one time in a Zodiac, which is like a rubber raft with an engine. That was on a trip to Nova Scotia and when that boat shot out of the harbor, it headed straight to open water. We pulled away from the beach, and then we left the harbor, and then I saw the cliffs recede and I started to panic. You realize how fragile you are, skimming the waves with nothing between you and the water but a thin piece of fiberglass or rubber or whatever it is. If something pierced the bottom, we'd be in the water, no land in sight, and no boats nearby to pick us up. My heart was in my throat and I thought I was going to have to tell the skipper to turn around and take us back to the shore, but then, just to our right, someone spotted a pod of pilot whales.

They're only about eighteen feet, small in the kingdom of whales, but when you're in a rubber boat sitting on the water and they're eye to eye with you, they take your breath away. One moment the sea all around you is whitecaps, something churning the water beneath the surface, and the next moment the dorsal fins appear, sleek and black, cutting through the chop. The body will break the surface, thick and round right up to the tail, which flips as the whale dives. They swam beside our boat, around our boat and beneath our boat and as self-absorbed as we are as a species, as blind and deaf as we are to other species, you couldn't miss that they were having fun escorting us at times, chasing us at others. I remember the look on Triona's face; it was like she was seeing the miracle at Fatima.

Sam called me right after he got off the phone with the reporter. He said an unfamiliar number had come up on his cell phone and he'd let it go to voicemail. When he went out for lunch, he called the number and it was a reporter who said she was working on the story with Betsy. They spoke for nearly an hour. First, a number of questions about his job. Then some about that disgusting list: who compiled it, how it was compiled, where the information was sent, who likely was aware of and/or had seen the list. Sam couldn't answer some of those questions, but he had a few of his own. The reporter said she'd checked the list against all the information she could find and some of the incidents matched; not all, but enough for the paper to pursue the story. And no, they wouldn't need to reveal the source.

"That doesn't mean no one will know," Sam said.

And that's the other set of scenarios that occupied my free time at the hospital. Newport isn't the Navy town it once was, but the Naval War College is still here, as is Naval Undersea Warfare Center. Military contractors like Raytheon remain on the island and employ a lot of locals. Drive around town in late January and you'll see a lot of out-of-state license plates, even though very few people are vacationing here in the dead of winter, and if you follow those cars eventually you'll see men and women in uniform get out of those cars. Go down West Main Road at the right time and you'll see cars pouring out of Raytheon. And if you think about the money the Navy and their contactors spend on Aquidneck Island, you get a sense of how many people will be none too happy if the Navy's new sonar system is scuttled.

Not wanting to pursue that line any farther, I'd speculate whether the system could be modified rather than scuttled. But I had about as much knowledge of sonar systems as I did about splitting the atom, so why was I wasting my time speculating? I didn't know what would happen, couldn't even guess.

Anyway, by then my stomach would be in knots again and I'd remember that I shouldn't stress Charlie. And that's the bad part about the October slowdown in the hospital: too much time to think. I thought about those people at NUWC and Raytheon and all the other contractors, people who had children to feed, and all the people who depended on the Navy and the contractors for their income. I thought about what it would mean to Triona and Willy if everyone knew who killed the system. Mostly I thought about Sam being hauled away to prison and what would happen to the kids if they sent him away for a long time. But then I thought about that trip to Nova Scotia.

Sam talked to Betsy and the other reporter a few times during the following weeks and then nothing happened. We didn't know if they were still working on the story, if the story had died, or even if they were still employed by the paper. Nothing. A week went by, and then a second and then a third. Another stranding happened, somewhere near Rio de Janeiro.

Sam was never a great sleeper: he'd spend the first fifteen minutes sampling the infinite variety of positions: left side, right side, stomach, back, two pillows, one pillow, one hand tucked under his face, both hands tucked under the pillow. Eventually he'd settle down and he'd sleep a few hours, wake up, power through the various positions and sleep again for a few hours before awakening and going through the routine one more time.

Now I was getting a whole night of that, violently, Sam hurtling from one position to another when he was half-awake and thrashing wildly while he was asleep. I thought I was going to pass out one night when his heel crashed into my patella. I was willing to put up with it because I figured it was a temporary aberration but Sam decided to sleep in a spare bedroom, where he could flop around all night without injuring Charlie. I told him that babies were tougher than you thought they were.

Children weren't, though. One Saturday at breakfast, I reluctantly announced that Dad was going to be sleeping in the pink bedroom for a while. Instant reaction from Triona, whose head jerked up from her cereal bowl, her face stricken. "Are you and Daddy getting divorced?"

"Caitriona Clarke does melodrama." But my sunny child was looking a little wary.

It was just about then that my brain gave up. Exhaustion, stress, no small amount of dyspepsia; I just couldn't make the leap from Triona's question to a reasonable response. From the other end of the table, Sam looked a question, a beat in which I had the chance to answer Triona. I stared back, totally vacant, like I had been pithed.

"Your mother and Charlie need to stretch out," he told the children. "There's getting to be less and less room in the bed, if you know what I mean."

For extra effect, he stood and poked out his stomach. While the kids laughed, Sam shot me a meaningful look.

I found my voice. "Daddy thinks he might accidentally roll over on me and hurt the baby. He or she will do just fine either way," I continued, forestalling the next question, "because babies are well protected in the womb. The hip bones provide a natural cradle, and the mother's layer of fat and muscle also protect the baby, and the womb has a thick wall of muscle. Babies are suspended in the amniotic fluid—"

"Too much information." Triona made a face.

Most times, grace comes to you and you don't recognize it. You think it's you, that you're suddenly smart enough, or strong enough, or lucky enough, or kind enough. But there are other times when it's like a shove between the shoulder blades, whacking you out of your stupor. Because we're all like that, or anyway, most of us are, walking around with our eyes half-open, dreaming our little dream of ourselves and the world. If God didn't give us a shot of grace now and then, we'd be totally hopeless and the world an even bigger mess than it is now. Anyway, I've always believed in God and in grace.

Across the table, Sam was happy; I could see it in his face. He didn't have much reason to be: the newspaper article was whirling toward us like a tornado. Sam expected to be let go and whether or not that happened, he intended to look for a new job, though what he'd do he didn't know. My brother was having psychotic episodes, and I was so distracted that I couldn't even answer a simple question. Little reason for Sam to be happy, but he was.

Then it was like a shade went up: I saw our breakfast table through Sam's eyes. Two kids who'd needed reassurance and had been given it. His partner in that reassurance. His partner, who now was sitting with him in the library every night after the kids went to bed, talking. Going over the options for Jimmy and for themselves. Imagining a million futures, trying to figure out the best ones for their family and how to get there.

It's odd but I suddenly thought of our trip to Italy. Willy was three and Triona had just turned six. Sam had done his usual thing, reading all about the geography and history and learning a bit of Italian, and we were in Florence, at the Uffizi, and Sam was in the middle of Renaissance history when Willy had suddenly piped up, "No more talk. Just facts."

Triona had demanded to know why Sam and I were laughing. But you couldn't explain it to a little kid; she wouldn't understand that it wasn't just humor, that it was humor mixed with wonder, and with joy, too: we had made this child, Sam and I, just the two of us. Sam and I had made this kid.

I looked over the cereal boxes and the bowls and the juice glasses and I met Sam's eyes. I have no idea what he saw in mine but I saw love, and I blinked a few times because even I know that kids get freaked out if they see grownups cry.

A few nights later, when Charlie was behaving himself and we'd talked ourselves out and the house was freezing, Sam stood and held out his hand and we shared a bed. And I sometimes think there's nothing in this life better than lying in bed, your husband's arms wrapped around you, folding you against him, feeling him smile against your cheek, his breathing in your ear as steadying as the world turning.

Sam called Betsy in mid-November. The sonar thing was being incorporated into a larger story. A three-part series, the subject of which she was cagey about. "Does she think I'm going to sell it to the competition?" Sam said, irritated.

Anyway, we knew it was going to happen but not when. So we waited.

31

Helen saved regional magazines and city magazines. They were stacked here and there, including on a dresser in the guest bedroom. In one of them I read a story about Catherine Lorillard Wolfe, daughter of one of the people who founded the Museum of Natural History and heir to a tobacco fortune. Catherine Wolfe never married; she didn't have to. Instead, she built a palace for herself in Newport. After she built it, she decided she needed mature trees to decorate the grounds. I guess she could afford to be impatient, too.

She chose a pair of thirty-foot beech trees from her father's place on Long Island. I don't know how easy it is today to transplant mature trees, but in the 1880s there were no backhoes and it was a good ten years before the horseless buggy was invented, so after they managed to dig up all the roots the trees must have been loaded onto horse-drawn wagons that were transported by boat from Long Island to Aquidneck Island. Wolfe had been warned by her friend Frederick Law Olmsted that the trees wouldn't survive, but instead of listening to the man who designed Central Park, Wolfe went her own hardheaded way. A year later, Olmsted was a guest at Wolfe's estate and was entertained in the cool shadows cast by two large, thriving, beech trees.

Sometimes, if you're hardheaded, you get lucky.

The day Peter had the stroke, I moved my clothes from the bed and breakfast to the Brennans' house. In the emergency room, Peter tried to speak but it was as if his tongue kept getting in the way, the words so garbled that it was impossible to tell what he was trying to say. Helen hovered over him, clutching his hand between hers, trying to understand. Eventually, Peter closed his eyes and abandoned the effort.

The doctor was a little woman with wild red hair and a big voice; maybe she was accustomed to speaking to the deaf. She took Peter's hand just as Helen had, and told him he'd had a stroke but they'd treated him in time and she expected he'd recover well. I thought that was pretty vague but Peter's eyes, which had been avid and furious, calmed a bit with that.

Then she turned to us and asked about what she called Peter's "level of activity." Actually, she asked Helen. I was prepared to tell the doctor that I wasn't the granddaughter but she didn't even glance my way, and my surprise at that made me realize something I've never thought about before: the only person lower in the food chain than a young woman is an old woman. People pay even less attention to an old woman than a young woman, and I'd observed it before without understanding what I was seeing.

When Helen said that Peter used a walker but didn't spend much of the day on his feet, the doctor said that's what she'd guessed: Peter had a clot that interrupted the blood flow to the brain, which caused muscle weakness and dizziness that likely resulted in his fall and impaired his speech. He hadn't broken any bones, and he probably "would get most of it back" but Peter should be taking aspirin to prevent blood clots and despite the arthritis in his hips and knees should be doing exercises twice a day and should get up and walk at least once an hour; once every thirty minutes was even better.

"When can he go home?" Helen asked.

"Hard to say," the doctor said. "Right now, if he tried to stand up he'd go down like a sack of potatoes."

Helen hadn't taken her eyes off him until the doctor came. She probably had forgotten I was there. Or, more likely, wished it. This was private, I thought, a husband-and-wife thing, and they didn't need some random person with them. Peter wouldn't want a random person seeing him helpless.

I had no reason to stay; Peter had been delivered to the hospital and was under a doctor's care. But I didn't leave.

The doctor said Peter would be transferred to the medical floor. Helen looked exhausted; normally pale, her skin was gray with fatigue. The wind had blown her hair when we were walking and it stood in little tufts like whitecaps. The circles below her eyes had turned dark purple. She was a sad little thing, sitting in the red sweater and pants that were too big for her. Her red sneakers broke my heart.

I'd brought her some water when we were in the emergency department, and when Peter got a room I'd offered to find something for her to eat. She'd shaken her head but I suspect she'd been too distracted to even hear me. As the hours wore on, she looked worse and worse and I began to be afraid that she might collapse. It took me a while to work up to it but I finally said I'd stay the night with her. I'd thought about it for a long time as we were sitting by Peter's bed, looking at it from Helen's perspective, trying to figure out whether she needed me or not. Peter had eased a little and the hospital was taking care of him but Helen had to get home, eat something, and sleep.

Helen roused at the sound of my voice. "I'll be fine," she said, giving my hand a pat. "You don't have to stay with me."

I hesitated just for a second, the old fear kicking in. Maybe she didn't want me. Maybe the fuss of having a guest was too much for her. Maybe she'd had enough of me for the day—or for a lifetime. But if I were in her situation, I'd want someone to take charge, just until I could pull myself together again. "I know I don't have to," I said. "I want to. Besides, I've never slept in an authentic colonial."

I drove her home, fixed her a cup of tea and then I took care of everything. Found sheets and made the bed in the guestroom, chose a couple of towels from the linen closet, which still had paintings stacked beneath the lowest shelf, and, searching the fridge, came up with cheese sandwiches with lettuce on wheat bread. Helen could only manage half a sandwich.

"I'm going to get my things from the bed and breakfast," I said as I was washing the few dishes. "I don't want you to do anything while I'm gone."

"I don't have the energy," Helen said frankly.

"Good. Then I won't have to worry about you."

The guest bedroom had light blue wallpaper with tiny yellow and white flowers; very feminine and not really me. I'm more of a gray, black, and white person, which is very Manhattan, though I favored those colors even when I was a child. A small window, the glass in it so old and wavy that it made you nauseated to look through it. The room probably was an oven in July and August, but in late September it was warm but not uncomfortable. The sheets smelled like lavender but the pillow was musty. And all around me were the paintings, shoulder-to-shoulder sentries on the walls. One a watercolor under glass and the rest unframed oil on canvas. I'd looked closely at the oils during my survey with Todd, and then with Clay, but the subjects remained murky under the old varnish and smoke; they'd be impenetrable by moonlight. I browsed through the pile of magazines, saw the article on the beech trees, and got into bed with that.

I hadn't realized Newport could be so quiet. Once in a while I heard Helen turn over in the bed at the end of the hall. Otherwise, the stillness was punctuated only by rhythmic thunks in the distance as cars traveled over the Newport Bridge.

Helen had asked me how I knew Father Ennis. We were talking for a while after I'd come back from the bed and breakfast. We were sitting in the living room, which was just large enough to hold a coffee table, small sofa, two wingback chairs, and a battered secretary. Helen had settled herself in a chair, and thinking that if I took the other chair we'd look like we were in the midst of a formal interview, I'd opted for the couch. I could see why Helen preferred the chair; the cushions and I kept going down. I wasn't quite on the floor but I wasn't too far above it, either. Even I found it difficult to get out of.

The bridge had been nearly three months before but in a way it felt like three years. Perhaps because my memories of that night were fragmented: the vision of Rob with my successor; a woman's laughter rising above the din of the bar I went to; the argument I'd had with myself when I was stumbling over cobblestones because if I didn't watch where I was going I'd fall and ruin the dress, but if I kept my eyes on the ground, the swirl of the dress would nauseate me to the point of vomiting; the priest's hand, oddly hairless, as he held the flashlight; the coarseness of wet silk against my back as the cop talked to Father Ennis.

Or perhaps it seemed years ago because I didn't exactly remember the jump.

Because at some point, I faced the fact that I had jumped. I hadn't fallen in. I also hadn't planned to jump. When I left the party that night, I had no plan, and then I was too drunk to make one. I wasn't familiar with the city but I happened to go in the direction of the waterfront, and there I found the bars. The only real decision that night happened when I was sitting at the bar, where some guy was chatting me up. I wanted to get away from him and the bar and when I was on the street I decided I wanted to get away from the crowds. That was my one plan. I walked north, along waterfront streets, and eventually I found myself in someplace quiet. I kept moving, as if by moving I could walk right out of my life. I found myself on a busier street, and then another street, which I discovered was actually the off-ramp of the bridge.

Unless you've been in my shoes, you don't know how it is. You're feeling too much and too hard to actually think, submerged in a stew of despair and anger and sorrow and self-pity. You sink deeper and deeper. You let yourself sink to the bottom. And then you just stay there. I could have remained that way for hours if the priest hadn't come. With the wind tangling my dress around my legs, the foghorns bleating into the night, the damp caressing my skin, my hand sliding along the railing as I took the smallest steps, barely moving, as if now, at last, I saw where I was going and was reluctant to go there.

The priest got my brain going again. He crept closer and closer, pretending he wasn't, assuming I was too drunk to realize that any decision was going to be taken out of my hands. That I was going to miss the unlooked-for opportunity that had been presented to me. That I'd never have the chance again. I tried to talk myself into some kind of courage but it was just words.

A bomb went off in my head and before the sound of it died away, I jumped.

Sitting in the hospital, I'd been thinking about what Helen said. About what she'd done with her life and what my solution had been. About the magnitude of my traumas compared to hers. I was smart enough to recognize the fallacy of the idea that any trauma is devastating to a sensitive soul. Rape was rape.

I told Helen I'd met Father Ennis around the Fourth of July, and to forestall more questions I talked around it, telling her I'd been in Newport for the weekend with friends. It was my first trip to Newport; I'd gone to college in Massachusetts but hadn't been to Rhode Island and I was originally from New York.

"And now you're in Manhattan and have a glamorous job. You must enjoy it."

I admired the strength of it: she'd had the world's worst day and she must have been reeling with exhaustion, but here she was, sharp eyes that were nonetheless warm, her expression holding nothing but interest.

Sitting in her living room, the house quiet around us, scores of old paintings looking down on us, I realized I was content. Content to sit there in the dim light, on the sprung sofa. I'd done everything I could do and it was enough for Helen, this woman I hadn't known six months ago, who offered her life to me generously because she thought giving it might help me. I told her the truth: "So, yeah, I should, but I don't. I don't think it's the right job for me."

She didn't try to talk me into liking my job, as most people would, thinking of the way the job appeared to them rather what it was like actually doing the job. "You know what I've always thought? I think God gives each of us a talent or talents and our life's work is to understand what we are to do with them. Maybe working for the auction company isn't what you're meant to do."

"I don't know who would be meant to sell the detritus of rich people's lives."

"So what would you like to do?"

The idea flashed on me, fully formed. It was like rounding a corner at the Metropolitan Museum and seeing the portrait of *Madame X*. The jolt of that long slope of nose, the skin tinted blue by arsenic, so familiar from books but suddenly the real thing is there before you and it stops you in your tracks. Then I remembered that I had to save money just to rent a car to Newport. My mother's voice in my head, I told Helen that my mother considered art to be a short, straight road to penury.

She remembered what I'd said about my mother, but I was shy; you could hardly tell someone who'd been raped about a mother who'd tossed out every gift you'd ever made for her. Not that I would have told her, anyway; I figured that if people knew my own mother didn't like me, they'd look more closely and discover why.

Instead, I launched into a few minutes of the patter I gave to Father Ennis, about the plays and the concerts. "I don't know when it started but now the audience does a standing ovation no matter how good the performance is. Every time. I've got two theories about that: either the audience is trying to convince themselves that the performance was worth the price of the tickets or the audience figures if they get to their feet they'll get out that much faster."

"Is there someone who takes you to all these places?"

"You mean a date? Sometimes there is and sometimes I go with friends. I don't have a boyfriend now. The last one was kind of a disaster so I'm kind of thinking I'm done."

Helen had been slumped in the chair, but now sat up, startled. "You're done? Done with dating?"

"Yeah." I don't know if it was the surroundings, or Helen, or pure exhaustion, but once more I told her the truth: "I'm totally done with it. There's some trick to it that I've never gotten. All my friends go out with the same guy for years and then they get engaged, and none of mine last more than a couple of dates."

I could have stopped there but now I wanted to hear what I'd say. "I don't think I've ever been asked out by a normal guy. They're drunks or they do drugs, or they're mean or they're egocentric jerks or they're train wrecks. I haven't had a single date with a nice guy. Not one."

"Perhaps the nice ones are a little intimidated," she ventured. "I might be if I were a young man and I liked a girl who was beautiful and brilliant and sophisticated, and had a successful career."

And here it was: I'd walked myself right up to it. I started to feel shaky because even though I was telling myself to keep my stupid mouth closed, I knew I wouldn't. I couldn't look at her while I said it, though, because I'd cry and I then I'd hate myself because what was my life compared to hers? "Intimidated because I come from Nowhere, New York and most of my crap salary goes to an apartment I share with two other girls even though it's the size of a jewelry box and I can't afford this year's dress which in any case would look terrible on me because I have this pasty-white face and fat thighs."

Helen was taken aback. "You can't believe that, can you?"

It was like pushing pins into my skin; it hurt but I kept on doing it. "I do. I think it's a fairly accurate assessment. There's something wrong with me. I don't know what, exactly, but there is. Not even my own mother loves me."

Then, I took a breath while I pretended to debate myself but I knew I'd say it. "I tried to kill myself in July. That's how I met Father Ennis. I jumped off the Newport Bridge and he rescued me."

"Oh, my dear," Helen said softly. I heard movement and thought she was going to bed, to get away from me. But then I felt her beside me and she sank into the sofa and put her arms around me.

Her husband had just had a stroke, she probably was spending her first night alone in more than sixty years, yet here she was. Stupid, stupid me.

"Tell me," she said.

It was selfish, but I did. She heard about my father who died and about my mother. What my mother told me about myself, how hard I tried to make her love me. Finally, having worked myself up to it, the most frightening thing of all: being told I was incapable of love. No one would ever love me, I told Helen, because I would never be able to reciprocate. When I ran down, I whacked the tears from my cheeks and made an attempt to shrug it off.

"It's okay. So there's something wrong with me. So I tried to off myself. Not a big deal in the great scheme of things, right? Despite my best efforts, I'm still kicking."

"If your mother were here, I'd shake her until her teeth fell out," Helen said with some asperity. "To tell her own child that. I can't imagine it. I just can't. I understand why you believed her: she's your mother, after all. But don't you believe her."

I didn't want to look at Helen. Couldn't bring myself to do it because then I'd see what was in her face and I didn't want to do that.

"Of course you can love. That's just pure nonsense. You can love and you can be loved. I don't know why she said what she did but it's complete and utter nonsense." I was still sniffling and thinking how hideous I must look but I heard the anger in her voice. "My dear God. You don't see yourself at all, do you? When you first came to the house I didn't think you did."

"I think I see myself pretty clearly."

"Obviously, you don't." She stroked my hair and then sat back to face me. "Listen to me: no matter what anyone says to you, no matter what anyone does to you, you decide who you are. You decide."

Her gaze wandered while she thought, then came back to me. "After I was raped, the thought of leaving the house was unbearable. When people looked at me, they wouldn't see me, they'd see the girl who was soiled. Some people might pity me; more likely they'd be disgusted by me. I told you how Delia pushed me out the door and Peter came along and swept me down that river . . . and now I'm mixing metaphors, aren't I? But here's the point: I might have kept that idea of myself my entire life, all because of something that probably took no more than a few minutes. I could always have thought of myself as this appalling creature that had been raped. But I didn't. And I thank Delia for that. She didn't tell me anything about myself and I wouldn't have believed her if she had. Instead, she gave me the example of her life."

Helen was rubbing my back, slowly, though I'm not sure she realized she was doing it. It was comforting, though I still could see myself, hunched and unlovely, being comforted by this small old woman I'd only recently met. "She wasn't some poor soul who'd suffered a catastrophic loss and spent the rest of her life mourning. After her first child died, she didn't shut herself away. She kept on being who she was and doing what she had been doing. If she hadn't done that, she wouldn't have met Mr. Heade when she was walking that day, and changed the course of her life.

There would have been no store if she hadn't bought that painting. She didn't accept the role her society would have given her. So I chose not to see myself as some people might have seen me. I stopped mourning. You should, too."

She leaned away and faced me. "This may be the most important thing to know about ourselves: we decide who we are. Nobody else. Not the people around town, at the grocery store, the post office, or wherever. Not our mother and father. Certainly not some stranger in an alley. We decide. We decide whom we love and what we love, and really, in a nutshell, that's who we are, isn't it? When I realized that, I started walking again. Just like Delia, though I didn't know it then."

I thought she was pretty smart.

"No, I'm pretty old," she said, taking my hands in hers. "And very opinionated. I don't know an awful lot but I do know a few things. So believe me about this: I can tell you in a million ways that your mother is wrong, but don't you listen to either of us, or anyone else for that matter. Decide for yourself who you are."

I asked what time she wanted to get to the hospital. When we'd ironed out the plans for the following day, which involved a quick breakfast, a trip to the hospital, and lunch in the cafeteria, after which I'd get my bag and drive home, it was nearly midnight. As Helen went up the stairs, I went from room to room, switching off the lights. At the top she turned to me.

"I have been lucky in life: I've had parents who loved me and a brother who did. I've had friends and for almost all my life I've had Peter. He makes me realize how lucky it was that I was open to love when it came to me. Because believe it or not, it comes to us all, my dear."

I watched her go slowly down the hall, her white hair picking up the hall light, the rest of her small, shadowed, and perhaps fearing that some part of her life was gone, as maybe it was. I hoped it wasn't, hoped that Peter would recover and be the person he was before the stroke. Even if he did recover, today, for her, must have been a taste of what was to come.

After I'd finished the article about the beech trees, I thought about the things I'd have to do to get ready for the week ahead: clothes to wash and iron, food to buy. That depressed me, so I turned off the light and slid down under the covers.

The waning moon outlined the dark forms of a dresser and chair and the paintings. I closed my eyes and felt I'd stepped into an alien life, the unfamiliar house all around me, the wingback chairs in the living room, a grandfather clock in one corner of the dining room, frozen to seven minutes past two. The narrow kitchen with a linoleum counter, relict of the 1950s, possibly one of the first renovations the Brennans had done when they bought the house, along with the kitchen cabinets which were horrible faux-country style, not in keeping with the house at all. Then I realized how unkind that was and my mind went to Peter as we'd seen him in the garden and in the hospital.

Had he known about the rape before he'd asked her out? If he hadn't, how had he felt when Helen told him? Angry on Helen's behalf or, selfishly, on his own? Had his feeling for Helen changed at that moment because she wasn't the person he'd imagined, though not by her own fault? In those days it must have made a difference; it still did. I tried to picture Peter as he must have been then: tall, slim, with that rounded forehead and the sharp nose that reminded me of the *Capitoline Brutus*, though Peter didn't have the weird eyes. What it must have been like for her to tell that young man. Yet after that, maybe not always happy—no one was—but having that security about someone else. Someone and something you could always count on. I could hear her voice: *He makes me realize how lucky it was that I was open to love when it came to me.* I let that roll around in my brain, wondering if somehow I'd missed my chance.

The house crept back in again, smelling musty, though with the thick odor of old wood that I'd always liked. Room after room made uncanny by the moonlight, crowded with dark paintings, less a simulacrum of the Frick or the Gardner than of something assembled for tours at Halloween.

I was half-asleep when I heard a noise that I thought at first was the house settling in the cooling air. It sounded like footsteps belonging to someone small and slight, and it would start and then pause and then start again, moving through the rooms downstairs. Then the stairs felt that soft, light weight, one and then the next and then the next, coming slowly. The hair rose on the back of my neck. I slid off the bed and crossed the room to the doorway. I could see nothing but they were still coming on, fractionally louder and surer than they had been downstairs. I peered into the hall and saw nothing as they came toward me but I felt something warm and benign. I had a sudden image of my father, a tall man with oddly delicate bones and gray eyes like mine, and my fingers went to the onyx ring I wore; it had been snug on his finger but I'd had to wrap string around it so I wouldn't lose it. He'd gone off the road in a snowstorm when I was nine and landed upside down in a ditch. Sometimes, when I was very low, he would appear in my mind, unbidden, and I'd feel embraced by the knowledge that someone had loved me very much.

The footsteps passed, fading as they continued down the hall and into Helen's bedroom. I could have followed them but there was no need; I was as sure of that as if a voice had spoken the words. Helen was fine. I went back to bed and almost immediately fell asleep.

A few weeks later I was on my way to Newport again, this time by train to Kingston then bus to Newport. Peter was going to be discharged from the nursing home on Thursday. I'd been calling nearly every day, and after Helen had given me the medical report, we'd keep right on talking. It was wonderful. I'd told her the very worst and she still liked me, which meant that I didn't have to be careful with my words. She heard about my days, and what I was thinking and feeling. She didn't get the entertaining reports I gave my mother and Father Ennis; instead, she just heard uncensored me.

One night Helen told me that Peter had to be persuaded to eat, and earlier that day he didn't seem to recognize her. Her voice was so uncertain that I felt I needed to go to Newport.

Todd asked me if I had a boyfriend. Actually, what he asked was whether I had a boyfriend or a drug connection in Newport. He knew the second was a joke and probably meant the first to be, too. Todd and I had commiserated now and again about our dating lives. Though as I said, Todd, who's not the handsomest guy on the planet, and not the youngest, either, has a boyfriend, and he recently celebrated his three-month anniversary with a guy he says is perfect, though I still haven't met him.

Todd's question came when we were having lunch in one of the million coffee shops in Manhattan. Todd likes coffee shops and while I'm not partial to them, I enjoy the waiters, who blow away all the pretensions of the tonier eateries in town. They take a zillion orders, remember them all, get the food out quickly, never give the wrong food to the wrong person, and, in short, handle ten times the traffic that the *chiceries* do and never bat an eyelash, unlike their tony counterparts, who seem to think that if they're slow and look pained, you'll be convinced their job is almost more than Man can handle and will give them a tip commensurate with their effort. I only wish the food was better in coffee shops.

"You move fast," Todd said admiringly. "You spend one weekend up there alone and you find a man? Or is it just a casual drug connection?"

"You can't tell but I'm laughing hysterically on the inside," I said. "I'm going to be staying with the Brennans. Helen invited me."

Todd sat back in the booth, felled by this information. "The old couple? You're joking, right?"

I explained, feeling defensive. After all, I'd only met them in July.

"Interesting," he said noncommittally, but I knew what he was thinking. It's what any born-and-bred New Yorker would think: she's getting sucked into some drab world populated by the Medicare crowd. Drab because nothing outside New York City was exciting or interesting—you had to go to a place like Paris or Tokyo or London to find something nearly equivalent, and even they couldn't hold a candle to the city. And old people were what gathered with their confreres to compare aches and pains, doctor visits, and ferret out news of recent hospitalizations and deaths. Todd was worried but not yet truly alarmed.

Helen said that Peter was about seventy percent of where he'd been before the stroke, which told me he probably needed help getting around. He was supposed to continue physical therapy as an outpatient, although Helen feared that seventy percent was all he was ever going to reclaim. "At our age, we don't bounce back so easily."

"It would be better if you had someone helping full time. I can come for the first few days, anyway."

Rather than telling me they could manage alone, Helen hesitated, and that told me how anxious she was. "Why don't I come up Friday and stay until Monday." And just like that, it was settled.

Todd tried to work it out for himself using his own reference points, as we all do. By the time the waiter slapped the bill on the table, Todd thought he had it figured out. "It's the priest, isn't it? Tell me, please, that you haven't slept with him. Though I wouldn't blame you. Not my type but he's hot in a way. All that nervous energy. Kind of a jittery, could-be-a-psycho vibe that would make some people want to get a closer look."

My turn to sit back. "He's not a psycho."

Todd redirected his speculation to this more interesting topic. "He's always hitting himself; did you notice that? The mosquitoes and whatever other nasty winged things flying around suburbia can't possibly be that bad. I wonder if he's a secret flagellant. Probably wears a hair shirt under that cheap polyester. Gets it tailored at the Vatican, or somewhere equally sinister. I can picture him with his arms out, a great big cruciform of anticipated agony, while some nasty little tailor takes measurements."

"Now you're just amusing yourself." I knew he didn't mean what he said but I felt disloyal just listening to it. "I thought you liked Newport," I said to get him off the topic.

Todd looked down his long nose, but not unkindly, because he wasn't asking me why I wanted to hang out with a couple of octogenarians, though I knew that's what he really found odd.

"You're too weird for Newport, Ems, and I mean that in the kindest way possible."

I laughed. "There is no kindest way with that comment."

"You going to put your brain in storage before you cross the East River? I just can't picture you in a sea of bilious pinks and greens. Black is definitely your color." Todd was shaking his head. "Two possibilities: a boy or drugs."

"Peter Brennan had a stroke," I insisted. "He's being discharged this week and Helen needs help. That's why I'm going."

"You'll tell me eventually," he said. "I'm your best friend in the city."

It's odd how you can tell someone the truth and something about them prevents them from believing you. I could have talked myself blue in the face.

I started feeling happy on Thursday but on the way to Newport I began to have second thoughts.

I don't know if other people do this, but sometimes it's like I'm out of my body, sitting near the ceiling in a corner of the room, looking down at myself. It happens to me all the time, when I'm laughing with Todd at work, when I'm at a restaurant with a guy I'm dating. I'll see myself from that height, and my laugh will come at me, harsh and ugly, or I'll see my stupid face, and my nice black pants and whatever top I'm wearing will look pathetic and cheap, and I'll see my fat thighs and I'll just hate myself. I'll think there isn't one part of me that's halfway decent, and why am I putting on this show like I think there is?

Somewhere in the middle of Connecticut, I saw myself sitting on the train, years-old white shirt, the yellow cashmere cardigan that looked so pretty when I bought it and now was completely pilled but I'd worn it that day thinking it may not be pink or green but it was as Newport as I could manage without spending money. I saw my gray skirt and my big feet in gray flats I hadn't been able to afford but that I'd bought when I was dating Rob because he liked me in gray, which had led to a flurry of monochromatic purchases: dresses, shirts, pants, and skirts that obliterated what was left in my checking account. I saw myself wearing these clothes that I'd bought in optimism but which now were the detritus of failure, as everything with me was a failure, and yet here I was, despite that bleak history, optimistic and happy as if this venture would end up any different from those in my past.

What did I think? That two old people liked me? I could walk Peter around the garden a million times, vacuum the whole house, wash every dish in the place, clean up the yard, and it would do no good. I knew that you couldn't make people like you; I had some experience in that area, after all. Someone had been nice to me, and stupid, stupid me was rushing back to two old people who had enormous troubles that overshadowed everything else in their lives, including me.

But she did like me. Somehow. Despite all the things I'd told her, she liked me. I knew it. I might bray like a mule and look like a beached whale but she liked me, anyway. Though she was duped by Taylor, she was no fool, and even so, she liked me. It was a little masterpiece that I owned, that I could take out whenever I wanted and look at with unalloyed delight. I'd told her more than I'd ever told anyone, I'd told her everything, and, still, she liked me.

What counted most, though, was that I had two hands to help, and that was the point of the trip, wasn't it?

That was the effect that Mass-going had on me. In New York, there's nothing but people, nothing, really, to distract you from yourself. It's not like you can take a walk on the beach to clear your head; you can't even walk in Central Park because the place is packed with people. And everyone talks about people: who's sleeping with whom, who's breaking up, who's put on twenty break-up pounds, who's had too many late nights. It's all about people and it's all superficial and gossipy. It's hard to escape and if you're not happy with yourself to begin with, nothing about New York discourages you from dwelling even more on your bad points. When I was in church, though, listening to a gospel, the message was always about the action of love, expressing it in everything you did. I heard that message over and over and at times like these, when I was wallowing, it came to me and sort of set me on my feet again. Instead of worrying about the amount of love coming my way, my job was to send it into the world, to practice it, share it, live it. So I was traveling to Newport to practice it and share it and live it—and hope that Helen's promise was true, that at some point in my life it would be coming to meet me.

Newport worked on me. Whether or not the Brennans figured into it, as the bus came down 138 to the Jamestown Bridge, Narragansett Bay was a million shards of glass in sunlight; that summer color, the pale green of new leaves, had deepened to dark sapphire. The view at the top of the Newport Bridge encompassing the squat lighthouse on Rose Island, the spires of Newport, and the mouth of the bay dissolving into the great blue horizon of Rhode Island Sound.

By the time I'd walked from the Gateway Center to the Brennans' home, happiness had returned. I was thinking that I could spare an hour or so on Saturday and Sunday to walk as much of the city as I could, dipping now and then into the guide I'd bought that wrote about the history and the architecture of some of the more notable houses.

As I turned off Thames Street, my heart sank. I recognized the car parked in front of the Brennans' house.

Bart Meagher, Harvard and Harvard Law School, was sliding a huge piece of plywood from the back of his car but he stopped when he saw me. "What are you doing here?"

I had a jacket over the sweater, carried my weekend bag in one hand and a large reusable bag in the other. Both were heavy; I'd brought New York bagels and a variety of pastries, a bag of designer pasta, a loaf of sourdough bread, and a jar of good tomato sauce—I wasn't a great cook but I intended to do my best. I looked like a refugee and though the air was cool and the walk from the bus station wasn't long, my face was damp and sweat was trickling down my back. I hated meeting the world underarmed and hated even more being in that state when I was meeting someone who didn't like me.

He reminded me of a Winslow Homer, one of those earthbound men, their feet solidly planted on the soil, double-dipped in brute energy. I took in the chinos and the blue-and-white-striped shirt, the loafers that he wore sockless in November; it was the uniform of prep school, Ivies, clubs, and privilege. He also had the confidence, the dazzlingly white teeth, the slight meatiness that was on parade at the Hamptons and certain blocks of the Upper East Side. Bart Meagher had all of those, plus a tan. In November. But he didn't come from money; Helen had said as much. So that was something.

I pulled myself up and straightened my shoulders. "It's so hard to resist charm." He'd probably never had a difficult day in his life. And had a mother who saved everything, including his used chewing gum. I crossed the lawn and rang the bell.

"They're not home." He slid the plywood halfway into the car and came up the walk. "Peter's back in the hospital. High fever."

"Oh, no." I stood on the doorstep, deflated.

"The door's open." He moved around me and pushed it. "If you brought something for them you can leave it in the house. I'll tell them you've been here."

He followed me into the kitchen, where a cup of half-finished tea sat forlornly on the counter, keeping company with a solitary piece of toast, one bite taken out of it. Everything else was just the same, the small paintings hanging in the gloom. The house had a strange feeling without Helen, bereft, shrinking away from Bart Meagher's sunny energy. I set the bag on the counter, thinking what to do.

I'd had an idea that I'd surprise Helen with the food and Helen would sit companionably in the kitchen while I made dinner, and she'd tell me everything that had happened since our last call. I imagined that I'd look through the magazines and take to bed any that had the trees or the houses or anything that I liked about the city. I imagined getting up Saturday morning and showing them four different kinds of bagels and my treasure of pastries. I was going to give them a great weekend . . . but now I wasn't.

I turned and he was right behind me, a probing look that vanished quickly, though not before I saw it. His eyes were brilliant, green irises with a thin band of dark blue around the perimeter. I said the first thing that came into my head. "So what's with the plywood?"

"I'm good-deed-doing. It's a break from all that unscrupulous lawyering I do all week."

My hair was sticking wetly to my face; with both hands I pushed back the hair and let it drop over my shoulders. "Ha, ha," I said.

"Peter's been using a wheelchair. I threw down a few boards when he was discharged after the stroke but it's not a solution. This time of year, they'd be waiting a month at least for a carpenter to get a ramp built. Well, so." He shrugged.

The back door was off the kitchen. I took a few steps and opened the door. I looked past the half-finished ramp to the rose garden, facing west, and the flower garden that faced east; Peter had been deadheading painted daisies when he'd had the stroke. I heard again Helen's small cry when we saw him. Newport hadn't had a killing frost; things were still growing but there were more spent flowers than blooms and the annuals were leggy, neglected. Maybe I could clean up the garden and prune the roses as I'd always done at my mother's house. And was that, in Bart Meagher's terms, a good deed, or did I expect the kind of recompense I'd never had from my mother? Did it matter, though, why I was doing it as long as I was doing it? I could exhaust myself, thinking. Did, frequently.

When I turned back, he hadn't moved. Still leaning against the counter, tanned arms folded, watching me, ready for a challenge. "The gardens look a little sad out there."

Nodding, he checked his watch. I have a friend who says you can tell everything about a man from the watch he wears. His wasn't the ultrathin kind or the two-tone alternative that usually accompanied the kind of clothes he wore. It looked like an ordinary, inexpensive brand. Maybe business in Newport wasn't very lucrative. "You in town for the weekend?"

"Three days."

A knowing look. "Big party?"

"Nope." I closed the back door. The kitchen was so narrow that we were separated by only a few feet. He smelled of fresh air and something vaguely sweet, most likely the shampoo he used. He was waiting for me to leave.

"Interesting ring," he said abruptly.

It sounded derisive or at least I took it that way because the ring was pretty ordinary. A rectangle of onyx set in gold with a diamond chip. Not particularly flashy but also not something a woman would wear. "It was my father's. He died when I was a kid."

Something stopped him from saying whatever he'd been ready to bring forth next. He gave me a long look. I waited because if you wait long enough, people start to feel uncomfortable and will talk. Most people need to fill in spaces.

He didn't. Just stood there in the chinos, which I now saw were not so crisp; he'd been kneeling in them. And the shirt was frayed at the collar. Old clothes, then. He checked his watch again. "I've got a bit of work ahead if I'm going to get the backdoor ramp finished today." A glance at me. "I'll let them know you were here."

"I'm staying with them for a few days." His eyebrows shot up. "To help out," I added. I reached for the bag and lifted it. "Dinner tonight and breakfast tomorrow."

Hard to tell what he was thinking but he made me uncomfortable, looking and looking. And thinking; you could see it. "I guess I'll bring the overnight bag upstairs and then go over to the hospital."

"You don't have a car."

"No point having one in the city."

He pushed himself away from the counter. "Give me a half hour, I'll drive you over."

"Another good deed?"

His face was impassive.

"Okay," I said.

— 32 —

When the day finally came, Peter arrived at the courthouse in a wheelchair and Jim almost envied him. A damp morning in the latter part of November, the sky as dull as tarnished silver, a gale blowing through the city; the wind tore at his coat and his clothing was a sieve as he pulled himself up the steps outside the courthouse. One leg had declared its independence; his options were to maneuver it a step at a time, as you would a stack of anvils, putting all your energy to the business of lifting and carefully setting down, or to gain a step with one leg and then half-turn so you could swing the other leg past the riser to join its mate on the next step. Half-man, half-crab, he would have been the cynosure of at least Washington Square except that, mercifully, the weather discouraged casual perambulation.

Inside the building, the windows shook and rattled. But he'd made it to the courthouse and he'd make it through the trial. The room was large and little warmth was to be had; he was pretending that if he kept his coat on, eventually he wouldn't have to concentrate to prevent his body from shivering. The fact was, despite his efforts, he'd lost weight. He'd been mildly surprised there was any more to lose but then he hadn't seen his body for months. Except for his hands, the skin shriveled and dry as last year's leaves. November shielded him from Lizzie's eyes and thank God for small mercies.

He sat alone, behind the others, who nevertheless knew he was there. Helen acknowledging him with a faltering smile, Meagher with a grin and a nod, Emily nearly as nervous as Helen. Maria was late, and he was beginning to think she wasn't going to appear but then she did. Everyone was wearing black, it seemed, Emily more stylish than the others. Or so he thought, anyway. A sober color or perhaps just a November color.

Taylor and his wife had looked around, too. She was more subdued than he remembered, wearing a plain black suit.

Three lawyers on Taylor's side of the room, Meagher defiantly solo on the Brennans' side. Before the judge walked in Meagher was chatting with the old couple, his voice low, the words themselves probably unremarkable, the music of them meant to reassure.

Meagher had predicted that the Taylors would build a case for conspiracy, but Jim still wasn't prepared for it. He could almost see himself as the lawyers painted him, avaricious as a crow, alert to opportunity and, when it came, preying on an old couple who'd signed a contract freely, without duress. Emily, who'd stiffened at the mention of her name, was someone he didn't recognize, predatory, motivated by an ambition as cold as the bottom of the bay.

It had been ludicrous in Meagher's office and would have been now except that the judge was impossible to read. Mary Iannota was sixtyish, with coarse, curly, black hair pulled tightly back from a forbidding face that could have been carved from stone: a long, straight nose, sharp jaw, and a hard mouth. In her dark robes, she could have been kin to Cotton Mather.

The Boston lawyers, fortyish, wore identical airs of confidence. One, blond hair and gold-rimmed spectacles that gave his eyes an owlish look, made the case while the dark-haired lawyer sat at the table taking notes and looking at his cell phone. Wade, the local lawyer, sat beside the note taker. He had a sheaf of papers that he barely glanced at and while he seemed to follow closely, he never said a word. Jim wondered how Taylor was able to afford all of them but then he remembered Meagher's speculation that one of Taylor's clients was footing the bill.

Taylor on the stand. Narrating a humble history that obviously had been rehearsed. He'd become acquainted with the Brennans through his work with the Colonial Commission, an organization seeking to preserve the architectural heritage of Newport, with a focus on seventeenth- and eighteenth-century structures.

"Initially, I approached the commission to determine whether part of their mandate was furnishing the buildings they acquired, but once you join a small society of volunteers, you can expect to be asked to pitch in wherever help is needed." The shrug of a foot soldier, duty bound. "I've done just about everything, from helping to organize fundraisers to identifying properties that may have been overlooked in the past, which was how I happened to meet the Brennans."

An air of vague distress as he pretended to work out how he had been misunderstood. “Quite honestly,” he said, “when I first called on Mr. and Mrs. Brennan, I was paying less attention to what was on the walls than whether the walls and windows were in good repair. I did mention to them that the commission has negotiated contracts that allow homeowners to remain in their homes for a period of time after ownership has passed to the commission. They are watertight agreements, but of course I understand the reluctance to relinquish ownership. It’s only natural, isn’t it? Historic homes are unique as well as beautiful. We all value them enormously. Then I noticed the paintings. Mr. and Mrs. Brennan were very grateful when I offered them an alternative and quite honestly, I was relieved that I was able to help them in some small way.”

Despite the undershirt, a wool shirt and clerical collar, a heavy blazer, and an overcoat, Jim’s muscles were locked against the urge to shudder his way into warmth. He heard only half of what Taylor said under his lawyer’s examination and Meagher’s cross-examination. He was afraid he wouldn’t be equal to the day, heard Lizzie’s voice: “You want to have some kind of psychotic episode and think something’s attacking you?” Part of his mind, the part that wasn’t subjected to the breathing or cataloguing the variety of pain, was sending words and more words to the deaf nonentities in the ether.

Words and more words when he knew better. Like playing hide-and-seek when you were the only player. Jumping rope when there was no rope. It was a magnificent thing that no one could see into your brain because the thoughts you had would shame you. He longed to be back at the rectory and sitting in front of a roaring fire. He had never felt so cold.

Helen resurrected her bank mien: attentive, considering, choosing her words with care as she narrated a brief history of her art collection, her introduction to Maria, her first meeting with Taylor. If she was anxious, she was hiding it well. Meagher led her easily, though Taylor’s lawyer had encountered something polite but immalleable.

The temperature dropped considerably when Taylor’s lawyer started on Maria. She’d deliberately looked him over when he’d approached the stand, and her features had resolved into open hostility. The lawyer proceeded with questions about her background; Meagher objected that her birthplace was irrelevant, as was her immigration status, which anyway was not at issue because she’d been granted citizenship in 2005. That settled, Maria turned an inquiry about her relationship to the Brennans into a discourse on Taylor’s threat.

"You say you wouldn't steal from anyone," the lawyer said, "but subsequently you were fired from two jobs. Can you relate the circumstances of that?"

It didn't matter that Maria had no explanation. There was nothing glamorous about her, nothing seductive about her manner, which was as stark and solid as a cliff face; the lawyer might as well have been using a fork to chip away pieces. In a way, Jim thought, she was like Lizzie, both of them so authentic as to be jarring. Nothing about them had been smoothed to fit society's expectations of them. And as with Lizzie, when Maria spoke you believed her. Maria said she'd found steady work since her termination from the nursing homes and her employers had no issues with the quality of her work. The lawyer pointed out that two of Maria's current employers were Father Ennis and his sister; Maria was unmoved by that revelation.

Jim had been steeling himself to take the stand after Maria. Leo would have been a better witness: he was dignified, even sporting a bib of confectioner's sugar beneath his chin or a bullseye of jam on his stomach. He would have been composed and his elocution immaculate. But Jim had to wait: Emily was called next.

Her eyes, as she took the stand, were dull as the day itself. Meagher must have warned her what might be coming. Was coming; she now knew it as well as Jim did and was she sorry he'd called her those months ago? Was she angry with him for involving her with the Brennans? When he'd given in to impulse, he hadn't been thinking she'd come back to Newport, but that was the problem, wasn't it? He'd been thoughtless and now she was on the witness stand and it was his fault she was about to be brutalized.

Emily became warier with each question from Taylor's lawyer, though he was gentle as a June breeze. Where she grew up, her education, her history with Metropolitan Auctions, her current position in the company. The salary he'd researched was correct. She lived with two other women but rents were high in the city and she was careful with her money. She said that she had a slight acquaintance with Father Ennis, who'd called her to ask for a professional opinion about the Brennans' art. Explained how a trip to their home followed that phone call and how the trip led to a visit to the Taylors' store.

The lawyer probed for her opinion of the contract, her experience with such things, and she reined in the response she no doubt wished to give. Pulled herself up a little, frosted every word that described Taylor's contract. She intended to skate her way to safety, then, and Jim believed that she could do it. The lawyer appeared to have gone down all the avenues he'd opened with his questions.

Then he backtracked. She characterized her relationship with Father Ennis as slight—what exactly did she mean by that?

"I'd met him once before."

A request that she describe the circumstances of that meeting brought Meagher to his feet. "Whether Ms. Bell had a cup of coffee or chatted with him in line at the grocery store is not germane to this suit or countersuit."

"I believe the court might be interested to find out why Father Ennis would call a slight acquaintance in New York rather than Mr. and Mrs. Taylor or any of the other respectable art dealers in and around Newport," the lawyer said mildly.

Meagher was overruled and Emily took a deep breath, her gaze sweeping the room, and anchored herself on her lawyer. "I came up for a party. I didn't enjoy the party." She shrugged. "So I left. After that I decided to take a walk and accidentally wound up on the Newport Bridge."

"You were on the bridge accidentally?"

Her gaze flickered to Meagher. "It was my first time in Newport. I thought I was walking along the waterfront."

"But when you realized you were on a bridge, you didn't immediately retrace your steps. According to the Newport Police Department's records, you were charged with trespassing."

"It didn't occur to me that I was trespassing." Shrugged again, and graced Taylor's lawyer with a grin. "As for reasons, you have to admit that the view from the bridge by moonlight is pretty spectacular."

"According to the police report, a passerby saw you and Father Ennis arguing but you didn't remain on the bridge. The report says that you both were pulled from the bay sometime between 2:30 and 2:45 that morning. Would you explain that sequence of events for the court?"

Meagher was on his feet again but whatever he meant to say was stoppered by a single shake of her head. She took a minute to consider it. "Father Ennis wanted to give me a ride home. I was afraid to get into the car because I didn't know him. He said he was a priest but as far as I knew, he could have been anybody. I just wanted to get away from him."

"So you jumped off the bridge?"

"I was drunk, okay? I've only been drunk about three times in my life. Bad things happen when you're drunk, but I was drunk that night. Is that what you want me to say?"

"So were you on that bridge accidentally or did you in fact have a reason for going there? Did you head to the bridge because you intended to take your life that night?"

Meagher jumped to his feet. "Irrelevant." He wouldn't be silenced this time. "This has no bearing on the case. It's been established that Ms. Bell met Father Ennis for the first time that night; the circumstances of that meeting are irrelevant."

Meagher wasn't angry, he was incandescent. Remembering Meagher's performance in his office, Jim wasn't sure that it wasn't manufactured, but it didn't matter; Emily had a little time to steady herself.

The objection was sustained and a few minutes later, Meagher was walking Emily through the bridge and the days after. His tone was impersonal but his questions were careful. She did not lose her composure again.

Then it was Jim's turn.

He willed himself not to shiver. Nothing he could do about the limp; swinging the numb leg it felt like years before he'd crossed the room. The judge looked him over as he approached and he knew what she saw: a skeletal figure in baggy clothes, white stripes across one cheek where the scrapes had robbed the skin of pigment. Sunken eyes, dark circles beneath them. As cautious in his movements as a centenarian. Whatever she thought, her face remained impassive.

Up close, the lawyer's cheeks were slightly pink, the skin as smooth as if it had been buffed. The lawyer up close as well. Jim felt the slight recoil as the lawyer took in every millimeter of skin on Jim's face. Jim wasn't sure whether his face argued for or against him, though could anyone imagine that he had any more energy than that needed to continue to live? That anyone who had to lug his body from here to there, who had to concentrate every bit of energy on that effort, would have strength remaining to entertain greed?

The first questions were the same as those posed to Taylor and Emily. Biographical data, though Jim had to concentrate before he spoke; finding the information in his brain was mining coal in an unlit cave.

The lawyer, still sounding casual as he said, "Ms. Bell has stated that the first time she met you was when you encountered her on the Newport Bridge. Is that correct?"

Jim nodded and was told he needed to answer verbally. He did.

"So you'd never seen her before. Can you explain to the court how you happened to be on the bridge at that hour?"

Meagher objected.

"We have named four parties in our suit and with this line of questioning I hope to establish cause for two of the parties involved in the breach of contract."

The lawyer was repeating his question and Jim inclined his head as if he were attending, though his leg had begun to throb in rhythm with his heartbeat. Still, it wasn't pain, exactly, and whenever his body's pains eased a little, exhaustion swept in. He felt around the tenebrous space that was his brain until he had a sequence of words.

"I received a call. They said a woman was on the bridge and I thought it was a mistake. I remember thinking that. That somebody misdialed. Or—" He closed his eyes to concentrate, to see something in that lightless space. Important that he disclose all the information because the sooner he did that, the sooner he could go home. "A joke. I thought it might be a prank. Some kid calling a random number." Though perhaps it didn't matter what he'd thought. "But then the second call came and that convinced me that something was happening. An accident, maybe. I thought it must be a bad accident, which is why he was calling a priest. So I drove to the bridge and I saw Emily Bell on the walkway."

His thoughts again, which probably didn't matter, but he groped around to see if he'd missed anything. Pleased that he hadn't, that he had nothing left to contribute, he opened his eyes again. Noticed for the first time that Helen had a little scarf around her neck. Red. Cardinal red, he decided.

Then he saw Meagher. And remembered too late that he wasn't supposed to bring up the second call. They'd discussed it. Twice, in fact. Meagher had impressed on him the importance of maintaining his credibility. Which already was damaged because he'd told the police he'd been called to the bridge but nothing had shown up on his phone log. He was supposed to believe a tech glitch accounted for the missing call. He was supposed to stay far away from the second call.

But hadn't he sworn to tell the whole truth? The whole truth was two calls. Surely he couldn't be blamed for telling the truth. But the thought did not soothe him.

He could see the moment Taylor's lawyer understood. Jim was nervous now and that was another thing he wasn't supposed to reveal.

The lawyer came to the witness stand. "Did you say two, Father? You told the police that you'd received one call but in fact there were two? Not one but two? Is that what you said? Were both calls to inform you that someone was on the bridge?"

"Yes."

"Are you aware that your phone's log doesn't record even a single call at that time, much less two?"

"Yes, I know."

"Don't you think that's rather odd, Father Ennis?" The unmistakable emphasis on his name. "Because plenty of calls were logged before that time, both incoming and outgoing, and lots of calls the next day and the days following that. Including some from Ms. Bell after that night. And one you made to her place of business. Your phone appears to have logged all those."

He was looking over people's heads. Trying not to appear nervous but also distracted because he was cold.

"Okay. Now I can believe that one call could possibly have gone astray. Technology isn't perfect, after all. But two calls?" The lawyer was enjoying himself. "As I said, your phone appears to have had no problem logging incoming calls earlier in the evening and calls the next day and the following days. But not two calls that came in sometime around two o'clock that night?"

"I can't explain it."

"So we don't have any way of knowing whether you were on that bridge because you received a call, or you were there for some other reason, or even whether you were alone in the car when you drove to the bridge."

Jim didn't think a response was called for, but he couldn't help himself. "I told you why I was there."

"The police report indicates that someone called 911 just before 2:30 that morning. The caller said that a couple was having an argument on the walkway. Is that an accurate description of what was occurring?"

"Yes," he said, and then, "No. We aren't a couple. It wasn't an argument. It might have appeared to be an argument but I was trying to get her off the bridge because it was dangerous."

"So whether she intended to kill herself that night—"

"Objection."

"Sustained." The judge intimidated him, her face inviolate, her consonants unyielding. She would not believe him. His appearance bad enough, nothing there to indicate that he was a functioning member of society, and then the two missing calls. Why would she believe him?

"We have to wonder why one individual who witnessed Ms. Bell responded in a way we would expect, and that was to call 911, yet another individual, seeing Ms. Bell alone on the bridge, decided to call a Catholic priest between two and two thirty in the morning. I imagine that you receive certain calls routinely. When people are dying, for instance, they would call you to administer last rites."

"Yes."

"I expect that happens every so often. But are people in the habit of calling upon you to pick up indigents, inebriates, and the like?"

He decided he hated the lawyer. The buffed face. The smug expression. Insinuating what wasn't true. "She isn't an inebriate."

"I see. And I'm sure the judge will appreciate that defense of Ms. Bell's habits." A long pause. "But if you didn't know Ms. Bell, and she wasn't at the point of death, why would someone call you rather than the police? Maybe there was no phone call. Which seems a more likely scenario than receiving two anonymous calls in the small hours of the morning about a woman you'd never met, which caused you to jump out of bed and drive straight to the Newport Bridge. Two anonymous calls that we can't document."

"I've told you the truth." His teeth chattered; he'd felt obliged to remove his overcoat before he took the stand. He locked his arms to his sides, willed the chattering to stop. "Someone called me. I don't know who called. It could have been someone passing by. It could have been anyone. I don't know and I'll never know."

He stared at his hands, noticed they were bloodless, shaking. He knew that words were being hurled his way but he was drifting. Maybe he was going to lose time again; he thought that might be the case. It didn't feel frightening but he knew he should be frightened. Some part of him recognized that.

He felt he'd lost the case. After all the work Meagher had done, after dragging Emily back through what had probably been the worst night of her life, after Maria sitting stoically while the lawyer insinuated lies and theft, Jim was going to lose the case and Helen's paintings would be carted away. With what was left of conscious thought he pleaded for help. Again. Words and words. He didn't deserve to be heard but still he asked for help. Not for him; little hope for him. Words and words that ran together like smoke, incense rising to saints who possibly never existed, to a deity that possibly was invented. Even now, he couldn't shake the habit of prayer.

"I called."

It was as if he'd touched a live wire. His heart thudding painfully, electricity coursing through his body and down both legs, fully felt. Jim hadn't seen him come in but there he was, in his rumpled slacks and a coat that looked to have been trampled by a herd of bison, skin sallow as always and nicotine-stained fingers.

The judge asked the newcomer to approach the bench. "If you please, Mr. Dyer?"

A quiet conversation followed. Meagher shot Jim a look of consternation as he and the other lawyers joined Mike. After a moment, Jim shuffled back to his seat and Mike was on the stand, being sworn in.

"You want the whole truth and nothing but," he told the courtroom. "So here it is. I made the call. I called Jim Ennis. He was none too pleased to be roused from his beauty sleep. Hung up on me that first time so I had at it again."

If Mr. Dyer had seen a woman on the bridge, the lawyer said, why hadn't he called the police, who presumably could remove her more quickly from any danger occasioned by vehicles or those in them?

"Who said I saw her?" Mike was scowling. "I didn't see her. Didn't need to see her; I knew she was there, all right." Jim's mind wasn't processing it. It was stuck a few beats back, still trying to match the voice he knew so well to that of his July Fourth caller.

The lawyer didn't seem to be too far ahead of Jim. He'd recoiled as if he'd been confronted with something feral. When he spoke again he was trying to recapture the tone of assurance. "You'll have to explain to the court how you knew—"

Mike cut him off.

"I wish I had time for a lot of palaver but I don't. I gotta be somewhere else, so here's the alpha and omega, free of charge: I called Father Ennis. I called him twice because it wasn't a question of the body. A soul was in mortal danger."

With that, he was out of the witness stand and halfway to the door, pausing briefly to say a word to Emily.

The double doors banged shut and just before the courtroom erupted, Jim scanned the room. Consternation, on both sides of the aisle. The only person who looked positively pacific, who wore an expression of great satisfaction, was Maria. Peaceful as a starry night, she caught Jim's eye and nodded sharply, once.

Judge Iannota called recess for two hours and summoned the lawyers to her chambers. Jim made good use of the time and returned to the courthouse in a different frame of mind.

The latter part of the afternoon went quickly because the judge announced an end to witness examination. The court would hear closing arguments.

Taylor's lawyer had much to say about his client's good intentions and his concern for an old couple who so obviously needed help. Jim had positioned himself between Emily and Maria, ready to support either or both when the lawyer waded into his slanderous tale of corruption, conspiracies, and instability. He was estimating how much emotional support the Brennans would need and how to insist on providing at least some financial support.

"He can't be done already," Emily whispered, "can he?"

Bart Meagher was collecting a handful of enlarged photos, setting some before the judge, holding up a duplicate set. Taylor's lawyer had joined his colleagues.

"I've printed a half-dozen representations of the Brennans' art," Meagher said, "but I'd like to draw your collective attention to one in particular. It's a view of Bellevue Avenue of one hundred years or so ago. The painting was subject to the same casual use as the others but it's easier to make out the scene because the colors are so vivid beneath the varnish. I am a lawyer and, as has been pointed out to me recently, lawyers aren't expected to know much about art. Nevertheless, I did recognize this artist, even though I only took a few courses in college and, I might add, I did so for reasons that had nothing to do with an avidity for the visual arts."

His tone became more businesslike. "This painting hasn't been authenticated but three people from the auction house have looked at it and believe it to be the work of Frederick Childe Hassam. I expect that if I recognized it, Mr. Taylor did, too. Childe Hassam paintings hang in the Museum of Fine Art, the Metropolitan Museum, and the Smithsonian, as well as museums elsewhere in this country and around the world. His paintings have sold for millions of dollars at auction, as Ms. Bell will tell you, and as Mr. Taylor certainly knows. That's not, as I understand it, the only valuable painting in the Brennans' collection. Though Mrs. Brennan's family weren't art collectors in the traditional sense, more than one obviously had a good eye."

Meagher took a folder from the table and handed it to the judge. "I have been able to obtain several bills of sale from Mr. Taylor's shop. As you can see, they are quite specific, detailing the name of the painting and the artist or, if both are not known, describing the painting and including the size, what medium was used to create it and an estimate of its age. On the other hand, I have not been able to locate another one-line contract for the entire contents of a property. You would suppose that at the very least, the contract would note the number of paintings being purchased."

Jim glanced at the lawyers flanking Taylor; both were stony faced. Taylor's face was flushed.

"Mr. Taylor's lawyers may argue that by signing this paper, the Brennans legitimized the contract. If it functioned merely as a receipt, the Brennans wouldn't have been required to do so. However, their signatures on the document were, they believed, verification that they sold one painting to Mr. Taylor. They thought they were legitimizing the sale for Mr. Taylor's benefit.

"A few of the paintings, as I have pointed out, appear to have significant value. Mr. Taylor's lawyers have alleged that a pecuniary motive led the Brennans to sell their art and, once they learned the value of their paintings, it also led to the breach of their agreement. But," he said, "there is another way to value things, one that doesn't consider dollars and cents, and this way may illuminate Mrs. Brennan's intention when she signed that piece of paper.

"If we're lucky in life, we have possessions we'd never part with. Maybe it's a watch passed down from mother to daughter. Maybe it's a ring that belonged to someone who loved you with all their might. I have a recording of a long-dead uncle. It's about two minutes long; he was singing at a family Christmas party. He had a good tenor voice and while that's why I recorded it, it isn't the reason I keep it.

"In her way, Helen Brennan valued the paintings much more than Mr. Taylor did. These oils and watercolors, rendered by talented and untalented hands, were collected by her father, her grandparents, and her great-grandparents. Some, at one point, had belonged to her brother. It is diminishing Helen and all of us to say these objects have sentimental value because that's a soft word, while what we feel is fierce and enduring.

What matters isn't the watch or the ring or the twenty-year-old recording. What matters is the people they represent and the love that binds us to them while they are alive and long after they've died. To Mrs. Brennan, the artists, the subjects, and the quality of the paintings mattered less than the people who once owned them. Helen Brennan is not an acquisitive woman; she is a loving woman. She held on tightly to them, just as she saved the ledgers from her family's store and the diary her great-grandmother kept.

"Neither Helen nor Peter Brennan recognized the monetary worth of the paintings, but that is not to say they didn't value them. It was difficult for Mrs. Brennan to sell even one; you'd have to have a heart of stone to believe that Helen Brennan would have allowed the house to be stripped of everything that connected her to her father, her brother, her grandparents, and great-grandparents. And to sell the entire collection for somewhat less than twenty-five dollars a painting? Helen Brennan wouldn't have done it. She loved the paintings because she loved the people, whether they had passed on twenty, forty, or nearly eighty years ago. I think we all would wish to be so present, so loved, so many years after our death."

Jim glanced at Helen, who was weeping soundlessly. And was caught by a movement beside him; Emily crying as if her heart would break. Meagher, coming back to the table, stopped, arrested by the sight of it. A flurry of emotions crossed his features; he sighed and sat down.

— 33 —

How had he felt? Face-to-face with Jesus after the resurrection, had Thomas been embarrassed as he was invited to touch the proofs of the crucifixion? Had Thomas been ashamed, or too overwhelmed to be anything but astonished? Or had he felt pure happiness, knowing the offer was one of love?

Jim hadn't believed, not really, even when the evidence was before his eyes. Though perhaps it was because it had never been before his eyes; everything had come to him second-hand. Except the demon. He'd felt that, had feared it but even so, he hadn't quite believed. So after Helen Brennan's protective spirit, after Bart Meagher's unseen guardian, after a long existence in the crosshairs of something that wasn't corporeal, and perhaps more tormenting because it wasn't something he could touch, he had come to the presence of God through a late-night phone call.

He turned it over and over in his mind, marveling. Something wondrous as sunrise, something that never lost its vigor, lighting up your brain as it warmed you to the bone. You couldn't know what would happen, from day to day and nearly moment to moment. You couldn't know what good might come your way, that a phone call could set you on a path you couldn't have imagined, to things that hardly seemed possible. But there it was.

"I think of myself as a mediator," Mike had said, irritated to be found before he'd closed up his bookstore. Jim had a hunch that Mike would disappear, so when the judge had called for a recess, he'd snatched his coat, hurried out of the courtroom and by the time he'd hit the courthouse steps he was running.

"You thought I was going to vanish? Maybe you'd come to the store to find out it was a pizza joint or a barber shop? What did you think I was going to do about all these books? Or did you think they'd vanish, too?" He snapped his fingers. "Gone. Just like they'd never been."

It did seem preposterous but after Mike's appearance in the courtroom, Jim was ready to believe just about anything.

"I'm taking a vacation," he said, hunting around behind the counter. At last he produced a battered sign that dangled at the end of a fraying length of rope. "I hate this time of year. Cold but no snow, damp that gets into your bones. I'll be in Florida right up until Christmas. I've said my piece to Mary Iannota. Nice woman, by the way; I've been in her courtroom a time or two before this appearance. That was the only thing that's been keeping me here, otherwise I'd have been gone a week ago."

"Why did you call me? Why me?"

He opened the register and removed the bills. Digging into his back pocket, he produced a wallet and, with great concentration, stuffed in the wad of money. "You come flying up here to ask me that?"

"No." But now he felt sheepish and silly, afraid he'd look foolish if he asked what he really wanted to know. He was glad Mike wasn't looking at him. "You called. Twice. Neither call showed up on my phone."

"The diocese doesn't pay you enough to afford a decent phone?" He leaned forward a little to return the overstuffed wallet to the pocket.

"Nothing's wrong with the phone."

"Look, I'd love to talk about phones but I gotta catch a plane. It's not like I can spread my wings and flap myself to Florida, you know?" Looking around, he found a paper cup of coffee, sniffed it, then walked to the door and threw the coffee into the street. Set the cup on the counter and found his keys.

"Actually, I don't know. I don't know anything. That's why I'm here. And how can you just come back after a few weeks?"

"Easy. Return flight."

They were both outside the store. Jim's body was screaming a variety of protests after the sprint but for once, he barely noticed. "Everyone in the courtroom heard you. Everyone heard what you said."

"Heard what?" Mike turned the key in the lock and facing Jim again, straightened up and shook his head slowly. "I said a few words to Mary Iannota, but you think you all heard the same thing? People are weird that way. You heard one thing, Emily Bell heard something else, the two WASPs from Boston and that joker Wade heard something else entirely. Same words but nobody heard the same thing. On top of that, you have a bad take on the attention span of the average twenty-first-century

American. In a few weeks, no one is going to remember a thing anyone said in the courtroom, least of all what I said. Believe me. Time goes by and things happen. Which reminds me, keep an eye on your sister's family, okay? Things may get a little rough."

"What?" Almost arbitrarily, he yanked a single question from the whirlwind in his brain. Not the most important; just the most urgent. "What are you?"

Mike's car was parked in front of the store. He opened the car door. "I think of myself as a mediator. That's all. Come see me in a few weeks. I might have some books for you and the kids. Unless the store has turned into a barbershop."

Lizzie was spying on him through Maria. As soon as he'd finished one of Lizzie's casseroles, his sister would appear at the rectory to whisk away the empty dish and replace it with one that was full to the brim. Problem was, Lizzie was not a good cook; sometimes things were burned or undercooked, and the ingredients must have been chosen because they were calorie-dense rather than because they blended well. Leo wouldn't go near them. Jim considered scraping them into the garbage but thought that somehow his sister would know. So he worked his painful way through one glutinous mess after another. Anything to keep her at bay.

Some days, he thought he was a little better, imagined he had some feeling in his left leg, judged the prickling and burning in the right leg to have abated marginally. His legs retained their scalded look, though, and just when he'd convinced himself he was improving, the air would gather substance near him, and he would close his mind to the possibility of another presence lurking nearby, though he couldn't shut out the uneasiness, a creeping expectation of doom.

The trial had felt like an ending. On his knees before the lowest shelf of the bookcase in his office, piling up all the psychology texts, which would return to Mike's shop when it reopened, he was acknowledging an ending, if only to uncertainty. A relief in one way, because no one wanted to think he was the agent of his own misery. Left with the one alternative, however, he did not feel comforted.

Prayer was the only defense he had, and if his petitions weren't answered, there must be a reason, one that he might yet discover. He believed in God's love. Now, he had to trust it.

Thanksgiving dinners were more palatable because Sam did much of the cooking, although when Willy went through a brief culinary phase, some odd side dishes had appeared on the table: kale and mushrooms, pureed sweet potatoes and apples, lavender rice. Triona had a lot to say about those concoctions but it hadn't discouraged her brother; Willy had just grown out of that interest and into another.

Leo was going to a fellow priest's condo for Thanksgiving. "Retired last year. He makes a chocolate torte that is heavenly. And I will be glad to leave the place to the rats."

Which were rats. The traps had yielded two and Jim hoped that would be it. He wouldn't acknowledge that he'd ever thought differently, but did admit to himself that almost always, a rat was just a rat.

He'd asked Lizzie to invite the Brennans for Thanksgiving. Her answer had surprised him. "Let me ask Sam," she'd said. "With the mob of Clarkes, two more people won't make much of a difference, but I'll check with Sam."

The house was full, every bedroom occupied. In one were Sam's brother and his wife, who had driven up from New Jersey. Their oldest son, who was eight, was bunked with Willy, and their two younger children had a room next to their parents. Sam's sister and her husband had arrived from New Hampshire and occupied Triona's bedroom with their nine-month-old son, who was fractious.

"He does not like to be awake," was Willy's opinion. It was as good a theory as any.

With Sam in the kitchen, the other male members of the Clarke family had drifted to that room, the older ones sipping wine at the kitchen table. "Triona's the only one who got a good night's sleep last night. Or would have if she hadn't been watching television in the living room until midnight. I'm not looking forward to screaming babies. Thought we were all done with Willy but in another couple of months, here comes Charlie."

"You know it's going to be a boy?" Jim's brother asked.

Sam lifted the lid of a pot and stirred the contents. "Lizzie wants to be surprised. We have no clue what it is but Willy's been calling it 'Charlie' for months now."

"It is gender neutral," Willy said.

Sam appealed to his brother. "How do kids know what they know? 'Gender neutral.'" He grabbed Willy's shoulder and shook it gently. "Go on, you, gender specific. Go help your mother."

"Aunt Jen and Aunt Lisa are helping Mom."

"There must be something for you to do."

"There is and I am doing it," Willy said promptly. "I am listening."

"No, you're not; you're yapping," Sam complained. "I don't know how I got such yappy kids."

"Mom said that when you were in college, you would talk on the bus all the way from Boston to Portsmouth. I do not talk that long."

"You talk long enough for someone with nothing to say."

That sally amused both father and son.

Fifteen minutes after Sam called people to the table, they finally were seated, except for Lizzie, who suddenly noticed the water glasses were empty.

"Nobody told me to do it," Triona said hotly. "I even asked if anyone wanted help."

"Maybe you didn't hear over the yowling baby," said the yowling baby's mother.

"Jim's going to say grace." Sam grabbed Lizzie's arm. "Sit; I'll get the water. After grace—or we'll never eat."

Lizzie was going to resist but changed her mind and sat, reluctantly. Pregnant women were said to glow but Lizzie looked as if every breath exhausted her. As she eased herself into the chair, she caught her brother watching her and mouthed the words *three months*.

The dining room walls were green, the dusty green of bayberry. The table, now covered with a linen cloth, had belonged to their parents, as had eight of the chairs. The sun came in thinly through a cloudy sky; Sam had remarked earlier that it smelled like snow.

But they were warm. Peter and Helen sitting side by side, Peter frail but Helen contented, her husband beside her and her paintings still in her possession. Sam's brother and sister and their families—a show of support and a show of force. Sam, Lizzie, Triona, and Willy. There was life in the room, from the ripening in Lizzie's womb to the squalling baby and the fidgeting children, the chattering adults, and finally, the Brennans. He felt himself blessed to be so surrounded.

And so he raised his hands, taking in the feast that had been ferried to the table on their grandmother's Limoges, which saw sunshine on Thanksgiving, Christmas, and Easter, and was packed carefully away the remainder of the year. He said what came to his mind about the bountiful Earth that was a sign of God's love, about the love of family and friends, which also was a gift from God.

And then he sat, trying not to brood though no one was noticing anyway. He had been afraid he wouldn't last until the birth but now he prayed earnestly and more mindfully, asking for a little more time because he felt he inflated his own importance by asking for more than that. Often, the niggling thought came that Mike Dyer hadn't explained anything, that he was interpreting Mike's words the way that best suited him. Doubt would creep in, and worry and fear would lurk in the shadows behind it, but Jim pushed it back; his particular gift was for pushing things away.

The *Globe* series occupied everyone during dinner. The first article had appeared the day before. It was the first of what was going to be a three-part series entitled "In for the Kill: Under the Guise of Military Superiority, Technology Developed by Government Scientists Is Silently Slaughtering Marine Mammals."

The first part covered the strandings that occurred simultaneously with tests of the sonar system and quoted marine biologists from Woods Hole and the University of Rhode Island. Peppered through the article, which had appeared on the front page of the paper, were photos of beached whales and of people trying to rescue stranded dolphins.

"You wouldn't believe the number of people who have reacted," Sam said. "More than five hundred comments online, last time I checked. If the info didn't get you, the pictures did."

The second part would cover the Naval Undersea Warfare Center, which received over a billion dollars every year and had a workforce of more than five thousand, and the veil of secrecy that cloaked the government's research in Newport and elsewhere. The last part was to be about Raum, Inc., the contractor that would produce the sonar system, and the cozy relationship between the federal government and its large contractors.

"I know that name," Jim said. "He owns Seawinds, out on Ocean Drive."

"According to the preview, Raum collects foreign women and American art," Lizzie told the table. "That's how they put it, which I think is more than a little misogynistic."

"American art? They said American art?" He tried to catch Helen's eye but she was passing the gravy boat to Peter.

"If the series shuts down the program, I'll dance a jig," Sam said, "though I'd be happier if we were developing technology that would obviate any variety of sonar."

"Dad is saving the whales," Triona announced.

"He is a whale hugger," Willy put in. "And a jellyfish hugger, even though no one actually likes jellyfish."

"I wish I could be a job hugger, too," Sam said ruefully.

"You think you've put yourself out of a job?" Jim asked.

"If my name surfaces, absolutely. It wouldn't happen overnight; that would look like retaliation. But it would happen. I should say *will* happen; if someone in my division hasn't figured it out yet, I'd be surprised. I'm still the new guy, or at least the newest guy, and I was asking questions. Someone will remember that. Doesn't matter, though. I'm ready for a new career." Sam paused. "Something that doesn't keep me awake nights."

Triona had chosen a seat near her father at the head of the table; she was eating slowly, absorbed in the conversation for once. Every so often, she asked her father to pass something—the bread, the salt—just so he would turn his attention to her. Sam saw it, and winked.

The gesture made the breath catch in Jim's throat. It was so easy to see God's love in the world. In the past, when he'd witnessed such moments, he'd sometimes felt the sharp stab of envy, and then he'd laugh at himself; he could have married and had children, but they would never be *these* children, would never be Triona and Willy.

He was thinking of them, his niece and nephew, when the doorbell rang.

"Who's this?"

"Maybe flowers? Did somebody order flowers?" Lizzie pushed her chair from the table but before she could struggle to her feet, Willy had spared his mother the effort and was out of the room.

Willy.

Jim's chair slammed against the wall.

"What?" Lizzie's voice, alarmed.

"Stay." The word hanging in the air behind him as he threw his body out of the room and down the hall, the roar of the engine coming at him like knives. The breathing was a scream over it, his heart beating so fast he thought it would explode. His feet might have been running over razor blades. Bugs crawling over his legs and under his shirt, everything telling him to stop, stop.

Something large and pitiless was on the other side of the door.

He was incandescent with rage that burned through him, brilliant as a magnesium fire, from his center out, burning through marrow and bone, blood and veins, through the stringy tissue of muscles and the very little fat that remained on his body, through his skin, singeing and purifying as it shot along every hair from follicle to tip. He was nearly past the point of seeing, and the howl of outrage that blew through his mind overwhelmed the breathing. But it also made him rougher than he'd intended. Willy's hand on the door as Jim grabbed his nephew's wrist and yanked it away, Willy's body shouldered to the side as Jim tore open the door to a blast of cold air.

The baby screamed. Chairs toppled, ricocheting off the wall and the floor in the scramble, the bottles of wine teetering and crashing against glasses and dishes as the tablecloth jerked, someone's body catching a corner, pulling the linen. Willy, who had fallen, was frozen on the carpet so that despite her bulk, Lizzie was the first to reach Jim, seconds only, but as she knelt beside him, the blood soaking into her pants was already cold.

— 34 —

The last funeral I went to was my father's. I don't remember it very well. Not because I was a little kid when he died but because I just wasn't there. You can be someplace and not be there at the same time, sort of the opposite of the looking-at-yourself-from-the-corner-of-the-room thing. I remember my father's skin at the funeral home, powdery with a ghastly pink tint. I don't know why they do that to dead people; it frightens you away from the people you love. I have no idea who was at the wake, don't remember the priest leading any prayers and I certainly remember nothing of the funeral except that the chill went right through the soles of my best shoes when I was standing in the grass beside the open grave.

He loved me. That I know. He took me to Howe Caverns. We learned how to paint Easter eggs like the Ukrainians do. He taught me how to ride a bicycle and how to cross-country ski and tried to interest me in basketball.

There's almost nothing of him left in the house in Schoharie. His clothes are long gone, there are no pictures of him in frames, and I'm the only one who ever mentions him. I stayed one night over Thanksgiving, long enough to help cook dinner, my sister on her cell phone while my mother and I worked in the kitchen, she telling me about Julia's plans to go back to college in the spring. She'd bought a car for Julia; not a new one, but nice enough. Julia planned to get a job and save a little money before she went back to school. I tried to tell my mother about the trial but she interrupted twice and after that I gave up. On Thanksgiving Day I stayed long enough to wash the dishes, then Julia took me to Utica to catch the train and I went back to the city.

I think of my father every day. I'm not really thinking of him, not really trying to call him up in a deliberate way. He just comes to me. I'll see his face, his gray eyes like mine. He had this tic: when he was telling a story, he would pause right before the punchline, and his hand would go up to his ear and flick the top of it, once, and you'd see the flash of his onyx ring.

No one gave me that ring. My mother never said I could have it. After the funeral I saw it sitting on their dresser and I just took it.

He told me where we'd find you. And rested a finger on that ring.

Bart Meagher called me. He said he thought I'd want to know. People always say that, even if you are perfectly fine not knowing and it doesn't really matter whether you know or not. When people tell you they think you'd want to know something, it means they want to tell you something and it's probably going to make you feel bad. Sometimes it's because they like to be the conveyer of news or they just want to see how you'll react. Other times, it's because they know the news will make you unhappy and they feast on that feeling.

It wasn't like that with Bart Meagher. He was right: I did want to know, even though after we hung up I curled up on my bed and cried until I ran out of tears. After that I fell asleep for a while but when I awakened, the news hit me all over again and I discovered I wasn't through crying. I kept thinking it wasn't fair. But fairness has nothing to do with anything that happens in life.

By the time I got myself a glass of water I'd started thinking about what I'd have to do. Of course I'd go to the funeral, but where would I stay? I didn't think it would be right to stay at the Brennans' house. People would be coming to the door and who would I say I was? Not a member of the family, certainly. The only reason I'd ever stayed at the Brennans' house was that I told myself Helen needed me. In fact, I'd needed her. I still needed her but she no longer needed me.

I looked up the same B and B I'd booked the weekend Peter had the stroke. Called and made a reservation for two nights. Then I phoned the office and left a message for my boss. There wasn't going to be a wake, just the funeral on Tuesday morning. I knew I'd still be no good on Thursday but I said I'd be back then. There was nothing to do the rest of the day so I waited until four-thirty and then I got dressed and went to the five o'clock Mass.

You feel them around you at Mass. You're sitting there with the rest of the congregation, and someone's coughing and someone's phone accidentally goes off, and some little kid discovers that his voice sounds bigger in the echoing chambers of the church and he just won't be shushed by his parents, and you feel them with you and with the rest of the congregants fighting colds and worrying about big things like bills and anxious about a hundred little things that don't really matter. They are the unseen celebrants, the generations gone to dust, the people who built the church stone by stone, who came to Sunday Mass wasp-waisted and bustled, with celluloid collars and brilliantined hair, with drop-waist skirts and peekaboo heels and peplum jackets and DAs and Beatle haircuts and big shoulder pads and jeans, jeans, and more jeans. And the things they worried about have dropped away and their anger and anguish have departed and their fads and loyalties have gone, too. They are the Church Triumphant, the dead and buried, who are linked in love, linked in that mystical union with the living, the Church Militant, the pilgrims on earth. They are with us always, loving us in our need, hearing us in our need, because all their anger and anguish and fads and loyalties have fallen away and they are purified and pure love.

And I saw myself at the end of my life and tried to look back to see what I'd become and I couldn't. Couldn't see what I'd been or where, couldn't see where I'd helped, couldn't see whether I'd mattered. Couldn't see whether I was alone. But as I sat there, the *Madame X* idea came back to me.

On Sunday I planned my future and got so depressed I had to take a walk. I'd need to save money, and the only way I'd be able to do that is to get a second job, possibly a few nights a week or maybe on the weekends, and move to a cheaper borough. I estimated how much money I'd need to save and came up with a barely-squeaking-by figure, as well as one that gave me a little breathing room. My lowest estimate added two years to my Manhattan existence and the breathing room added at least two more.

Manhattan is at its best between Thanksgiving and Christmas. Even the meanest stores have some decoration, the big department stores create elaborate window displays, and the tree at Rockefeller Center towers over the skating rink. It's party season for the locals, Radio City Music Hall for the out-of-towners. Christmas music spilling into the streets when shop doors open, people with packages smiling at nothing. I hadn't bought anything for my mother or Julia but I'd have to get them something. The only person I'd bought for was Helen.

I walked a mile south, then across town, then up to 57th Street and back to the East Side, where Christmas was more subdued. The air was so cold it hurt to inhale and I stopped at a coffee shop just to warm my fingers around a cup of hot tea. I'd cheered myself up a little but then I saw myself in the naugahyde booth, alone in the world, my nose crimson, stubby fingers red as radishes. I went home and made art nearly through to Monday.

The bus pulled into the visitors' center and he was waiting for me. Leaning against a beam, hunched against the cold in a mustard-brown canvas jacket that looked like it was a hundred years old, faded and frayed and with a tear on one of the pockets. I saw him a moment before he saw me and his expression was resolute, like he didn't know what kind of reception he'd get but he'd be ready for it because he was here, picking me up, and that was what people did for one another. Sweet, Helen had said. Suddenly, I could see it.

When he spotted me, a smile flickered and died and then flickered once again. "How was the trip?" Leaning in to take my weekend bag.

"Shrieking babies and boisterous undergrads. Next time I'll rent a car."

"Not exactly high society on public transport." And then he heard what he'd said and was trying to think of something else, quickly, before I could respond.

I knew he meant nothing by it. "As long as I don't get mugged en route, I'm good."

I'd never been in his car. On the back seat was a wetsuit and a couple of old towels that may have accounted for the briny smell. "I tried to get the worst of the sand off your seat," he said. "I'm not much of a housekeeper."

It was different, being in the car with him. The darkness, the cold, the smell of the sea was part of it but not all of it. All that male energy was muted, tamped down. He wasn't comfortable, I could see that, but for once I wasn't worried what that meant, whether he'd felt obligated to fetch me, or irritated because he wanted to be doing something else, or any of the other scenarios I could invent to make myself anxious and depressed.

I'd been thinking about him on the way up. Remembering what he said in his closing argument. All those first dates, a slightly smaller number of second dates, and how many of those men had not only listened to me but thought afterward about what I said? And how many would have known exactly why? He was right about my father's ring. I wore it not just because my father loved me but also because I loved him and I wasn't relinquishing that love just because he was dead.

Being told it was as enduring in him, wherever he was in death, was beyond my understanding. It was like trying to imagine how gravity bends time: someone tells you it's real but your mind can't accept it. The shock of it had flared for a full day and then it had subsided, steady and warming as May sunshine. Helen had been right, after all: love brings them back.

Bart had given me an abbreviated story on the phone. About the man who came to the door on Thanksgiving Day and shot Father Ennis. Helen had risen from the table and followed the stampede to the front door, and when she saw the body she'd collapsed. Two ambulances had been called and two went to the local hospital, but only one went to Rhode Island Hospital.

"They couldn't revive Helen. They worked on her for a while, but she'd had a massive heart attack. Jim was shot in the shoulder and the stomach. He's in intensive care."

"Two days," I said. "She had two days to be happy." But I knew that was wrong as soon as I'd said it: she'd been happy for many more days than that.

We stopped in front of the B and B. I'd liked the look of it online: a three-story Victorian with a huge mansard roof and lots of gingerbread. Garlands had been hung from the porch railings, a spotlight illuminated the Christmas wreath on the front door, and candles glowed from every window. I was completely unable to face it.

"Did they get the shooter?"

"In a way. Friday morning. Jim's sister thinks the guy blamed Sam—that's the brother-in-law—for a story that's running in the *Boston Globe*. I haven't seen the story but the sister says it's going to scuttle a Navy project that's killing marine life. Good riddance to it."

"Will they try him for first-degree murder?"

"Ah, no. No. He's dead. A jogger came across his body on Second Beach. He'd shot himself."

Had he planned to kill himself all along, or had he done it because he'd shot the wrong man? I could picture the long stretch of beach, how the waves would catch the moonlight, and a solitary form, dark, motionless, growing cold. A lonely way to go. "How's Peter?"

"Not good. I sat with him Thanksgiving night." He leaned in to switch off the engine and then it was quiet. Peaceful, almost. "Jim had his sister call me from the hospital; I have no idea how he managed to think of that. Jim was in rough shape to start, and then to take a couple of bullets. Well."

My first friend in the city. The gentle van der Weyden whom I'd frightened practically out of his wits. Who'd hurled himself off the bridge to save me. Who'd listened while I talked myself out during the warm months. I'd been drawn to him because he'd worried about me.

Todd had been fascinated by him because, he said, the priest was a complete innocent. And maybe he was: with most people, you didn't let them know your bad stuff because you didn't want them to think badly of you but if you didn't let the priest know your bad stuff, it was because you didn't want him to think badly of the world.

I'd watched him lurch to the witness stand, moving as if he'd already been riddled with bullets, sure he'd collapse before he got there. The sunken eyes, the long, livid scars under one. Shaking or shivering in the chair under that nasty interrogation. You could see it was an effort for him to listen, a greater effort to speak and I was sick with the certainty that whatever illness he had was killing him. When Bart phoned with his news, I saw Father Ennis exactly as he'd been at the trial, and I'd been frightened.

I didn't have the courage to ask when Bart called, but now I wanted to know everything. "Is Father Ennis going to make it?"

"I hope so. I went up Friday afternoon but he was sleeping. They said he'd been sleeping pretty much nonstop for most of the day." Then a bit of that energy came roaring up. "So, I've had a few chats now with the sister. Have you met her? She's like General Sherman, marching through the wards, laying waste to all ills. I don't think she's going to give him much choice."

I knew he said it just to cheer me up but it did make me feel better.

"Bad as Jim looks, Peter's the one you worry about. Frankly, I thought you'd be staying at the house again. If you want to go over there after you've checked in here . . ."

"Tonight? I don't know if that's a good idea."

"Why wouldn't it be?" And then he supplied his own reason. "If you're afraid you'll break down, he won't mind. He's mourning Helen, too."

If Helen were alone in that house, I would have barged in, just the way I had before. But I didn't know Peter well. I didn't know Bart Meagher well, either, but I decided to be frank. "It's not like I'm a relative, or an old friend, or even a neighbor. He might not want me there, bothering him."

"You think an old man prefers to spend the evening rattling around the house all by himself the night before his wife's funeral?"

"That doesn't mean I should automatically assume he wants to see me."

"I didn't ask him if he wanted me to take him home Thursday night. Maria didn't ask him before she saw him on Friday. And Saturday. And yesterday. And I seriously doubt Jim's sister asked, either; she doesn't seem the type." He looked at me. "It's not you, is it? It's company. Easy company. Someone who'll come in and chatter away for a little while, get him a beer if he wants it or fix him a cup of cocoa if he wants that. The man is eighty-seven years old and he's all alone. He had a stroke not too long ago, his partner of sixty-odd years is gone and he's been alone in that house for four days. For fuck's sake, why wouldn't he want to see you?"

"I'm sorry," I said, though I wasn't, and opened the door.

His arm shot past me and closed it. "Wait."

"No." My hand on the door again. "I'm going. Thanks again for the ride. It was good of you to pick me up."

"Wait," he said. "Please."

And to my surprise, I did.

He let out a long breath. "I didn't mean to bark."

"Well, you did."

"Sorry."

The wail of an ambulance made me think of Helen, of her face as she listened to me that night. For some reason I'd told her all of it—and selfishly, at the worst possible time for her—and none of it had made any difference in her feeling for me. I wished I'd met her years ago but that was another selfish thought.

"She was so smart and so *nice*," I said, because I couldn't tell a near-stranger that she'd never again put her arms around me, listen to me, and take my side. "There isn't a lot of nice in Manhattan. Maybe there is, somewhere, but not in my world. She was the reason I liked coming to Newport and now she's gone."

The engine turned off, cold was creeping into the car again. Raw ocean air.

"Well, so," he said, "I'm not going anywhere."

He was half-turned in the seat, his eyes glinting in the Christmas lights from the bed and breakfast.

I glanced out the window, at the festive, front-door wreath, all fake starfish and phony shells. A hundred ways I could interpret that comment, but I thought of all the Fridays at Metro when I watched everyone else begin their weekends, and I said, "You're braver than I am."

"Comes of all that unscrupulous lawyering I do."

I didn't want to make a joke of it and didn't want him to, either. "I ought to toughen up but oddly, I don't."

"You sounded plenty tough on the phone that first time."

"I didn't know who you were, then."

We sat for a while, looking out the front window at the houses lit by the streetlights. Every house was different; a Gothic revival beside a Queen Anne, a Federal beside an Italianate. A car slid slowly by us on the narrow street. I felt him smile.

"So, here's a plan," in a brisk voice. "I was going to see Peter anyway. Maria has been stopping by in the morning and I usually do late afternoon or evening. So you and I will go together. Any objections to that?"

I shook my head.

"And suppose you went to fix your hair in the powder room and I asked him if he'd like you to stay there tonight, which I think he would like. But would you want to do that?"

"I can ask. If he says no, he says no, right?"

"Good woman," he said approvingly. "Either way, we'll visit and take Peter to dinner if he has the energy for it, and if not, we'll bring something back for him. You'll feel better on a full stomach—I always do. You do eat, right? You're thin but you don't starve yourself . . . or do you?"

"I'm not thin."

I felt his hand cover mine, just long enough to give it a reassuring squeeze. "That's all right then: we have a plan."

Helen's funeral Mass was at St. Patrick, Father Ennis's church, and Father Sullivan said the Mass. An older priest who sounded almost British, he tended to talk in considered sentences, like he was reading from an old book, Samuel Johnson, maybe. About fifty people in the pews, more than I'd expected. A few people looked to be friends of the Brennans, others who might have known Helen from the store or the bank or Peter from the construction company. They weren't the only mourners, though.

"I know a few of the old ladies; they go to every funeral in Newport, and often it's then they become acquainted with the deceased." Bart told me that while everyone was eating sandwiches at La Forge, after we'd been to the cemetery. What he didn't tell me—what I learned much later from Father Ennis—was that Bart had paid for the collation and had made most of the arrangements himself.

The thing about Bart was that he didn't go away. I'd been dismal company at dinner. I'm not sure if I was mourning Helen's death, or Helen's death and the end of my beginning in Newport, or Newport as Paradise Lost, without Helen. My eyes would fill now and again and the room would swim. In the middle of dinner, at a restaurant that displayed a large Christmas tree and overlooked empty docks and dark water, I saw myself from a corner of the room but it was just a flash and then it was gone. Not even enough time to inspect my nose, to see if it was red; all that male energy was like a wind that pushed you if you tried to linger in one spot.

Helen had loved my phone calls, Bart said.

"She told you about them?"

I'm not stupid, but at times like these I see how simple-minded I can be. Helen talked to me about Bart; why hadn't it occurred to me that she'd talk to Bart about me? Because it never did occur to me that anyone talked about me, even thought about me, unless I was right in front of them. I was a little worried about what she'd said. She wouldn't have recounted the long conversation we'd had the day Peter had the stroke but I wondered what she'd told him, and what bits and pieces he'd put together to construct his version of me.

I searched his face and saw that my fears weren't justified. It wasn't a little dart or an arrow or a bullet. It was a gift. "Thank you," I said.

We discussed the trial, and the guy who dropped his bombshell and left. I thought he was a street person. Bart told me the man actually owned a used bookstore. Bart said he remembered him from when he was a kid and he looked just the same as he did now. I think Bart was fishing—he wanted to know what the man had said to me—but I wasn't ready to tell him, not then.

I was going to hate to leave Peter. The night before, he'd talked about Helen. Little stories. Little things she did. How she always had to stand right in front of him and give him a look before he remembered she'd had her hair done that day. Sometimes he did remember but pretended he didn't, just to see what she'd do. She loved to swim laps at Hazard's Beach;

by the time she dragged herself out of the water her lips would be blue with cold. He always told her she had no sense. She always told him she also had no stomach, and that was because she was a swimmer.

He was so forlorn, a small, stooped figure in the front row of St. Patrick, his head bowed right through the Mass. No one from his family came; there was a great niece in Oregon and a distant cousin who lived in England, and I don't know if there were others, but no one came so I sat beside him on one side and Maria sat on the other. Jim's sister approached him at the collation, handed him a plate of food, and sat right down and complained how everything she ate gave her heartburn or made her feet swell. I think he realized she was trying to distract him, but she kept on, nonstop, and finally got a laugh out of him.

Bart drove us both to the house and the closer we got, the smaller Peter looked. I was talked out and I think Bart was, too. When we were getting out of the car, a man erupted from the house across the street, jabbering on his cell phone and he didn't end the call when he reached the car, just sort of held the phone away from his face.

"I've been watching for you," he said, not sure whom he should be addressing. "I saw the funeral was today so I thought I'd keep an eye on the house. You know how people are."

Bart had Peter's arm as we went up the walk and it was a good thing. As soon as we opened the front door, chaos lay before us. It looked like the house had been picked up and shaken.

"They didn't get anything. Two guys in a van." The neighbor was behind us, craning his neck to get a good look. There was a lot to take in. "I saw the van and I was going to go out there and ask what they were doing when the two of them came out of the house like a shot. They took off fast but I got the license plate. You can call it in if you don't know them."

Bart surveyed the living room, totally bewildered, but Peter glanced at the paintings on the floor, one of them half covered with a black tarp, and the smashed glasses and broken mugs, a box of cornmeal spilling onto the sofa, a container of flour splattered against a chair, another chair on which a box of spaghetti apparently had exploded, and he looked happier than I'd ever seen him.

"She'd never throw her mother's china. Looks like she threw everything else, though, and I'd bet good money she didn't even nick them," he said, laughing. "Lousy aim but you've got to give her credit for trying."

35

This time of year, the feeders were boiling with activity. While the second pot of coffee was brewing, he'd slid into the shoes that had the thickest tread, stepped carefully over the dew-laden grass, and filled the feeders: sunflower seeds for the chickadees, mixed seed for the sparrows, and suet for the woodpeckers and the wrens. He'd also hung a seed block for whatever wanted it. Apparently, the squirrels did, because they ran up the pole, encountered the baffle, went round and round beneath it, and then scrambled down again, defeated.

The scar along his shoulder wasn't painful but made him shiver when he touched it; bright red, it was numb, and at first he feared the hard clerical collar would tear it open somehow. But that hadn't happened. Wouldn't, he knew.

He walked over to the church and turned on the same lights he'd switched off after the nine-thirty Mass. St. Pat's was dark, chilly, and silent; just how it should be. And fragrant with flowers. Rows of potted lilies surrounded the altar and massed beneath the statues of Mary and St. Patrick. He crossed to the altar and knelt. Closed his eyes and gave himself to an endless gratitude. For life, and everything that went with it.

When he'd come to consciousness at the hospital, he hadn't immediately noticed the absence. You tended to notice what was there, before you realized what wasn't. No breathing but his own. At first, he didn't believe it. Listened carefully, getting under the jabbering machines in his room, the voices beyond the door. Heard his own breathing and thanked God for the unlooked-for marvel of his continued existence. Heard no more and then he moved his mind tentatively, as if somehow it would sense his consciousness and react.

But no. It was gone. There was nothing but his own painful breaths. He couldn't decide whether it felt worse inhaling or exhaling, but it didn't matter, since neither was optional. Someone had taken a crowbar to his shoulder and stomach, but his legs felt intact. No numbness. No itching, crawling, tingling, or cold. He reached out a hand and pain came rushing at him, his shoulder bursting into flames, and, as if in response, a torch blasting through his stomach.

He had, despite that, a peaceful feeling. He'd done what he needed to do. And he turned over and over in his mind the knowledge that had arrived so suddenly. He'd been mistaken. Or, more precisely, misled. He'd thought he was a target. Couldn't understand why he was. But he hadn't been. All along, he'd been a shield.

An instrument of God, as everyone was called to be. He wouldn't flatter himself: he wasn't rare and certainly wasn't unique. Nor was he any stronger than anyone else; he thanked God, the sister saints, and whoever else had watched over him.

Willy was alive.

And then, because it hit him so suddenly, he wept.

While he was recovering in the hospital, the world was spinning on. Lizzie came every day at first, waddling into his room looking furious, and usually for what she declared were good reasons: they were giving him the wrong pain meds, they should have run this scan or that test. She bullied the doctors and nurses.

Sam had brought the children. A hand on each child's shoulder. He was smiling but he looked stricken. "I don't know what to say."

Jim shook his head.

The children stared silently at the fresh reminder of Thanksgiving Day. Judging by the expression on their father's face, Jim didn't think Sam would pull them back to the present as he had after the ghost tour.

"You know what?" Jim said. "Your mother is prescribing full body armor for me." Nothing; not the hint of a reaction. Triona's freckles a sweet constellation across her cheeks, Willy's cheeks baby-smooth, vulnerable. "One of those black suits that covers you from neck to ankle and a helmet with little slits to see through. I'm going to order some Frankenstein shoes to go with it because sneakers would look stupid with body armor. What do you think? Think I'd look like the coolest uncle that ever was? You can flip a coin and whoever wins can wear it for Halloween next year."

And there it was—a glimmer in Willy's eyes as he considered the possibility. "People will think that a space invader is saying Mass."

At the end of their visit, Triona dipped into her pocket. "Mom took it last Christmas. Willy and I gave her a selfie stick." She propped the photo against a styrofoam cup and set the small tissue box against it, holding the photo in place. "Can you see it?"

He let the moment fill him. Then, "Yes." Lizzie had positioned her family in front of the tree. The children were laughing at something Sam was saying, and Lizzie was trying to be good-humored despite the fact that her family weren't behaving so she could get a nice picture. "It's perfect." He glanced up, into eyes that were the mirror of his: light blue, orange flecked. "Thank you."

Triona became shy, and shrugged.

Lizzie was the one who told him about the man who'd shot him.

That was how it happened. Something worried at you, gnawed its way into your brain, harried and harassed you until you acted. Shot someone who had destroyed your life and only then realized you were the one who'd killed it. Or found yourself standing in the darkness of a bedroom, pulling on the clothes that would be plastered to your body when you were pulled from the waters of Narragansett Bay.

How close he'd come to that ending.

At long last, lying in bed, he dared to look full on at Blessed Sacrament. The murmuring, the argument. Anselm Chace standing in front of it, blocking the sight of it. The moment the old priest had turned. Anguish on his face like an open wound. The darkness behind him so thick it felt alive. But it was empty. Thirteen years old, he'd imagined something out of his nightmares because he didn't know then that presence didn't always mean form.

He saw the boy, halfway into a growth spurt, legs not much broader than his arms, skin livid where it was taut against the protuberances of knees and elbows. Awkward, but unaware that he was. Shivering, frightened, but not yet knowing that he'd come to an ending. And all he'd missed—thousands of days, the choices that he might otherwise have made, the pleasure of just being—it could blind him with rage if he let it. But he wouldn't let it.

He'd never had Anselm's pride. He'd never thought for a moment he was equal to it. Pleading with God, imploring the saints, but never realizing how much help he was receiving. From so many sources, but foremost from Lizzie, whose love wouldn't let him shut her out, who forced herself and her family into his life, even though he tried to push her away. She had given him so much to love. Had given him herself and

Sam. Triona. Willy. And love was the ballast that had prevented him from flying apart.

He'd asked Lizzie to write down the name of the suicide. He added the man's name to his prayer list.

Meagher came in once, bubbling with laughter, to tell him about the attempted theft. The license plate had been traced and two men arrested. Two men, it turned out, who'd been hired by Alborn Raum. "Sole owner and proprietor of Raum, Inc, the company contracting with the feds to produce the killer sonar. The thing your brother-in-law blew the whistle on. Remember the story I told you about Seawinds? Raum was the one sitting there with a face like thunder the day I went down with the contract. Gives me hives just to think about it. I don't know how our friends the Taylors got mixed up with him, but I don't expect they'll be appealing the verdict of their lawsuit. Raum is wanted for questioning but apparently he's skipped town."

Leo made the trip off the island, bearing cookies decorated in reds and greens. "Bilious," he said, wiping crumbs from the corners of his lips, "but Christmas has ever been the season of vulgarity and immoderation. You appear to be improved since Friday."

"I don't feel better," he complained.

"One must consider where you started. Have a cookie."

Jim pondered the plate Leo held out.

"I should tell you I spoke to Father Reilly. I gave some thought to whether it was your prerogative to call him but concluded that it is a kindness to relieve the anxiety of the elderly, if one can."

Jim's eyes filled.

"None of that, now," Leo said. "Moderation. In everything but our gratitude for God's goodness."

No one told him about Helen Brennan until he was out of the hospital and recovering at the rectory, though Leo had blandly suggested the sisters and Lizzie more forcefully proposed her home. He knew he wasn't responsible for Helen; he still felt it, though. No matter that Peter was convinced she was still present for him. Maybe she was.

Leo had assumed the responsibility of the feeders. Jim lay on the couch for much of the day, dozing with the images of cardinals and finches imprinted on the back of his lids. He awakened one afternoon to find Maria standing over him, hands on her hips.

"Your sister say you getting better but I brought something that hurry you up."

"Not cake, I hope."

Maria grinned. "Ahh, I know you no like cake. *Cocido*. Guatemala soup."

Maria was still cleaning houses and she said she liked making her own hours and naming the price for her work.

Emily had visited him in the hospital and twice at the rectory. "You'd be surprised how much money you can make selling your old stuff online. I had all these designer shoes I'd worn once or twice. I thought the gowns would be out of style but apparently not. I'm trying not to go too crazy. I don't want to wake up one morning and discover my closet is a big black hole, but once you start selling it's addictive. I have bought one or two things, though. Things that I like and who cares if no one else does, right?"

On her last visit to the rectory she laid out her plan for the future.

"I don't want to auction art. I want to make it. That's who I am but somewhere along the way I got sidetracked. So, yeah, I sidetracked myself. Stupid. I could kick myself when I think about it.

"I'm selling all my dressy clothes and just keeping my absolutely essential work clothes, and besides Metro I'm also working at a gallery two nights a week. I'm saving every penny I can. I figure I'll put together a two-year cushion and then I'll move to Newport. Bart said he'd keep an eye out for a decent apartment but I told him there's no hurry."

There had been snow the night before, and she had brought that cold, clean smell with her. Serene as she watched the mob at the feeders, content just to see. Traces of that look around the eyes but she had lost the urgency to speech.

"If I can help—"

"I'm doing the RCIA thing at my church." She was full up with the wonder of it. "I'm going to be a full-fledged Catholic. That's what I wanted to tell you. I'm enlisting in the Church Militant and getting my weekly dose of the Church Triumphant. So, yeah, there are two other people my age and they can't figure out why I'm there; I told them I wasn't engaged or anything like that, which I guess is the main reason people in their twenties do RCIA. They probably think I'm demented or something, but so far no one has tried to kick me out."

The shoulder had taken months to heal. He'd been lucky that the surgeon had been able to repair it because replacement wasn't recommended for someone so young. "I'd say it was your own fault, Jimmy," Lizzie said, "except that I don't know what to think. The whole thing is completely nuts. How did you know who was at the door? Sam thinks it was some kind of divine intervention because if Willy had opened the door he would have been killed. I told him the kids are freaked out enough without seeing their father get on board the Crazy Train." Then, without waiting for response, "Listen, Jimmy, no one's going to make me believe that Satan catapulted up from hell and decided to attack you. I mean, it's not like you're the pope. Anyway, you were in such poor condition when you were shot that your shoulder shattered in three places. The surgeon did a great job patching you up but if you don't do the exercises you'll never regain full function of the joint."

Rehab was monotonous and painful. But he had a great fear of his sister. And just like Emily, a goal in mind.

He hadn't really tested the shoulder but he was taking the eleven o'clock Mass, ready or not. *I'd like a little help, though, if you can manage it. Please let everything go well, if not for my sake then for Lizzie's.* And as he rose from his knees he heard the main door open. Impatient as always, Lizzie charged down the center aisle.

"Mom, we are so early that it is practically Saturday." Willy had a cassock and alb over his shoulder.

"You're here," she said to Jim. "Good. I want Willy to go through it one more time so he doesn't forget."

"Actually, it is so you can take a movie of my first time as an altar server," Willy said, accurately—Lizzie had dug her phone from her bag. "In fact, you are taking a movie of a practice, not a Mass. Practice does not count."

"Well, I'll have the baby then and your father—" Lizzie caught herself. Fought a silent battle with herself and shoved the phone into the bag again. "Well, anyway, you might as well get dressed as long as we're here."

Jim gave his sister a kiss and put his arm around his nephew, just for a moment; ten-year-old boys and twelve-year-old girls, he'd discovered, tolerated only the briefest hugs. "Where is Charlie?"

"Sam's got him. He's picking up Peter Brennan and then they'll all come to church."

"His name is not Charlie." The words emerged deep and fractured as always. "It is James Ethan Clarke but I think I will take that name when I am confirmed. Samuel William Charlie Clarke, first man to go to the Andromeda galaxy and claim it for Aquidneck Island."

Sometime later, as the epistle was being read, Jim looked around him. To Willy; to Sam and Lizzie and the new baby in the pew nearest the baptismal font; and behind them, the godparents and Peter Brennan. He spotted Maria and her family, Maria looking as grim as ever, though the family recently had received the best of news.

The experts had been right about the paintings; Metro sold the Hassam, which would allow Peter to renovate the house and restore the rest of the collection. The Heade, the first painting Helen's ancestor bought, was on permanent loan to the Newport Art Museum, courtesy of the Helen Eagan Brennan Estate. Peter had won the fight with Maria and established a trust for the children's college tuition and, Meagher told Jim with a note of satisfaction, Peter had made Emily Bell cry.

Triona caught his eye from the choir loft and lifted her hand in a little wave.

And rows and rows, more people than he'd ever seen at St. Patrick. The churches were always full at Easter; Christmas and Easter were the only days some people crossed the threshold of a church. He wondered how many had come out of curiosity, to see the priest who'd been shot eating dinner at the home of his sister, the hospital's ER doc, on Thanksgiving Day. It didn't matter why they came, though; they were here.

He stepped to the pulpit and read the gospel, the miracle of Easter morning. And then began his homily, which was about the transformative power of love.

His voice caught as he began his sermon. And then started up again, strength surging out of the ether.

He'd seen Emily Bell, elegant as a heron, gray eyes watching him, reach out a hand. And Bart Meagher take it and fold it into his.

CPSIA information can be obtained
at www.ICGtesting.com
Printed in the USA
BVHW012101150821
614464BV00020B/221

9 781666 703320